THE FOREMAN AND THE DRIFTER

ALSO BY JACKIE NORTH

The Farthingdale Ranch Series

The Foreman and the Drifter

The Blacksmith and the Ex-Con

The Ranch Hand and the Single Dad

The Wrangler and the Orphan

The Cook and the Gangster

The Trail Boss and the Brat

The Love Across Time Series

Heroes for Ghosts

Honey From the Lion

Wild as the West Texas Wind

Ride the Whirlwind

Hemingway's Notebook

For the Love of a Ghost

Love Across Time Sequels

Heroes Across Time - Sequel to Heroes for Ghosts

The Oliver & Jack Series

Fagin's Boy

At Lodgings in Lyme

In Axminster Workhouse

Out in the World

On the Isle of Dogs

In London Towne

THE FOREMAN AND THE DRIFTER

A GAY M/M COWBOY ROMANCE

JACKIE NORTH

Jackie North

MM Romance Author

The Foreman and the Drifter
Copyright © 2021 Jackie North
Published March 15, 2021

Cover Design by AngstyG

The Foreman and the Drifter/Jackie North

ISBN Numbers:

Mobi - 978-1-94-280940-1
Print - 978-1-942809-41-8
Epub - 978-1-942809-42-5

Library of Congress Control Number: 2021904476

For all those who know that love is love...

And to Randall J, who asked brilliant questions about Honey From the Lion,
the answers to which inspired the Farthingdale Ranch series.

"Never give up on something you cannot go a day without thinking about."
~~ Cowboy Quote, Anonymous

"Gentle in what you do. Firm in how you do it."
~~ Cowboy Quote, Anonymous

CONTENTS

LELAND

*S*ettling back in the saddle, Leland pulled the reins gently across the mare's neck to see how she would handle. She had new iron shoes and a borrowed saddle, saddle blanket, and tack. All of this was different from what she was used to, and any of which might throw a horse off, but poor Gwen had to deal with all of this all at once.

When Gwen executed the turn, he patted her neck, clucking in a gentle way to let her know she was a good girl and had done well, then urged her to trot in a wide circle. Again, she did what he asked her to do, and chuffed as she trotted, as though to get him to pay attention to how well she was going.

"I know you're going good, girl," he told her, patting her neck again. "You're so good, you're going to be perfect for Dorothy."

Finally satisfied, he pulled up in front of the tall open doors of the big horse barn, where Brody, the ranch's horse wrangler, waited. Brody was angular and thin inside of his t-shirt and jeans, having not yet grown into the shoulders nature had blessed him with. He was the best horse whisperer Leland had ever encountered and, for all he was so young, there was nobody Leland trusted more to take care of the horses on the ranch.

"Hey, girl," said Brody, as he came up to them. He lifted quiet hands to pat Gwen's neck and stroke her soft nose, by habit greeting the horse before the man. "Hey, Leland," he said now. "I still think Travelle's a better horse for that lady."

"It's not just the horse, Brody," said Leland. He thought to dismount and get on with other work, but if he stayed astride, he could really make sure Gwen was okay with the borrowed saddle and tack, and then maybe he'd even get his daily ride in. Some days, especially at the tail end of the first week of the season, it was hard to find the time. "It's everything else."

"I know it, boss," said Brody. He looked up at Leland, his cowboy hat perched back on his head, his dark eyes keen as he looked at the horse and at the man. "It was never your fault, eh? Just damn luck that kid disappeared on your watch."

Leland did not need reminding of the incident that had thrown his pretty comfortable life into the air and dumped it into a metaphorical wood chipper waiting below. Even before he'd graduated high school, all he ever wanted to do was work on some kind of ranch, but the disappearance of Laurie Quinn at the end of last season had threatened to kill that dream dead.

That dream had always been to work out of doors with horses and cattle, and so that's what he'd done, the life he'd gone after. After years of working on ranches in Yellowstone and Santa Fe and even Durango, his parents realized he was serious and helped him pay for a degree in ranch management at Iowa State University.

When his dad had passed away unexpectedly during his first semester at Iowa State, Leland had come home, telling his mom he'd give it all up. She encouraged him to go back, to finish doing what he loved, telling Leland it was what Dad would have wanted.

With that kind of support, Leland had kept his eye on the prize: to be ranch manager at Farthingdale Dude Ranch, where he'd worked during his summers in high school. As an additional bonus, the ranch was only a thirty-minute drive from his childhood home. Stubborn woman that she was, Mom still lived in the farmhouse she and Dad had shared before he'd passed away.

The farmhouse needed maintenance every season, and while he was happy to do it, he always told her she'd be better off and live with less fuss in a patio home, one of the new ones in Cheyenne, on the outskirts. But she was determined to stay in Chugwater and tend her garden and sell rhubarb compote and sugar-preserved cherries at the farmer's market in the fall.

So after he graduated, he worked at a few more ranches before finally getting his dream job as ranch manager at Farthingdale Ranch. He'd just turned 30 in the spring, and it had been like coming home after years away.

Tragically, at the end of his first, proud season, Laurie Quinn, and all the strange events surrounding him, had happened. Quinn had gone to sleep near the campfire, like all the other guests, but unlike all the other guests, in the morning he was gone.

Not that Leland had known what havoc the young man would wreak when he'd met Quinn at the first night's chuck wagon event. As they were getting guests settled for the night, Quinn had come forward, eyes wide in the shadows of the firelight, his movements quick and graceful. He'd wanted to talk to Bill, that much was obvious, so Leland had made his escape, and strode in the darkness to the barn to make sure everything was properly shut down for the night before turning in himself.

Normally, Leland wouldn't have such a vivid memory of a single, particular guest, but he did of Quinn because after falling asleep on top of his sleeping bag, Quinn had been gone by morning. He'd shown up a week later, only to disappear again into the night, leaving his belongings and a mystery behind.

Quinn had left his cell phone plugged in so the local police were able to track down any known associates. At the same time, the investigation left the ranch after two detectives discovered there was nothing to find. Quinn's footprints had been discovered heading away from the campsite but then vanished, and the end of the season became a tangle of legal obligations and heartache.

As the ranching community learned of the tragedy, most sent their sympathies, while some expressed misgivings about what kind of ranch Bill Wainwright was running. Curious thrill seekers booked rooms in the bunkhouses and the cabins above the river months in advance, which made a kind of promise that everything would be all right in spite of Quinn.

But then, one by one, so many of the guests had canceled that only 30 guests had shown up for the first week of the spring season, and only 35 guests were set to arrive on Sunday morning for the second week. This was under half the ranch's normal number, which dried up most of the money to invest in repairs and upkeep at the ranch.

Leland stayed up many sleepless nights trying to figure a way out, a way back for the ranch from the edge of bankruptcy so they could give guests the quality vacations they'd signed up for.

He needed to make sure every last detail was seen to, so had held meetings about everybody taking on extra tasks. He'd sent out low-ball bids for contractors for painting and basic landscape and other general work, most of which had already come back negative. He even gently fired the ranch's accountant, and took up the task himself, spending time each evening on the books, making sure the numbers were in good order.

It was a lot of extra work he'd not counted on, but for Farthingdale Ranch to come back from the brink, it needed to be done. Luckily the staff that he had kept, including ranch hands, the cook, the wrangler, the blacksmith, were willing to wash dishes or paint fence posts, doing chores completely outside the scope of their job descriptions, whatever was needed. He had a good team, and they were willing to do the hard work necessary to keep the ranch running.

Everything else on the ranch had been pared down to the essentials. He'd auctioned off all but 100 head of even-tempered, sweet-faced cattle. He'd sold half of the horses, and farmed some of the horses that remained at his mom's ten-acre backyard, keeping only the best, people-friendly horses for guests. He was going to save the ranch and his job. Then, come the next season, they could think about expanding.

In addition to all that, he intended to review each and every horse to make sure they'd be a perfect fit for a specific guest. Which was why he needed Brody's input all that morning, even as the first week's guests were still checking out.

"That guy was fey," said Brody. He patted Gwen's neck in long, slow pats, telling Leland his opinion in his matter-of-fact way.

"Fey?" asked Leland.

"You know," said Brody. "Like he was switched at birth and the fairies took the real one."

"I know what it means," said Leland, doing his best to keep the irritation out of his voice.

He'd heard this same story from Bill, when he'd visited him in the hospital in December. Quinn's disappearance had brought Bill down sorely low as the season ended. Then, just before Christmas, Bill had experienced shortness of breath. Maddy had raced him to the hospital in Cheyenne. There, he'd been checked in, looked over, and, having closely averted a heart attack, spent a few nights hooked up to machines and tubes.

Bill had been given some good drugs, and told Leland all about it, how Quinn had wanted to know more about some guy named Old Joe, who'd been looking for his little red fox. Quinn had also wanted to know how to wish upon a star, Bill added. That's when it had gotten more strange than Leland cared to deal with, for Bill had insisted that there was a ghost story he'd personally been telling all the guests for years on chuck wagon night, setting the mood and the tone so he could get people to look up at the stars rather than at their phones.

Only thing was, Bill had never told *any* such story, not to Leland's recollection, and he'd been hanging around the ranch for years. Even Maddy had no idea what Bill'd been talking about.

Sure, Bill told the guests marvelous stories, and tall ones, too. And yes, some of those stories were about vivid encounters with a herd of wild ghost horses, or a pair of buffalo wolves along Chugwater Creek, which would then typically lead into a lively discussion about land conservation and the sad plight of animal extinction. But none of the stories were or ever had been about a guy named Old Joe, and certainly none included anything about a little red fox.

In spite of being quite certain about this, Leland had stopped arguing with Bill about it when Bill would bring it up, which he did at least once a month. Leland didn't think Bill was going either crazy or senile, but maybe the heart attack scare, along with those very good drugs, had danced this story into his brain, where it refused to leave. And now it looked as though Brody was taking up the baton of the story.

"I know what fey means," said Leland again. "How does it apply here, with Quinn?"

"It was the look in his eyes," said Brody, in the same story-telling voice Bill used around the campfire. "When I was helping pull the chuck wagon in, he was standing right there by the fire pit. He was looking right at me, you see, but it really felt like he was looking through me, like there was something more important behind me, only there wasn't."

This wasn't any kind of explanation that cleared things up or told Leland what he wanted to know to even begin to believe Bill or Brody. It was the same fairy tale it always was: Laurie Quinn knew about his own impending doom. Which was impossible, and certainly nothing anybody at the ranch needed to be spending their time and attention on.

Everyone at the ranch, from the greenest ranch hand to the experienced trail boss, needed to focus on running the ranch, and on delivering individual care to each and every guest. Everyone Leland had kept on the payroll needed to be concerned with the length of stirrup on each guest's horse, the quality of their coffee at breakfast, and their ability to see nice sunsets over Iron Mountain. Those were the memories Leland wanted the ranch to give guests, for it was such positive, glowing images they'd share with their friends, which would then, in turn, bring the ranch bookings for next summer.

He couldn't make Brody and Bill stop talking about Quinn, except in the presence of guests, which he insisted on. There was no point dragging the awful events at the end of last season into this new, shiny one. No point in scaring the guests, some of whom were already full of trepidation about riding a horse for the very first time.

Like Dorothy, who he was developing a special affection for, even before he'd met her. She and her husband had booked a spot in week three at the ranch, and had been planning on staying in Cabin #1. This was the smallest cabin the ranch had, but it was the cutest one with the best view of the river, the best view of the valley stretching out to the foot of the mountains beyond.

Sadly, Dorothy's husband had suddenly passed away, and a tearful Dorothy had called about her husband's death. Only it became apparent during the conversation that one of Dorothy's friends had convinced her to come on her own, as a tribute to her husband and as a way of making her way in the world, now that she was alone.

He and Maddy and Bill had discussed the situation at length. All of them had agreed that even though, given the refund policy, they could not have refunded her for her husband's portion of the reservation, they told her they would. Only Dorothy had insisted on not taking the refund and suggested maybe they could donate her husband's week to someone in need?

That wasn't how things normally worked, but it had been nice of Dorothy just the same, and they assured her they'd do their best to set up some kind of grant of a free week. Currently, Dorothy was expected on the bus from Cheyenne a week from tomorrow, with the shadows of her recent widowhood swirling all around her. If anybody deserved a fresh start, it was Dorothy for being so brave. Hence, she was going to get to ride Gwen, the best of the best of the best the ranch had to offer. Or maybe Brody was right, and she should ride Travelle.

"You remember him, right?" asked Brody, as though Leland's lack of response indicated a kind of amnesia about the tragedy surrounding Quinn. "He had really dark, red hair, and the most expressive brown eyes—"

"Let me stop you there," said Leland, holding up a hand, palm out. "You met him *one* time—"

"Guy like that," said Brody. He shook his head, hands on his hips. "Sometimes, that's all it takes."

"Well, he's gone now," said Leland, pushing his most pragmatic tone into the words. "And we need to get on with things. Need to get the ranch ready for the guests of week two. And we really need to make the Ayers family pack up and go home."

"Their chauffeur is still waiting?" asked Brody. The main lodge building wasn't quite visible from the horse barn, so Brody'd not been seeing what Leland had seen, that Mr. and Mrs. Ayers were still drinking on the shady wooden porch of the dining hall. Their luggage, evidently, was still in Cabin #2, which was larger than the other cabins, and had a wider, less sloped walkway to the road, and their chauffeur was in the parking lot with their sleek black Cadillac Escalade.

"Yes," said Leland, sighing. "Maybe I'll swing on over there and put a bug in their ear."

"I could do it for you, boss," said Brody. His smile was a bit on the sassy side, because maybe he'd get a bit more enjoyment from kicking two rich folks and their daughter to the curb than he ought to have done.

"I'll take care of it," said Leland. "But thank you."

"Who's that?" Brody jerked his chin at the road leading through the trees to the parking lot to indicate where he wanted Leland to look.

Leland shifted in his saddle, looking down the dirt road as it curved beneath the pines and aspen trees. A small breeze swirled the dust, and it took him a minute to realize that a young man was emerging from the shadows and into the sunshine. He looked road-worn, Leland could see that, even from this distance. His shoulders slumped, and he looked down at his feet as he walked, as though uncertain of the surface. All he was doing, though, was kicking up dust and kicking up *more* dust—

Then the young man looked up, as though feeling eyes upon him. Leland couldn't truly see the expression on the young man's face, but as he looked over his shoulder, a bit of wind swirled his long hair around his temples and forehead. Sun glinted on that hair, as though painting strands of bronze, and if that wasn't fey, Leland didn't know what was.

"Damn it," he said. He took off his hat and wiped his forehead on his sleeve, then put his hat back on. "Damn that Eddy Piggot." As Brody looked up at him, a question raising his eyebrows, Leland shook his head. "Over at the Rusty Nail. He's been sending us drifters all week, telling them that there's a job to be had. And now he's sent us another'n."

Leland needed to get rid of the drifter and then pay Eddy a visit, to clear things up. The ranch needed a sterling reputation if it was to stay in business. They couldn't be seen hiring drifters who thought they could just show up with no experience in guests, cattle, horses, or anything related to a ranch and expect to get a job.

It was one more thing on his long list of things to do. Just one more thing between him and that long, peaceful ride.

2

JAMIE

*J*amie had his hand on his back pocket as he walked into the Rusty Nail, ready to pull out his driver's license if he needed to. That license was about to expire tomorrow on his birthday, but he was a little excited to legally be able to go into an actual bar, even if the bar was on a back street in a small town at the end of the world.

Well, not the end of the world exactly, but so far from the world he'd come from he might almost be on a different planet. That was pretty dramatic, but after a long, bumpy Greyhound bus ride from Greeley that left him seeing the mid-morning sky as a hazy narrow line stretching toward the horizon, it was hard to believe he'd arrived. The unending openness of the high prairie flung itself all around him like a blue bowl full of strange promises.

It'd been such a long journey, in more ways than one, a journey that started almost two years before when his parents had announced they were getting a divorce. He couldn't blame them for that, as it had been easy to see they'd not been happy with each other. But the result had been jagged endings he'd been unable to tie up that left him running into mental barriers, rattling inside his own life.

His two-year stint at Red Rocks Community College came to an abrupt end, as the divorce seemed to swallow all the money. And after? He'd lived with Mom for half a year until she kicked him out. Then he lived with Dad, and the same thing happened. Both of them had started new lives, rocketing off into shiny futures, leaving him stranded on some metal-sheened launching pad with no way to lift off.

And here he was, at the end of the road. At least he wasn't still trapped within the cement walls of the meat packing plant in Greeley. At least he wasn't still sharing an old, rattle-walled house with three other guys from the plant, guys who thought it was okay to take his carton milk from the fridge and drink it in front of him, as if daring him to object. No more would he have to sit at the table trying to eat his breakfast, shoulders hunched, hoping that one of them wouldn't take it in his mind yet again to spit in his half-eaten bowl of cereal as they walked by.

The last straw had been when, after a 12-hour shift at the plant, the usual length, one of his housemates had clocked him out early, getting him in trouble with the foreman and losing him hours of pay. He'd explained it, the foreman had adjusted the time card, but from then on out, the foreman eyed him askance, always shaking his head, and didn't trust him. The guys from the house, greaseballs all, snickered as he walked past, and splashed blood at him with their rubber boots when he was on the assembly line, cutting up meat.

Since he couldn't take a break, the blood had dried in his hair, and he had his pay docked for being untidy. Then the guys told him he was short on the rent when it was obvious his check had already been cashed, and that was about all he'd been able to stand. He stuffed everything he owned into his one faded green duffle bag, slapped last year's sneakers on his feet, and bought a ticket to the first ranch that showed up on his internet search.

"You gonna buy a drink or what?"

Jamie looked up, pushing his dust-coated hair out of his eyes. It was going to be tricky. Normally he would already have his new license in preparation for tomorrow, his twenty-first birthday, when he would become legally an adult, so there shouldn't have been a problem. At least not back in Colorado, where he figured bartenders would cut him a break and serve him, anyway. In Wyoming, he had no idea. But his throat was dry, and if he bought a beer, then maybe this guy would tell him where the ranch was.

"Lemme see that license."

Obligingly, Jamie pulled out his wallet and sucked in a breath as he handed it over to the guy behind the counter.

The guy took it and huffed a laugh, and only too late did Jamie realize his mistake. Only an idiot would hand over his whole wallet. Someone more savvy would have pulled out the license and handed that over. There were rules in the real world, rules he was on his own to learn. The ones he did know had come painfully, and he knew, he just knew, that the ones he didn't already know were going to cost him.

"Not quite," said the guy, folding the wallet shut, tossing it on the bar with a hard flick of his wrist, like he was throwing away trash.

Jamie didn't flinch, though he wanted to. Why was it that the more north he went, the men seemed to get tougher and more mean?

"I'll be twenty-one tomorrow," said Jamie, doing his best to push casual strength in his voice as he stuffed his wallet into his back pocket.

"Come back tomorrow, when you're older." The guy's rangy, straw-colored hair hung in his pale blue eyes, and he looked at Jamie with a complete lack of interest and a whole lot of disdain.

"I don't really want a beer," said Jamie, though that was a complete lie. He wanted beer, or a glass of water to drink, at least, but he didn't think this guy would give it to him without charging him for it. "I'm looking for directions to the ranch."

"What ranch?" asked the guy. His mouth twisted downward as he said the word *ranch*.

"The one—"

Jamie thought about the day when a representative from a nearby ranch in northeastern Colorado had come to the meat packing plant with special instructions on how to slaughter his grass-fed beef. The rancher wore a crisp-collared blue denim shirt, standing out from the grubby slaughterhouse workers like a handsome, well-groomed beacon. While the foreman sneered at the rancher and basically told him to take his business elsewhere, the rancher remained calm and businesslike and, settling his shoulders as he left, didn't seem at all bothered to have been refused a spot in the meat packing plant's slaughter schedule.

Thinking about the rancher, and the kind of man he seemed to be, the thought had been planted in Jamie's mind that not all cattle came from feedlots up near the Nebraska border. Searching on the internet, he discovered that some herds of cattle were raised differently than feed-lot cattle. These cattle were fed solely on grass and lived out their days in peaceful, grass-green fields. His mind easily imagined an idyllic green field where happy brown cows twitched their tails as they grazed in the sunshine.

If he could get a job working with cattle at a place like that, he wouldn't have to wade in blood up to his knees every day and cut apart beef ribs and hunks of flesh that were still warm, blood beading on his knife blade and spraying into the air each time he raised it.

"Farthingdale Ranch," he said. "I'm looking to get hired there."

"That's not a *real* ranch, kid," said the guy, his disdain brimming along the top of the words. "It's a fuckin' dude ranch."

"A dude ranch?" asked Jamie, confusion taking over his idyllic image of the place. "I thought it was a cattle ranch, where they raise cattle."

"No." The guy shook his head and looked ready to turn away from the conversation rather than engage in any more of Jamie's foolish notions. "It's a place where idiots from the city come to play at being cowboys."

"Still." Jamie's late-night internet search at the library had obviously given him wrong information. Or maybe he'd read the online brochure wrong. Keeping his hope firmly tucked tight, Jamie cast a look around the bar. It wasn't hardly past eleven o'clock in the morning, and so only a few customers sat in the dark booths along the wall, nursing beers. "It's what I came all this way for. I'd like to give it a try."

"Sure, kid," said the guy, laughing. "Maybe they're hiring, after all. You'd be the third I sent up to them this week, and I ain't got no complaints yet."

"How do I get there?" asked Jamie, feeling buoyed up once more.

"Go up Latham Street," said the guy, pointing out the window. "Go south to Main Street, then go west. Just follow the road, it'll lead you right to the gate."

Jamie opened his mouth to remark how differently people in Wyoming gave directions than people in Denver. Telling Jamie to go south or west made it sound like he was about to embark on an adventure, rather than just walk along a sidewalk till he hit the middle of town. West was where the mountains were, that he did know, making it easy to get where he was going, if he just stayed alert. So with a nod of thanks, he hefted his duffle bag over his shoulder, left the bar, and started walking.

Following the directions was easy enough, and he found himself headed west on Main Street inside of two minutes. What the guy at the bar hadn't told him was how long it was to the ranch. He had to walk a good mile beneath the bowl of blue sky before he reached the bare-board sign that said *Farthingdale Ranch*.

He paused at the sign, which stood on top of two rough poles on either side of a green-painted metal gate. Dust coated him all over and he was tired. There was gravel in his old sneakers, the left sole flopping against the duct tape he'd wound around the toe. He sighed as he looked beyond the gate at the dirt road that meandered through the low scrub, a road that seemed to go on and on and was, yes, uphill. Going through and shutting the gate behind him, he changed his duffle bag to his other shoulder, and kept on walking.

Inside of half a mile in the blazing sun, he entered a group of trees and crossed a stone bridge, where water spun itself around in the air and sprayed up gusts of coolness. It was nice to finally be in the shade as he walked, and the slight June breeze through the pine trees smelled nice, much nicer than the diesel fumes of the Greyhound bus he'd taken from Greeley.

He scraped his hair out of his eyes as he walked. His feet ached, and he cursed the holes in his shoe, and the flopping sole of his left one as he went up the dirt road. The sun shone through the branches of the pine trees like dappled lace, and he might have been able to finally draw a deep breath if he wasn't so tired. Here and there, squirrels darted, and altogether it was a whole lot more nature than he was used to.

It had been desperation that made him shell out a chunk of cash for that bus ticket to the end of nowhere, which had landed him at the edge of the world in Farthing, Wyoming. He hoped for a better life, but he had damn little hope left after learning what kind of ranch it was. What was he supposed to do now? Staring up at the sky as he paused in a bend in the road was like staring up at the opening of a deep well he was at the bottom of.

Desperation would turn into insanity because what if the guy at the Rusty Nail had been lying to him and there was no job at the ranch? Then he would be stuck in the hind end of Wyoming with no other prospect but that of returning to Denver to take up cheap work like a delivery job and maybe find another apartment to share with strangers.

At least he'd have a roof over his head. At least he'd be in a city he knew. Maybe he could even figure out a way to go back to college. But at the end of getting his degree, where would he be? Probably right where he was this very minute, walking along a dirt road, kicking up clouds of dust as he walked, no job, no home, no hope.

His sneaker came untied just as he got to the edge of the glade. Setting down his duffle, he bent to tie the laces, and then straightened up. To the left was a narrow dirt track leading up and around a small hill. Another dusty road went off to the right around a low hill that flowed along a glassy calm river. Beyond the glade, the trees opened up to a field of tall grasses, green and pale yellow in the sunlight, going on forever as fresh and as new as an untrammeled promise.

Ahead, the road went up to a round area, a dusty, lightly graveled parking lot where a few cars were parked. A low split-rail fence curved around the edges of the parking lot, with small stones lined beneath the fence, sort of as decoration. Two buildings sat side by side, tucked into the arms of a low hill. There were wooden barrels lined up in front of one of the porches for no particular reason, at least none he could figure out.

Three flag poles stood between the two buildings, one flying the American flag, the other flying the state flag of Wyoming, and a third flying what looked like the flag for the ranch, with the name of the ranch in red against white, and three pine trees curving around those letters. Beyond the parking lot, amidst cottonwoods and aspen trees, budding green in springtime, were a few more buildings. Beyond that were even more buildings, and a corral perhaps, but the trees got in the way and he couldn't be sure.

Nothing was like a ranch as he'd imagined it, or like he'd seen in the movies, except maybe in a Disney movie. It wasn't a cattle ranch, that was for sure. It was more like what the guy at the Rusty Nail had described: a place for fancy people to go to escape their own lives, spread over acres and acres of land.

One of the closer buildings had a sign on the door, so he figured he would go up to that and check it out to see if anyone was inside who could give him a thumbs up on that job. Not that he had any experience with ranches at all, no way. But here he was, all walked out. What other option did he have?

As he mounted the wooden steps of first building, he would have paid his last dime for a glass of water, which would be stupid, because where was more cash going to come from if they didn't hire him? A friendly moose?

The wooden sign on the wall next to the door indicated the building was the ranch office and welcome center. But the paper sign on the door said someone named Maddy had gone on an errand and would be back later, and that Bill had gone to Chugwater to take care of some permits and would also be back later. Which was when, exactly?

The place looked deserted. Although he could hear sounds in the air, they shifted around him and he couldn't pin them down. It was not quite lunchtime, but maybe people were eating already or something?

He had no idea how ranches worked, or even, really, what it would feel like to have a regular sit down meal again. His last sit down meal had been days ago, the night before he'd handed in his notice. He'd eaten his favorite meal at a diner, breakfast for dinner, biscuits and gravy. His mouth watered as he thought of it, the salty taste, the spices. Then he'd headed to the Greyhound station and shelled out cash for as far as he dared go.

Giving himself a shake, he hefted the duffle to his other shoulder, and went back down the wooden steps to the parking lot.

The other building was a store of some kind, but though it was open, people in stores rarely liked people coming in without the intention of buying anything. Though he probably could get a bottle of water, in a place like this, with sky-high prices, well. He was better off finding a water hose and getting a drink off that. Water from a hose in early June was just about the best tasting water anyhow, and he would save a few bucks besides.

Going on up the road, he staggered through a little copse of aspens, bright green at the tip of each slender branch, and found himself in another open area. The blue sky blazed above him, and a jagged, rusty-edged mountain stood stark against the cloudless sky in the distance to the west. Ahead, through the trees, he could see more buildings. A lodge maybe, or perhaps it was a barn, people in cowboy hats going into them.

He thought he could smell something cooking, but he couldn't tell where that was coming from, though his stomach stood up and growled and demanded to be fed. To the right, as he walked along, was something that looked like an open fire pit with hay bales and rocks circled around it. Beyond that was a glassy pond, fed by the creek water, draining away to a bright, sparkling creek. Beyond that were more trees, open fields, and a whole lot of sky.

It was all quite pretty and somebody had probably put a lot of thought into the layout, planting trees between buildings all the time, but it also meant he had no idea where to go next. The ranch seemed to spread out forever and forever, and he was just too tired to want to walk any further.

He passed what looked like a giant hotel made of logs and stone; two people sat on the shady porch with glasses of wine and laughed out loud, maybe at him. Jamie kept walking, eager to enter the shade of pine trees once more. As he stepped out of the glade, he saw a barn-looking building, where one man on a horse was talking to another man standing next to the horse.

The tall guy on the horse had long legs and broad shoulders, and wore the same kind of crisp-collared blue shirt that the ranch guy at the meat packing plant had. This man looked completely at home as he patted the neck of the horse, which was a tan color with a black mane and tail. The other guy looked up at the taller guy as they talked, their cowboy hats bobbing as they nodded in agreement over something.

The tall guy pulled on the reins to circle the horse around, and the other guy pointed at the horse's hooves, or maybe he was pointing at the saddle, which looked shiny and new.

As Jamie got closer, he could see that the guy on the horse was handsome in a tough, cowboy way, sitting there in that saddle on that horse like he knew he was cock of the walk. Or maybe that's just the way it was with cowboy guys when they sat in saddles, which made his shoulders look even more broad than they probably were, his hips tucked beneath him, rounding his ass, drawing his blue jeans tight.

Jamie shouldn't be staring, but of course he did, at that hard jawline and those blue eyes glinting at him from beneath the brim of his straw cowboy hat. Jamie recognized the posture right away. It was one of appraisal and, of course, a total lack of approval.

He looked down at himself, at his scuffed sneakers where the one shoelace was already coming untied again, at his dust-covered blue jeans, his thin black leather thrift-store jacket with the ragged cuffs, and finally, his t-shirt. He had purchased an egg sandwich from the bodega at the bus station, but he'd been startled to hear the bus was leaving, all of a sudden, and so the sandwich had fallen out of his hand, leaving stains on the shirt. He felt a bit like a bum in their midst.

He'd not taken the time to clean up, even though he had a clean t-shirt in his duffle. Well, it was too late now. Mr. Tall was riding right up to him, directing the horse with a purposeful air, probably with a broad-shouldered intent to throw Jamie out on his ass, right then and there.

3

JAMIE

r. Tall came to a halt, the horse's hooves kicking up a little dust. His face was half shaded by the brim of his hat, and beneath that brim, two steel-blue eyes glared at Jamie.

"Did Eddy Piggot send you?" asked Mr. Tall, though by the grim line of his mouth it was easy to see he already knew the answer.

"Who?" asked Jamie as his mind chased visions of people he'd talked to that day. The Greyhound bus driver, the lady at the bodega—

"The idiot who owns the Rusty Nail," said Mr. Tall. "You're the third drifter he's sent us this week."

"I'm not a drifter," said Jamie, even as memories of all the places he'd slept in the last year danced in front of him. "Sure, I'm *drifting*, but I'm not a drifter. I'm just looking for a job, is all. I saw your website and thought you were a cattle ranch—"

"Look," said Mr. Tall as he leaned forward in the saddle, looming over Jamie just like he knew he was a barrier to all of Jamie's hopes and dreams. "This is a dude ranch, not a cattle ranch. It's a nice place for decent people to come and take a break from their busy lives. Either way—" The man paused to look Jamie up and down. "Either way, I doubt you have any experience with any of that."

"I'm decent," said Jamie, blinking his eyes against the sting of the words. Heat rose in his chest. "And I'm not looking for a handout. I'm looking for work."

"It's fine by me you're looking," said Mr. Tall, though it was easy to see it wasn't fine. "But you can't just march in here like this. We go through the Templeton Agency in Chugwater. You can apply there. If you're qualified, they can find you something."

"Chugwater?" Jamie asked. How was he going to make this work, heading there and back again? On the heels of that, after his experience at the meat packing plant, why on earth would he want to work someplace with a guy like this, who was glaring at him extra hard with a mouth that curled up at one edge like he was stopping himself from saying something even more scathing? "How far is that? Is there someone I should ask for, once I get there?"

"It's thirty miles or so," said Mr. Tall. "But it's Saturday, so they're closed today and tomorrow."

Mr. Tall appraised him from the back of his horse. When he clicked to the horse to move closer, it was all Jamie could do not to take a step back. He could smell the leather of the saddle, horse sweat and dust, and a bit of the man himself, and maybe the soap he'd used that morning. At eye level were those thighs, muscled and long, pressing against the horse's sides, controlling it perfectly.

"I get that," Jamie said. He put on his best smile, looking up at Mr. Tall, squinting, trying to catch his eye, trying to figure out what he could say to make this work. "Sure, it's the weekend and all. But maybe you've got some work that needs doing today? You could pay me a couple of bucks and a meal? Maybe a place to sleep? What do you say?"

"Pay you in food and lodging?" The question rose in the air as Mr. Tall tipped back his hat and appraised Jamie all over again. "I don't think so. I'm sorry."

Biting his lower lip, Jamie registered Mr. Tall's casual dismissal. There was no getting Mr. Tall to change his mind, and no getting around the fact that he now had to march back into town without a place to sleep or a job to earn money so he could eat. He was so tired.

Coming up against such a definite nope was the last straw, though he probably shouldn't have been surprised. He knew he looked like he'd just stepped out of a trash can like some walking, talking Oscar the Grouch.

He wasn't going to keep drifting. Or at least he hoped not. All he needed was a chance, though it looked like he'd come to the ends of the earth for nothing.

"So," said Mr. Tall. He had one hand on the saddle horn and with the other, he waved in the direction of the small glade, beyond which was the road back into town.

"Yeah, okay," said Jamie, keeping his frustration out of his voice as he swatted a fly out of his face and turned on his heels to start walking down that dirt road.

In his mind, he measured the distance. Half a mile to the gate. Another mile in the heat of the long afternoon, to the town. There, he'd try to find a motel room, if there even was a motel, something with a shower. Grab a hot meal and then figure out what he needed to do in the morning.

Maybe he *would* go to Chugwater and go through proper channels to apply for a job, maybe even at the ranch. Though he'd not the faintest idea what that job would be, and he certainly wasn't qualified, he was willing to do anything they asked of him if they just gave him a chance.

Wouldn't it be funny if he got the job? Not to mention if he was on the ranch, he could grab another eyeful of those long legs. Even if Mr. Tall was straight, which he probably was, those legs would be bonus enough for Jamie.

He shouldn't be thinking like that, not at all. Telling his mom and dad he was gay had probably led to their divorce and certainly was the reason behind neither wanting him to live with them. But even though he'd known he'd liked other boys, and had attempted to go on dates with a few guys at the community college, his love life always seemed to arrive at a dead end. With these ideas hanging over him like a sad weight, he started walking, not even turning his head when Mr. Tall shouted out to him.

23

"Don't forget to close the gate behind you as you leave."

Yeah, sure. He wouldn't forget, and couldn't wait to put this place behind him. Chugwater it was because even if he didn't apply for a job on the ranch, maybe they'd have something else going. He could always hope.

4

LELAND

*P*ulling Gwen's reins, Leland settled the horse as he watched the drifter walk away, heading into the glade with an insouciant walk that seemed to evidence youthful years of defying authority and skirting the rules. It wasn't that Leland was against free will or young people piercing their nipples or whatever they wanted to do, but they needed to do it with style.

It was obvious the stains on the drifter's shirt had not been done with style, they'd been done with negligence and a hurried decision to walk and eat at the same time. His dark hair had been a long, curly mess over his eyes, and by the looks of him, the bruise on his cheek, he'd been in a brawl of some kind.

The pained way he'd hefted his green canvas duffle bag and the stiff way he'd stood there, panting, as though he'd not had water to drink in a good long time, spoke of even more neglect, probably self-imposed. Had the drifter been an employee of the ranch, or a guest, or a horse or any of those under his care, Leland would have pulled the young man aside, found out what he'd needed, given it to him, and then made sure he had work to do to earn his keep.

There was nothing wrong with hard work, and nothing wrong with traveling a great distance to get it. But he was frustrated with

Eddy Piggot, so his reaction had been strong and his dismissal quick. Both of which now seemed out of proportion to the simple request for a job.

The other part of his reaction was harder to explain. It hadn't happened when he spotted the drifter standing in the middle of the road, looking around him like a lost thing, no. It had happened when Leland had gotten close enough to see the flash in the drifter's eyes, a spark of energy that exploded things in Leland's chest he didn't quite know what to do with.

Again, he should have offered the drifter a glass of water, at least, before he'd sent him packing. And maybe he envied the drifter, just a little bit, the freedom he seemed to have to just turn and walk away, going wherever the wind took him.

It wasn't that Leland didn't love his job at the ranch, because he did. He loved everything about it, from the time he got up in the morning, to when he went to bed at night. He'd gained even more responsibility while Bill had been recovering in the hospital from his near heart attack, and now, even with Bill getting better and taking back some of his old tasks, running the ranch was what Leland was made for. Bill often said Leland should delegate more. Bill was probably right, but today wasn't that day, and tomorrow didn't look so good for that, either.

"Mr. Tate?" said a voice behind him. "Excuse me, Mr. Tate? You got a minute?"

Leland tugged the reins on Gwen's neck and looked down to see Clay, one of the ranch hands, holding his straw cowboy hat in his hands as he looked up. He was an eager young man, easy on the eyes, and a hard worker, too. He'd only started the summer before, though Leland remembered Clay had graduated from college and was now considering starting a ranch of his own, and was doing everything possible to gain as much experience as he could.

"Yes, Clay," he said, focusing on the bright-faced young man. "You can call me Leland, don't forget. What can I do for you? And put your hat back on. It might be only June, but it's too sunny and hot for such niceties."

"Maddy said to tell you that the guy from the grounds maintenance company called." Clay put his hat back on, straightening it with an efficient tug and a bright, cheery smile. "And she said to tell you they're raising their rates."

"What?" he asked, going over the figures in his mind as he settled back in the saddle. "By how much, did she say?"

"She didn't say exact amounts, but she said specifically that the rate for hand scything was going to be double what it was last year and that we probably can't afford them."

While Clay looked at him as though he really hoped Leland wouldn't be mad at him for being the bearer of bad news, he considered the matter. He'd tried to contract out some of the groundskeeping to save more experienced hands for the work that applied directly to the ranch, taking care of the horses and tending to guests. But it wasn't a good, long-term plan because though the ranch hands and the trail boss and even the blacksmith were able to step up and help when they could, it wasn't an efficient way to run a ranch.

He'd already talked to Maddy about this, that hiring a single groundskeeper would be better than contracting out to a company. Plus, the work would be done to the higher standards ranch guests expected, so he needed to keep trying.

"Can you take a message to Maddy for me, when you find her?" he asked, knowing already that Clay would be on the task right away. "Tell her to call Templeton's in Chugwater and ask them to open the position for one groundskeeper again. She'll know what to tell them about the skills we're looking for."

"Sure thing, Mr. Tate, I mean, Leland," said Clay with a friendly smile. "Is there anything else you need?"

"Yes, please," he said, returning Clay's smile. Would that he had a hundred more like Clay on the ranch. "We've got new guests arriving tomorrow. Most are staying in the lodge, and some are in the cabins. Can you check with Stella in guest services to make sure everything's set up? I'm sure it will be, but as the guests won't all be in one place, it'd be nice to have it confirmed."

"I've already done that." Clay reached into his pocket and handed

Leland a folded piece of paper, reaching up. "Here's Stella's checklist. She says everything is ready. And she says, though I'm not supposed to tell you, that she's glad there're no kids this week, 'cause she needs a break."

Clay winked at him, and made Leland wish he was a few years younger to be able to follow up on that kind of flirting. Not that he'd ever get involved with another employee on the ranch. But it was young, vibrant men like Clay who kept reminding Leland he was on his own, and working away toward a future that didn't involve anyone else. What would it be worth in the end if he had nobody to share it with? But, what with putting in twelve-hour days pretty much every day of the week, he was working too hard to worry about that now.

"She loves kids," Leland said with a laugh, pushing those darker thoughts away. "So do the wranglers and the cook and the trail boss and even the blacksmith."

"Jasper, you mean?" Clay tilted back his hat and snorted. "He hates everybody, don't you know that? Everybody."

"Beneath that hard exterior lies a heart of butter, I assure you," Leland said, and though he tried to keep a straight face, it was hard.

Jasper produced excellent work as both blacksmith and farrier, and knew how to shoe a horse like nobody's business. He was also willing to do demonstrations for local kid's groups, pioneer re-enactors, Girl Scout troops, and the Fresh Air people that brought city kids from Cheyenne for a bit of country life.

Though Jasper pretended he hated doing the demos, hated donning frontier garb to replicate the excitement of frontier days, he always provided top-notch performances and everybody always came away happy, the clang of the hammer on the anvil ringing in their ears. Leland's next task with him was to get him to take on one of the parolees from the ex-con rehabilitation program Bill had decided to participate in, on account of the tax break benefits it would bring.

"I doubt that," said Clay, shaking his head. "Okay, I'm off. There's a load of salt blocks coming this afternoon and those gently used saddles you ordered. I plan to be at the barn when they get here."

"Sounds good and thank you," Leland said, clucking to Gwen to soothe her. "But make sure you take a break for lunch. If there's a delay in the delivery, have them call me on my cell, and I'll take care of it."

"Will do, Leland."

With a tip of his straw hat, Clay was off, hustling down the dirt road to the office where Maddy was probably back from her errand.

Maddy was the ranch's administrator, part-time nurse, dance organizer, and a whole host of functions that, once she'd done them, the ranch simply could not do without. She'd usually swing by the local farms once or twice a week to see if they had fruit and vegetables for staff and guests.

Maddy had a thing for farmers, it seemed. Luckily there were a few of them in the area, all vying for her attention and willing to sell her tender young onions and potatoes for pennies. Plus, the guests seemed to like the local produce, and the ranch was known for providing the best at their tables, so he was glad Maddy was willing to go the extra mile. Everybody on the ranch was, it seemed, even if they groused about it like Jasper did. Or didn't say anything, and just got to work, like Levi, the cook did. Leland was lucky to have them working for him, and he'd do whatever it took to keep them.

5

LELAND

*L*eland trotted Gwen up the road and through the trees to the dining hall where Mr. and Mrs. Ayers were still in residence on the front porch, making the most of their country adventure, as they called it. Staff had been good at keeping the couple well supplied with martinis watered down to an appropriate level, so there was that to be grateful for.

The main trouble was that the Ayers and their daughter Monica were the last to leave. It was long past time for housekeeping to get into the cabin they'd stayed in and prep it for the next guest.

"How's it going, folks?" he asked as he pulled Gwen's reins and patted her neck. He leaned forward, his arm on the saddle horn, to make the inquiry casual. "Just about ready to head out?"

"Monica's gone for one last horse ride," said Mr. Ayers as he raised his martini glass from the comfort of the wooden rocking chair on the porch.

"She's been smelling like horse all week," said Mrs. Ayers, taking a sip of her drink. "But if she's happy, I'm happy. Do you think she'll want to come back next summer, dear? We could bring her for her twenty-first birthday."

Leland waited while they chatted about it between them, drinking their drinks, lollygagging when they should be packed up and ready for their driver, who, even now, was waiting in the parking lot. There were ranch hands standing by to help remove the luggage from the cabin. All the Ayers had to do was get moving. While they were nice enough, rich city folks such as the Ayers traveled on their own schedule. Still, it was time for them to get a move on.

"I'll just go and fetch her," Leland said. "That horse deserves its rest in the stable. Then I'll let her know you folks are ready to go."

"Thank you, Mr. Tate," said Mr. Ayers with his usual formality, his voice slurred from the drink in his hand. "I know we spoil her, I know we do."

With a nod, Leland trotted Gwen back up the road to the barn, enjoying the fresh air, the movement, the steady feel of the horse and the hard saddle beneath him. When Leland arrived at the barn, Brody was holding two new iron horseshoes in his hands. With him was Jasper, the ranch's blacksmith, and together the two men seemed to be discussing how many of this size they should order, how many of that.

Just on the other side of them, Monica came riding on Old Blue, a blue roan gelding. Monica was giggling with a ranch hand and generally goofing off and certainly not paying attention to the gelding beneath her. Then it happened. The horse gave a sharp buck and Monica shrieked. This startled the horse even more and off it went, first at a canter, and then at a gallop with the bit in his teeth, his head lowered, ears back.

As Old Blue galloped past Leland, he tried to pivot Gwen so he could grab Old Blue's bridle, but the gelding's head was too low and he was going too fast. Giving Gwen a kick, Leland urged the horse to catch up, and since they were herd-mates, it wasn't hard to get Gwen going. The only problem was, Old Blue was galloping full out, and had the jump on Gwen, who had shorter legs.

If he could catch up to the gelding, he could ride alongside and grab his bridle that way. It was obvious Monica was of no use and was too frightened to slow Old Blue down. She was not a horsewoman, just a guest at the ranch, a city girl with a dream in her head of what it was like to be a cowgirl.

Gwen did her best to close the distance as they raced past the dining hall and into the trees. As soon as they crossed the stone bridge, they were on Old Blue's heels.

Up ahead, the drifter had just opened the gate. If Old Blue went through the gate, he could run for quite a long way. Monica might get thrown, or the horse would hurt itself, and then Mr. and Mrs. Ayers would be very unhappy and might sue the ranch. All of this went through Leland's head as he leaned forward to get Gwen to go faster.

"Close the gate," he shouted to the drifter, his breath coming hard, heart hammering. "Close it!"

Everything happened at once, fast, but time seemed to slow down as the drifter looked up, startled, saw the horse and Monica at the same time, and closed the gate, latching it shut. The gelding came up to the gate, and luckily, not being a jumper, dug in his hooves and slid into the metal bars, jangling the gate on its hinges.

Monica was flung from the saddle and, unbelievably, the drifter caught her in his arms as he too banged into the now-closed gate.

Riderless, the gelding danced about, then stopped abruptly and lowered his head, chuffing at the grass and the dust at the edge of the road, as if nothing had happened. That's how it was with horses sometimes.

As for horses trained at the ranch, they knew nothing truly bad would happen to them, and so were seldom fractious or got out of hand. What had set the gelding off? Leland needed to find out. But first he needed to make sure of Monica.

"Are you all right, miss?" he asked. He eyed Monica clinging to the drifter as he placed her on her feet. There was a green duffle bag in the grass, where the drifter had dropped it.

"Y-yes," said Monica, sniffing hard as she straightened her fancy, feather-laced cowboy hat, scraping hair back from her face. "But it wasn't the horse's fault, okay? It wasn't. I don't know what happened. I was just sitting there and—"

"That's fine," he said, taking a deep breath. "You need to get back on that horse, now, and gently ride him to the barn. Can you do that for me? Hey, can you help her mount?"

"My name's Jamie," said the drifter. He lifted his chin as the wind danced his hair in his eyes, making Leland want to stare for longer than was appropriate. "And sure, I can help."

As Jamie tried to grab Old Blue's reins, the gelding skittered away from his outstretched hand, telling Leland in one quick minute that Monica would have a hard time of it with the horse.

Normally, Leland would be very insistent about getting back on the horse after a dismount like that, teaching both yourself and the horse that everything was okay, that nobody was hurt.

It was an important lesson to learn, yet, given the fact Monica and her family were leaving soon and would probably never go riding again, how important was it? Important enough, perhaps, even in this small moment, for him to make sure it happened as it should.

Jamie reached for Old Blue's reins again, doing his best to approach the gelding, though it was obvious he had no idea how to handle a horse. With a quick, hidden sigh, Leland dismounted from Gwen and handed her reins to Jamie.

"Jamie, can you guide Gwen to the stable while I help Monica with Old Blue?"

"Sure," said Jamie again, taking the reins. "A horse is like a large dog, right? I can walk a dog. Anybody can walk a dog."

Ignoring his internal bit of laughter at Jamie's small joke, Leland grabbed Old Blue's reins and soothed him and urged Monica to come close. Together they petted Old Blue, making much of the gelding, and quickly Leland discovered a bump just at the edge of the saddle blanket where a wasp had stung the horse.

"He got stung," he told Monica. "That's why he ran. It was nothing you did."

Monica nodded and sniffed, and he helped her mount up, figuring that at least this final lesson might help her not be afraid to try again, if she ever decided to live out more of her cowgirl fantasies. Gathering Old Blue's reins in a way he hoped was an example to Jamie how to do it, he clucked to the gelding and began walking. Behind him, leading Gwen in a hopelessly loose manner, came Jamie, kicking up dust as he went.

"Let's go," said Leland. "I think the horses have had enough for one day."

They walked along the dirt road through the trees to the main parking lot, where the Ayers and their driver and their big black car were waiting. From the looks of it, all their luggage had been loaded, for which he was very grateful to somebody. He'd find out who and then profusely thank them. Clay, probably.

"Is she all right?" asked Mrs. Ayers, coming up in a rush, waving her arms. "Tell me, Leland, is she hurt?"

"She's all right, folks," he said, pulling Old Blue to a stop.

Monica slid off the horse and ran into her parents' arms as though she'd returned from a long and arduous journey. The Ayers petted her and cooed over her while Leland waited with the mare.

"Looks like the horse bolted when he got stung by a wasp," he said. "She had a scare, and I apologize for that, but your daughter is okay and the horse is okay."

"Thank you, Mr. Tate," said Mr. Ayers, his face red from drinking.

The wasp nest was a problem, and Leland fumed at himself for having missed it. Usually he took a horse from the barn or the herd each evening, saddled up, and rode around the perimeter of the main part of the ranch. Partly the ride was for his own pleasure, but he took time to check everything out, from the state of fence lines that bordered the property, and along the creek, looking for anything that needed fixing or was out of place.

Still, because of his lack of time to go riding, he'd missed the nest. He'd have to take time to find the nest, now, and destroy it before another one of the horses or one of the guests got stung.

Mr. Ayers talked to his driver as they walked with Monica to their large black car in the parking lot. Meanwhile, Jamie waited with Gwen, letting the horse slobber on his shirt in a way that showed he wasn't afraid of horses, at least, and knew how to stand still around them.

"I'll take that horse now," he said, going up to Jamie with Old Blue in tow.

Jamie handed him Gwen's reins, and in his eyes was a question

35

about the job he'd asked for earlier. There was an agency in Chugwater for jobs, and Jamie already knew that. Leland had set up hard guidelines about how they would staff the ranch, so even though he felt bad Jamie had a good distance to walk back into town, Leland had to shake his head.

Just before Jamie turned to go, a brisk breeze stirred his dark hair into his sad eyes, and Leland felt like the worst of assholes. But rules were rules, and he needed to keep the ranch running or everyone who worked for him would lose their jobs, and Bill would risk losing his beloved land. With all that at stake, Leland made himself stay silent as Jamie walked away, and walked away himself, leading Old Blue back to the barn.

Just as he got there, up the road came Bill driving his old blue Chevy truck, bouncing to a stop in the small gravel area next to the barn. He strode over to Leland with his half-hitch limp, his felt ranch hat tipped back on his head.

"What's this I hear," said Bill as Clay came up and took Old Blue into the barn. "I was just on the phone with Maddy, and she says there was a runaway. And who was that kid?" Bill jerked his thumb over his shoulder to point at the direction Jamie had gone, as though he'd just ghosted into the trees to disappear from sight.

"Old Blue got stung by a wasp," said Leland. He took off his hat to wipe at his forehead with his sleeve, then put his hat back on again. "The kid was one of the drifters Eddy Piggot's been sending me this week. Mind you, this one closed the gate in time to keep Old Blue from running off, and then caught Monica before she broke her neck."

"Sounds like he did us a favor." Bill looked at Leland with narrowed eyes, as though taking in the story while having all kinds of ideas about it in his own mind. "What did he want, anyway?"

"A job, like the other drifters Eddy Piggot sent us," said Leland, half-shrugging. "But I sent him away. We go through Templeton's, you know that."

"I do know it." Bill nodded firmly. "But it sounds like he did us a favor. And Maddy says the bid for that groundskeeper contract is a big no, so why don't we hire the kid and pay him under the table? We'll save some money that way."

"You know we can't do that, Bill," said Leland. He shook his head because paying under the table was no way to run a business, even if the idea appealed to him, too. What's more, Jamie had been different from the other drifters, had remained polite even when the answer was no. There'd been such hope in his eyes, such an eagerness to earn his keep that now, standing there with Bill and mulling the idea over in his mind, a sense of regret filled him that he'd not already said yes to Jamie's request.

"Rules, rules," said Bill with a rough laugh, eyeing Leland from beneath the brim of his battered felt hat.

"I don't have a stick up my ass, at least not all the time," said Leland in his own defense.

"Sometimes, young fellow, you do."

Bill let this idea float on the air for a bit as he looked out over the slope of the hill and across the river to where the sun blazed on the low plateau and the spring-green hills that seemed to stretch out forever beneath the blue sky. Behind the foothills, Iron Mountain pushed rocky shoulders, cutting a hard horizon line. There wasn't a cloud in the sky, and the air was sharp and clear and smelled of pine trees and young aspen leaves.

Leland was lucky to live where he did, lucky to have grown up with supportive parents who loved him, lucky to have a job he adored. He was also lucky to work for a guy like Bill, who knew how to point out what worked and what didn't, never pulling any punches, but without being cruel. And now, as he always did, he was telling Leland without telling him that he needed to change his mind.

"What if—" Leland felt his heart start to beat a little faster at the idea forming in his mind, which felt new and fresh. "What if we hired him for two weeks, a trial. He could paint the border rocks in the main parking lot, cut the long grasses around the fire pit and beside the river. Groundskeeper work."

"And the more experienced hands can do the jobs we hired them to do." Bill nodded, tugging on the brim of his felt hat as though bidding welcome to Leland's marvelous idea. "We have plenty of room in the staff quarters, as you know. And the kid looked like he could use a few hot meals in his belly, besides. Maddy can get the paperwork together easy, so it'll all be above board."

"Now I feel like an ass." Tightening his jaw, Leland prepared himself for Bill to agree, expressing himself quite succinctly, as was Bill's way. But even as he regretted again the fact that he'd not offered Jamie some cool water to drink, or a step to sit on while he rested in the shade, Bill was shaking his head.

"You were doing what you thought was right. You're looking out for the ranch, and the staff, and for me and my place, the way you always do." Bill patted Leland's shoulder with a hearty slap. "Nothing wrong with doing what you think is right. Now, why don't you ride out and bring him back, and I'll alert Maddy that there will be one more for lunch."

"Sure thing, Bill, and thank you." With a lighter heart than he'd had all week, Leland mounted Gwen, settled himself in the saddle, and tugged the reins against her neck to get her to turn. He nodded to Bill, and scanned the horizon, taking in the view across the valley and the blue sky above.

Fresh air rushed around him like a gift, one that he never stopped appreciating. It was selfish of him to keep that for himself, and so now he would offer it to a young stranger who had come looking for work. He imagined in his mind's eye how the expression on Jamie's face would change with the offer of a job. And he remembered the way the sun had bronzed through Jamie's dark hair when he stepped out of the glade of pine trees.

Riveted by that image, he clucked to Gwen to get her to move into a trot. He needed to catch Jamie before he got to Farthing and caught the next Greyhound out of town.

6

JAMIE

With his head down, Jamie walked along the dirt road to the gate, passing in and out of the shade as he went, not even stopping at the stone bridge to let the spray of water cool his hot skin. There was no point in sticking around to see if anybody changed their mind, no point in dawdling. He needed to pick up his duffle bag from where it had fallen near the gate, and return to Farthing. From there he'd have to decide which direction he needed to go.

He had two options. Either he could hitch a ride to Chugwater and fill out whatever forms were needed at Templeton's and try, at least, to get a job on a ranch, like he'd planned. Or, he could hitch a ride back to Denver and start his life all over again, staying in the city, and maybe getting a job in a convenience store or something. Neither of which sounded very promising. He'd probably end up sharing an apartment with guys who would be jerks, and spend all his money on rent and food.

His dream of finishing college and making something of his life would turn out to be just that, a dream, one that would never come true. And who was to blame for that? Part of him felt like he should be angrier at Leland Tate for saying no about the job, but he wasn't. He'd watched Leland taking care of Monica, settling her from her fright. And he'd seen how Leland handled the horses, horses which were calm in Leland's presence, heads down as they nosed him in a gentle way.

Leland had seemed so steady, so kind, that even without knowing it, Jamie knew for a fact Leland hadn't refused him out of meanness, or his frustration with Eddy Piggot at the Rusty Nail, or even because he thought Jamie was a drifter. No, he refused Jamie a job because that was *his* job.

And then, for an entire hot minute, Leland and he had looked at each other, and he'd been sure Leland had been on the verge of offering him a job, anyway. Except Leland had shaken his head, and any sympathy he'd had vanished beneath the glitter of his hard blue eyes.

Not that Jamie needed sympathy. He needed a job and fast. His stomach was growling and his ribs hurt and he was so footsore he wanted to collapse then and there. And he smelled like horse now. While it wasn't a bad smell, he wanted a shower more than anything. The other part of him wanted to prove to both himself and to Leland that he wasn't a drifter, wasn't looking for a handout. He was trying to make his way in the world, and he just needed a chance.

By the time he got to the gate and picked up his duffle bag to sling it over his shoulder, he realized the duct tape on his left sneaker had broken and the sole was now almost completely detached from the canvas. He was basically walking on a bare foot; he had a hole in the sock where his big toe was poking out, and he still had a mile to go to town, and then unknown miles after that. In his wallet was twenty-five dollars and twenty-two cents, barely enough to buy fries and a coke to keep his stomach from growling. Barely enough for a night in a cheap motel. Certainly not enough for new sneakers.

The sun was blaring overhead, and his mouth was so dry, he could taste dust. There was nothing for it, though, but to open the gate and limp that last mile into Farthing. He couldn't think further than that, as the last bit of hope he'd clung to that day as he approached the ranch seemed to have vaporized in the heat.

From behind him he heard the churn of an engine and when he turned to look, he saw the sleek black SUV that had been in the parking lot before. Now it was coming down the road at him, and didn't look to be slowing at all, with spins of dust clouds churning from the wheels before settling on the spiky grasses alongside the road.

Out of courtesy, Jamie opened the gate wide for them and stood aside. He remembered Leland shouting at him to shut the gate, and it seemed important, so after the SUV passed through, he shut and latched the gate once more, coughing as dust settled in his throat.

To his surprise, the SUV pulled to a stop and the passenger door opened. The man who'd been sitting on the front porch with a drink in his hand leaned out and gestured to Jamie to come closer.

Thinking that he'd now get a lift into town, thus saving his feet, Jamie hustled over, swinging his duffle bag back so it wouldn't hit the man or the car. Sitting in the back seat was Monica and the woman who'd also been sitting on the porch drinking.

"Here you go, son," said the guy who was obviously Monica's dad. He held out a fold of bills. "You did a good job rescuing my daughter, and you deserve a reward."

"Give him more than that, hon," said Monica's mom from inside the SUV. When Monica's dad reached back into his wallet and pulled out more bills, Jamie hesitated before taking the money.

"Thank you," he said, shock moving through him like a low but energetic hum.

As the door closed and the SUV pulled away in another cloud of dust, he looked at the bills in his hand. There were many bills, most of them twenties, a few hundreds, and a couple of fifties. It looked like there was just about a thousand dollars in his hand.

As he shoved the fold of bills in his front pocket, he realized with a small jump of hope that he could do so many things. He could get one of those rent-by-the-week motel rooms, if Farthing or Chugwater had one. He could even get new sneakers. He could really work at getting a ranch job and save for going back to college. He could, finally, start turning his life around.

This lent a spring to his step, even if he had to limp a bit, but he'd not gone ten feet before he heard galloping hooves behind him. Jerking around, he was surprised to see Leland Tate riding Gwen. He slowed her at the gate and opened it without even getting off his horse. He carefully closed the gate behind him, which told Jamie that yes, he'd been right about that small detail being important, even as he watched Leland trot right up to him and stop.

Jamie looked up, squinting into the sun and was surprised when Leland moved the horse so that it was Leland facing the sun. He looked down at Jamie, eyes shadowed by the brim of his cowboy hat, and leaned forward on the horn of the saddle.

"I'm headed to town," said Jamie, in a hurry to make sure Leland knew he wasn't loitering or trying to stir up trouble. "I just saw Monica and her folks." He pointed his thumb up the road at the cloud of dust that was only now settling back down.

Opening his mouth, he tried to swallow as he prepared himself to tell Leland more of his plans, and how he meant to spend the money in his pocket, though why he felt the need to do that was beyond him. Or maybe he did know. He wanted Leland to think well of him.

"The Ayers didn't give you a lift?" asked Leland, with a long, hard stare up the road, as though the Ayers had just exhibited the worst manners.

"No," said Jamie. He shrugged to excuse them. "I think they were in a hurry."

"Still." Leland shook his head at his own private thoughts, then nodded at Jamie as if they'd come to an agreement between them about the Ayers.

Jamie waited and watched as Leland shifted in the saddle, not having any idea why a man who wanted him gone had now ridden out to see him, unless it was to make sure that Jamie stayed gone. Jamie shifted his duffle bag on his shoulder and was about to say his goodbyes when Leland straightened up.

"Listen, Jamie," said Leland. "Bill and I talked about it, and we're going to give you that job. It's just doing chores for two weeks to see how you work out, but it's a job."

Jamie's mouth fell open.

"I didn't mean to be so brusque before," said Leland. "I was frustrated with Eddy Piggot, but I took it out on you and for that I apologize." Straightening his shoulders, Leland sat back in his saddle, tightening his long legs against the horse's sides, as though pleased with himself he'd gotten the most troublesome part of his errand out of the way.

"Okay," said Jamie. In a rush, he realized he didn't have to take the job, now that he had money in his pocket. He could just say no and keep on walking.

Only—at the end of that walk was a whole lot more uncertainty than he wanted to deal with right about now. Besides, there was something about the way Leland was looking at him, as though he expected Jamie would say yes, which of course he was going to. Beyond that, Leland's expression seemed to indicate he also expected Jamie was up to the task, and right then and there, Jamie knew he wanted to get that stamp of approval that seemed to be waiting just behind those hard grey-blue eyes.

"I don't know anything about cows except how to cut them up," said Jamie, his own nature pushing at him to be terribly, terribly honest, as it usually did. This typically had proven itself to not be a very good idea of late, except here, it seemed to the exact right thing. "I worked at a meat packing plant and there was this guy who came in —" Jamie paused before blurting out that the guy reminded him a whole lot of Leland. "He talked about grass-fed cattle and how they should be slaughtered, sort of out of respect for the animal, and it was so different from what I was doing—"

"That you came away with the idea of working on a ranch." Leland nodded, and he was watching Jamie as though listening, really listening, to every single word he was saying.

"Yeah," said Jamie, swallowing a sudden jangle of nerves. "Only I thought you were a cattle ranch, and not a—whatever the guy at the Rusty Nail called it."

"A dude ranch," said Leland. "We call them guest ranches nowadays."

43

"Right, a dude ranch." Laughing a little bit, Jamie felt his nervousness start to fade away. "He doesn't like them."

"No, he does not," said Leland. "But if you want a job on one, it's yours."

"I don't know anything about horses, though." Jamie couldn't lie about that either.

Jamie looked at the horse Leland was riding, at her long horsey lashes and the soft leather strap across her nose, and the way she blinked and sighed, as if tired of their chatter and wanting to get a move on. Then Jamie looked up, right into Leland's eyes. Just as he was thinking about what he needed to say right then, the horse took a step forward and bumped her nose against his belly, as though she wanted him to pet her.

"Well, I'd say you know more than you think," said Leland. "She likes you, anyhow, and that stands for something with me. So what do you say?"

"I say yes," said Jamie before he could second-guess himself and probably walk away from the best offer he'd had in a long time. He watched while Leland pulled on the horse's reins and seemed to gather the animal beneath him. "Guess I'll see you at the ranch, then," Jamie said, petting the horse's nose as he shifted his duffle bag on his shoulder and thought about how long it would be before the stones in the road cut into his foot.

"I'll give you a ride, Jamie; you don't have to walk." Leland leaned forward and patted the horse's neck. The leather of the saddle creaked slightly. "Gwen can carry double that far, for sure."

When Jamie tried to imagine how he would get on top of an animal that suddenly looked very tall, Leland took his booted foot out of the stirrup, and held out his hand.

"Give me your duffle, then I'll help you up."

Jamie handed over his duffle bag and watched as Leland slung it around the saddle horn so it dangled on the other side of the horse. Then he held out his hand. It was obvious he meant Jamie to take it, so he did, a little shocked at the warm strength of it, the callouses. He put his left foot in the now-empty stirrup, wincing a bit at the stretch in his thighs, and let himself be pulled up.

For a wild second, he wasn't sure where he was supposed to land, and felt he was going to get astride the horse only to fall off on the other side. But Leland didn't let go of him, and Jamie was able to settle himself on Gwen's back, right behind the saddle, half on the saddle blanket, half off.

He was quite close to Leland's back, even before Gwen shifted into action. When she moved, his entire body moved forward, banging into Leland. He could smell the day's sweat on Leland, the trace of soap from an earlier shower. He had to grab onto Leland's waist to keep from falling off as Gwen trotted to the gate, and then he had to let go again as Leland leaned down to unlock the gate.

Leland made a clucking noise and shifted sideways as he straightened up, and Gwen suddenly moved beneath him. Flailing, Jamie's hands landed on Leland's thighs, both of them, and he scrambled to sit back, his hands slipping on Leland's blue jeans, which were warm from the sun, and warm from the taut muscle beneath.

"Easy now," said Leland. "Let's get through and I'll shut the gate. Then Gwen'll just be walking and it won't seem so unsteady."

"Okay," said Jamie, though it really wasn't okay at all. He couldn't seem to let go of Leland's waist, and couldn't seem to draw a single breath that didn't carry with it the scent of Leland's skin, the dash of faded shaving cologne, couldn't move a single inch without feeling Leland's strong muscles shifting beneath his touch. It was almost too much, almost enough to make him want to jump off then and there, to land in the road, shaking and confused.

Just then, as if she wanted to cover the distance between the gate and the shady glade before the stone bridge, Gwen burst into a small canter. Inside of a quick minute, they were in the cool gloom of the glade with the spray of water from the tumbling river blowing up at them. Jamie whooshed out a breath as Leland reached back to pat his knee.

"She just wants to get back to the stable, is all," said Leland in that

45

same calm voice he'd used with Monica. "This is your first time on horseback, I gather."

"Yes, it is." Jamie tried to unclench his hands from where they were gripping the front of Leland's shirt, and he figured Leland would be mad about it, but Leland patted his hands and clucked to Gwen.

"You'll be all right once you settle in," said Leland. "You'll be all right."

And he sounded like he believed it.

7

JAMIE

Once they arrived in the parking lot, Leland patted Jamie's knee again as he pulled Gwen right up to the porch of the office, where only a little while ago, it seemed, Jamie had read the sign about Maddy and Bill being gone and wondered what to do next. The sign was gone now, and beyond the screen door was an open wooden door, where he could hear someone talking on the phone. Then a woman came out and held the screen door open halfway. She wore blue jeans, and a pink cotton snap-button shirt, and her hair was in two blond and grey braids over her shoulders.

"There you are," she said, jingling keys in her hand as though Leland had kept her waiting for hours. "Tie that horse up for a minute. This paperwork won't take long. Then Bill said something about boots and a hat?"

"Thank you, Maddy," said Leland. "Slide off, Jamie, and we'll get you checked in."

It felt like Leland was treating Jamie like a guest, and that he most certainly did not want to be. He was being given a chance to work on a ranch, just like he'd wanted, and he was going to prove he was worth the risk, even if he had to work from sunup to sundown to do it.

When Leland turned to see why Jamie wasn't moving, Jamie scrambled down from the horse, his knees wobbling as he landed on solid ground once more. His ribs and shoulder ached from where he'd banged into the gate, but he kept silent about it, not wanting to let it get in the way of his newfound hope.

Stepping back, he watched the way Leland dismounted, studying how Leland balanced himself with a booted foot in one stirrup, not letting go of the saddle horn until his other foot touched the ground. Leland now loomed above Jamie, all length and muscle and surety, and he seemed to smile a little bit as he watched Jamie try to back up without falling over.

"Don't worry, Jamie," said Leland as he tied Gwen's reins to one of the poles supporting the roof of the small porch. "Your legs will get stronger. The more you ride, the less they'll wobble."

They went inside the office, where Maddy made Jamie sit down in an old leather chair and pushed a pile of papers on a clipboard at him to sign. When she took his driver's license into a little side room where a copier was to copy it, she looked at the date and made *tsk tsk* noises under her breath. As she came back and handed Jamie his license, she waved the copy of it in front of Leland.

"This expires tomorrow," she said. "Can you help him get it renewed? He can't drive any of our vehicles until it's up to date, as insurance won't cover it. And Jamie, I'm going to need routing numbers for your bank account, so I can send your wages there." Maddy sat back down at her desk and opened a manilla folder, then wrote Jamie's name on the tab with a black marker. "Jamie Decker," she said as she wrote it. "Yes," she said to him, shaking her head as though he'd been arguing with her. "Folders are old-fashioned, but they work for me. Don't they, Leland?"

"Yes, ma'am," said Leland. He'd taken off his hat and stood by the chair, watching Jamie fill out the paperwork. "That they do."

Jamie finished the paperwork as fast as he could, populating little boxes with all the information about his previous employment that he could remember, and signing his name so many times his fingers began to ache. But he had a job, now, and his growling stomach, sensing that, sent up another rumble.

"I'll take those," said Maddy, reaching over the desk and taking the clipboard from Jamie with an efficient snap. "Bill says to take him to the store and get him boots and a hat, whatever he needs—and I'd say yes, within reason."

"I-I can pay," said Jamie, thinking of the thousand dollars in his pocket. He'd rather save it than spend it, but he also wanted cowboy gear like Leland had on. "But how much—?"

"Oh, no," said Maddy, her mouth pursing as though he was demonstrating the worst manners she'd ever seen. "The first round's on the company. That's what Bill said. If you need anything after, we deduct it from your pay. So I really need that routing number; you didn't fill it out."

"Uh, I don't have a bank account." He looked up at Leland, anxiety tightening his shoulders because if Leland thought Jamie was too much trouble, he might just take back that job offer and send Jamie on his way. "I mean, I used to, but not anymore." Not since he took all his money out so he could pay for a Greyhound bus ticket to Wyoming so he could take a chance on a wild dream.

"Leland, can you help him with that, too?" asked Maddy. "And I'll need to add your name to the Friday announcements at dinner." She scribbled in a small notebook, then looked up at him. "We usually have a sheet cake, and everyone comes up while we sing happy birthday to all the folks who had a birthday that week."

"You don't need to do that," said Jamie, the words coming out in a rush.

His face grew warm at the thought of someone going to so much trouble just for him. In fact, everything was overwhelming him with a small avalanche of kindness that threatened to undo him if it didn't stop. Which it wasn't because Maddy was still talking, mostly to Leland, about boots he needed, and what kind of hat. She was handing over a set of keys as she rattled on a set of instructions to Leland about which room Jamie was to have, and to make sure about those clean sheets.

The room seemed to spin a little and the sound of Maddy's voice sank low until it was barely a buzz, and all Jamie could focus on was the shaft of sunlight streaming in through the panes of glass, where it settled on the corner of a display case beneath sepia-toned photographs arranged on the wall.

"Okay, Jamie?" asked Maddy.

She was standing up, so Jamie stood up, nodded at her, and then followed Leland out of the office. He thought they were going to get back on Gwen and ride to the barn or something, but Leland led him into the building next door, and together they clomped up the steps to go where Jamie hadn't dared go before.

The store was a little different from he imagined it would be, a shiny, compact space that was longer than it was wide. It seemed to sell everything from chilled bottled water to beef jerky and other snacks, and included on its shelves boots and hats and touristy trinkets, as well as sweatshirts with the ranch logo on it, and snap-button cowboy-style shirts on hangers.

Every corner seemed packed with anything anybody visiting the ranch might need. Jamie watched as Leland picked out a pair of lace-up brown leather boots so new they almost squeaked when he put them on the glass-topped counter.

"Don't worry," said Leland, smiling at Jamie as he pulled two shirts from the rack. "We have cowboy boots in the barn that prior guests sometimes leave behind. Some are shiny enough for dancing, which is good because these days we need all hands on deck on dancing night. These boots are just for everyday use."

Overwhelmed again, Jamie couldn't even find the voice to protest as the pile on the counter grew. It included new white t-shirts, a packet of underwear, a toothbrush, a thick dun-colored jacket. There was everything he might need and, in fact, did need, since his duffle bag, still hanging on Gwen's saddle horn, only contained a single change of clothes.

Best of all, Leland asked the clerk to bring down several cowboy hats for Jamie to try on. Together they selected a crisp-edged straw hat with a narrow leather band and a twist of brass in the front that looked a little like a pine tree. Jamie felt a burst of excitement as the clerk put the hat back in its tidy box, and couldn't wait to wear it.

"We better try those boots on, make sure they fit," said Leland, then he turned to the young lady behind the counter. "Can I get some socks, too, please?"

When the young lady handed Leland a packet of socks, Leland handed the socks to Jamie, and grabbed the new lace-up boots.

"Over here," he said, leading the way to a pair of chairs beside a rack of leather moccasins. He sat in one chair and patted the other one beside him. "We need to make sure they fit or else you'll get blisters."

Jamie did as he was told and sat down to drag off his sneakers and thin socks. The right sneaker came off just like it should, in one piece, but the left one was almost cracked in half, and there were two sizable holes in the bottom of his socks.

"What the hell?" Leland took the sneaker and shook it at Jamie, like a man about to scold a dog over a shoe it has just chewed up. "How long have you been wearing these in the state that they are?" He turned the sneaker over to look at it more closely. "Did the sole crack or something? I notice traces of duct tape here."

"Um." Shrinking back against the chair, Jamie tried to dig up an explanation that wouldn't sound like he was a complete idiot who hadn't noticed his sneaker was falling apart. "A while," was all he could say, leaving out the part where his plans to buy new sneakers had been foiled because the guys he rented a house with said he owed them money.

That was all far behind him now, so he should be able to get over it, only it was difficult. And here was Leland, seemingly pissed, looking at Jamie with hard eyes because Jamie hadn't been able to make things work on his own. Only what Leland eventually said was not what Jamie had been expecting.

"Look, Jamie," said Leland, in the same calm, steady voice he'd used before. "On the ranch, it's important to have good footwear and to take good care of your feet. We do a lot of walking and a lot of riding so, in future, if you need new boots, you need to speak up. Got it?"

"Yes, sir," said Jamie. He wanted to squirm in his chair, and he would have if Leland's scrutiny had gone on much longer. Instead, Leland waggled the packet of socks in front of Jamie, took the other sneaker from him and threw both in a small, round, metal trash can next to the rack of moccasins. Then, with his booted foot, he scooted the new boots across the linoleum floor closer to Jamie.

"Put those on, then walk back and forth so we can see."

Feeling a bit like he was on trial, Jamie slipped off his old socks, and didn't say anything when Leland threw those away, too. Then he put on the new socks, and laced up the new boots, and was just about enjoying the small squeaking sounds the new leather made when Leland bent down to push on the toe.

"Yeah, that looks about right. Now, get up and walk."

Jamie felt like he was on parade, or a small show pony being asked to trot in front of the judges. Or maybe he was just very tired, very hungry, and completely out of his depth to be thinking such thoughts. Luckily, Leland seemed to approve of how the boots fit, and stood up and gestured that Jamie should stand up, too.

"Bag those up for me, will you?" he asked the young lady behind the counter as he pushed all the items toward her. "Bill says to put them on the company tab." He turned to Jamie. "If you need anything else, just come get it. The cost can be deducted from your pay."

"Thank you," said Jamie in a very small voice as he watched Leland heft the large, plastic bag the clerk handed him. The box with the hat in it, Leland handed to Jamie.

"You'll need that to keep the sun off. And though it might seem too warm for 'em, you'll need to wear long-sleeved shirts when you're working, too. Okay?"

"Okay."

Bearing the hatbox in his hands, Jamie followed Leland out of the cool, air-conditioned store to where Gwen patiently waited, still tied to the porch, flicking her tail behind her. Stomping in his new boots down the small flight of wooden steps, Jamie almost stepped on Leland's heels when Leland suddenly came to a stop.

"Up you get," Leland said.

"What?"

"You ride, and I'll lead. Gwen's done enough work carrying two for one day, I think."

Leland helped Jamie get his new boot in the stirrup. They were almost too big and round to fit into the stirrup, and Jamie could easily see why they would be good work boots but not good riding boots. Once Jamie was astride, Leland tied the plastic bag of new gear to the saddle horn. Untying Gwen's reins, he led the horse along the road and into the glade of trees that grew between the parking lot and the lodge.

Jamie was pleased that the layout was becoming more familiar to him and even more pleased to see the quiet moment Leland took to pet Gwen and whisper something to her as they went. He felt a thrill at being so high up, high enough to look down on Leland's broad shoulders, to be able to measure the length of his stride. It was a completely different world, being on horseback, and it was nothing like he'd expected it would be. Maybe buying that Greyhound bus ticket to the back end of nowhere had been the best idea rather than the worst, after all.

They walked along the road through the glade. Jamie clenched the saddle horn and held the box with his hat in it close against his stomach, where the corner poked him every now and then. Once out of the glade, they passed the dining hall, which was now bustling with cowboy-type people who were going inside. How different it looked now that he'd secured a job and belonged there, more solid, more approachable. More like home.

Leland led Gwen past the dining hall, where they turned into the shade of a group of pine trees to follow a wide path to a building that stood against a hillside.

"This is the staff quarters," said Leland. "Can you manage all of this?" he asked Jamie as an older woman with a flowered apron and a tight bun came out of the building. "Hey, there Stella."

"The room's all ready," she said. "Do you have the key?"

"Yes, I got it from Maddy. Here." Leland waited as Jamie dismounted, once again to unsteady knees, his new boots feeling like they weighed a ton. "These are your keys. Looks like you're in room 301. Why don't you head up and grab a quick shower, and I'll meet you in front of the dining hall when you're ready. That's the building we just passed."

A small wave of dismay swept over Jamie, though he scolded himself for it. Leland wasn't dismissing him, he was telling him to take a shower and meet up for something to eat. All of this was so good, so wonderful and amazing, that he hardly knew how to take it all in.

"Thank you," he said as he took the keys and juggled the hatbox in his hands as he tried to take the plastic bag from Leland, and his green duffle bag, as well.

"Here," said Leland. He put the plastic bag on the ground while Gwen nuzzled him from behind as though looking for treats. Slinging the duffle bag over Jamie's shoulder, he took the new straw hat out of the box and plonked it on Jamie's head. He tucked the now-empty box under his arm. "You might as well get used to wearing it. I need to take Gwen to the stable and get her unsaddled and watered. See you in a bit."

"See you," said Jamie, echoing Leland's words, trying to make them his own.

As Leland gathered up Gwen's reins and headed back down the small path between the trees, Jamie hefted the plastic bag and smiled beneath the brim of his new straw hat. The keys to his new life dangled from his fingers, and he smiled even wider as he stepped inside and looked at the number on the wooden rectangle attached to the keys. It said 301.

That meant he needed to climb three flights of stairs, but he didn't let that bother him, and sprinted up as fast as he could. By the time he reached the third floor landing, his thighs were aching, and his throat was dry as paper. Quickly he searched for the room with the same number as the key.

The building was simple, built of wood, but everything was sturdy and clean and he found the room at the very end of a long, narrow hallway. He dumped the plastic bag and the duffle bag on the floor and hurried to unlock the door to his new room, his new life, and, with a sigh, stepped inside.

The room was small with bare white walls and a plain wooden floor. It was a corner room with a window on each wall, each with a thin cotton curtain. A door led off to a little bathroom.

On the bed were clean sheets, with one corner of the bedclothes turned down as though inviting him to slide in and have a nap. His rented room back in Greeley hadn't been as nice as this, nor as clean, or as quiet. The last time he'd slept in a place this nice was when he'd been living with his dad, and even then it'd not been as homey or as welcoming.

He went over to the window to peer out. His room occupied the corner of the building, overlooking a low hillside of trees and wild green grasses and a short row of small wooden cabins, each with a front porch. It was the best view he'd ever had access to in his entire life.

Sliding open the window, he could hear birds and see the breeze stir through the trees, and wanted to cry with happiness. He'd landed in a blissful bounty of wonderfulness, that was for certain. All he had to do was work his ass off so he could keep it.

He grabbed his things from the hallway and shut the door behind him, reveling in the quiet, simple space that was all his own. He put his straw hat on the bed, and stored everything away in the dresser and the narrow closet, and arranged his new toothbrush and tooth-paste and other items in the small mirrored cupboard above the sink. Then he took a fast hot shower, and buffed himself off and dried his hair on a pair of fluffy, white towels.

He put on one of the new pairs of blue jeans, one of the new t-shirts from the packet, and then his new socks and boots, and a long-sleeved shirt, as Leland had instructed. Then he pulled out the wad of cash from the blue jeans he'd flung across the bed and looked at the bills as they unfolded in his hand. He stored the money in the top drawer of the dresser. He had a key to the room, and so the money would be safe until Leland helped him set up that bank account.

Satisfied with that decision, he put his straw hat back on, and went out, locking the door behind him. And then clomped down the stairs with his stomach growling in anticipation of the fine meal it would soon have. His life was turning out much better than he ever thought possible, and silently he thanked that un-named rancher who'd come to the meat packing plant, wanting special treatment for his grass-fed herd of cattle.

8

LELAND

When Leland met Jamie at the bottom of the steps of the dining hall, he was struck by how well the young man cleaned up. He'd washed all the road dust off him, and was wearing a new white t-shirt and a pair of new, dark blue jeans. His dark hair curled around his forehead in a sweet way, glinting with bronze at the edges. He had his hands in his back pockets as he bounced on his toes and was very easy to look at.

"That room is great," Jamie said with a shy smile, his green eyes sparkling from beneath the brim of his new straw cowboy hat. "So clean and nice. All my stuff fit in the two top drawers."

Leland had to pause. The rooms were quite spartan and plain, but Jamie was talking about his room as though he'd moved into a palace all his own.

Maybe to a drifter like him it was a palace, but unlike any other drifter Leland'd chanced to meet, Jamie seemed to appreciate it. Maybe the ranch would be a new start for him and, if so, it was Leland's job to help him make the most of it. And to make good Bill's suggestion at repaying Jamie the favor he'd done them.

Jamie was quiet as he followed Leland into the dining hall, shadowing his movements as they hung up their hats on handy wooden pegs on the wall, and stood behind him in the buffet line. Usually, the ranch provided different ways of feeding guests, but since last season, they'd had to economize by having all buffet meals. At least, thanks to Maddy, it was all good, fresh food.

Leland took a plate, some cutlery, a cloth napkin, and nodded at Jamie that he should do the same. Together they went through the buffet line.

Jamie took a mound of everything, and then served himself another large spoonful of fried mashed potatoes, enough so that the food spilled from the plate and onto his tray. Where had the young man come from, what had he experienced, that he felt the need to take more than a man could actually eat?

"You can sit with me, if you like," said Leland, gesturing with his tray.

His single thought was to save a newcomer from sitting by himself so he wouldn't feel like a stranger in a new place. Jamie had a slight look of panic on his face, which he quickly covered up by looking away from Leland and at the dining hall, as though he was searching for somebody he knew so he could sit with them. But there was nobody he actually knew, so when his attention turned to Leland again, he looked flushed.

"Okay," said Jamie. Then, "I'm sorry, I'm just overwhelmed."

"Not a problem, Jamie." It was obvious that Jamie'd been on his own for a while.

Leland led the way to one of the tables along the bank of windows, where he liked to sit for pretty much any meal, when he wasn't sitting with guests or his staff. The view was of a lush green hillside. Along the other side of the dining hall, the long side, the spaces between the pine trees provided glimpses of other buildings, but mostly the view was of the rolling hills and a whole lot of sky.

"How about here?" Leland asked as he set his tray on the table. Jamie seemed to be hesitating, so Leland sat down and unfurled his napkin to show how it was done.

"This is nice," Jamie said, as though he'd been provided with the best seat in the house. Then he sat down as well.

Jamie was focused on his food, so as they ate together there wasn't much conversation. Leland had questions in his mind about why the young man had come all this way looking for a job, an uncertain prospect at best. But he seemed willing at the same time to learn something unfamiliar and new. Grit and determination had taken him this far, qualities Leland had always admired.

"We'll give you an orientation this afternoon," said Leland into the small silence, which seemed to have created a bubble around them amidst the general chatter and low sounds of the high-ceilinged dining hall. "Take you around, show you the layout of the place, spell out some ground rules. Then in the morning, after the general meeting outside the barn, we'll put you to work."

"Okay," said Jamie between quick bites, finishing the last of what was on his plate in a hurry, as though he feared he'd never get another hot meal as long as he lived.

While Leland finished a slice of strawberry-rhubarb pie, home-made and locally grown, Jamie went and got another helping of the meatloaf and mashed potatoes, as if he'd not just had a huge serving. As he came back and put his tray down, his face turned pale, a sheen of sweat on his forehead.

"Are you all right?" Leland asked, unsure, in that moment, what was going on.

"I shouldn't have eaten so fast," Jamie said. Without another word, he turned and went out of the dining hall through the double doors at one end.

Quickly, Leland followed him, ignoring the startled looks of the staff in the serving line.

Just as Leland stepped through the double doors, he found Jamie by an open trash can, bending over it, retching. All of Leland's sympathies rose in a way he'd not expected. Moving close, he patted Jamie's back and stayed near as he threw up. There was nothing more lonely than being sick in a new place, and there was just so much he didn't understand about Jamie's situation.

"Easy now, easy," he said, sympathy rising inside of him in waves.

Jamie finished throwing up and groaned low in his chest, resting his head on his arm along the rim of the trash can. His dark hair trailed about his head, threatening to get dragged through the vomit.

"C'mon, now," Leland said, tugging on his t-shirt, noting the heat of Jamie's body beneath the cotton. "Let's get you cleaned up. Get you some ginger ale and crackers."

Jamie looked up, his eyes full of a kind of low surprise, as though he couldn't believe anybody cared enough to look after him in this way. His body shivered in the cool air that came through the breezeway off the dining hall, where shipments came in and where the dumpsters were stored. Guests never came back here, so it was a little more workaday than most parts of the ranch. It was also not the place to linger if you'd just been sick.

"Come with me," Leland said, quite gently. "We'll use the staff restroom."

Jamie seemed a little resistant to this, as though he thought he was about to be tricked and led into an even more dismal situation.

"I was hungry," he said in a quiet voice as Leland guided him back inside.

It was easy to see that Jamie's mind was whirling with ways to explain his behavior without giving too much away. His life before coming to the ranch had obviously made him cautious. Any upbeat smiles from earlier had now worn away to nothing. He was exhausted, through and through, building in Leland more of those same feelings from earlier, that of wanting to help.

"Don't worry about that now," Leland said. He led Jamie back through the dining hall to the service area, where staff was cleaning up from the lunchtime meal. "Here's the restroom. Go get cleaned up."

As Leland watched Jamie go into the restroom, he knew that had Jamie been anybody else, whether a new ranch hand or an experienced trail boss, he would have left it at that, a direction to wash up and instructions for one of the kitchen staff to fetch him that ginger ale.

It was not his style to linger like this. He trusted his staff to look after these kinds of small details. His job as a foreman was to delegate, and to expect that his more experienced employees would then, in turn, run their departments.

It was not his job to fetch and carry for a newly hired hand who didn't know the size of his own belly. So why was he doing exactly that? Why did he have the ginger ale poured and ready when Jamie came out of the restroom, the ends of his dark hair dripping as though he'd stuck his face beneath the tap with the water running at full blast?

The center of his t-shirt was damp, etching the lines of his ribs and sternum. He was on the thin side, still growing, still on his way to becoming a man.

Leland jerked his eyes away and focused on handing over the can of ginger ale and the glass of ice.

"You can drink that," he said, nodding as one of the white-aproned kitchen staff came over with a small bowl of salted crackers. "And eat those, slowly."

He was used to being obeyed, but as Jamie looked up at him, ready to follow orders, something bright shone in his green eyes, as though he trusted anything that Leland might tell him to do would be the right thing.

There was a pile of accounting and other paperwork waiting for Leland in his cabin, and he needed to make a few phone calls about delayed orders before finally calling it a day. He didn't have the luxury of lingering, yet he lingered. Lingered and watched Jamie while he nibbled on the crackers and sipped on the ginger ale.

"I'll take you around for a bit. A walk in the fresh air will do you good. Then I'll hand you over to Clay," said Leland, smiling, as he knew how good Clay would be at this task. "We'll find out what you're good at. Do you need a clean shirt?"

Jamie lifted his can of ginger ale, holding it high as though he was afraid of spilling it on himself.

"I think I'm okay," he said, looking up at Leland again. "I'm sorry to be so much trouble after you gave me the job without sending me to Chugwater first."

Again, Leland wanted to know how Jamie had come to such a

state, with worn out sneakers and an about-to-expire driver's license. Sure, he'd worked in a meat packing plant, which was a rough way to live, no matter how you looked at it. But that didn't explain everything else.

"You sure you're up for this tour?" Leland asked, gently.

"Yeah, I'm up for it." Jamie swallowed the rest of the ginger ale in one gulp, too fast for Leland's comfort, then put the can and the now-empty bowl on a nearby metal counter. He wiped cracker crumbs from his mouth with the back of his hand. He finished the gesture with an exhausted nod as his dark hair fell over his eyes. "Just show me the way."

For a long, terrible instant, Leland had to stifle the impulse to brush away the last bit of crumb that still clung to Jamie's mouth, but this was hardly the time and, in the breezeway of a common work area, hardly the place. Besides, what was he having such tender instincts like that for?

"Let's get to it," Leland said.

He was tempted to pat Jamie on the shoulder as a kind of reassurance that things would look better in the morning, and to say something encouraging, but he wasn't a small talk kind of man. He explained how things worked, gave orders, received information, and ran one of the sweetest ranches in Wyoming.

His world was the Farthingdale Guest Ranch, just as he wanted it to be. Only now someone had stepped inside that space, creating a small ripple effect that even if it had only just started, didn't look like it was going to stop.

"Let's start at the back end of the ranch," said Leland, again questioning his motives. He usually had a ranch hand do the general tour, then would meet with the new hire at the end of that to have a final meeting about rules and expectations. This time, he wanted to do part of the tour himself to share with Jamie the beauty of the ranch.

Jamie nodded, and after they grabbed their hats from the wooden pegs, he followed Leland out of the dining hall. Together they walked along the shaded path that curved between the trees, up past the barn to the first corral. Cottonwoods and willows grew along the tributary of Horse Creek that ran through the property, but the slope at this end of the ranch was decked with pine and aspen both, and the breeze was sweetly scented.

Briskly, Leland described the layout of the ranch, starting with the corral.

"Notice the unpainted wood, Jamie. You won't be asked to paint it, because unpainted wood seasons better. The round rails between round posts are not the most efficient, but look nice and it's what guests at the ranch expect."

Jamie nodded, stuffing his hands in the back pocket of his new jeans. He looked a little lost in his new clothes, as though the fit was just a bit too big. The jeans, especially, would shrink in the wash, though. Leland clamped down on the impulse to take Jamie to the laundry room in the staff quarters to get that process started.

"We mostly do riding lessons in the corral," said Leland, pointing to the area. "But sometimes, if the group of guests might like it, Brody comes out and does some of his rope tricks, and demos his fancy riding with his special saddle."

"Oh, yeah?"

"He's about your age," said Leland, mentally shaking his head, because why was he talking about age at all? "Maybe a little older. Best wrangler I've ever worked with."

Moving on from the corral, Leland pointed out the acres of open fields behind the barbed wire fence, some of which belonged to the ranch, and some of which belonged to the Bureau of Land Management. They were always careful not to leave any trace behind, so the BLM had never given them any grief about taking long cattle drives across their land into the hills. It was a truce of long standing Leland was proud of, as was Bill.

"The barn's this way," said Leland, pointing down the road.

He led the way and took Jamie inside to show him the large area where horses were groomed, or where demonstrations could be held when the weather was bad. There was a row of box stalls along two walls, and a large tack room whose open door showed neatly arranged saddles and other tack and grooming supplies.

"That's my office, over there." He pointed to the corner of the barn, just to the side of the big open doors. "I'll hand you to Clay in a minute, when he gets here," he said, inhaling the scent of dried hay and leather oil, which helped to settle him some.

"Clay?" asked Jamie.

"Clay Pullman's my right-hand man," said Leland with a nod, for he didn't know what he'd do without Clay. "He'll show you the cabins along the river, and all the other nooks and crannies, and the laundry room in the staff quarters, where you can wash your clothes. There's a box of quarters next to the soap, so you don't need to worry about paying."

"It's free?" asked Jamie. "Doesn't anybody steal the quarters?"

In Jamie's world, it was easy to see, any money left out got taken. Here, on the ranch, there was plenty of everything, and no sense of want.

"No, they don't," Leland said. "Sure, sometimes the final count at the end of the week means we'd gone low a quarter or two. But the ranch hands and everybody who uses the machines usually leave their spare change, so it all works out in the wash, so to speak."

There were purple smudges under Jamie's eyes as he looked at Leland, though he tried to smile like everything was fine, just fine, and that nobody needed to worry about him. Then his exhaustion seemed to overcome him, as though this small display had tapped the last of his energy.

"You okay, Jamie?" Leland asked. He wanted to gently push for the answer, but Clay came up twirling his straw cowboy hat in his hands, whistling under his breath.

"This is Clay," said Leland. "Clay, this is Jamie Decker, our new groundskeeper and general ranch hand."

"I'm a ranch hand?" asked Jamie, now lighting up in a way that was hard for Leland to look away from.

"That you are," said Leland, secretly pleased at Jamie's response. "You're just starting, but if you listen to what Clay tells you, you will do very well, I'm sure of it. You got this, Clay? Show him the ropes, now. Show him everything he needs to know."

"Can do, boss," said Clay. With a bright smile, he put his hat back on and clapped Jamie on the shoulder in a friendly way. "I'll take good care of him."

"Make sure he knows how to take breaks and drink enough water." Leland turned his attention to Jamie. "We're up at altitude here, so it's easy to get dehydrated. That's why we've got coolers of bottled water set out at various places. If you're working out of doors, you'll see one. Okay?"

"Yes, sir," said Jamie, wide eyed.

With a small wave, Leland bid them farewell and went up the path between the trees and the buildings to the little cabin tucked in the hillside that was all his own. The cabin had a porch where he could sit and watch the sunsets, if he had the time, and a small flagstone patio in the back where he could watch the sunrise over the low hills and have his coffee in the morning.

Or, like now, he could hang up his keys on the little hook on the wall just inside the front door, pull off his work boots and cowboy hat, yank off his socks, and walk barefooted into the small cafe kitchen. There he could grab a bottle of ice cold locally-brewed root beer and drink it with the fridge door standing wide open. Now, in his own place, he was no longer the ranch manager, or the boss of anyone, didn't need to be on his best game or set a good example.

He sucked back half of a bottle of root beer before taking a single, gasping breath after he swallowed it down. This was one of his favorite moments of the day, when he was just Leland, just a guy who loved his mom and who loved working out of doors. A guy who loved root beer and sunsets and sunrises and the way the chinook winds rushed down from Iron Mountain as though on their way to someplace new and exciting. Leaving behind the sweet, pure scent of spring and growth and green.

Amidst all of that, like a strange, leaf-rustling breeze, came thoughts of Jamie Decker. Who, with his dark bronze-touched hair and bright green eyes, seemed to be cutting a shape for himself in Leland's world, changing his vision of it. Leland imagined Jamie pushing his hair out of his eyes, shocked at the idea that he had any effect on Leland, because how could he, being so newly arrived?

But he did have an effect, and the results were already there, for anyone to see. For starters, Leland had changed his mind about hiring drifters, which he never thought he'd ever do. Then he'd tended to Jamie after he'd been sick, like he'd known Jamie for years instead of only a few hours. And now he was worried about Jamie on his tour with Clay.

Clay would do an excellent job, of course, being sure to tell Jamie everything he'd need to know to be a success on the ranch. But Jamie had looked tired, still strung out from his travels, perhaps, or, like he said, simply overwhelmed. Would he be okay all on his own his first night in a room he described as his own personal palace?

Maybe Leland should check with Clay at dinner, just to see how the tour went, and then check with Jamie to see if he had any questions. Yes, that's what he'd do. In the meantime, he needed to move on from worries that would probably amount to nothing. He needed to take a shower and get to that paperwork so he could keep up with the daily accounts.

Nobody had asked him to take on such work, but he'd decided to save the ranch money by doing it himself, so now it was his responsibility. He needed to focus on that and not on how Jamie had smiled and tossed his dark hair out of his eyes, and looked around him as though the ranch was the prettiest place he'd ever seen.

Drinking the rest of the root beer, Leland rinsed the glass bottle, put it in the blue plastic recycling box, and padded to the small but serviceable bathroom. There he stripped, threw his dirty clothes into the hamper, and stepped into the shower, turning the dial as hot as it would go.

The moment the hot water hit his shoulders was a sigh-worthy one, and he shuddered as his body released all the tensions of the day. He still had some hours to go being on duty as ranch manager, but in this shower stall, his thoughts could be all his own.

As he washed, the sweet smell of soap drifted up in rising swirls of air, and he inhaled deeply. Then he let out his breath quite slowly and closed his eyes as his mind drifted to where it would go. Which was, he was not surprised to admit, to Jamie wearing his new straw hat with its narrow leather band around the crown and the twist of brass in the front that looked a little like one of the pine trees on the ranch that grew so proudly and smelled so nice.

Beneath the brim of the straw hat, Jamie's hair tumbled in loose, loping curls past his ears, turning this way and that, dark against the pale skin of his neck. Green eyes looked at Leland, as though through the mist of the shower, wide with wonderment and surprise that something good had happened to him.

That's what the expression said to Leland now as he turned the soap over and over in his hands. He wanted, suddenly, to hop out of the shower and find Jamie to ask him what had happened to him to make the simple act of getting a job and a place to lay his head at night such a miracle.

He couldn't ask that outright, of course, but perhaps over time he should find out. Then, having solved that mystery, he could move on and stop obsessing over a young man who probably did not know he was causing Leland's mind to dwell on the curve of his cheek. Who did not know that the memory of him, covered in road-dust and leading a horse in a hopeless way, was making Leland smile in spite of himself.

Who had no idea, none at all, that Leland had his hand on his own soap-covered belly, clenching every muscle in his body to keep from doing what he very much wanted to do. Which was to give in to the spark of lively desire he felt at the thought of how he might, quite gently, ask Jamie to sit at dinner with him. Or maybe go for an inno-cent walk after.

Innocent it would be, for Leland was not the type to fraternize with employees, especially not ones almost ten years younger than himself. And who, at the end of all of that, was probably straight as an arrow, with no interest in single-minded ranch managers who felt the love of the land, of horses, of hard work, too deeply to let go without a fight.

With an odd pang in his heart, he finished his shower as fast as he could, buffing himself afterward with a towel. The ranch was the prettiest place in the world, with green prairie grasses and aspen trees and a clean-running creek. It was everything to him. He would not risk it by flirting with someone he'd just hired that very day. Sure, he was willing to share the ranch, share his joy in the wild country all around, but that didn't mean he could play fast and loose with his responsibilities. Fast and loose with the emotions of a young man who'd come through a rough patch and just needed to get his life together.

The last thing he wanted to do was be reckless with the ranch. With himself. With Jamie.

He resolutely fixed his mind on what he needed to do, and he changed into clean blue jeans and a t-shirt.

Later, after he was done with the paperwork, he'd put on socks, and add back his cowboy hat and a long-sleeved snap-button shirt, turning into a ranch manager once more. But for now, he took the ledger, the calculator, a stack of receipts, and a scratch pad out to the little table on his back patio, settling himself in to update the accounts, to make sure of the books. And then he needed to show up at dinner looking like the ranch manager he was, even if there weren't any guests in residence, setting a good example for ranch hands and staff.

Jamie Decker was a mystery he wanted to solve, but in the meantime, he still had work to do.

9

JAMIE

*M*orning brought Jamie to bleary-eyed wakefulness accompanied by a knocking on the door and a stiffness along his ribs. He should have asked for aspirin or something when he and Leland had been in the ranch's store, but he'd been given so much already he hated to ask for more.

"Hey," said Clay from the other side of the door. "Better get a move on or you'll miss breakfast."

"Coming." Jamie sat up, rubbing the sleep from his eyes, wincing as his sore shoulder protested. "Coming."

As fast as he could, he scrambled into the clothes he'd worn the day before, and scraped his hair back from his face. There wasn't time for a shower, but he took a swallow of water from the sink in his little bathroom and scrubbed his teeth with his finger. It would have to be enough.

He tied his boots and proudly put on his straw hat. When he looked at himself in the mirror, he smiled. The hat made him look like a genuine cowboy—a real ranch hand—and the little brass pine tree on the narrow leather hat band made the hat look special.

Thumping down the stairs, he raced to the dining hall, but found that they were already clearing up the buffet warmers and wiping down the tables from breakfast.

"Sorry, kid," said the white-aproned guy as he paused with a tray of dirty glasses. "You can grab a glass of milk from the dispenser, at least."

"Thank you," said Jamie, breathless.

A glance at the clock on the wall told him he was already late to the meeting, but he downed a glass of milk and scrubbed his mouth with the back of his hand. Then, as fast as he could, he raced out of the dining hall and up the dirt road to the barn.

The night before, he'd been so tired after his tour with Clay that he'd skipped dinner and gone straight to bed. Now he was starving even before he got to the barn and shaking beneath his skin because he was going to be late, already on his way to screwing everything up.

The outside air was chilly. The skin on his bare arms prickled in the cold, even though it was June. The ranch was near the mountains and high up in altitude, so that must be the reason, though he honestly hadn't expected any of this when he'd bought that Greyhound ticket.

He rubbed his arms as he arrived at the barn where all the other ranch hands were already gathered in a group. All of them wore sturdy boots and long-sleeved shirts and felt or straw cowboy hats. Chatting with each other, joking around, they all looked like they belonged, and Jamie wondered how long it would be before he felt like he fit in.

The tall doors to the barn opened, and out stepped Leland Tate, drawing Jamie's eyes to him with a hard snap. Leland's blue jeans were tight on his long legs, his flannel shirt with pearl-snap buttons as crisp as though he'd ironed it that morning before putting it on.

Leland started talking to an older guy and two other men. Then he scanned the crowd as if to see who had shown up, and Jamie froze. The day before, throwing up everything he'd eaten, with everybody watching, had left him feeling like he'd crawled through a bush backwards, all sweaty and gross. Leland hadn't seemed to mind that and had been nicer about it than Jamie had expected. That would end, of course, when he remembered Jamie was a drifter that someone named

Bill had made him hire, and not someone who'd gone through official channels.

Turning his attention back to the small group of men, Leland took off his hat to scrub at his hair. As the sun came through the trees, it sparkled in Leland's hair, turning it to bright gold.

He was really quite gorgeous, all blue eyed and broad shouldered, but his expression seemed to change from easy going to hard-assed in under a minute when lifted his head and looked right at Jamie. But instead of hauling Jamie out of the crowd to holler at him for being late, he merely nodded, put on his hat, and continued talking to the men.

Jamie exhaled a breath and rubbed his arms, hopping from foot to foot to get warm, even as he noticed that as the sun got higher in the sky, it got warmer, and was getting warmer, bit by bit. Maybe he should have worn that long-sleeved shirt like Leland had said, but it was too late to go back for it now.

The air was fresh and so clean it hardly seemed real. In the distance, he could hear horses whinnying, and birds singing, the nearby sound of a creek running. It was all pretty amazing, and he smiled to himself, glad, after all, that he'd bought that Greyhound bus ticket.

The woman from the day before, Maddy, came up to Leland and handed him a clipboard. Then Maddy whistled for everybody to be quiet, and listed the plan for the day, the times when guests were arriving, where they would need their luggage taken to, and who was responsible for what.

There seemed to be a lot of prep work to be done before guests even started arriving that day. Feeling a little lost as the information came at him, Jamie figured he'd be put to work doing the most miserable of tasks. He wasn't high on the ladder, so that only made sense. He just hoped what he was asked to do wasn't truly horrible.

One by one, the ranch hands got their assignments and walked away from the group till only Jamie stood by himself. He thought for a wild second Leland would come up to him and say something about what he wanted Jamie to do, but he'd already gone into the barn with Maddy and the older guy.

Jamie stood there alone, his arms criss-crossed over his chest, halfway on his way to shivering again, wondering what he should do.

"Hey," said Clay, coming up to him with a smile. He was dressed like all the ranch hands had been, in a crisp button-down shirt, his hair tidy beneath his straw hat.

"Where'd you come from?" asked Jamie.

"From the barn," said Clay, jerking his thumb over his shoulder. "I have your assignment for the morning, you'll be pleased to know."

"I am pleased," said Jamie, and he meant it. He would feel more settled once he got to work, he just knew it.

"We need to have the area around the fire pit scythed clear," said Clay. "Cutting the grass away from the area keeps it a little more bug free. Plus, we don't want the fire leaping into the grass and setting everything ablaze when Bill tells his ghost stories. You see?"

"Okay."

"I'll take you there now," said Clay as he started down the road. "Jasper is waiting with the scythes. Do you know how to use one?"

"No," said Jamie, following. "But I can learn. I'm a fast learner."

"Good. He's tough, but he'll take good care of you."

They walked beneath the group of trees alongside the road, the cool air making Jamie shiver. Clay looked at him and shook his head, and it was easy to see he figured Jamie already realized he should have worn that shirt. But maybe for today, it would be okay.

When they arrived at the dining hall, Clay stopped and pointed over a low field where the fire pit was. A dark-haired man wearing overalls and a straw hat was waiting with two long poles with shiny curved blades on them.

"Just go on down," said Clay. "Jasper will show you how to use the scythe, okay?"

"Okay," Jamie said, his voice faint in his ears.

The scythes looked heavy, and he didn't know if his shoulder and ribs could take it. But he couldn't very well say no, not when Jasper might go complaining to Leland about Jamie's lack of cooperation.

Which really wasn't fair, as nobody on the ranch seemed to be the same type of people he'd worked with at the meat packing plant. He needed to give people at the ranch a chance, just like Leland had given him a chance.

The fire pit was a wide, flat area that overlooked a slope that led down to a road, and from that, a river. Tall, wheat-looking grasses grew high around a large, rock-lined pit that held a thin layer of ash. Hay bales and old logs were ringed around the fire pit, and it looked like it would be a cozy place to gather and tell stories.

As Jamie walked through the grasses to the fire pit and over to where Jasper was standing, he couldn't shake the feeling he was about to mess something up, and almost turned around and walked back to the barn to ask for different work. Except he'd already been seen by the glower-eyed, black-haired Jasper, who held a scythe cradled in his arms like he was some old west version of the grim reaper.

"You here to do this?" Jasper asked, almost grunting the question.

"Yeah," Jamie said.

"Yeah?" Jasper asked, his dark blue eyes glaring.

"Yes, sir, I'm here to help," said Jamie quickly. Then he pointed to the wicked-looking blade, not quite wanting to touch it. "I've never used a scythe before, though. Can you teach me?"

"Yes," Jasper said, the word short and clipped.

He gestured Jamie closer, and Jamie went up to him, leery of having his head taken off the first time he made a mistake. But Jasper, while he didn't say much, was calm as he demonstrated how to stand, how to swing the scythe back and forth slowly, how to walk backward while cutting, and how to straddle the thin, green layer of newly cut grass.

He showed Jamie how it all came together by cutting an entire row with the blade, using quick, deft motions. Then he stepped back and handed Jamie the scythe.

"Now you try."

Jamie cradled the scythe against his forearms and winced as the weight pulled at his shoulder. Jasper corrected Jamie's stance with surprisingly gentle hands.

"Now swing and let me see."

Doing his best, Jamie straddled the grass and swung the scythe, stepping back, swinging again, then stepping back again. He thought for sure Jasper would say something about how messy the line of cut grass was, but he nodded.

"I'll leave you to it then," he said. "Be sure and cut the grass all the way around the pit." Then he pointed up the hill at the dining hall. "There's a cooler of water at the lodge, so be sure to hydrate. Got it?"

"Yes," said Jamie. "Yes, sir."

Jasper started walking up the dirt road toward the parking lot without another word. Which left Jamie on his own in a wide circle of very tall grass. The grass smelled nice, and the air was very fresh and sweet, even though the task seemed overwhelming. How long would it take him? And what was he supposed to do when he was done? Should he report to Jasper, wherever he'd gone, or head back to the barn?

The sun had risen above the trees and the air quickly grew hot as Jamie swung the scythe and stepped back, swung the scythe and stepped back. In short order, he was thirsty. His ribs and shoulder hurt, and as he'd had no dinner the night before and no breakfast that morning, his stomach was growling like a live thing. All he wanted to do was lie down in the shade somewhere, block out the sun with his forearms over his eyes, and think long and hard about how he could get some aspirin.

But he needed to get a move-on with the scythe, needed to get this job done so Leland would know he'd not wasted his time hiring Jamie, wouldn't regret taking a chance on a drifter. At some point, he would take a break, then work some more, and then it'd be lunchtime. Maybe he'd again get to sit across from Leland, looking all dapper in his crisp snap-button flannel shirt, and this time not throw up after. But between now and then was about a hundred miles of very tall, very tough prairie grass that needed cutting.

So he bent and cut, bent and cut, sweating buckets the whole while, cursing the weight of his new straw hat even as he blessed it for keeping the sun off his face. Not that the little bit of shade beneath the brim of the hat made any difference. The entire area was becoming a banked oven, and he was baking inside of it.

His throat was raw by the time he finished cutting half of the area around the fire pit, and his shoulder was screaming at him, and his ribs were protesting with every other breath he took. He stopped to take a breather, propping his elbow up on the top of the handle of the scythe, and lifted his hat to scrape his hair out of his eyes.

A small breeze whispered around his temples and, deciding it was cooler without the hat, he placed it on a patch of newly cut grass. After a minute of rest, he set his feet the right distance apart, lifted the scythe, and swung it. Somehow he'd misjudged the distance and sliced through his brand new hat, the silver blade of the scythe winking against the crisp, yellow straw like it knew what it was doing.

With a shocked sound escaping him, he dropped the scythe and reached for the pieces, thinking wildly that he could somehow glue them back together. What would Leland say when he found out Jamie had cut his brand new hat in two?

Just as his hands touched the cut straw, his heart began to race, and he felt a cold sweat all over him as the sky above him reeled out of place and he fell backwards. Then all of him went from being cold to being encased in fire, and he lay there, blinking up at the blazing sun, trying to figure out what had just happened.

Had he fallen on the scythe and cut himself? Leland would be mad because he'd have to assign someone to clean up the mess. He might make *tsk tsk* sounds and shake his head and assure everyone else it was okay because Jamie was only a drifter and should have gone through Templeton's anyway.

It was hard to focus as he pushed up on his elbows, struggling to get to his feet. The ground seemed to move beneath him, and then a man appeared on the edge of the small rise beyond the fire pit. The sun was directly behind him, so the edges of his silhouette blazed like the man was on fire. He came up to Jamie at a fast pace, swearing as he bent down amidst the heat of the grasses baking in the sun.

"Holy Christ, Jamie," said the man as he swept Jamie up in his arms, holding his face in warm, strong hands.

It was Leland. His eyes were a very grey blue and Jamie focused on them like he could use them to track himself back to a safe place where nothing hurt.

His mouth opened to explain that he'd not been slacking, no, not at all, but that he was hot and tired and very thirsty. No words came out, of course, only a faint sound that wanted to be words only couldn't be.

Leland was saying something Jamie couldn't exactly understand, but his body reacted when Leland lifted him up in his arms like he weighed nothing. With strong strides, Leland carried him out of the fire pit and across the road to the dining hall.

He didn't have to do anything, just lean back, feeling Leland's arms around his shoulders and beneath his knees, like they'd been connected that way forever somehow. Without fully dismissing these crazy, crazy thoughts, Jamie clasped one of Leland's hands, his fingers turning white.

In another second, Leland was mounting the steps of the dining hall, the sky spinning around and around as they stepped into the blessedly cool darkness of the porch. Then Leland placed Jamie on one of the wooden benches, and everything became quiet.

"Get me some water and some of those salt tablets," said Leland to someone who'd just come out of the dining hall. Then he bent close, his hands on Jamie's shoulders, cupping the back of his neck.

"I'm okay," said Jamie, whispering.

"No, you're not, Jamie," Leland said, scolding, his grey-blue eyes flinted with worry. "What's going on, Jamie?" he asked, quite gently. "When did you last eat or take a break? What happened to get you in this state?"

What state? He was thirsty, and his head, now that it was still and cool, decided to pound and pound, all out of proportion. Then he was hot all over, then cold, and on the verge of shaking.

"Drink this," Leland said.

To Jamie's surprise, Leland sat down next to him on the wooden bench. He curved his arm around Jamie's shoulders and urged him to drink something from a glass.

Leland could have made him do just about anything at that

moment, just for bringing him out of the sun and into the shade, though he didn't have the words to say it. So he drank the salty liquid and enjoyed the feel of the cool cloth Leland pressed against his forehead. And enjoyed tucking his face in the curve of Leland's shoulder, sighing as the heat seemed to ease out of his body, slowly, as though it was reluctant to go.

Someone was taking off his boots and sweaty socks and wiping his feet with another cold cloth. Leland started pulling up Jamie's t-shirt as if he meant to take it off. Only when he did this, Jamie hissed, and Leland paused.

"And where did these bruises come from?"

"Bruises?" Jamie asked, feeling dumb.

"On your ribs," Leland said, pointing to Jamie's side. He touched a spot with his finger and though he was so, so gentle, Jamie winced. Then Leland pulled the t-shirt back down. "Here, drink some more of this. You've experienced heat exhaustion. You should be okay; you're responding well to the water and the cooler air."

Jamie took the glass and drank the rest of the water. And shivered as Leland placed a gentle hand on his side.

"Tell me about your ribs, Jamie," he said, and while his voice was stern, his eyes were quiet as he looked at him.

His skin sizzled where Leland touched him, and he took a deep breath. He pressed his palm against the back of Leland's hand, to keep him there, just for another minute.

"It was when I fell against the gate," he said. "When the horse ran away."

"*Jamie.*" Leland's voice rang with dismay.

"I thought it would get better, but it hasn't. It just keeps hurting worse."

Before Leland could say anything, Maddy came walking up the road and marched up the steps as though to announce she was in charge now.

"I got a phone call about this," she said, her mouth a tart line. "Are you cooled off?" she asked Jamie as she looked him up and down. When he nodded, she shook her head, but to his surprise, her scolding wasn't aimed at him. "You worked him too hard, Leland," she said, a grumpy frown on her face. "He's not used to the altitude, and you should have known better."

"No harder than I work myself," said Leland, drawing back from her at the accusation.

"Which is too damn hard," said Maddy. Then she shook her finger at Jamie. "Now, he's going to take the rest of the day off. Bed rest all day and that's final."

"That's what I was going to suggest, Maddy," said Leland, and his tone was quite mild with her. "Thank you. I'm going to get him to his room to rest and bring him something to eat. He'll be in bed all afternoon, I promise."

"I'll call Clay to take care of your horse," said Maddy. She shook her head as if in despair over Leland's daring rescue of the idiot who didn't know enough to take care in the heat.

"That's fine and I appreciate it," said Leland. "C'mon Jamie, get up. I'll help you."

Blurry around the edges, Jamie could feel the warmth of Leland's arm around his waist as someone helped him with his socks and boots. Then Leland helped him back to his room, walking with him slowly through the shade and up the three flights of stairs. Once in his room, Leland made him sit down and bent to take off his boots and socks.

"You should take a quick shower," said Leland. "I'll bring you something to eat right away and check on you later. Okay?"

Leland's hands had been gentle, and he still had that concerned look on his face. As much as Jamie hated to be a bother, it made him feel better just to have him there, caring and kind. Which wasn't how he expected any of this to go when he'd first stepped off that Greyhound bus in a strange town with no idea which way to turn.

10

LELAND

*A*s Leland hurried to the dining hall, he berated himself for letting Jamie get to such a state where he'd collapse while working. The work didn't matter; it was Jamie that mattered, and not just because he was an employee of the ranch.

When Leland reached the steps of the dining hall, he knew it was early and that the kitchen staff would have lunch just underway, and nothing would be quite ready. That's when Jasper caught up with him, carrying the scythe in his hand, brandishing it at Leland as though he was the town's monster and Jasper, the angry villager.

"What's he playing at, leaving a tool out in a field like that?" Jasper's scowl said everything about what he thought about that, and how he was one step away from making sure Jamie was good and fired before the sun went down.

"He collapsed from heat exhaustion," Leland said, keeping his voice quiet so Jasper would have to lean close, and in leaning close, it took some of the bluster out of him. "I'd thought he was taking breaks, drinking enough water, like we tell everybody to do up here. But he wasn't. It's my fault entirely, so if you want to blame someone for the tool getting left out in the weather, blame me."

There was a long pause as Jasper considered the words, then he shook his head and lowered the scythe.

"I did not know," he said, the growl gone from his voice. "I told him about the water in the cooler on the porch here. I should have made sure, but I went to my cabin to get that paperwork for the ex-con program, which I'm still pissed about, by the way."

"I know," said Leland. "You're doing the ranch a favor, and we appreciate it."

"Well, the work he did was top notch, even if he didn't get very far." Jasper rubbed his chin with his thumb and nodded slowly. "I'd have him back for more, if he's willing."

Jasper was so sparing with praise that Leland only sent the best of the best to work with him, though ranch hands never lasted more than a day or so. That he was willing to have Jamie help him out again was a green stamp of approval nobody ever got.

"I'll let him know, and thank you," Leland said. "Now I need to get him something from the dining hall and make sure he eats it."

Jasper nodded his goodbye and headed back to his forge, carefully shifting the scythe so the blade angled away from his body. Then Clay came up, leading Beltaine, the sweet, dark mare Leland had been riding down to the parking lot to meet and greet with arriving guests.

"Can you hold on to her while I grab Jamie something to eat?"

"Sure," said Clay, though Leland could see the questions in his eyes.

"He passed out in the field." Leland shook his head. "You and I both told him about the rules about water."

"Yeah, boss, I did," said Clay. "He wasn't at dinner last night on account of he said he was so tired."

"I noticed." Rubbing his thumb along his jaw, Leland looked down the road to where it wound into the trees. "I'll take care of this and meet you back here in ten minutes. Can you walk her so she doesn't get restless?"

"Yes, boss," said Clay with a mock salute.

Going into the dining hall, Leland went past the buffet area where staff was setting up for lunch and made his way back to the kitchen. There, he coaxed Levi into making up a hearty BLT, and giving him a slice of his famous strawberry-rhubarb pie and a glass of milk. Then he went over to the first aid box on the wall and grabbed a few packets of ibuprofen, and grabbed a bottle of water from the cooler. Placing all this on a tray, Leland went out the back door, past the dumpster area, and hurried up the path to the staff quarters and up the stairs to Jamie's room at the end of the hall.

Before he knocked, he paused for a good long minute. What was he doing? Sure, he should take care of an employee, and sure he should give Jamie the afternoon off after experiencing heat exhaustion. But nowhere in any rule book did it say he had to bring him his lunch on a tray. At most, he might have asked one of the kitchen staff to do this, but there he was, waiting on a new employee like he'd not told Jamie to leave the property only the day before.

He balanced the tray on his forearm as he knocked on the door, but there was no answer. Opening the door, he saw Jamie was on the bed, right where he'd been left. Leland opened the door wider. Jamie was curled on his side, bare feet tangled in the sheets, head tucked against his chest, his dark hair spilling across the white pillowcase.

He'd not taken a shower, let alone moved from where he'd been. No, he'd made himself a nest of the bedclothes, as though that was all he deserved. And in a way that told Leland that Jamie quite expected to tend to his own needs once he woke up. Like he expected nobody would ever care. Like he was all on his own.

Which couldn't be further from the truth. Unexpected feelings tumbled through Leland's chest as he made his way quietly to the dresser where he placed the tray. Then he bent over the bed and very gently cupped his hand around Jamie's shoulder.

Jamie looked up at Leland, blinking, shoulders curled like he was one second away from ducking a blow or shying from very bad news. The idea of it struck through Leland's heart like he'd been stabbed by a spear.

"Jamie," he said, making his voice soft. "Can you sit up? I've brought something for you to eat. Then I want you to take a shower and get some rest. Can you do that?"

There was a shine of surprise in those green eyes. But Jamie nodded as Leland helped him sit up, and arranged pillows behind his back, all the while looking at Leland as though he was some kind of magic trick. Which he wasn't. This was just how people treated each other, and Jamie needed to learn that. Nowhere in Jamie's world, it seemed, had anybody taught him to stop and take care of himself. That was Leland's job, now, for a while at least.

Going to the dresser, Leland brought over the tray and placed it on Jamie's lap, taking the glass of milk and the bottle of water to put them on the little nightstand next to the bed.

"Can you eat that?" Leland asked him, stepping back. "Is there anything you need?"

"Maybe some aspirin," Jamie said, his voice low.

"I've got some ibuprofen right here," said Leland. "Take two of them first, then eat. Then shower. Then rest."

Pulling up a chair next to the bed, Leland opened the packet of ibuprofen, and handed Jamie the bottle of water so he could wash them down. As Jamie took the pills, he looked at Leland out of the corner of his eyes, as though startled to have him so close.

"Those should kick in fast," said Leland. "If your ribs aren't feeling better by tomorrow, I'll take you to the clinic in town to get x-rays done."

"I don't have health insurance," Jamie said, and Leland could see he thought it was yet another black mark on his record.

"The ranch'll cover it," Leland said, leaning forward. He had advanced first aid training and knew ribs could heal on their own, if the patient rested. "If you're feeling better, you can get up for dinner."

"But what about my job?" With his hands on the tray, one on each side, Jamie looked up. He'd not started eating, but seemed to be waiting for some kind of permission.

"You get the afternoon off." Leland shook his head, wanting to reassure him. "That's what happens when you're hurt. You rest up. Then on Monday, if you're feeling better, light work for a few days. Ease into it. Okay?"

"Okay," Jamie said, his mouth pulled down in the corners, like he was unhappy about it all. "If you're sure I won't lose my job."

"You won't," Leland said. "But you're to rest now, and I mean it. You don't want me to tell Maddy you weren't following orders, do you?"

"No," said Jamie with a little laugh.

There was a small smile in those green eyes of his, as though he was amazed that anyone would worry so hard about him. Well, Leland was worried and, at the same time, he was a little amazed he felt so strongly about it.

What if he'd not been riding Beltaine on his way to the parking lot to greet the arriving guests? What if he'd not paused on the rise on the road above the fire pit? Life on the ranch was full time work, hard work, from sunup to sundown. Jamie was a city boy through and through, and so Leland had stopped to check on him, and considered it lucky he had.

The other question was: why this one? Why was he so affected by Jamie when there were a dozen or more young men, cowboys, ranch hands, staff, who were capable and hard working—but no, this was the one who drew his eye and his attention, stirring up his heart, making him want to take care of him.

"Now," said Leland. He pointed at the as-yet untouched tray. "Start eating so I can faithfully report back to Maddy that I saw you eat."

"Okay." With a smile Jamie picked up the BLT and took a bite and his entire body seemed to sigh with contentment. After he'd eaten half the sandwich and some of the strawberry-rhubarb pie, he settled back in his pillows.

"So how did you end up on the road, Jamie?" Leland asked, figuring that this quiet moment between them was a good time to get some of his questions answered. "I know you came from a meat packing plant, but what made you leave there?"

"Well, the guy I told you about." Jamie polished off the rest of his pie in three quick bites and scrubbed at his mouth with his forearm. "He kind of impressed me when he was talking about his cows. Kind of reminds me of you." A quick flush raced across Jamie's face as he scraped his hair back. "But part of it was I was tired of the guys I shared a place with. They'd spit in my cereal and lied about whether I paid the rent. The foreman at the plant always believed them over me, so I left there and came here."

"And before that?" asked Leland, now, doing his best to keep a rein on his temper about abusive bosses.

"I worked at a bodega on Colfax for a while, and before that, I worked at a bookstore." Jamie looked at him carefully, as though wondering what Leland might make of his journey.

"And before that?" asked Leland, thinking there must be more to Jamie's story, as he was too smart and too hard working to have ended up drifting without a good reason.

"Well, my folks got divorced about two years ago, and there was no more money for me to go to college." Wrinkling his nose, Jamie looked down and brushed the crumbs from his t-shirt. "And I know you're going to ask, so I'll just tell you. I don't know they got divorced because I told them I was gay, but sometimes I think that was why. Neither one of them wanted me to live with them after that."

"Oh, Jamie—"

"I had to leave the meat packing job," Jamie said with a gulp. "So I bought a Greyhound bus ticket as far as it would take me."

"Which was to Farthing," Leland said, slowly.

"And I guess you don't want gay guys working on your ranch any more than you want drifters."

"That's not true, not true at all," said Leland. Where only seconds before his heart had started tightening up, now it expanded, both with fury at such unfeeling parents and a sense of wonder that Jamie had done so much on his own. "Nobody on this ranch tolerates any kind of discrimination, understand? Besides." Leland put his hand on his heart. "I'm gay, and I run the place."

At Jamie's astonished expression, Leland nodded, pleased to have gotten the message across. But, at the same time, should he have opened that particular door?

"Listen," he said, standing up. "I need to go down and greet guests, but I'll check on you later," he said "Feel better, okay?"

"Thank you, Mr. Tate," Jamie said, looking at him, his hands fiddling with the sheets. "I feel better already."

"Good," Leland said. "And it's Leland. You hear?"

With a nod, Leland left and shut the door behind him. And stood there for a good long minute, feeling a bit relieved that all was going to be well but not understanding anything about why he kept thinking about Jamie the way that he was. Regardless of the fact Jamie was gay, he was off limits. Those were his own rules, and he needed to stick to them.

Slowly, his heart doing unexpected things in his chest, he walked back down to where Clay waited with Beltaine. Mounting up, he settled his shoulders and lifted his chin. Week two was getting underway. He needed to greet the guests with a smile and make sure they knew they were going to have a very good time at the ranch and that their money was well spent.

JAMIE

*W*hen he woke up, Jamie took a quick, hot shower, dried off and got dressed as fast as he could. Slugging down two more ibuprofen with the rest of the bottled water, he bemoaned his lack of a cell phone to tell him what time it was. Was he going to be late for dinner, or too early? And how was he going to get another hat? All the ranch hands had hats, and Leland was probably going to be pissed that his brand new straw one was lying in pieces in the newly shorn grass near the fire pit. He'd have to get a new hat before Leland noticed.

Pounding down the stairs of the staff quarters, he raced through the trees to the dining hall. The front porch was busy with activity, with ranch hands standing to one side while the guest got in line for the buffet. Everybody looked happy, and the air was filled with excited chatter.

Going to the very end of the line, he relaxed his shoulders. He wasn't too late, so that was one problem solved. Odors of salt and fried onions and good strong coffee floated out of the open double doors. The ibuprofen was kicking in, too, and he didn't feel sick or too hot.

When it was his turn at the buffet, he picked up a tray and loaded his plate with fried chicken and cornbread, and carried everything to the nearest table, plunked it down, and began to eat. But, being more aware, he ate at a more sensible speed than he had the day before, pacing himself rather than shoving it in. Life was looking good. He had a job, a place to sleep, food to eat, and a thousand bucks hidden beneath the underwear in the top drawer of his dresser.

"Hey, new guy."

Looking up, Jamie saw Clay amidst the bustle of the dining hall. He was smiling as he came over, letting Jamie know he was being teased, but gently, which made a pleasant change from the guys at the meat packing plant. With Clay was another guy, slender and lanky, with messy hair and a casual walk.

"Can we sit with you?" asked Clay as he put his tray on the table.

"Of course," said Jamie, terribly pleased to have been asked, to have the company. "I was hoping to see Leland and invite him to sit with us."

"Oh no," said Clay as he sat down. At his side, the other guy was shaking his head as he, too, put his tray down and sat. "Leland never sits with ranch hands. He usually sits with his team leads, and especially tonight, he's got to mingle with the guests, make them feel welcome."

"We had lunch together yesterday," said Jamie before he could think about how it might come across as bragging. "I mean, maybe he was just making me feel welcome on my first day."

"That's probably it. He's nice like that." Clay shrugged as he began eating. Then he gestured at the other guy with his elbow. "This here's Brody, he's our horse wrangler. Brody, this is Jamie, our newest ranch hand."

"Hi," said Brody, without quite looking at Jamie, but not in a rude way. Maybe he was shy of strangers.

"What does a horse wrangler do?" asked Jamie. He crunched into his fried chicken, enjoying every bite.

"Uh." Ducking his head, Brody scrubbed his hands with a napkin and nodded, like he was forming an explanation in his head and wanted to have it all ready before he started talking. "I'm in charge of choosing horses for guests, and for leading the horse procession each morning and the retreat at night."

"Horse procession?" asked Jamie, feeling his eyebrows go up.

"That's when we bring the horses down from the upper fields. They kind of race into the main corral and we make a big show of it. Guests love it." Brody nodded. "I also work with Jasper to make sure the horses are all properly shod and in good health."

"Jasper can shoe a horse like nobody's business," said Clay. He took a long swallow of his ice tea. "And there's nothing on this ranch he can't fix." With a laugh he added, "Except maybe that stupid ice maker, which is always breaking down."

"Everybody's got so many skills," said Jamie, trying to make a list in his mind as to what he could say his skills were, but other than cutting up hunks of raw meat, he came up blank.

Looking around the dining hall at the variety of guests, all smiling and talking, at the row of cowboy hats hanging on the wooden pegs along the wall, Jamie saw Leland come into the dining hall. He was with Jasper, who didn't look too happy as Leland talked to him earnestly. They both hung up their hats on the pegs before getting in the buffet line, which moved quite briskly. Then, when they came out of the other end of the line, trays in hand, Leland went up to a table with a pair of older couples and smiled as he sat with them.

"See?" said Clay. "That's part of his job. He sits with guests, mostly, but sometimes you get lucky."

Clay winked at him, and Jamie pulled back, not really understanding what that meant.

"I guess I was lucky," he said, buttering his cornbread with way too much butter to try and cover his own confusion.

"You have skills," said Brody, somewhat unexpectedly into the small silence that fell. "Jasper told me you did a good job cutting the grass, at least before you collapsed."

"Hey," said Clay, jabbing Brody in the ribs as he snickered.

"I'm just teasing," said Brody, smiling. There was a smile in his dark eyes, so Jamie knew he meant it. "Same thing almost happened to me my first week. What was it, beginning of last season? They lecture you about those dang coolers full of bottled water and snacks, so—"

He looked at Clay with expectation on his face and the two of them said together, *"Always hydrate. Always take breaks."* Then they laughed and returned to their dinners, leaving Jamie realizing he'd been included in a long-standing joke, like he was one of the guys, part of the team.

Oh, this was nice, so nice, and so different from what his life had been like for the last two years. Maybe he could just stick that thousand dollars in the bank and work really hard and save up and go back to college. Maybe it would take him a year, maybe two, but at least now it felt possible, as long as he could work on the ranch to do it.

They ate their dinners together, with Clay making jokes while Brody smiled at his tray, as though unwilling to let on that he found Clay funny. Jamie ate slowly, and when Clay and Brody got up, he got up too.

"We've got to go help in the barn," said Clay.

"What about me?" asked Jamie.

"You're not on the roster till morning," said Clay. "But you might go down to the office, if you're up to it, and see if Maddy needs help greeting arriving guests. Handing out water, that kind of stuff."

"Okay." Feeling pleased with himself, his belly full, his shoulders relaxed, Jamie watched as they hurried off, then bussed his own tray, and went outside, clomping down the wooden steps in his sturdy new boots. He smiled as he got out of the way of guests who were too excited to be paying attention to where they were going, and started down the dirt road to the parking lot and the office.

From behind him, he felt a rush of movement, and a warm hand on his shoulder.

"Hey, Jamie, hold up."

Jamie turned. Leland stood there, and because he was on a little rise, he was taller than Jamie, taller than he normally was. And while that might have been imposing in any other circumstance, here on the ranch, it felt less so, much less so than had he been at the meat packing plant with the manager coming up to grill him about some fault, real or imagined.

"How are you feeling, Jamie?" asked Leland, tipping his hat back from his forehead so his eyes weren't in the shade of the brim.

"Good," said Jamie. "I had dinner with Clay and Brody and they said I could head down to help Maddy hand out water and stuff?" He turned the answer into a question, just in case Leland didn't like the idea of him greeting guests like that, since he was the newest ranch hand.

"That's fine, as long as you don't overdo." Leland nodded. "But where's your hat? Did you leave it in the dining hall?"

"No, I—" Jamie had to take a deep breath. The hat had been brand new, and maybe his plan had been to make sure the store was open before grabbing some money from the drawer and buying a new one. Maybe he'd been hoping nobody would notice, but it was too late for that. A sense of honesty pushed to the fore, as it always did. "I sliced through it accidentally with the scythe."

"That's a shame," said Leland. "That hat looked good on you."

Leland stepped back to let guests pass by them on the way to the dining hall, and Jamie stepped back, as well. It gave him a sense of belonging that felt weird but good at the same time. Then Leland pulled out his cell phone from his back pocket and looked at it.

"It's after five, so the store is closed." He looked at Jamie and nodded, as if it was the most sensible of things for a store to close at five on a Sunday. "But I can get the keys from Maddy. It's going to be sunny tomorrow and you will need that hat."

"Okay, thanks," said Jamie. "I can pay for it, right?"

"Yes," said Leland. "It'll come out of your pay, though, which might teach you to be more careful in future." The words were said in Leland's steady way, like he wasn't judging Jamie, just reminding him. Then he jerked his thumb at the newly shorn fire pit. "Is the hat still out there? Maybe Jasper picked it up. We better go check."

It only made sense that Leland would want everything on the ranch to be tidy but, at the same time, he didn't seem bent out of shape about the whole thing. Instead, the two of them looked in the short grass around the fire pit until Jamie found the two pieces of the hat, neatly stacked on one of the hay bales, as though Jasper had intended the pieces be found. When Jamie gestured, Leland came over and shook his head.

"That scythe is damn sharp," he said. "Here, we can throw this away at the store."

He handed the two pieces to Jamie and put the thin leather hat band with the small bit of brass shaped like a pine tree into his pocket. Together they walked down the road, and through the glade of trees, where the sun slanted through the spring leaves, and the warmth of the day was whisked away by a sprightly breeze around their shoulders.

At the office, where Maddy was helping a guest with paperwork, Leland nodded at her, and grabbed the keys to the store. At the store, Leland unlocked both locks and turned on only one of the lights. The store was quiet and cool, and in the semi-darkness, Leland went behind the counter and started tugging on boxes high up on the shelves.

"You want the same kind?" he asked, reaching up.

"Yes, please," said Jamie, smiling as Leland brought down a box that was a replica of the one from the day before. But this time, it was Leland opening the box and gently pushing it across the glass-topped counter at Jamie. Feeling rather like he was opening a very special birthday gift, he found he was smiling and his hands were shaking.

"Try it on," said Leland. "Make sure it fits."

Jamie raised the hat and put it on his head, looking up at Leland. In the shadows of the half-lit store, Leland's eyes seemed to sparkle like grey diamonds, and in the stillness, he reached out and pushed some hair away from Jamie's forehead. The movement was quite slow and gentle, as though Leland didn't realize he was doing it, and for a moment they were quiet together. Then Leland shook his head as if pulling himself out of his own private thoughts.

"Looks like it fits," he said. "Make sure you take better care of it this time, right? I'll write it up for Maddy to deduct out of your pay, so you'll see that info on the statement."

All of Leland's words eased over Jamie, laying themselves down like a gentle blanket. Sure, he'd messed up, cutting his hat in two like he had, but Leland was treating it all so matter-of-factly, as though it was a mistake anyone could have made, a small one, at that, and didn't warrant Jamie getting yelled at or written up. The tightness in his chest that always came when he thought about the meat packing plant loosened even further when Leland smiled at him.

"Don't worry about it, Jamie," said Leland, jingling the keys in his hand as he scooped up the box and placed it on the floor next to the recycling bin. "We've all been there."

"Did you ever cut your new hat with a scythe?" asked Jamie as he followed Leland out of the store and waited while he locked up.

"No," said Leland. As they stood on the wooden porch of the store, and Leland looked out over the parking lot, where a lone van was dropping off a few people with their suitcases, he shook his head. "But I've had my share of mishaps. As long as you learn from it, you'll be fine. Now, if you'll pardon me, I've got to go and help those guests."

Before Jamie could say yes or no, Leland hurried down the stairs and over to the people, his long legs eating up the distance in short order. He pointed to the glade of trees and took the handles of two suitcases. Jamie could hear Leland telling them about which cabin they would be in, and what kind of view it had.

Jamie walked to the office, where Maddy was standing on the shaded porch with a clipboard in her hand.

"Evening, Jamie," she said. "How are you feeling?"

She asked it like she really cared, and not like she had to ask. That was another difference between the ranch and the meat packing plant, and hopefully, soon, he wouldn't be making any more comparisons like that because he never wanted to think about the meat packing plant again.

"I'm good," he said. "Clay suggested I come down and ask if you need help greeting guests, or handing out water, stuff like that."

"That's like him, bless him," said Maddy. She shook her head as she looked at the clipboard. "We're all checked in for the week. Those folks were the last." She appraised Jamie with a quick up-and-down look. "You're off duty till 8 o'clock tomorrow, when Leland runs the general meeting in front of the barn. Breakfast starts at 6:30, so you should have plenty of time to eat beforehand."

"Yes, ma'am," said Jamie, making a mental note to ask Clay to bang on his door. As soon as he could, he'd find an alarm clock of some sort. Or maybe he'd learn to wake up with the birds, bright and early, instead of dreading the day like he used to.

"I'm sorry I couldn't do anything for your birthday today," she said. "There's just too much happening on Sundays. But don't forget, we do a group thing at dinner on Friday with a sheet cake, as there are guests with birthdays this week."

"That's fine," said Jamie, meaning it. "I don't mind." And he didn't. Getting a new hat without getting yelled at was the best birthday present he could ask for. Plus, working at the ranch was turning into something good, and each day something he could look forward to. Plus, he wanted to earn more of those approving nods from Leland, and glances from those grey-blue eyes of his.

12

LELAND

*A*fter getting the guests' luggage to Cabin #1 and Cabin #2, and briefly talking with them about the lovely view and the activities planned for the week, Leland felt satisfied they were settled in, and bid them goodnight with a tip of his hat. Then he walked up the slope behind the cabins to the barn, going over a mental checklist in his head about everything he'd tended to that day, tasks he'd delegated, errands Clay had run for him. All was well, and now he could go for that ride he'd been hoping for.

Brody, ever efficient, waited at the open barn doors with Buster, all saddled and ready to go.

"Thank you, Brody," he said as he mounted the bay gelding.

"You bet, boss," said Brody as he patted Buster's neck and played with the gelding's black mane. "I know how you like your rides."

Tapping his hat brim, Leland urged Buster into a fast walk, heading down the dirt road toward the gate. Buster wasn't very energetic, but he was responsive and sweet and seemed willing to go where Leland wanted him to, easing into a canter as they followed the road through the trees.

They cantered some and walked some while Leland surveyed the terrain and checked on the height of the grasses around the parking lot and the condition of the split-rail fence that followed the creek, which was mostly for decorative purposes. Then he guided Buster back up the road, riding all the way through the ranch, going as far as the low hills above the corral. There, on the top of a small rise, he settled back in Buster's saddle, where he could see everything from Iron Mountain all the way out to the plains.

The sun was coming through the clouds like soft, grey bars of metal against the pale blue sky, touching the landscape to silver as it set. A bit of a wind picked up, making the air turn cool quite fast.

Buster snorted and started to walk back to the ranch all on his own say-so, though Leland had not given him the command. He patted the gelding's neck anyway and didn't pull back on the reins because the horse knew it was time for him to get that saddle off and relax with his pals.

"There you go, Buster," he said to the gelding as he tucked his legs in close, enjoying the strength and movement of the horse beneath him. "We'll get you home, right quick."

As they trotted back to the barn, Leland saw Jamie heading through the trees. He had barn dust on his shoulders, and strands of hay in his hair, and must have disobeyed orders and helped with evening chores in the barn.

Making a mental note to scold his newest ranch hand in the morning, Leland took Buster into the barn, gave him a good grooming, put the saddle on its long peg on the wall, and nodded at Brody who came over to wipe the saddle down. Then he headed along the same path Jamie had taken as he went back to his own cabin and told himself he wasn't hoping Jamie had lingered on the steps of the staff quarters so they might have a chance visit.

At his cabin, he went inside, doffed his boots and hat and, sock footed, grabbing a root beer, walked back out to the front porch. There, he sat in one of the Adirondack chairs and drank his root beer, enjoying the tang on his tongue while the darkness grew around him. When the automatic porch light went off, it got even darker. A cool wind blew through the tops of the trees as the stars flickered brightly among the top branches.

Balancing the bottle of root beer on one armrest, he held onto the other armrest, gripping and letting go, gripping and letting go, letting his mind wander. And thought about the ranch and all the land around as it sloped down from Iron Mountain. He pictured the herd of horses, all different colors, some brown, some speckled, some white, manes tossing, ears flicking for danger. And smiled at the idea of so many guests from all over the world, bringing with them a range of expressions and smiles, all of their hearts open for a new adventure. And dipped his chin as he thought about the people he worked with.

Sometimes he could not imagine doing anything else with anyone else, brave, funny souls, every single one. And now they had added Jamie to their number, Jamie who had shown up unexpectedly and who was already looking like he felt more at home. He was confident in some ways, gentle in others. That dark, curly hair over his green eyes. Those shoulders that needed muscle and food to fill out. A half-empty duffle bag full of broken dreams.

Oh, Leland was tired, that's what it was. Tired and still wired from the day full of guests arriving, everybody busy, as it usually was on a Sunday.

He took another swallow of his root beer and winced at the bite of it at the back of his throat. Standing up, he scraped his hands through his hair and blinked as the porch light came on, triggered by his sudden movement.

The light showed Leland the porch with two empty wooden chairs and the empty path leading through the trees. Beyond the porch light was a resting world, waiting for the sunrise to become active and alive. And somewhere, a young man was going to bed, seemingly grateful he had a job, but for some reason, not reassured, had worked more than he'd been told to.

The concern wasn't just about helping Jamie understand what to do to keep that job, it was more. It was about showing Jamie that not only did he have a fresh start, but that people at the ranch wanted to help him. They weren't all out to get him, and certainly Leland wasn't planning to trip him up at the first opportunity. What he wanted for Jamie—

What did he want? To help him? Or was it something else?

Typically, when he hired staff from Templeton's, they arrived fully aware of the standards the ranch expected from them. This young man, this city boy, was not only out of his depth as far as working on a ranch, his life had been rough up to this point. And why was he thinking about Jamie so deeply?

Leland's impulses were honorable, of course they were. He was going to teach Jamie what he needed to know in order to help him be successful, whether on the ranch or off it.

He dipped his head at the thought of Jamie going on his way at the end of the season, never to be seen again. He couldn't be thinking like that. Jamie was a member of staff, and Leland was in charge. It was his job to be responsible for everyone on the ranch. And that included looking after a wide-eyed youngster who could not possibly know he was the focus of such nighttime thoughts.

Nighttime thoughts that included the memory of the two of them alone in the ranch's store together. They'd been close, and Leland had taken a good hard look at Jamie, seeing details about him the way he'd not noticed before.

Jamie had green eyes, yes, but they sparkled in the electric light, his hair curling over one eye like it had a mind of its own. Leland's body also had a mind of its own, reacting with silent, just-below-the-skin impulses he'd not quite known what to do with. They'd been alone in the store, and there was only one overhead light on, filling the corners with shadows, as though they were in a secret place, all their own.

Leland sighed and looked out through the trees and inhaled the crisp pine scent of the breeze. Maybe some of his impulses weren't honorable. He needed to be wary of where his thoughts might take him. Needed to make sure that any attention he paid Jamie was because it was necessary, to instruct, to guide, to teach. Just the way he always did with new ranch hands. Trouble was, this one was different. This one had broken through barriers Leland had not realized he'd built.

Needing to re-erect those barriers, Leland finished his root beer, took a quick shower, and worked through paperwork before calling it an early night. Each moment, he focused on what he needed to do for the ranch, how he needed to expect problems before they happened, how he needed to make sure guests were having a good time.

All of this was to the good, for when he woke in the morning and had breakfast, he showed up in front of the barn at 8 o'clock sharp, earlier even than Maddy, who was usually first on the scene. He surveyed his team, all of whom were looking to him for direction. Every single one of them, from Jasper, the blacksmith, on down to Clay, a ranch hand, was capable and prepared. All of them knew what to do, even if he never said a word, but Leland liked to bring them together so they could have this quick meeting, and the ranch always ran better for it.

As Leland spoke about the tasks for that day, he spotted Jamie at the back of the small crowd, a little to one side, as though he felt he didn't quite belong. But then, just as Jamie was adjusting his new straw hat, as though to give his hands something to do, Clay sidled up to him and nudged him with a gentle elbow. That brought the smile to Jamie's face, but it was when Jamie smiled at him that Leland realized he'd been staring.

"Thanks, everyone," he said, returning his attention to the group before him. "Be sure and check with Maddy for special requests from the guests. Also, I'll need some folks to help Brody with getting guests connected with their horses."

As hands raised to volunteer, Leland pointed at three of his ranch hands. Then, gratefully, he turned to find Levi, the ranch's head cook, at his elbow, hat in his hands. He was a quiet man with dark hair, and while he never had much to say out loud, his brown eyes usually spoke volumes.

Sometimes Leland got the impression Levi was as lonely as he was, though he never complained and never seemed to join the ranch hands and other staff when they went into Farthing on a Saturday night. He was like Leland, in a way, with work to be done during long days, or maybe he was too reserved to reach out casually. Not that Leland could ask him about this, as he was a very private man.

"What can I do for you, Levi?" he asked him. Out of the corner of his eyes he could see Jamie walking off, rubbing his ribs a bit, then dropping his hand as he continued into the barn. Were his ribs still bothering him? Leland needed to ask him about it to make sure he was okay, but meanwhile, he had Levi's question to attend to.

"Question," said Levi, as he put his hat back on. "We're at half-capacity for guests and there's an overnight trail ride on Tuesday night. So, should I pull out the chuck wagon or just take the pack horses?"

Leland knew, without Levi saying it, that he would be quite willing to use the chuck wagon, even if it caused extra work. What he was asking, without words, was whether it would be more prudent and cost effective to just take pack horses.

"Why don't you ask the guests on Monday night, just before the line dancing?" Leland asked, leaving the decision fully in Levi's capable hands. "I'm sure it'd be fine either way, but see what they want."

"That's a good idea," he said with a nod. "Why didn't I think of that?" Then he smiled, a twinkle in his dark eyes, a small twinkle, like a secret he was sharing just with Leland.

With a laugh, Leland patted Levi's shoulder and wished again that he didn't have a rule about flirting with fellow employees. Levi was lonely and Leland was lonely and they'd make a good team, even if he knew full well and good that hooking up out of loneliness was never a good idea. Besides, he didn't just want a hookup; he wanted someone to be with, to work together with toward some kind of shared future.

And he knew, with a shake of his head, that he'd not had these kinds of thoughts before Jamie had arrived.

At any rate, it was time to take care of Monday's events and activities. It was always busy on a Monday, busy with the bustle of new guests and their excitement over the ranch, and their eagerness to partake in the fun and breathe in the fresh air.

Leland spent most of the morning shaking hands, making himself

THE FOREMAN AND THE DRIFTER

available at the barn to say hello and good morning to each and every guest. Later, while drinking a quick bottle of water, standing in the shade of the barn, keeping an eye on things, he went over the checklist with Maddy as to what had gone right and what process needed improvement.

When Levi rang the iron triangle announcing lunch, everyone went into the dining hall, which was full of good smells of cooking, and the energetic din of guests chatting with each other.

Leland sat with a small group of ladies, and ate his lunch quickly. Then he walked around the dining hall, making sure everything was going as it should, then slipped outside into the fresh air and relative quiet.

Making a note to check for wasp nests during his next ride, he strode up to the barn to see how the morning's riding lesson had gone. Afterwards, he wanted to head to the dining hall to check on the leak he'd noticed beneath the ice-making machine. And no, he did not look for Jamie along the way.

13

JAMIE

*J*amie's morning had been filled with work at the barn, where he'd been assigned the interesting but sweaty task of learning how to groom a horse and saddle it up so that each guest would have a well-turned out horse for their lesson. Going as fast as he could, he tried to keep up with Brody and the other ranch hands, but though his arms were used to hacking through raw cow ribs, they weren't used to the steady continual motion of the brush across a horse's side, or the slow way he was supposed to move around the animals.

The first time Clay came over with two bottles of water in his hands, Jamie tried to put him off.

"I have to finish this," he said. "You assigned me two more horses after this."

"We'll help each other," said Clay brightly. "But you have to take a break now. Can't have a repeat of yesterday." The smile Clay gave him as he held out one of the bottles quite insistently took the sting out of the words. And it was nice to stand there, letting the breeze from the open doors wash over them as they drank their water.

He hustled to finish his horses, smiling when Clay gave him the thumb's up and led all four out to the corral so the day's riding lesson could begin. After a quick lunch, Clay told him he had to rake the corral before the afternoon lesson began, so guests didn't have to trot their horses over piles of manure. It wasn't anything anybody else hadn't done before him, so he worked hard, raking and shoveling, pushing the wheelbarrow to the dump area behind the supply barn.

It was hot work, but it was nice to leave a tidy corral behind as evidence of his hard work, rather than a pile of bones and bloody knives, the way he would have had he still been working at the meat packing plant—no, he would not think about that anymore. He was going to focus on where he was and enjoy the fresh air and plentiful sunshine, even if the heat of the day made him have to drink a bunch of water, and he quickly sweated through his t-shirt and his long-sleeved shirt.

Then he had to help get horses set up for a trail ride for more experienced riders. When the guests rode back, those horses had to be groomed, the tack cleaned and oiled. He felt he might want to be done for the day. Still, he struggled on, and kept telling himself he had a thousand bucks and could leave at any time. Except he didn't want to leave. Even if the work was hard, the ranch was better than anyplace else he'd worked.

"Hey," said Clay from the doorway of the tack room. "The dinner bell is about to be rung, so hustle and get a shower. You can't go to dinner looking like that."

"Oh." Jamie looked down at himself. His once-white t-shirt was streaked with sweat and dirt, and the sleeves of his long-sleeved shirt had grime along the edges.

"It's especially important on account of there's a dance afterwards," said Clay. "Let's get moving. We don't want to miss out on the fun."

Trotting behind Clay, they went to their rooms, both on the third floor, and Jamie nearly collapsed once he got inside his own room. Both from exhaustion and from the fact that someone had made his bed and opened the windows to let the breeze flow through. In a panic, he checked the money in his top drawer, and let out a whoosh of air when he found it was still there.

The bathroom was sparkling clean, so he took a quick hot shower, and felt better about it all as he got dressed, clean socks, clean every-thing. His muscles would get used to the hard work, and as long as he worked as hard as he could, he'd be fine.

When he heard the dinner bell, he clomped down those wooden steps in his still-new boots and joined everyone in the dining hall. The place was loud with all the excited chatter and festive with guests dressed in their new western gear looking a little overwhelmed by it all. He couldn't blame them, as he was still getting used to it all himself.

He didn't see Clay or Brody, so he took his tray of food and found a place at a small table near the window where he'd sat with Leland on Saturday. The view was beautiful, with long shadows stretching out as the sun was going behind the low mountains to the west, all purple and blue. It looked like one of those postcards you could buy at a gas station, and it was nice to be sitting still.

His body shook as he sat down, as though ramping down from a hard day's work, and he started eating, so tired he could barely taste the food.

Across the dining hall, he spotted Leland, and it was as though a charge of electricity went through him. There Leland was, all dapper and groomed, looking like he'd never done a hard day's work in his whole life. He had already hung up his hat, so his blond hair was sticking up as he talked to someone from his staff. Two guests stood nearby, waiting to talk to him like he was some kind of rock star.

Leland did draw the eye, and it was easy to see Jamie wasn't the only one looking at him, with his broad shoulders and wide, bright smile. And those forearms of his. He'd rolled up his sleeves again and was talking to one of his staff and laughing. Then he turned to the guests and talked with them a bit, though it was easy to see he wanted to get on with having his dinner, only he was too polite to break away.

On impulse, Jamie pushed back from the table and went up to him, like he had important business to conduct. Leland's eyes focused on Jamie as he walked up, but he looked puzzled, his brow furrowing.

"Hey, Leland," Jamie said, casual. "I saved you a spot."

"A spot?" he asked, giving the guests another smile.

"You know," Jamie said, pointing at the table by the windows. "We were going to talk about, uh. Things. You know. Like we said we would."

"Things?" he asked, surprised.

"We should let you go," said one of the guests. "You've got business to take care of, and we didn't mean to keep you."

With a quick wave, the two guests got into the buffet line, which left Jamie and Leland standing there, looking at each other. His heart was pounding a little, and he wasn't sure why he'd done it. Leland was fully capable of rescuing himself from over-needy guests, so why had he done it? And was Leland going to be mad at him about it?

"Did we have things to talk about?" Leland asked, arching an eyebrow.

"I figured they were keeping you," Jamie said. It was a little white lie, meant to help.

"They weren't, actually," Leland said. "I typically sit with guests and rotate around."

"Oh." Now he felt stupid and lame, all at once, making assumptions about what Leland needed, and jumping in to fix something that wasn't broke. It was only then that he remembered what Clay had said about Leland sitting with guests as part of his job. "I'm sorry," he said, trying to smile.

"Not a problem, Jamie," said Leland. "Have a good dinner."

With this dismissal ringing in his ears, he went back to his place at a table at the far end of the room to eat his dinner all by himself.

The food was wonderful, but he hardly tasted it as he ate and watched Leland take his tray and join a group of guests, which had been his plan all along. Sitting with Jamie on Saturday had been kindness, and nothing more. But what was it he'd been expecting, anyway? Leland had a job to do, and sitting with Jamie at dinner wasn't part of that.

Feeling glum, he finished his dinner, then took his tray up to the bussing area and left it there. When he turned around, he almost bumped into Maddy, clipboard in hand.

"There you are," she said. "We missed some paperwork I need you to sign. Here's a pen."

"What is this?" he asked, taking the clipboard and pen.

"It's about tips," she said, clucking under her breath as she watched him try to read the single sheet of paper.

"Tips?"

"You know, if a guest gives you money as a tip," she said. "We have a policy that you can't keep tips. You turn them into me, and at the end of the year we have a party for staff, and hand out whatever cash we don't use."

Jamie leaned the clipboard against the metal bussing table, and not really thinking about it, signed at the bottom. Sure, a place like this wouldn't want to encourage tipping so guests wouldn't feel obligated.

"How's it going so far?" she asked him as she ruffled through other papers in her hand.

"Pretty good," he said, lying about it. "I think I'm going to turn in and get an early night, I'm that tired."

"Oh, no," she said, peering seriously at him through her eyeglasses. "You don't want to do that. We've got a new program for line dancing in the evenings. Got a dance instructor and everything. It takes place right after the dining hall closes, and it's a lot of fun."

"Sure," Jamie said, feeling drained not only by the amount of energy she had but by the idea of doing something that would require him to keep moving, long after his body just wanted to quit. His ribs hurt, his feet hurt, and he had blisters where none should be. The last thing he wanted to do was dance.

Besides, Leland would probably be there, and the last thing Jamie wanted to do was face him after having interrupted Leland while he was trying to mingle with guests. On the other hand, maybe Jamie could sit on the sidelines and watch from afar.

It was only after he handed her back the clipboard and pen did he remember the thousand bucks Mr. Ayers had given him. But Maddy walked away before he could say anything, and as he watched her go, he felt like a thief keeping what wasn't rightfully his. He'd just signed the policy, so it wasn't like he didn't know. But if he gave up the thousand dollars, he'd be giving up part of his future dreams of going back to college.

In the end, he stuck around for the dance, and got roped into setting up the little twinkling lights hung on poles around the open space in front of the dining hall, and on the front porch of the dining hall. When the lights were turned on, it really did look festive and sweet.

Grabbing a can of soda from the big barrel full of ice, he propped himself along the edge of the porch where the band was finishing setting up.

All the guests came and huddled in the open area until the dance instructor, a sprightly older woman all decked out in cowgirl gear, came up, grabbed the microphone, and told them what to do. *Move this way, move that, spin about, and don't forget to smile!*

When the band played, it all got pretty lively and nobody seemed to mind that he was just sitting there. Maybe he added to the atmosphere, or maybe nobody noticed that he wasn't joining in. None of that mattered as he drank his soda and watched everybody having a good time. It was a pretty sight, watching everybody whirl and step on each other's toes and laugh and bow to each other and try again.

The sight got even better when Leland showed up, wearing a fancy red cowboy shirt with pearl-snap buttons. He got in one of the lines, and some of the staff, Clay included, went with him to mix and mingle and show the guests how to have a good time.

A sigh went through Jamie's whole body as he watched Leland dance. Leland knew the steps, knew how to move those long legs of his, and it was hard for Jamie to look away, to look anywhere else. When Leland rolled up his shirt sleeves and scraped his hands through his stand-up hair, Jamie almost wanted to get up and join him.

In a pause in the dancing, Leland scanned the crowd as though making sure everybody was having as good a time as they ought to be having. When his eyes rested on Jamie, who suddenly felt like he was sitting there like a pile of mud, there was a question in his grey-blue eyes as to whether Jamie would be getting up to dance, though really Leland looked away too fast for Jamie to be sure.

All the same, Jamie's body seemed to shift all on its own, a reaction to that quick glance, that imagined question. But he couldn't respond. Leland was his boss, and approaching him outside of a certain context would get Jamie turned away. Leland had only sat with him the one time because it was part of his job. That was the way with bosses, and he needed to stay the hell away from any other kind of thinking.

On top of which, he was in possession of a thousand bucks that wasn't rightfully his. What would Leland say if he knew Jamie wanted to keep the money? He'd get one of those disappointed looks, with Leland narrowing those grey-blue eyes of his. Then he'd set his shoulders back and look down his nose, like Jamie'd crawled out from under a rock.

Starting to sweat, Jamie clenched the empty soda can in his fist, his body reacting to the sugar like he'd dumped it into an empty gas tank. He didn't want that look, never wanted that look, but he was going to get it if he didn't figure out something fast.

On one hand, nobody would ever know about the money, not if Jamie didn't tell them. Of course, Mr. Ayers might make a casual mention about it, and somehow it might get back to Leland, though that wasn't likely.

At any rate, turning over the money because he might get found out was *not* the right reason to turn the money over. Turning it over because it was the ranch's policy was the right reason to do it.

He would be out a thousand bucks if he turned it over. But there was something else, too, that might happen. He'd get a different response from Leland, one that would be like finding a buried vein of gold. Leland would say *thank you* and *well done,* and he'd know how much Jamie could be trusted.

A more sensible person would have stopped Maddy earlier as she walked off with the clipboard and told her the truth. But there was another way he could take care of this.

Slowly, he got up, disposed of his soda can in the recycling barrel, and walked to his room. It seemed like a long way to go as he left the dancing and fun behind to grab a thousand bucks that would have done him a whole lot more good than it would the ranch. Except it wasn't rightfully his money.

All the way to his room, he thought about it. Thought about giving half to Leland, or maybe even just a few hundred of it, and keeping the rest for himself. He thought about what Leland would say, the look he would give him, if he ever found out Jamie had held some of the money back. Besides, he knew he would feel like crap if he outright lied to Leland like that.

Once in his room, with the soft, gentle breeze coming through the open windows, ruffling the thin white curtains, he stood there at the dresser with the folded bills pressed to his forehead.

Since his parent's divorce, and he'd been on his own, he'd never held that amount of money, never had a decision like the one he had now. But he knew what he needed to do. If he wanted to turn his life around and stop drifting, then he needed to follow the rules of the ranch. It was the right thing to do. It was what Leland would say was the right thing to do. And then, when he did it, maybe Leland would smile at him, maybe.

LELAND

*T*he first full day of week two was well underway, with the guests having a quick lesson in line dancing on the large porch in front of the dining hall after dinner. The air was cool, and the flickering small lights gave the porch an atmosphere of a shared secret celebration. Lanterns, handmade out of iron by the ranch's very own Jasper, added a rustic air.

"Quint and Brody are going to take everyone on a half-day trail ride tomorrow," Leland said to Maddy with a tired smile. He'd done his bit and danced with the guests, and now he could call his evening his own, once he finished up going over arrangements for the next day with her.

"If the weather holds, which it should," she said, checking the item on her clipboard and sounding for all the world as though the weather better hold or she'd have something to say about it. "How's Jamie doing? He looked a little tired when I spoke to him earlier."

"Good, as far as I know," he said, somewhat distracted as he thought about Jamie. "I'm just going to check with Clay, who was taking him under his wing."

"Don't forget, he needs a new driver's license. He needs to have that, so don't forget." She shook her head at him as though worried about his forgetfulness. "Remember to help him with the bank *and* his driver's license."

"Yes, ma'am and I will," said Leland. Maddy was a stickler for following procedure, for which he was glad. Without her, the ranch would not have been as well run. "I'll take care of the account and the license, end of the week by the latest."

With a nod, she was off, and he went down the steps from the porch of the dining hall, going to the barn where some of the hands were just finishing the last touches to prepare for the trail ride the next day. There he found Clay, working late as usual, just coming out of his office.

"I put those receipts in your accounting book," he said. "For the saddles and the salt."

Clay made a very good unofficial right-hand man. He was young, but he was eager to learn all there was to know about a ranch and how to run one. He was also too cute for words, blond haired and blue eyed, and way too young for Leland. Not to mention he had very strict ideas about fraternizing with employees who reported directly to him and even those who didn't. Those kinds of complications were unnecessary and easily avoidable.

"Thank you," he said, taking off his hat, now that it was the end of the day. "How's Jamie holding up?"

"He's a hard worker, all right," said Clay. He echoed Leland's movements, holding his hat in his hand. "But he didn't want to take breaks. I had to explain to him all over again about the altitude and all."

"Thank you for keeping on top of that," Leland said. "I'll speak to him about it when I see him."

"He's new," said Clay. "When he did drink some water, it was too fast and he almost barfed. You know how it goes."

"I do indeed." Shaking his head, he knew he would have to have a talk with Jamie. "You boys off to town after the dance?"

"Yes, sir," said Clay, almost proudly as he put his cowboy hat back on. "The Rusty Nail is holding us a table."

"Not too late now," Leland said. "Trail ride tomorrow."

"Yes, sir," said Clay again, and with a cheeky wink, he was off.

Leland made his way through the growing darkness to his small cabin, grateful, as he always was, for the privacy and the quiet. Sundays, the day guests arrived, were always busy, but now that Monday, the first full day, was at an end, the week's events planned and underway, he could relax. Kick his boots off. Hang up his cowboy hat.

After a quick shower, he went to the front porch in his sweats and t-shirt and sat in the Adirondack chair, propping his bare feet up on the rail. He might have gotten himself a root beer to enjoy, but it felt like too much work to get up and fetch it.

While he thought he was all alone enjoying the quiet gloom, looking up at the stars among the pine branches, he heard footsteps on the little gravel path that led up to the cabin's porch. There, to his surprise, stepping into the circle of bright air when the porch light came on, was Jamie.

He was wearing the shirt he'd had on at the dance, a pale yellow snap-button shirt that made him seem to glow like a slender firefly.

"Hey, Jamie," Leland said. He stood up, surprised at his own plea-sure to find him there. "What can I do for you?"

Jamie came closer and mounted the two wooden steps to the porch. Then he just stood there, his eyes wide, breath coming a little quick. There was no way of telling what he wanted, but he was pale, as though something truly bad had happened.

"It's okay, whatever it is," Leland said, coming to the edge of the porch to meet him halfway. "Tell me what I can do to help."

"I didn't know," Jamie said, his voice ghostly faint. "Honest I didn't. And I didn't know what to do, but I figured—"

He stopped to take a breath as his voice grew thinner with each word.

"I figured what *you* would do," Jamie finished with a gasp. And with that he reached into his pocket and pulled out a thick fold of cash, which he held out to Leland. "I didn't know. I honestly didn't know."

"Didn't know about what?" Leland asked as he took the money, a stack of fifties and hundred-dollar bills. It did seem to be an awful lot for Jamie to be carrying around, especially since he'd arrived at the ranch footsore, looking like he'd not had a hot meal in days.

"Maddy came to me just after dinner with more paperwork and explained the rule about tips," Jamie said. "She said we weren't supposed to keep tips, but had to turn them in. So I'm turning it in."

"Where'd you get the tip?" Leland asked, as it wasn't usual for guests to tip on the first day.

"Mr. Ayers gave it to me when they left that day," said Jamie. "Only I swear I didn't know about the policy when he did it."

Seeing as how Jamie's background seemed to be rather troubled, the fact that it had taken him such a short while to hand over the money spoke of a conscience well-wrestled with. *And* he'd said he'd done it because it was what he thought Leland would have done.

All of this spoke to Leland's heart in ways he'd not expected upon first meeting Jamie. Leland liked to set a good example to the younger staff on the ranch, but never before had he seen the results of this in such a determined way. The thousand dollars would have gone a long way to seeing Jamie down the road. Nobody would have known.

"That's right," Leland said, curling the money in his fist. "There'll be a party at the end of the season and we split up whatever's left and hand it out."

"So I'm not going to lose my job?" asked Jamie.

It was clear this was important to him, and Leland realized Jamie was looking upon his position as an opportunity for a new start, not just a job to get cash before heading out again. At least that's what it seemed like. Leland wanted to find out more, wanted to ask Jamie up on the porch. Then maybe Leland could fetch two root beers and dig a little deeper about Jamie.

"No, Jamie, you aren't." Leland smiled, wanting to be encouraging. "Besides, they gave you this money before I hired you, so it's rightfully yours. Here."

He held out the money and when Jamie didn't take it right away, he clasped the back of Jamie's hand and pressed the money into it. Held his own hand there until Jamie's fingers tightened around the bills. His face flushed in the soft light and he looked up at Leland. His

114

eyes told Leland he hung the moon, and the thought of this twisted deep inside of his heart.

"Clay said you did a good job today," said Leland, switching the conversation to more mundane matters and away from all he wanted to say. "The only thing is, you need to take breaks. It's easy to get dehydrated up here. Understand?"

"Take breaks?" he asked. "I thought—I thought. Well, there was so much to do in the barn, I was afraid I wouldn't get it all done. And then I'd get fired. And when Maddy came by about the policy, I thought—"

Jamie had worked hard that day and now had come to Leland in the darkness to hand over money he thought wasn't rightfully his. He was worried about the repercussions of this, worried about taking breaks. Just plain worried about everything.

Again, Leland wanted to invite him up to the porch to sit in the other Adirondack chair so they could talk, or maybe just be as the evening turned into full darkness. But he couldn't do any of that.

"It's okay to ask for help," Leland said, gently, dipping his head so he wasn't looming over Jamie quite so much. "If the task is too much for one man, always ask. We're a team here, and you're part of that team."

"I am?"

The question came quite softly, and they were close enough so that when he blinked, Leland saw the surprise in Jamie's eyes, the sense that he'd found out he was a part of something.

"Yes, you are. I told you, remember?" Leland took another step closer, and the look on Jamie's face was so raw and vulnerable Leland knew if he took another step, he'd be in danger of breaking one of his own rules. Something pulsed in the air between them, a scent, a sigh, an unspoken longing. But that was all his imagination, it had to be. "You're a ranch hand. Just keep in mind the ranch becomes a part of you the longer you are here."

Leland stopped himself from going on in this way, too poetic for words spoken out loud, words he usually kept hidden in his heart.

Jamie's behavior, the way he stood there, told Leland without words that he simply wasn't used to being cared about or looked after. That he expected to be rebuffed and turned away out of hand, simply because he was a drifter. Which was exactly what Leland had done upon meeting him.

Now he knew differently. But what could he do about it? Jamie was like anyone who worked on the ranch, off limits to Leland, regardless of the fact he could picture it in his mind's eye the two of them on the porch, talking over some cold root beers. Or teaching Jamie how to ride, for he certainly didn't know how. A closeness could grow between two people in those circumstances, though it certainly couldn't grow with Leland as his boss. And yet, that's what he was.

All of this, these images, swirled around inside of him, and he realized he'd been standing there, looking at Jamie in the glow of the porch light without saying a word. And that all the while, Jamie'd been standing there, patient and still, like he was waiting for something from Leland. Not anything Leland could define, but something.

"You did right by bringing me the money," Leland said, nodding at Jamie's hand, which still held the bills clutched between tight fingers. "Seriously, well done, but keep it. You earned it."

A change shifted through Jamie when Leland said *well done*, like he'd been waiting for it to open a door that had been shut for a good long while. Leland was given a smile, like a gift, and that smile reached those green eyes of his in a way that tugged at Leland's heart.

Jamie should smile more, for he had a lovely one. And as he scraped his hair out of his eyes, Leland wanted to ask him never to cut it, for it was lovely as well, draped like liquid ink. And again, his mind was going on when it should not have been.

"Well, good night," Leland said. "After the meeting tomorrow morning, check in with me, so I can lecture you about taking breaks and drinking enough water."

Regular hydration was the last thing he wanted to be talking about with Jamie, but it was necessary and so there they stood.

"And how are those ribs?"

"I'm fine," said Jamie. "I guess moving all day eased the soreness."

He smiled as he looked down at his boots, as though somehow fascinated by them. "And thank you for the new hat and not being mad when I ruined the first one."

"Happens more than you might think," Leland said, a little surprised that Jamie'd think he'd get mad. Then again, at their first meeting he'd been frustrated with Jamie, and sent him packing.

Part of Leland wanted to convince Jamie he wasn't that straight-laced all the time, and explain he needed to be in foreman mode *most* of the time. There was so much he was responsible for in making the ranch run as it should. And being responsible made him strict and careful.

He was not the kind of man who got mad at the drop of a hat, but that's what Jamie thought, what someone had taught him to think. Leland wanted, needed, to teach Jamie to think differently about himself and the world, and to know he could come to Leland if something came up, that he wasn't simply going to lash out for no reason. Leland knew he never did. He wasn't like that. But Jamie thought he might be.

"My first week here," Leland said conversationally into the small silence that had grown between them. "You wouldn't believe it, but I backed a brand new F150 Ford truck into the wooden porch of the office. You know, where Maddy works? That's why the wood railing looks so new."

"You busted it?" asked Jamie, his eyebrows going up, his sense of humor coming to the fore and relaxing the worry from his features. "What did Bill do?"

"Oh, he hollered a good bit, but then I offered to make it right." Leland smiled at the memory of it, his horror at having messed up so badly his first week, and Maddy's calm nature, which had taken over the conversation between him and Bill. "Which I did, in my off hours."

"And you didn't get fired?"

"No," he said. "Nobody's perfect. When you make a mistake, you offer to make it right and get on with things. And that's how we operate on this ranch."

He hated to think that when Jamie'd made mistakes in the past, someone had decided that asking for his head on a plate was the best solution. What Leland also found himself not enjoying very much was the banal nature of the conversation, when what he wanted to do was to get to know Jamie better, to find that closeness that teased him with its fickle nature.

"Well, you look tired. Better get some rest," he said instead of everything else he wanted to say. "Work starts early on the ranch."

"Okay." Jamie turned to go then paused and looked at Leland over his shoulder with such a sweet expression, his mouth curved into a smile, that it jump-started Leland's heart. "Thank you, Mr. Tate."

"It's Leland, Jamie," Leland said. "Always Leland. Okay?"

"Okay."

With that he was off, disappearing into the low gloom beyond the porch light.

Leland stood there for a good long minute, tracing the spot where Jamie'd been. Missing him already.

15

JAMIE

*J*amie hurried to finish raking the corral just before the horses were assembled for the trail ride. Then he had to clean it again after they left, hustling as fast as he could, skipping lunch because every other ranch hand had already finished the tasks assigned to them that morning. But every time he tried to hustle, he'd get a hitch in his side, and his head would start pounding, and he felt like he was moving through a river of sand.

It was as though his muscles had reached their limit the day before. Maybe he'd needed to take a break, like everybody'd been telling him. Heading into the shade of the barn, he blinked as his eyes adjusted to the low light, and nearly got himself run over. Someone caught him, just in time, wrapping two powerful arms around him, holding him close for a brief second before letting him go.

"Jamie," said Leland in his ear, his body close enough so Jamie could smell the morning's sweat on him, the last traces of soap from his morning shower. "Are you okay?"

"Sure," he said, as breezily as he could, though his hands tightened on Leland's arms longer than he'd intended. "I'm fine, I'm fine. I'm taking a break, just like you said I should."

"Did you get lunch?" he asked.

"Yeah," Jamie said, though that was a lie. He wasn't hungry anyhow, and a low headache was making him feel sick to think of food.

"Fair enough," said Leland. "Check in with Clay when you're done here. I've got to meet with Jasper about those horseshoes."

With that, Leland strode out of the barn, and Jamie realized he should, perhaps, finally take that break. Yes, he'd been lectured about this on multiple occasions, but he kept falling further and further behind. Still, he grabbed a bottled water from the cooler by the closed door of Leland's office and drank it down, feeling it gurgle unpleasantly in his empty stomach.

When he finished, he put the empty bottle in the recycling bin and went out to make sure the corral was raked and ready. One of the hands asked him to help pick up trash and empty soda cans from the front of the dining hall, which he did, though as his headache got worse, it became harder and harder to bend at the waist over and over, to the point where he wondered what was wrong with him.

Maybe he should have eaten lunch, at least. Or maybe he could grab something from the ranch store and have it taken out of his pay, that or break one of the fifties tucked in his top dresser drawer. But just as he was about to head down the road in that direction, the trail ride came back, and there were horses to unsaddle and groom, tack to wipe down and put away.

Some of the ranch's guests helped out, but it was a lark to them. They only did the easy stuff, and mostly stood around petting the horses they'd been riding like they were old pals, and talking to their fellow guests, all the while getting in Jamie's way.

It felt a little like being back at the meat packing plant, doing all the worst jobs while the shift foreman sat in his booth and laughed with some of his favorite cronies. Jamie did his best not to go that direction with his thoughts, but it was hard, so he kept his head down and worked as fast as he could and was able to take care of two horses out of the dozen or so, while Clay and another ranch hand finished five each.

"Thanks," Jamie said to Clay as he wiped the leather oil from his hands with an old rag. "Anything else I could do?" he asked, doing his best to make up for his slow speed.

"Sure is," Clay said. "You can stop working so damn hard. You can start asking for help, saying when you need help. Plus, I just figured out you didn't go to lunch. And I can see by how much you're not sweating that you're not drinking enough water. Now." Clay tipped his head back and looked at Jamie appraisingly, not smiling. "What do you want me to tell Leland about that?"

Jamie hung his head.

Leland had said if he needed help he should ask for it. That he needed to take breaks. To drink water. He'd wanted to show Leland he was somebody that could be depended upon. And he was still reeling with Leland's response to his bringing the tip money to him. That smile, the approval in his eyes, and the way he'd taken a step closer to Jamie as though he wanted to tell him something else—all of this felt so new, so very special, he could not quite explain it to himself.

He would be completely willing to listen to Leland go on about hay bales or wheelbarrows or whatever. Didn't matter. Only that his ears liked the sound of his voice, and something deep inside of him responded to Leland, and whether it was waiting for more approval, or the hope of something more, he couldn't quite figure out.

His arms still felt the ghost of that quick embrace. Well, not an embrace, really, not when what he'd been doing was keeping Jamie from falling on his ass. But Leland's touch—one touch—on his skin, and his body reacted as though he was starving for it.

"I'm sorry," he said to Clay.

"Well, sorry's not going to cut it if you collapse on my watch."

"I was just trying to catch up."

"That's fine and all, but you seem to keep forgetting that you don't work here alone. No one at the ranch works in isolation." Clay's voice went from sounding strict to being kind.

"I know." Looking down at his sturdy boots, still new for all they had a few scuffs on them now, he tried to think about how he could explain it to Clay. How yes, he'd been told these things over and over, but how hard it was after the meat packing plant to believe that they were true. That he was a valued member of the ranch, and that he didn't need to be Superman to prove his worth.

There'd been moments when he believed it was true, and everything seemed like it would work out. But sometimes, like that morning, when he couldn't keep up, nothing in the world could have convinced him he was earning his keep.

"I feel like I'm falling behind," he said, settling for something simple.

"Well, you *are* falling behind," said Clay with a small laugh. "But this is, like, your third day, and nobody expects you to keep up with ranch hands who've been doing this for a few seasons. When you fall behind, let someone know, so someone can step in and help, so things can get done on time."

Now Jamie felt worse than ever, his eyes growing hot at the thought that not only had he not been able to keep up, but that he'd given someone else extra work to do.

"Listen," said Clay. "Falling behind is not a big deal. You collapsing again, that's a big deal. So here's what I want you to do. Listening?"

Jamie nodded, swallowing hard. This was so different from the meat packing plant, the bodega, even the bookstore, that it was hard to believe it was real.

"Go to the dining hall and get a glass of milk, and get them to make you a sandwich. Eat that, and then come back, and you can sort horseshoe nails for Jasper or something light."

"But there's hay. Someone said something about hay being delivered."

"There's plenty of work to go around." Clay shook his head. "Just do as I'm telling you. Don't forget, there's dinner and then a dance and guests to take care of. You need to go all day, but you can't do that if— say it with me now."

"I don't take breaks and I don't hydrate?" asked Jamie, his voice coming out quite thin.

"That is right. Okay?"

"Okay."

Clay waved him off, so he headed down to the dining hall and did as Clay had asked him. No, *told* him. He sat on the porch munching on a banana and having a tall glass of cool milk, which was all he was hungry for. All the while, he thought about Leland. How he looked at him with those grey-blue eyes of his. How he'd fussed and worried about him, scolded. How he'd caught him in the shadows of the barn.

Everything. All of it. Wound up inside of him. He did not know what to do with what he was feeling.

He finished up and went back to the barn where Clay set him in the tack room with a cardboard box of nails that needed sorting into small wooden bins. By the time the dinner bell sounded, he was bored with the tack room and the nails, but felt more rested.

When Jasper came by to inspect his work, he dismissed Jamie with a silent nod, and Jamie gratefully got up to go outside and take a breath of fresh air and feel the blue-sky breezes on his skin. The ranch was a different place. A better place than where he'd come from. He just needed to do his best to earn his keep.

Clay came rushing by.

"Get a shower before dinner," he said. "There's another dance after."

"Yes, sir," said Jamie, feeling more like smiling than he had all day.

JAMIE

eeling hopeful, Jamie looked around for Leland while he stood in line at the buffet and got himself some chili and cornbread, found a place at a long table, and plonked his tray down so he could eat. It was foolish to imagine they might sit together, like they'd done before. Foolish to think that when he thanked Leland for everything, he'd smile that rare smile, and give Jamie a nod of approval.

Why did he need all of that from Leland? What he needed to do was take a step back and focus on his work, his own life, and not on his boss. Besides, what could he offer that Leland Tate could possibly be interested in? When he was in college, Jamie had gone on a few dates, but he'd never—never done *that*. Never been with a guy.

Leland had probably dated many men, all as handsome as he was, so there was no way he'd want to spend time with someone like Jamie. Except if he did, he'd be patient, surely he would be. Patient and slow, his eyes kind as he explained how things worked. And he'd smell good, he'd smell *so* good up close—

With a snap, Jamie turned his attention back to his dinner, and tried not to keep an eye out for Leland. Except when Leland did enter the dining hall and hung up his hat, it was all Jamie could do not to stare. Instantly, Leland was surrounded by a small group of guests, who chatted and laughed like Leland was a prince distributing favors. Then Brody went up to him for a quick talk, and then someone else after that. It was easy to see Leland was not alone and did not need company.

After dinner, Jamie bussed his tray and went outside and got busy helping staff who were setting up for the line dancing in front of the dining hall. They accepted his presence so easily, it felt like he'd been woven into the life of the ranch, just as natural as breathing.

"Don't overdo," said Clay from behind him. "Feeling better?"

"Yes, thank you," Jamie said, turning around to greet Clay properly. "It was stupid—"

"Actually, it was stupid of me to not make sure you were drinking enough water."

"You *did* tell me," Jamie said.

"Well, I didn't make sure," Clay said, smiling that easy smile of his. "And you'll make sure in future, right? Leland gave me a talking to about it, and no, it wasn't fun."

"He gave you a talking to?" Jamie asked, and once again his mind danced around. He was sorry Clay had gotten in trouble on his behalf, but was pleased at the same time because Leland had followed up on what had happened. "That's my fault, I'm sorry."

"Well, we live, we learn, right?" Clay reached over to the barrel someone had just filled with ice and cans and bottles, pulled out two bottles, twisted off the tops, and handed one of them to Jamie. "This is homemade root beer. A local guy makes it, it's real good," he said. "And it's Leland's favorite."

"Thank you," Jamie said. He'd learned something new about Leland, and tucked it away like a secret to take out later.

As Clay swallowed his first sip, he tapped the brim of his hat and went off to chat with some of the guests who were assembling for the dance. Which left Jamie all on his own, to be sure, but he felt lighter inside, knowing Leland hadn't forgotten him.

Whether he would go on not forgetting was another question he didn't really want to ask himself. It was better to stay in his own head and picture little scenarios, Jamie and Leland, working together. Taking breaks together. Sharing a cold root beer together.

As it got slightly darker, someone turned on the string of lights and iron lanterns, which were hung between poles around the dance area and rose to line the edges of the porch of the dining hall. The lights twinkled like shining fireflies, bobbing a little in the slight breeze, setting over the area like a beacon, drawing guests to the dance.

Jamie situated himself on the corner of the porch as he'd done before, grabbed another bottle of root beer, and watched because he had an idea that if he got up to join the dance, someone would be sent to tell him to sit down and rest. This made him smile, his lips curving around the bottle of root beer as he thought about it. How it might get back to Leland. How he might come over, that scold in his voice as he—

"Feeling better?" a voice asked from behind him.

He turned and stood up, and there was Leland, wearing a dark blue shirt with pearl-snap buttons with the sleeves already rolled up to reveal his corded forearms. He held his hat in his hands, his fair hair standing up like a baby duck's behind.

Those grey-blue eyes of his were looking at Jamie, twinkling in the lights strung overhead. He stood there, hip cocked, ready at a moment's notice, as always, for whatever action was needed. Jamie had never met a guy so ready and at attention. Never had a guy like that looking at him like he was.

"Yes, thank you," he said, trying to be casual about it when his heart was actually racing. "Thought I'd come and add to the atmosphere."

"You look better," Leland said. "So much better. Next time, you'll check in with someone if you're not feeling well. Check in with me—" He stopped himself, and seemed a little confused, though Jamie didn't know why. Then he straightened his broad shoulders and smiled at Jamie, a genuine, warm smile that he wanted to reach out and grab and keep with him forever. "Now, no dancing tonight, okay? But tomorrow, you can dance."

"Okay," he said. "I didn't mean to be so much trouble."

"Not a problem, Jamie," he said, then pointed at the dance area. "I've got to join the fun, now."

Off he went with those long strides of his, taking his place in the line, going through the motions of practicing the steps when it was easy to see he already knew them. He joked with the guests on either side of them, his smile easy and broad, including guests in front and in back of him in the fun.

When the older lady dressed as a cowgirl sang out the steps and the music started, everybody whirled and moved and shimmied. Beneath the lights twinkling overhead, it became kind of magical, in a way, regardless of the grace or talent of the dancers. There was energy in the fun and laughter, and Jamie promised himself that tomorrow he would pace himself and join the dance when the stars came out.

But right then, he wanted to sneak into the line beside Leland and tug on his shirt to let him know he was there. To laugh with him, and smile back at him, all nice and easy and handsome as he laughed with other people, and confident with the guests of the ranch.

A little glum, Jamie finished his root beer and walked into the darkness to cool off a little. By the time he got back to the dance area, the music had changed to something more swirly, and the cowboy lady was giving directions for a couple's dance.

Leland had gathered a beautiful older red-headed woman in his arms, and together they danced, moving around the dance area, drawing everyone's eyes to them. Jamie couldn't imagine anything more lovely, but when one guest, a young man, came up to Leland and asked him to dance, Leland bowed, and took the young man in his arms like he'd done with the red-headed lady. As if there were no difference at all, and nothing special about him dancing with a man instead of a woman.

The young man wasn't as graceful as the lady, but the two of them were having a good time. They laughed at each other's mistakes, though Jamie suspected Leland pretended to suddenly forget everything he knew about dancing just to put the young man at ease.

If Jamie'd known it'd be okay for gay couples to dance, he'd have been practicing in his room this whole time while gathering his courage to ask Leland to dance. All this time and he'd never known— he could just *ask* him. Or maybe he couldn't because the rule might be that Leland only danced with guests.

Someone on the dance floor stumbled over someone else, and laughing, they helped each other up. The musicians, all standing on the wide front porch of the dining hall, stopped for a break, tuning their instruments, doing whatever it was musicians did. To Jamie's surprise, in the quiet hush of a pause, Leland came over to him.

Sweat gleamed lightly across Leland's forehead, and he wiped at it with his thumb. His smile was broad as he undid the bottle cap on his bottle of root beer and drank a swig, sighing deeply as it went down.

"I love this part of my job," Leland said with a laugh, as though embarrassed to admit it. "Just love it. The atmosphere, the lights. Everything."

He waved his hand at the dance floor that was actually dirt, but seemed, in the lights and the laughter, to be about as elegant and graceful as anything Jamie had ever seen. Beyond the dance floor, in the dark night, he could see the edge of the horizon between the trees, all dark blue and darker blue, and all at once the world seemed an enormous place, full of possibilities, full of happiness that he might find. And all because Leland had come over during a break in the dance. Had come over to *him*, Jamie, now he was holding out an opened bottle of root beer for him.

"This root beer's pretty good," Jamie said, taking it, wincing as he realized how lame the words sounded. What he wanted to say was everything else. How handsome Leland was. How stirred up he was, just looking at him. "And you're a pretty good dancer." His face got instantly hot as he said those words, which were exactly what he'd been thinking. But of course Leland surprised him with his response, never saying or doing what Jamie expected him to.

"Thank you," Leland said. "When I started last year, I was terrible. Over the winter I took a class with my mom, which kept us both off the streets and out of trouble." He smiled that wide smile as questions buzzed in Jamie's head.

"Your mom?" he asked, taking a huge swallow of the root beer. When it fizzed out of control, he had to wipe his lower lip with the back of his hand, feeling lame and clumsy all the while.

"She lives in Chugwater," Leland said easily as he looked out over the crowd who were lining up once more. "Refuses to move out of a house that is entirely too big for one person."

With a small shake of his head he seemed to dismiss this concern and turned to Jamie once more, his attention fully focused now, as though Jamie was the only person who existed on the whole entire planet.

"But she's happy and healthy and has her garden, so really why would I want to uproot her life just so it fits more comfortably with what I think she needs?"

This statement was almost too much for Jamie to figure out but it told him, all over again, that to Leland, helping others be happy was something that drove him and drove him hard. Which was probably part of the reason he was a foreman at a guest ranch, rather than a foreman at a meat packing plant or whatever.

"Listen," Leland said. "I've been thinking about it. I've got to deliver some salt blocks tomorrow. Maybe you can help me."

"You're asking for *my* help?" Jamie asked, his eyebrows going up, his hand pointing to his chest.

"Yes, I am," he said, gesturing at Jamie with his half-drunk bottle of root beer. "It's ranch policy to go in pairs for jobs that are distant from the main part of the ranch. Horses need salt when the weather gets warmer, and those salt blocks need to be set out for them in the fields." He seemed to stop himself from saying more on the subject and leaned close as though the answer Jamie would give him was something he very much wanted to hear. "You'd get to see parts of the ranch most guests don't," he added.

"Sure, I'll go," Jamie said, never even considering saying no. And who would? Errands with Leland Tate? Sign him up. Which was not something he thought he'd ever be thinking only days ago. "What time do we start?"

"We'll head out just after the general meeting." Then he seemed to think about it. "Stick by the barn. I'll get Clay to load the truck, and you and I will head out when the meeting is done."

"Okay," Jamie said, feeling buoyed by the bubbles of expectation zooming around inside of him.

"Well, I better get back and help finish out the evening," said Leland, with another easy smile and a swallow from his bottle of root beer. "Eat a good breakfast, as we'll be gone till lunch. If you're not feeling up to it tomorrow, you need to let me know. Deal?"

"It's a deal," Jamie said.

"Goodnight," Leland said, and with a wave he moved from the soft porch light and into the darkness.

"Goodnight, Leland," Jamie said with a little wave, though there was no-one to see it because absolutely nobody was paying attention to him. Which was fine.

JAMIE

*J*amie woke up feeling like a million bucks, no, make that a billion. His headache was gone and his ribs hurt only a little bit. Plus, as he took a shower and shaved carefully, he knew the reason he was looking forward to the day was because he was going to spend at least part of it with Leland. Just him and Leland, working together. As to what that might lead to, he did not know, but the possibilities felt good, just the same.

He ate his breakfast, quick as he could, and went to the barn to stand with the other ranch hands while the day's tasks were read out. His chest puffed out as Leland read his name and said what they'd be doing that day, which was, to his amazement, not just delivering salt blocks to the furthest points of the ranch, but also hunting for wasp nests.

He could barely wait for the meeting to be over, but then Leland went off with Maddy, their heads down in what looked like a serious discussion about split-rail fences. By the time Leland came back, waving to Jamie as he came up, it was nearly nine o'clock.

"I'm sorry, I had to take care of that," said Leland, as he came back into the barn. "Well, come on, Jamie. We're going to find that wasp nest."

"That's okay," said Jamie, pleased to have Leland to himself at last.

Together they walked out of the barn and into the bright sunshine. It was warmer than it had been before and Jamie was already sweating and hardly knew what to do with himself.

"Wasps like to build nests in corners and crannies around wooden buildings." Leland took off his hat, ran his fingers through his golden hair, and scanned the ranch, his eyes following the road as the dust from a passing truck settled. "So we'll go around every building and, when we find the nest, we'll get some kerosene and burn it out. No sense in guests getting stung, or any more horses running away on account of a wasp stung it."

Leland was even more handsome, all serious and intent on the work they were doing. Jamie made an effort to focus on the task at hand, and followed Leland around the ranch, helping by not getting in his way as they both looked for the nest.

By the time they made it around the dining hall, climbing through brush on the south side, where it went into the hillside, he was sweating buckets. They took a quick break to get some water and were back at it.

It hardly made sense that he was getting paid just to follow Leland around, but he was. Maybe Leland wanted to spend the time alone with him. Or, what was more likely, maybe Leland just wanted to make sure Jamie didn't end up sprawled in a field suffering from heat exhaustion again.

They found the wasp nest on the south side of the barn, between the barn and the staff quarters, underneath a low part of the roof. It wasn't a very big nest, but enough of one to cause a problem. The wasps flitted about silently in and out of the shadow of the roof, deadly yellow in the still, warm air behind the barn.

"I do a walk around and a ride around almost every day," said Leland, and it took Jamie a minute to realize he was talking to Jamie and not himself. "I can't believe I missed this one."

"Well, the wood is faded here," Jamie said. "The nest blends right in. And the roof hides most of it."

"That it does," said Leland. "Nicely spotted. Well, the barn could use a fresh coat of paint anyhow. Let's go get that kerosene."

They walked beyond the staff quarters to the supply barn, a huge wooden building that was painted the same greenish-tan as the local grasses, which were growing high, spread out along the hillside.

Leland didn't seem gleeful to destroy the nest, but instead showed Jamie how to soak it with kerosene and then smack it to the ground, where he lit it on fire, killing all the wasps. It was gross, but as Leland stomped out the flames, he sent Jamie to the supply shed to fetch a metal trash can so they could scoop up the remains and dispose of it.

"I'll assign some hands to clean the area along the wood where the nest was and to paint this side of the barn." Settling his hat on his head, he nodded at Jamie. Then the cell phone in his pocket rang, and he answered it. When he was done with the call, he looked at Jamie. "I've got to sign some paperwork for Bill," he said. "Can you wait for me at the barn?"

"Sure," Jamie said, pleased that they weren't done for the day.

Leland walked down the road to the office, and Jamie headed back up to the barn. There, he helped take care of tack by rubbing neatsfoot oil on the saddles and bridles that weren't being used that day. When someone asked if he could help groom horses after the trail ride, he shook his head.

"I'm helping Leland deliver salt blocks," he said, puffing his chest out a little. "If we get back in time, I'll help." That's what Leland would have said, he was sure of it. The response he got to that statement was a pair of raised eyebrows, and he smiled.

When Leland showed up in the barn, he was carrying a small ice chest, which he held out to Jamie.

"Can you carry that?" he asked.

Jamie took it. He hefted it in his hands and nodded, pleased with the task.

"What's in this?" he asked as he hurried to keep up with Leland as they walked to the truck.

"Lunch and snacks and cold water," he said. "It's important to keep hydrated, remember that."

"Lunch?" Jamie asked, hope rising in his chest.

"Well, we're running behind, and those salt blocks aren't getting any younger," Leland said with a small laugh. "By the time we get back, we'll have missed lunch at the dining hall."

Leland strapped the ice chest next to the rows of salt blocks in the truck bed of a new-looking F150 Ford that had four doors and shiny black tires. Jamie got in the passenger side and inhaled the new car smell as he buckled himself in. It was an enormous truck and one of the nicest he'd ever been in.

Leland got in with his long legs, and they placed their straw hats on top of each other in the seat between them, and Leland smiled at Jamie as he started the truck's engine. Then he drove along the dirt road that led up the hillside to the gate, where Jamie got out and opened and shut it again behind them.

There wasn't any conversation between them as they drove, but it was nice to look at the wide open sky and to feel the sun on his skin when he opened the window and rested his elbow on the ledge. It was nice to be alone with Leland like this, in the silence, a cool breeze coming down from the low mountains.

The truck bumped from time to time, but the road was well maintained, as everything on the ranch seemed to be. The sky went on forever, and the tall green grasses swayed in the low wind. Everything smelled open and wild, and he took a huge lungful of air.

"Nice, huh?" asked Leland. "The views are amazing out here."

Jamie looked at Leland, narrowing his focus to the cab of the truck, and realized how alone they were together. Just Jamie and Leland driving along. Two regular guys on a job. Two cowboys delivering salt blocks.

Jamie had new boots on his feet, a decent breakfast in his belly, and he was happier than he could remember being in a good long while. Leland had been so nice about the tip money. He'd seemed to understand about Maddy bringing him the policy papers so late. And now he was giving Jamie a smile that reflected in his grey-blue eyes.

"Yes," Jamie said, not adding that while the views were amazing and prettier than anyplace he'd ever been, the view inside the cab was pretty nice, too. With his tanned jaw, Leland was handsome, and the sleeves of his plaid cotton shirt were rolled up to his elbows, showing the strong cords of his forearms.

"There's a place up here where we can stop and have a drink of water." Leland pointed ahead of him with one finger, keeping both hands on the wheel.

They'd only been driving about an hour, and it seemed a luxury to stop. But when Leland parked, and they got out, Jamie understood why.

The truck was alongside some rocks in a little rough-edged parking lot out in the middle of nowhere. Beyond the rocks, the land sloped away and rolled out like a carpet of green and gold and brown and grey, all drenched in sunlight and disappearing to the far blue horizon.

Jamie held his breath as he looked at it, as it was more land with nothing on it than he'd ever seen. Farthingdale Ranch was more than he ever thought it could be, and he closed his eyes and made a wish that it could last, that they could stay there forever.

"Here's some water," said Leland, suddenly beside him, holding out a plastic bottle.

Taking the bottle, Jamie unscrewed it and took a nice, long drink while the wind danced around him, pushing his sun-warmed hair against his face. Leland didn't have his hat on either, and Jamie liked the way his hair turned to gold, and how blue his eyes were as he looked at him.

"Thanks," Jamie said, gesturing to the view. "I think I could get lost out here, if I was on my own."

"Oh, I don't know about that." Leland took a drink and then pointed at the landscape. "If you look, the mountains run north to south. You can always tell directions on the high plains if you remember that."

He talked for a bit about the prairie and the mountains, how big the ranch was, how it abutted BLM land. How the horses were pastured in the winter and in the summer. How the ranch provided jobs. How much Farthing had grown over the years.

All the while, Jamie looked at him, drinking it in, everything he had to teach him. Which was what he was doing, teaching him, though why he seemed to enjoy it so much, Jamie had no idea.

When Leland finished talking, they stood side by side, admiring the view. Jamie's skin drank in the sunshine as he finished the water Leland had given him. And it was nice, real nice, to be in a place like that with the blue sky all around, the breeze rippling through the prairie grasses, skirting the rocks that turned into low, grey mountains.

"We'll head down along that road," said Leland, pointing into the long valley. "As we go, we'll drop off blocks of rock salt one by one, so the grazing horses can congregate without crowding. They like that."

With a smile, Leland gestured it was time to get going. They got in the truck, and Leland drove down the road. While they didn't talk much as they went, it was nice just the same.

Jamie wasn't used to being with men like Leland, who said *we are doing this*, and then did it. In Jamie's world, his old world, back in Denver, or at the meat packing plant, everything was a promise that never came true. Out here, it was different. Leland was different. And Jamie was starting to feel different about himself.

They dropped off the salt blocks, one by one. Leland would stop and tell Jamie where to place the blocks, and Jamie would jump out of the truck and make it happen. Sometimes, Leland got out too, and walked around checking for bear scat, he said, or gauging the level of moisture in the grasses. Mostly it was Jamie doing the work, but he didn't mind, because it wasn't very hard.

They delivered the salt blocks until the truck bed was empty and they were in the middle of nowhere. At least that's what it felt like to Jamie, with the blue bowl of the sky overhead. There was no sound except for the low, almost-silent whistle of the wind over the tall prairie grasses. No presence except for Jamie and Leland, all alone in the middle of it, as though they were the only two people left on Earth.

It was there, way out there on the high prairie, that Leland folded down the tailgate and opened the cooler.

"Eat up," he said as he brought out the sandwiches and cookies and cans of soda. "You've got room to grow in those shoulders of yours," he said, and for a moment it seemed like he wanted to pat Jamie on the shoulder, only he didn't.

They sat on the tailgate in the blazing sun, the wind rushing around Jamie's ears as they ate. The wind whisked away any sounds, and they had to keep a hold on the sandwich wrappers to make sure they wouldn't litter the landscape.

The best part was when Leland smiled at Jamie, and wiped away a bit of mayonnaise in the corner of his mouth, and then dabbed playfully at his face with a paper napkin. Was he flirting? At least it felt like flirting, but where would it lead? Leland didn't seem like the kind of guy to do casual hookups. Jamie couldn't imagine him unbending those rules of his to lower his guard for a quickie behind the barn.

Driving back was fun, as Leland went a little faster without all the salt blocks in the back, and it was nice to see the ranch rise into view and to recognize it as home. Leland dropped Jamie off at the barn, told him to check with Clay for work, and drove off to park the truck.

Feeling pleased, Jamie went into the large, airy barn, somehow seeing it with fresh eyes. He was really a ranch hand now and had delivered rock salt to the fields where the horses grazed. Now, with his straw cowboy hat firmly on his head, he found someone who could direct him to Clay, who was out by the corral, helping Brody, who was instructing a small class of guests with their riding lessons.

"Hey, Clay," Jamie said, putting his booted foot up on the wooden rail, like Clay was doing. He pushed his straw hat back and watched the lesson for a minute. "Leland said to check with you for work."

"You can rake this corral after the lesson," Clay said, giving him a bright smile. "You remember to dump the manure?"

"Yes," he said. Raking a corral wasn't as exciting as being with Leland all day, but he wanted to be helpful, wanted to keep his job.

"Make the sand smooth as you can after," Clay said. "And be sure to stop for water. Every hour, pretty much, understand?"

"Yes, sir," Jamie said with a mock salute.

"Just Clay," Clay said.

"Yes, just Clay," Jamie said, laughing to himself.

Raking the corral after the lesson was over was sweaty work. Flies buzzed around him in the heat, and while horse manure didn't smell so bad, Jamie felt sticky and dusty all over by the time he stopped for water.

He drank an entire bottle while standing in the shade, then went out to finish the job. The sunshine, once bright and breezy, blazed down on the crown of his straw hat as he took the rake and turned it over to smooth the sand in the corral, which was pretty huge.

After that, Clay set Jamie to picking up stray leaves and branches around the barn, making everything tidy, which, after the morning's outing, felt boring. He wanted to deliver salt blocks with Leland again, or help saddle up the horses for an afternoon of trail riding, like he saw some of the ranch hands doing.

Feeling a little hard done by, he threw away the last of the trash in the bins near the supply barn, then went back to the main barn where he thought to find Clay and ask for something more interesting to do.

But instead he found Leland in his office. His hat hung on a wooden peg in the wall, and his sleeves were rolled up, and it looked like he'd run his hands through his hair again. He had a bottle of iced tea at his elbow and was going over a stack of papers on his desk. The office was plain, but there was a shelf full of books about ranching and horses, and everything had the air of hard use about it.

"Hey," Jamie said, and while he felt better just looking at Leland, he also knew he wanted to do something more exciting than picking up trash. "I'm done picking up trash. Is there anything more I can do? Like break a horse or something?" He felt foolish the second he asked it.

"Break a horse?" Leland asked, as he finished what he was writing. When he looked up at Jamie, he smiled. "We don't break horses anymore, at least not at this ranch. We only buy horses that are gentled in, and then we train them. That's how you get the best horses."

Leland reached into a small brown fridge that sat along the wall and pulled out a bottle of water, which he handed to Jamie.

"It's good to take breaks," he said.

Jamie took the bottle of water and leaned against the door jamb and drank it half down, all in a few gulps. When he wiped his mouth with the back of his hand, Leland was looking at him in that way he had. Half appraising, half something else. Jamie couldn't even begin to figure him out, but he wanted to try.

LELAND

*T*ypically on Thursdays, Maddy didn't set up a dance in front of the dining hall, but she'd organized a nighttime hike up to the ridge and back for some stargazing. That wasn't for hours yet, and Quint and Brody were leading that hike, so by the time the dinner bell rang, Leland was done for the day. Except for his usual ride around the ranch later, he was off duty. It was a good feeling and a nice treat mid-week, letting him catch his breath.

In the dining hall, he piled his plate with the lasagna and garlic bread they were serving, and also got a salad. Standing there with his tray, he saw Jasper and Brody at a table near the windows.

He might go sit with them, and make sure he was seated at the end of the table, in case any guests came by to chat. Then, out of the corner of his eyes, he saw Jamie standing at the end of the buffet line with his tray. He was a little grubby from the day's work, but he looked good, like he'd taken breaks and had plenty of energy to spare. When he saw Leland, his eyes lit up, shining like beacons.

What Leland should have done was nod and Jamie and gone to sit with his other co-workers, the ones who were like him, in charge of various functions of the ranch, in charge of people. What he should not have done was gesture to an empty table further along by the windows, with a smile to welcome Jamie to join him. But that's exactly what he did, and he felt a kind of joy seeing Jamie hurry over to the table even as he chastised himself. His rule was never to play favorites, but he was breaking that rule now.

"Hey, Jamie," he said as they sat across from each other. "Saw you working the corral again."

"I took breaks, every hour," Jamie said, nodding. His hair spilled in his eyes and Leland wanted to push it back, but that was him being ridiculous.

"That's good," Leland said, instead. "Eat up, we'll put some meat on those bones yet."

They ate in silence, much as they had when they'd been delivering salt blocks earlier.

Leland didn't know exactly why he'd asked Jamie to help him with that particular task. He'd written Jamie's name on the roster the night before, crossed that out, and written down Clay's name. Only to, in the end, call out Jamie's name.

He was glad he had, for it had been such a perfect time, the weather sunny and bright, just the two of them out there. Leland could never get over how beautiful the front range was, especially in early summer, and it gladdened him more than he could say to look at Jamie and see him taking in the view with wide-eyed wonder.

It made him glad all over again that they were starting that ex-con program and other community outreach programs. Bill was right. It was selfish to keep this all to themselves, and important to share it carefully, slowly, with minimal impact on the environment.

But more, it had felt significant to share it with Jamie, being together like they had been. It took all of whatever Leland possessed to not suggest to Jamie, then and there, that they should do the same the next day and the next and the next. But he couldn't. There was always other work to do, and besides, it could never be the same perfection. The landscape shifted, and the clouds moved, and it was always different each and every day.

Like the expressions on Jamie's face now, as he dug into his apple crumble and looked at Leland like he didn't know what to expect from him, but might welcome it. Leland didn't know what to expect from himself, so he could well appreciate what Jamie was going through. All he knew was that the affection he felt was solid, and beneath that was something more fleeting but quite powerful, if he let it come to fruition. He didn't know if he dared. Didn't know if he could resist following through, as he was only human after all.

"You're doing good work, Clay says," Leland said, reaching for his own apple crumble, trying to distract himself. "My, look at this. We have the best cooks at the ranch, just the best."

Jamie smiled, and the smile reached his eyes, and Leland wondered how many people had seen this smile since before his parents had gotten divorced. Not many, that's what he figured. But he was seeing it now, and it made something come alive inside of him. He was such a stickler for rules, but could they be broken or bent for such a smile as this? Maybe.

In the midst of his musings, Jasper came up and wanted to talk about new bellows for his forge. While Leland had already told him no, as he really didn't need a new one, Jasper patiently explained that what he wanted to get was an old-fashioned, wood-and-leather set of bellows that would be perfect for demos and would give the right atmosphere. Then Clay trotted over and wanted to know whether he could help with cabin assignments for the next week's group of families and singles.

In the middle of that, Jamie nodded at Leland, gathered his tray, and left. Which left Leland bereft and oddly unable to focus on Jasper or Clay. Or the other three ranch hands who came up to him with questions. And the pair of guests after that. Well, he was the foreman, so it was his job to answer their concerns, which he did, as patiently as he could, all the while hoping he'd catch another glimpse of Jamie before he left the dining hall. He did not.

After dinner, he went to the barn where a horse was waiting for him, all saddled and ready to go. This one was Travelle, a nice quiet bay mare who loved to run, when anybody would let her, but who was gentle and perfect for kids, for all she was a little lean in the withers.

Leland mounted up and went down the road, past the dining hall, cantering sometimes, or strolling in the cool air beneath the trees along the road to the gate. He checked the gate was closed, then turned back up the road and over the bridge.

From a little rise, he could see that the water from Horse Creek was collecting nicely in the pond on the other side of Jasper's cabin. The grasses along the river were high, except around the fire pit where Jamie had so obligingly scythed them back.

Someone, probably Jasper, had come in and finished the job and so now the fire pit was ready for the regular Friday night cookout. Some groups wanted scary stories, some wanted singalongs, and Maddy took a vote for preferences at the beginning of the week. This week was song week, which, luckily, he was not on tap for, as he was a horrible, truly horrible, singer.

He guided Travelle to the left and took the narrow, almost invisible dirt road that led up to the Surveyor's Cabin, a lonely spot tucked behind a hill. For over a hundred years, a log cabin had stood on that particular spot, falling into disarray over time. Finally, when the ranch could no longer insure the structure, Bill had it torn down, some seasons back. It had been a wreck anyway, with the roof caving in and the walls crumbling into the earthen foundation. Someone, probably Maddy, had collected artifacts and such and set them up in display cases in her office, and put pictures of the original cabin and occupant on the walls, as a kind of shrine to the old days.

Over the winter, when Bill had taken a trip out to assess the ranch, he'd come across the site, and dreamed up a plan to rebuild it, just as it had been. Even without a whole lot of money to spare, Bill had hired carpenters. They'd worked like fury during early spring, and now here the cabin was with a tidy roof that looked like wooden shingles but were actually cement, fire-safe and to code.

The air smelled like pine as Leland rode up to the cabin. There was a lock on the door, as the inside still needed some work. Someday, Bill hoped to rent the cabin out to folks who really wanted to get away from it all, live simply for a day or two, and stare up at the brilliant stars that could be seen overhead at night.

The structure had seasoned for a little while and now needed painting. Bill had ordered the color he wanted for it, which he insisted should be very natural looking and fit in with the wild prairie landscape. The gallons of paint were in the supply shed, and Leland knew that yes, he was going to ask Jamie to help him. The task would only take them a day or two, and while it might not be like their trip to deliver salt blocks, it might be something else.

Turning Travelle back to the main part of the ranch, he shook his head as he scolded himself. These weren't the thoughts a foreman should be having about one of his ranch hands. But he was having them. All kinds of thoughts and feelings he'd not had in a good long while.

Maybe he felt close to Jamie because he needed someone in his life, and maybe Jamie needed him. And maybe Leland needed Jamie to remind him it wasn't all rules and regulations, that life could be fun. That smiles could be shared over slices of apple crumble.

To soothe his troubled thoughts, he made another circle around the ranch, wide, to the north, going on the other side of the river from Jasper's cabin and his blacksmith forge, up along the hill above the pond. There he could see the spread of the ranch, the barn, the roofline of the staff quarters above the pine trees, the smoke rising from the dining hall's chimney, the majority of the building completely tucked away behind aspens coming to full leaf.

And there, just on the other side of the river where Horse Creek led into the pond, was Jamie. Maybe he'd come out to watch the sunset in the beauty of the evening. Or, possibly, he'd come out to watch Leland ride. Sometimes guests did. It had the air of the romantic about it, Clay assured him, even though he was doing it for very practical purposes.

Jamie spotted Leland and waved his straw hat in the air, a greeting and a welcome all at once. Joyous. Full of life. And a far cry from the young man who'd come through the gate to the ranch looking for a job, pale and practically shoeless.

Leland was a firm believer in work as a cure, the right work for the right person. He also knew that sometimes work could and should easily take second place. Or third. Or last.

147

Leaving off the rest of his ride, Leland trotted to the bank of the river, and urged Travelle across the creek. She went forward willingly, snuffling at the water that came up to her knees. Going through the rushing water, she trotted up the far bank when she reached it, splashing water as she went. Jamie laughed, jumping back, making a show of protesting, though they both knew damp clothes would dry in a heartbeat up here.

Pulling Travelle up, Leland settled her with pats to her neck, and took off his hat to wipe the faint sweat from his brow. Then he put his hat back on and leaned down, one arm on the saddle horn, one hand resting on his thigh.

"Not going on the star walk, Jamie?" he asked. "It's a fun hike, an easy hike."

"It sounded like it would be," he said, ducking his head but looking up at Leland from beneath the brim of his straw hat.

Leland's breath caught in his throat. Sweet, that's what Jamie was, sweet. He'd probably always been that way, but life had dealt him a rough hand and threatened to take away that sweetness. And now, here on the ranch, with its soft, warm breezes, the sweetness was strengthening into something stronger, something that could last, no matter what life threw at him.

This was how it always happened to Leland. His life would go on, as it should, as he'd planned, and then it would happen. The poetry in his soul, the poetry that he kept squashed, would creep up, swirling around like ribbons of pleasure and softness and sweetness. Cowboy poetry, he called it, full of lonesome cries along the ridge from coyotes calling to the moon, and whippoorwills down by the banks of the creek, sleepily wishing each other goodnight as the sun went down. It filled him, almost taking over as he looked at Jamie.

He sat back in the saddle because that was not how it was supposed to go. Except part of him, deep inside, wished he was brave enough to ask Jamie out on a moonlit night, and find some cowboy poetry and read it out loud to him. What would Jamie's response be? Would he laugh and walk away? Or, abashed, would he shrug and not know quite what to say? What young man wanted poetry from another man?

"Well," Leland said, cleaning his throat, gathering up Travelle's reins, signaling her to walk. "I better finish up my rounds."

"You ever take anyone with you?" Jamie asked, a bright eagerness in his face as he looked up at Leland. "On those rounds of yours?"

For a moment Leland hesitated, pulling on Travelle's reins as he looked down at Jamie. Nobody had ever asked him that before. Maybe everyone thought it would be presumptuous, and maybe most guests just liked to watch him ride. But he had been asked now. By Jamie, right out loud and brave as anything.

What he should have done was say no, a definite no. But what he did was nod slowly, pushing back the brim of his hat with a finger.

"Travelle's a bit more sprightly than Gwen," he said in warning, looking Jamie up and down as though judging him for his ability, and not, as was actually the truth, for the simple pleasure of looking at him. "You ever had lessons?"

"No," Jamie said, and his face fell, shoulders slumping.

Jamie was about to turn away and head back to the main part of the ranch, and Leland could imagine him taking a lonely shower and being glum as he went to bed. Only he didn't want that. He wanted Jamie's smiles and his joy, radiating off him like a little kid. He wanted Jamie wide eyed with wonder and happiness. He wanted all these things and pushed aside any hesitation he had as he reached out his hand.

"We'll get you set up with lessons as soon as we can," Leland said. "In the meantime, I'll give you another taste of riding. Take my hand and put your foot in the stirrup. I'll pull you up."

As he'd done the first day they met, Leland slipped his booted foot from Travelle's stirrup, and reached down, clasping Jamie's hand, sliding it up to his elbow, a forearm grip that was sure and strong. When Jamie got his boot in the stirrup and hopped on his other, Leland hauled him up behind him, where Jamie settled on the saddle blanket, his arms slipping around Leland's waist.

Leland squeezed his hand as he looked back at Jamie to make sure he was okay, and smiled, feeling it spill out of him, all unexpected and unaccounted for, but spilling everywhere, like rays of the sun after a storm. The smile he received in return came back at him, just like that, Jamie's eyes wide with pleasure and surprise, all at once.

"You ready?" Leland asked him. "She moves a bit fast, but it'll be fun, you'll see."

When Jamie nodded, Leland clucked to Travelle, and eagerly she trotted and then smoothed into a canter. For such a mixed breed of a horse, no breed really, she had a canter like silk, and could go on that way for a good long while. She would have made a terrific Pony Express horse, but here on the ranch, nobody would ever ride her that hard, and she could go on forever.

Jamie clung to Leland, pressing his body tight, making Leland's skin warm where he pressed. Jamie was trembling with excitement, peering out from behind Leland's arm to see where they were going. His dark hair flew about his ears, and Leland could just about feel him smiling as they cantered up the low ridge to the top where the land spread out in the long shadows as the sun started to set.

Leland didn't head Travelle down into the valley, as it was a little steep for two on a horse, let alone an inexperienced rider, but instead went up the ridge, following the riding path. And there, at the top, they met up with the stargazing hikers, all ten of them, decked out with protective gear like they were heading for pure wilderness, rather than a hike in the soft darkness that would take them no further than a mile or so from civilization.

"Hello, folks," Leland said, pulling Travelle to a stop. She trotted and chuffed, but obeyed, like she always did, though he knew she wanted to keep running. "Jamie and I thought we'd catch up and see how it's going."

"We got an early start," said Quint, and Brody, alongside him, nodded in agreement. They both eyed the two of them together on Travelle's back, but, being very tactful employees, didn't say anything.

Quint was Leland's trail boss, but unless there was a trail ride going, he usually helped with various tours and guided folks around when they needed it. He was as handsome as all get out, with jet black

150

hair and blazing blue eyes, and he was smart and tough. Leland appreciated him when the ranch had hired him last season, and each day that passed, he'd never regretted giving Quint the thumbs up, along with Bill's stamp of approval.

"Some of these folks wanted some ghost stories, so we're going to build a fire near the rocks at the base of the western ridge and tell them before we stargaze." Quint looked out over the ridge and then at his small group.

Leland nodded his approval without saying anything. That area was sparse for grass and trees, and a really nice location for stargazing, as the mountains made a delightful contrast in the night sky. Plus, Quint knew fire safety as well as anyone on the ranch.

Leland looked at the ten folks who were in this little band and considered the kind of folks they were, the kind who would remove themselves from what they were familiar with, game to try something new. Maybe someone else might have thought their outing was lame, but if they were city dwellers, which he expected some of them were, he thought it was mighty brave of them to try it, try the ranch, and breathe fresh air, and see the beauty of purple mountains majesty, all for themselves.

"Well, have a good time, folks, and let Quint here know if you need anything, though, I expect he's got you all set. Enjoy!"

With a wave, Leland turned Travelle and clucked to her.

"Hold tight," he said to Jamie, who was clinging to him even tighter as Travelle gathered her long legs beneath her.

She burst into a canter, and settled into a smooth rocking motion, nice as you please, and away they went with a flick of her tail, lovely in the low light of early sunset. Nobody knew that he clasped Jamie's hand in his, to hold him close and keep him safe, but nobody needed to know. Just Jamie and him.

JAMIE

*H*alf dizzy by the time they got back to the barn, Jamie slid down from the saddle, his thighs wobbling beneath him. His hand still tingled from when Leland had held it. It might have been his imagination that Leland's hand lingered for a good long while as he helped Jamie down from the horse, and that his fingers curled around Jamie's wrist in a kind of embrace before letting go. But maybe he didn't imagine it.

Jamie opened his mouth as he took off his hat in the cool shade of the barn. He wanted to say something to Leland. To thank him for the ride, the job, for everything. And he wanted to say more than that, only he didn't know what he wanted to say, really, or how to say it.

And then, of course, Brody came in to take care of the horse, and when Leland got off the mare, he and Brody talked about the saddle, and the condition of her coat, and how smoothly she cantered. How they should make a special note in her chart that she should be reserved for the shyest of riders, the ones who needed extra coddling. And how Brody was right, that Travelle would be perfect for Dorothy.

By the time they were alone again, all of the words in his heart, the jumpy, excited feelings, had stepped back to be replaced with practicalities. Leland was the foreman of the ranch, and Jamie knew it. He was just being nice to Jamie, making up for their first meeting, when he'd dismissed Jamie from the ranch with barely a second thought. They could be friends, maybe, but nothing more, and Jamie knew it.

"Thank you, that was fun," he said, rubbing the inside of his sore thighs, stopping when he realized what he was doing, how it might look.

"We'll start your lessons soon as we can," said Leland. He took his hat off and ran his fingers through his fair hair, and as he put the hat back on, seemed to consider the matter with his usual seriousness. "Possibly starting Sunday, so we'll need to get you some cowboy boots, as you can't ride in those."

Jamie looked where Leland was pointing, which was at his still-new boots. They were on their way to getting broken in, and there was already a neatsfoot oil stain on the toe of the left one. Then Jamie looked at Leland's boots, proper riding boots, western boots, with pointed toes and a stacked heel. He could hardly believe he would get a pair.

"Those are pretty expensive, huh?" Jamie asked, thinking of how long it would take before he could pay them off.

"Actually, guests sometimes leave boots behind," Leland said. "Remember? We have a lost-and-left behind box in the storeroom next to my office. We can find a pair that fits you. How does that sound?"

While Jamie would have liked brand new boots, it was better this way because he wouldn't owe the ranch any money. But he was disappointed, too, that they were talking about such practical matters, when all the while, he wanted to share what was inside of him. He wanted to share feelings he didn't quite understand, but that felt good and sweet and powerful, lingering just beneath the surface of his skin.

"Well, goodnight, Jamie," Leland said, touching his fingers to his hat. "See you in the morning."

With that, he left, striding out of the barn as though he had some-place to be, and maybe he might have. All Jamie knew was that he was alone with his thoughts and jumbled feelings. His legs ached, and his heart felt a little empty, and while he knew what to do about the first, he did not know what to do with the second.

A month ago, even a week ago, he would have stuffed his things in his green duffle bag and hightailed it out of there, looking for new horizons, promising himself that one day he would stop and put down roots. He would not do that now, though. He wanted to stick around and try his hardest to either come to terms with how he felt about Leland or get over him and find someone else.

There was probably a rule about employees hooking up with other employees, and probably one about bosses and workers—which explained a whole lot, now that he thought about it. Even if Leland liked him, and maybe even felt stronger than that, there was no way he was going to break a rule. Not for Jamie. But they could be friends, right? Even that would be better than nothing.

Jamie walked out of the barn, his knees quivering, and nodded at other members of staff who were on the path, finishing up evening errands, helping to pick up trash or whatever. But nobody asked Jamie to help, so he climbed the steps to his room and took off his straw hat and placed it carefully on the dresser.

He stripped to the skin and stepped into the hottest shower the plumbing would give him.

He knew he should never want what he absolutely couldn't ever have. Hope had not been a part of his life for a good long while, and he should have known better than to invite it to stay. Now he needed to get rid of it so he could keep everything else he'd been given.

He had a good job, his own room, and horse riding lessons coming his way. Leland probably wouldn't be the one to teach him, but he'd check in on Jamie, that was for certain. At the very least, Leland would get reports from whoever taught Jamie, and he'd have conversations about him, be thinking about him.

It was foolish to consider all of this and not be happy he was getting that much, not when it was so easy to see how it might be if there was more between them.

As the water flowed, hot and fast, he reached down between his legs and did what he could to get that sense of longing out of his system, out of his heart. And came in his hand, feeling lonelier than ever.

The night was warm, so he slept in his skin, on top of the bed with the sheets and blanket folded back. From the open windows came a slight breeze that cooled his skin and eased him into sleep. And in the morning, everything looked a little better, a little brighter. He showered and shaved, had breakfast, and was in front of the barn for the morning's meeting before Leland and pretty much everyone else.

Leland and Maddy went over everything for the day, the current fire danger status, the chance for rain, and that Leland wanted everyone at the fire pit come sundown to join the guests at the ranch for the singalong, and to be sure to be upbeat about it, even if they couldn't sing.

"Like me," said Leland.

Everybody laughed at that, and though Leland was blushing a little, he didn't seem to mind the teasing.

"Now, I've got a painting project today," said Leland, holding up Maddy's clipboard. "I need someone to help me paint the newly built cabin."

"What cabin?" asked Clay from the front of the group.

"You remember, the one Bill had built," said Leland.

"It's where the old surveyor's cabin used to be," said Maddy. She took the clipboard from Leland and gave him a look that clearly indicated she felt better with it in her own hands. "We tore it down a few seasons ago, so some of you newer folks might not know about it."

"Who wants to help me paint today?" asked Leland again as he looked out over the crowd. Into the bit of silence that fell rose murmurs and small questions, and then Leland looked right at Jamie and nodded his head, as though actually pointing to him.

"Me," said Jamie, raising his hand so hard and fast that something in his shoulder felt like it popped.

When Leland pointed at him, and dismissed everyone else, Jamie knew a little bit of his wish from the day before was going to come true, even if only for a little while. He and Leland would spend time together and, if a month ago someone had told him he'd be glad to be working with the boss for a whole day, he would have laughed out loud. And now here he was.

He kept himself busy helping in the barn until Leland was free from guests coming up to him and ranch hands asking him questions. Finally, Leland gestured to Jamie, his eyes shaded by the brim of his hat, his smile wide and welcoming, and Jamie went to him readily.

"Change into your oldest jeans," Leland said. "Wear a t-shirt you don't mind ruining because paint gets everywhere, even if you're careful."

"Okay," Jamie said and ran to his room to change, hurrying back to the barn so fast he was out of breath.

And there Leland was, waiting in the shade, dressed in old jeans and a threadbare white t-shirt that sculpted close to his back and his shoulders, so thin in places Jamie could almost see through it. Leland's jeans hung on his hips, and the elastic on his briefs were just visible.

In that moment, Jamie stood there with his mouth open. This was more than a wish coming true, it was a bit like a fantasy. But he shook himself because it was one thing to have the dream of spending time with Leland come true. It was another thing altogether to imagine it could come to anything more than that.

They walked to the supply shed and loaded an older truck with cans of paint, brushes, paint cloths and the like.

"You ever paint before?" Leland asked him as he grabbed a cooler Jamie *knew* was full of stuff for lunch and for breaks and put it on top of the paint cans.

"Yes," Jamie said, getting in the passenger side of the truck, inhaling the smell of old plastic and years of dust. "Just one time painting a house on a job I got through a temp agency in Denver." The painting job hadn't been as bad as the meat packing plant, but it had been pretty rugged, as they'd sent him up a tall rickety ladder and told him he couldn't come down until he'd finished the side of the house.

Leland drove the truck down the dirt road that went through the middle of the ranch and then through the parking lot and up a narrow dirt road that went up a hill. Beyond the hill was another low rise, and as the road curved around, ahead of them was a wooden cabin. It wasn't a log cabin, but one built of new boards, with simple lines and little square windows with shutters on the outside, framing each one. The roof looked sturdy, and as they drove up, the cabin seemed to watch them, waiting for what they might do.

"This is in the middle of nowhere," Jamie said as Leland parked the truck and they got out. "Why would someone build a cabin in the middle of nowhere?"

"I'll tell you," said Leland. "Help me unload; we'll arrange the equipment and then start."

They laid an old, paint-splattered canvas tarp on the grass, and lined up the brushes and cans of paint. Leland easily opened two cans with the metal bar, stirring each one with a thin wooden stick from the paint store. The smell of turpentine rose into the air.

"It's brown," Jamie said, looking at the color of the paint, wondering why it was so plain.

"Actually, it's a stain," said Leland. He handed Jamie a new brush, a can of paint, and a new, rough cotton cloth, which he stuffed into Jamie's waistband. "And here's the story."

They started painting the south side of the cabin before it got too warm, their paint brushes going in sync as they started applying stain beneath the eaves.

Leland told Jamie the story of John Henton, an ex-soldier who'd come out after the Indian Wars to look after the surveyor's cabin. How rough the winter had been, how he'd come out on his own, wounded. How a local Native American woman from the Arapaho tribe helped him get better. And how John and his companion survived the winter together before moving down to Trinidad. And how Bill had decided to re-create the cabin on the spot where it had once stood.

"How do you know all of this?" Jamie asked, laying down a swath of stain with a broad stroke.

"It's Maddy, really," said Leland. He stopped to get some waters and handed one to Jamie, and together they stood in the narrow shade and drank that water. All the while, Jamie watched Leland swallow and wipe his mouth with the back of his hand and had to look away.

"She's the history buff. All those pictures in her office? They're of the cabin and of John. All the stuff in those glass cases? That's from the junk she grabbed from around the foundation when they tore it down. She's got stuff from Farthing, too, when the town was first getting started. That woman loves history."

"Who was the companion?" Jamie asked, thinking about two men living in the wilderness like that, and how it would be if Leland and he shared the winter in such a small space, just the two of them sharing a bed.

"Oh, I don't know," said Leland. "Maddy would know, for sure." He made a gesture as though he was trying to get Maddy to let him finish telling the story. "She once told me John was lonely, then this other guy shows up, and he's not lonely anymore."

"Were they—were they close?" Jamie asked, feeling quite bold and daring, enjoying Leland's expression when he asked it. His eyebrows went up and a sort of sweet reflection danced in his eyes.

"I don't know," he said. "Maybe they were. Maddy would know."

He smiled and Jamie smiled back and for a moment, there was an idea between them. There were no words in this idea, just an idea of an idea, and he was glad to share it with Leland. Then they got busy painting.

The cabin was small, but they used up a lot of stain before they took a break for lunch. They sat in the shade of the cabin, on the flat patch of grass to the north, and ate their sandwiches, and had cookies and soda, joy rising inside of Jamie the whole while.

20

LELAND

The afternoon grew a little cloudy, which was good for painting, but it also meant it was hot. By the time they finished two-thirds of the cabin, they'd gone through nearly all the water. The smell of paint was thick in the air, with only a little breeze from the mountains to cool things off. That's when it got difficult.

Not the painting, no, it was never about the painting. It was about coming up with a way for Leland to be able to spend time with Jamie, to get to know him better. To see if he could figure out what he was feeling, what he wanted.

Jamie, as if he knew, decided to shake things up, and that's when he took off his t-shirt. The t-shirt was new. It was one of the ones Leland had bought for him, rather than an old one that wouldn't be missed if it got ruined.

When Jamie put his paintbrush down, bending to balance it on the edge of the can, Leland had no idea that Jamie would curl his fingers around the hem of that t-shirt and slide it up his torso. And just like that, the t-shirt was in the grass, and Jamie's ribs and slender shoulders and that tiny bit of downy hair on his chest was in full view.

Leland could hardly look away, but now he knew. Jamie already had a farmer's tan, his forearms dusky, with everything from his neck to his belly button pale as a lily.

Now Leland could see the remains of the bruises from the gate. Now he could see where the tender muscle ran from Jamie's neck to his shoulder. Now Leland had something to take with him so he could imagine what Jamie would look like laid out on white cotton sheets. The contrast his body would paint, like a dappled young horse, a sunny tan in some places, his arms, or his neck, pale in others, his long legs, his hips, the skin soft over his belly—

Jerking himself back from these thoughts was hard, harder than it ought to be. Hard as the cock in his jeans and certainly nothing he should linger on. Jamie was his employee. He was depending on his job to help him make a new life, which Leland knew he was working very hard at.

The last thing Jamie needed was someone like his boss making eyes at him, leading him on, and leading him on it would be, because what else did the two of them have in common except the job? That was no kind of relationship, and Leland was hardly one for casual hookups. For him, it was all the way or no way.

"Are you okay?" asked Jamie, his hair ashine with bronze in the sunlight, his smile wide, eyes innocent as a new day.

Leland blinked to focus. Jamie came up and reached past him, his breath soft on Leland's arm as he grabbed another bottle of water. Stirring him up in all kinds of ways, and he had to reach to adjust himself in his thin blue jeans. Jamie did not know what he was doing, and Leland knew that because Jamie looked at him with some surprise, as if he'd stirred himself up at the same time he'd stirred Leland up.

There was no one around. No one would know, save for the cabin and the spring-green prairie grasses, barely stirred and smelling warm in the heat of the afternoon as the clouds gathered over the mountains.

"Jamie," Leland said, low.

"Yeah?" Jamie asked, which made Leland realize he had no idea what he wanted to say to him. That Jamie should put his shirt back on? That Jamie should stop looking like a mixture of vulnerability and need and wonder at the world, all wrapped in his slender frame, making it so Leland couldn't stop staring?

They were unequal in terms of power. Leland was the boss. Jamie was his employee. He had his shirt off, while Leland still wore his. That was it, then.

Leland put his paintbrush down and grabbed the cloth over his shoulders to pull his t-shirt off. It was warm, so he used the t-shirt to wipe the sweat from his neck. Jamie's eyes tracked his movements the entire time.

If he was smart, he would have stopped it right then and there. Maybe he wasn't as smart as he ought to have been, for he grabbed a bottle of water and drank it slowly, and together they stood there, half-naked, the golden sun on their skins, the faint, warm breeze washing over them like a balm.

Leland watched Jamie watching him drink that water and watched him in return. His gaze lingered over Jamie's throat as he swallowed, the way his dark hair stuck to his temples with faint sweat. The smile that played over his mouth when he wiped it with the backs of his fingers.

Leland was lonely, that's what it was, and it had taken this drifter coming on to ranch property to show him that. And now he had all kinds of ideas in his head about taking Jamie out to see the moonrise, when the moon was full, or taking him out at dusk to watch shooting stars come over Iron Mountain. With grit teeth, he forced himself to turn back to the task at hand: painting.

They finished the first coat by the time the wind picked up and grey clouds came over the mountains like soapsuds. It might rain, or it might blow over; out where they were, it could go either way, especially in early summer.

"Let's start on the second coat," Leland said. "We might not get done, but we can finish tomorrow."

"Okay," Jamie said, as always willing.

As Jamie turned to his task, Leland reached out to sweep away a small butterfly, a yellow and blue one, that had landed on his shoulder. Jamie looked over his shoulder and Leland very gently pushed the butterfly from Jamie's skin.

Jamie's whole body twitched as Leland touched him, and it ran through him how much Jamie trusted him. Leland had only touched his shoulder, sure, but as Jamie pivoted on his heel, his eyes had darkened, and Leland had a feeling he would have trusted him with more. Only trouble was, Leland couldn't trust himself with more than this. Didn't want to break the trust Jamie had in him.

"Better get painting," Leland said, meaning it, even if the words came out like he was talking about something else altogether.

They painted, got brown stain on the green grass, on their jeans, and on the cabin, most of it. Sweat grew and dried and itched along the back of his neck, it was just that hot. He stopped for water twice during that last hour, though mostly it was to take a deep breath and a mental step back. Which helped some, though not enough. Jamie had a swath of stain on his belly, though how it had gotten there, Leland did not know.

When they were out of paint, he stopped them, and gestured for Jamie to come closer. The last thing he should do. The only thing he wanted to do.

"What?" Jamie asked, looking up at Leland, his face flushed, a rosy glow of a narrow band of sunburn along his shoulders.

"Paint," Leland said. Feeling rather like he was about to fling himself off the cabin's roof, he took one of the cloths, flicked a little turpentine on it, and wiped at Jamie's belly, back and forth, one way in each direction, then wiped the turpentine away. His breath was coming hard up his throat, and he had to put the brakes on fast. "That'll fix you up. Let's head back and get washed up for dinner."

Jamie seemed as reluctant to leave as Leland was to make him, but the wind had kicked up and it was time to go back to the ranch. They packed up the paint cans and the splattered canvas sheet, stored the paint brushes in old plastic bags so they could be used the next day, and put everything in the back of the old truck.

Just before they got in the truck's cab, Leland to drive and Jamie to sit in the passenger side of the bench seat, they grabbed their sun-warmed t-shirts to put them on. Leland found himself pausing, with his hands on the shirt balled into fists.

"That was fun," said Jamie. He was holding his t-shirt in his hand, and it was obvious that he didn't intend to put it on. Leland had to *make* him put it on, because that was ranch policy. Leland had to make him because he didn't think he could stand one more minute looking at Jamie's skin, the slope of his side, without doing something about it. "Are we going to finish up tomorrow?"

Leland tugged on his t-shirt, looking down to realize that the cotton cloth was quite thin and left very little to the imagination. What had he been thinking when he'd changed into clothes for painting? He'd not been thinking, that's what. Well, he needed to start.

"Actually, I've got other things to tend to, so I'll probably send some hands out to finish tomorrow." Leland shook his head, wishing it could be different but knowing that wishing never made it so. "Ranch policy," he said, pointing to Jamie. "Put it on."

Jamie was quick to put his t-shirt on and to get in the passenger seat, and Leland drove them back to the ranch and parked the truck near the supply barn.

"Get washed up and changed for dinner," Leland said, not moving from where he was on the bench seat, waiting for Jamie to get out.

"Did I mess up?" Jamie asked. "Are you mad at me?"

Leland looked over at Jamie's sad face, where the light had dimmed from his green eyes. Jamie looked to be two seconds from slinking away like a scolded hound. He had, in that moment, more in common with the drifter who'd shown up at the gate than the young man who'd raised his hand when Leland had asked for volunteers.

If he was careful. If he was careful. Maybe.

"No, I'm not mad," Leland said, resisting the impulse to tousle Jamie's hair, though he did reach out and touched Jamie's bejeaned knee. "Painting just takes it out of me. And it might rain and ruin the Friday night campfire and singalong—"

He stopped because that wasn't at all what he wanted or needed to say. It was what he *should* say, sure, but nothing that was in his heart. Which evidently had been a deep empty well just waiting to be filled, and he with no idea that the person coming along to fill it would be Jamie.

"C'mon," he said, reaching over to give Jamie's knee a hearty pat. "We need to get cleaned up, and I need to check on the weather and consult with Maddy."

"Do you need help putting the stuff away?" Jamie asked as he got out of the truck, standing on the footrest on the passenger side, his hands on the warm roof of the truck.

"No, we'll leave it, keep it covered till tomorrow," Leland said. "No sense unpacking and then packing again the next day. Now, go take a shower."

With a wave Jamie was gone, leaving Leland to his confused whirl of thoughts. The best thing for those, as he well knew, was to keep busy. So he went to his office and checked on the weather report on his computer, called Maddy, signed a few delivery receipts that Clay'd left for him, any paperwork he could find. Then he headed off to his cabin, quiet and snug beneath the rustling trees as the wind blew over the top of them. It would not rain, but it was going to get cooler, which was fine.

In the shower, he washed up, not touching himself, not having little fantasies about Jamie, being strict. And felt better for it as he got dressed and headed down to the dining hall. There, he got his tray of food, Friday night ribs and cornbread, and headed over to the table where two of his leads, Quint and Brody, were already in a friendly discussion about who was the better dancer.

"Depends on the dance," Leland said as he slid his tray across the table and sat down.

"What do you mean?" asked Quint as his sharp, white teeth bit into a rib.

"Line dancing, it's you," Leland said to Quint. "Couple's dance and swing dance? It's Brody, all the way. I've danced with both of you and I know which one of you stepped on my toes."

Between them they laughed and protested that it had never been them, and Leland was just relaxing into his meal when Jamie showed up at the end of the table, his tray in hand, piled with food, as it usually was.

"Can I sit with you guys?" he asked. He held his tray against his belly as if he didn't dare lay it down without permission. Leland sat with everyone and anyone, changing it up each night, but usually he sat with his leads or with guests, never with staff. What a snob he'd become. Maybe it was time to change that.

"Sure," Leland said. "Join us."

Jamie sat down next to Quint, on the diagonal from Leland. He seemed quite pleased at how brave he'd been to come over, and Leland realized that while he'd segregated himself, there wasn't any need for it.

"This is Jamie," Leland said. "You fellows already know each other, right?"

"Hi," said Jamie, his voice only a little shy.

Quint and Brody waved hello, then there was a long bit of silence while everybody ate, and then Leland remembered.

"Jamie needs some riding lessons," he said. "One of you want to help me out?"

"Ranch hands need to know how to ride before applying," said Quint. He was a rule follower too, but there was a bit of a question in his voice, because if Jamie didn't already know how to ride, how had he gotten the job?

"It's a favor to Bill and to me," Leland said, enjoying a large mouthful of buttered cornbread while he let that sink in. "Maybe you can put him in with the intro lesson on Sunday, with the guests. See how he does."

"Can do," said Brody, as he saw which way the wind was blowing. Then he turned to look at Jamie on his left. "We keep it real simple around here. You'll get a gentle horse and start learning little by little."

"Sounds good," said Jamie, and his smile was bright.

His eyes sparkled as he looked across the table at Leland, as though he'd made a miracle happen. Well, the miracle would be Leland not giving into the expression of hope that seemed to cover Jamie all over. Hope for what? For them to hook up? For Leland to dig out his old paperback of cowboy poetry and read it to Jamie under the moonlight?

No. That's not what he was going to do. He was going to finish his dinner and then help Maddy gather some hands to pull hay bales close to the fire pit so Bill could tell ghost stories and lead the singalong, that's what he was going to do. Then he was going to bed, by *himself*, and hope that by morning he'd have more sense than he did right that minute.

"Will you come watch me ride, Leland?" asked Jamie, his voice sweet and hopeful.

Brody and Quint gave Leland the side eye, both of them, with expressions a little knowing and a little surprised. The three of them had worked an entire season together, and they knew Leland never went anywhere with any member of staff. Especially not with someone as new and as green as Jamie so obviously was. But nowhere on their faces did Leland see even the remotest amount of recrimination or anything like it. Not even when Quint looked at him and made that face, the one he did when he had opinions but wasn't going to express them.

"Sure," Leland said, and what else could he have said with Jamie looking at him like that, like Leland's attention was his present on Christmas morning.

Leland couldn't lead Jamie on like this. Couldn't lead himself on like this. It was foolish, and it was cruel. He needed to put a stop to it, and he would. First thing in the morning.

"Better get at it," he said as he grabbed his tray and stood up. He pushed in his chair with his leg, Jamie's eyes on him the whole while. "See you at the campfire."

And with a nod, he was off to find the coldest setting on his shower.

21

JAMIE

*W*hen Leland left like that, all sudden and distant, Jamie was sure it was something he had done. Like when they'd been painting, and he'd taken his shirt off to get cool, Leland's eyes had been on him the whole time. They had been working together, and it had been great, just the two of them in the middle of nowhere, with the sky all to themselves. Jamie had echoed Leland's movements, painted the way he painted, took breaks when he took breaks.

And then Leland took his shirt off, leaving Jamie hard in his jeans. Not just because Leland was good looking and half naked with a trail of dark gold hair leading from his bellybutton to the brass button on his jeans, no. And not just because he had shoulders that went on for miles and muscles that covered every inch of him and long arms corded with muscle and vein.

No, more, it was him getting half naked with Jamie like he trusted him enough to do that. He had been naked to the skin, nary a pearl-snap button in sight, unabashed, the tan on his shoulders darkened by freckles like he'd taken his shirt off at some point, at many points, and forgotten to put it back on.

When Leland had looked at Jamie, he'd blushed, sweet and rosy.

Not that he'd been shy, or ashamed, at least it didn't seem that way to Jamie. More, that he'd been flustered.

Jamie had seen Leland was hard when he adjusted himself in his jeans with a quick hand. But he never acted on it. Never drew attention to it, and he could have so easily. Or maybe he didn't know he could have?

Maybe Jamie needed to make sure that he did know. Or maybe he needed to mind his own business and get on with his work. This was the best job he'd ever had, and the best opportunity to take his life away from the direction it had been going, which was straight down the gutter.

Deep in his own thoughts as he finished his ribs and cornbread, he slowly realized the two men, Quint and Brody, had both cast glances his way and then looked at each other as if sharing a secret, coded message. Well, Jamie wasn't much good at puzzles, and he was out of place. What had he been thinking asking to sit at the cool kids' table when he was obviously the new guy, and certainly not one of Leland's team leads?

"Did you know him from before?" asked Quint. He had such an intense gaze that Jamie almost pulled back. "I mean, how did you get this job if you don't know how to ride? It's one of the first things a ranch hand needs to know how to do."

"Um—" Jamie waved his fork as he swallowed, flinging a bit of beans around, then scrubbed at the table. "I came looking for a job and Leland said no, but then I guess he met with Bill and—"

"I see," said Quint. "And Leland didn't object to Bill telling him what to do?"

"You know better than that," said Brody, slow and careful, like he'd been thinking it over this entire time. "Bill doesn't tell Leland what to do. Bill suggests what Leland should do, and then Leland does it. It's Bill's ranch, after all."

"I know, but—" said Quint. He leaned forward and looked at Brody sitting across from him. "We've got policies in place for a reason, so I don't see why Leland wouldn't—"

"It's because he's sweet on him, that's why." Brody took a long swig of his iced tea and smiled at Jamie. "He's sweet on you, for sure," he said. "I've never seen him so flustered."

"That doesn't mean anything," said Quint, and he frowned, as if only a moment ago he'd been sure of himself and now, being presented with new information, didn't quite know anymore. "Though his cheeks *were* red."

"And there you have it," said Brody. He made a motion with his hands, as if that settled the argument, then returned to eating as if the entire conversation had never happened. Or, if it had, was of no special significance.

Jamie squirmed in his seat, horrified and delighted at the same time. He liked it that they thought Leland was sweet on him, but he didn't like it because Leland had seemed rattled when he left the dining hall. The last thing Jamie wanted to do was cause Leland any trouble.

What he wanted, really wanted, was more of what they'd had that day and the day before, just that, the two of them together. Two men, working hard. Sharing echoed motions, sharing the pauses in between, sharing all of that beneath a blue bowl of sky.

Jamie hung his head and scrubbed at his mouth with a paper napkin and struggled to figure a way to make a hasty exit. Maybe he could find Leland and apologize, and explain what he wanted and what he didn't want.

"I have to go," Jamie said as he stood up, grabbing his tray.

"Be sure and head down to the fire pit to help them set up," said Quint. "This your first Friday? The campfire events are kind of fun."

"Yes," Jamie said, and then added, "I'll go down and help."

Jamie bussed his tray and raced out of the dining hall so fast, he was on fire. He looked all around for Leland, but didn't see him, and so headed out to the fire pit and helped arrange the hay bales and patterned blankets in rings that went around and out from the fire pit.

One of the guys from the kitchen, wearing a long white apron that flapped around his knees, came pushing a huge cart that turned out to have all the makings for s'mores and hot apple cider. And then, as the sun started going down, guests started to gather and take their seats.

The air grew chilly, so Jamie ran up to the staff quarters to get his long-sleeved shirt. When he came back to the fire pit, long purple shadows had laid themselves over everything, making it dark.

A low wind blew. It didn't seem like quite the night to sit out in the open, but guests were chatting amongst themselves, faces aglow in the firelight when they got up to grab a roasting stick and supplies for their s'mores. Two ranch hands had built a fire in the middle of a ring of pink and white stones, and against the backdrop of the darker night, it was really quite cozy.

Almost all the hay bales were occupied, and a few chairs, too, which someone had brought out. About half of the staff was there, filling in any blank spots so nobody had to sit by themselves. Jamie took a seat in the back row on a hay bale with a red woolen blanket, but he was close enough to feel the warmth of the fire, and felt the anticipation building, not quite sure what was to happen.

What happened was that Bill came out, dressed pretty much like the first time Jamie had seen him, except he was wearing a canvas jacket like many of the ranch hands were wearing. Jamie should have worn his, but it was too late now to go get it.

Bill got himself a cup of hot cider and drank it while chatting with Brody and the guy with the apron standing near the cart. Then, just as Bill walked to stand by the fire and take center stage, someone sat down beside Jamie and held out a cup of hot cider. It was Leland.

"Here," said Leland. He was wearing one of those canvas jackets too, sturdy and warm. "You should have worn your jacket."

"Yeah, I'm realizing that. Thanks for the cider," Jamie said, taking the cup of cider. He curled both hands around it to warm his fingers, and took a sip and sighed as the warmth moved through him, the sweetness. "I didn't mean to butt in on your dinner with those guys."

"Don't worry about it," said Leland.

Jamie looked up at Leland as he took a sip of his cider. He had showered and shaved, and maybe Jamie could smell cologne, or maybe it was some other guy wearing it. Leland probably had to get cleaned up for the evening's activities so he could make a good impression on guests. That was it.

"Here," said Leland. He slipped off his jacket and placed it around Jamie's shoulders, where the heavy weight of it surrounded him with Leland's warmth. "Put your arms in."

Jamie did as he was told, carefully holding his hot cider away so he wouldn't spill it on the jacket. Was Leland doing what he'd do for any of his ranch hands? Or did it mean something else?

"You missed the happy birthday song in the dining hall," said Leland, leaning close. "I looked for you to come up, but you were gone."

It was almost a question. Jamie shrugged and tried not to latch on to the idea that Leland had been looking for *him*. Had stood there and wondered where he was.

But Leland had been looking, and the image of it whirled in Jamie's head as Bill started talking, introducing the story he was going to tell, something about wishes made on Iron Mountain when there were shooting stars overhead. Then he told a spooky story about a herd of ghost horses that raced across parts of the ranch when the moon was full.

"Please don't tell the one about the missing guest," said Leland, under his breath.

"What?" Jamie asked, leaning close. "Missing guest?"

"We had a guest go missing at the end of last season," said Leland, leaning just as close, so close that Jamie could smell his cologne, all dusky and lovely. "It's what put Bill in the hospital, the anxiety of it all. Don't know how the ranch pulled back after that, but we did. Bill tells it like a ghost story, but who wants to hear about a guest wandering and disappearing forever?"

Bill started telling a story about Tommyknockers who roamed the mines just on the other side of Iron Mountain, and Leland breathed a huge sigh, like he was relieved. Then Bill told another story, and another after that, and then led the crowd in campfire songs, making them sing rounds until everybody couldn't sing anymore, they were laughing so hard. Then someone turned up the lights on the front of the dining hall, and Bill thanked everyone for coming, and said it was time for bed.

The guests dispersed back to their cabins or the main lodge, and Jamie helped tidy the hay bales and fold blankets. Leland stuck close the whole while, and as they worked in the chilly air, it began to rain a little. Jamie would have been shivering without Leland's sturdy jacket, and he still couldn't believe Leland had lent it to him.

"Don't forget next time," said Leland, as he came up to Jamie.

"What?" Jamie asked, blinking up at him, feeling like he wanted to yawn.

"This," Leland said. He tugged on the sleeve of the jacket. "At night at this altitude, it can get pretty chilly, even if it's not raining. You need to stay warm so you don't catch a chill." Leland seemed to stop himself from something he wanted to say, then tugged on the jacket once more. "Anyway, you can give it back to me in the morning. Right?"

"Sure," Jamie said, pleased and flustered at the same time, and found he loved looking up at Leland while he looked down at Jamie with his serious grey-blue eyes flashing in the dying firelight. What he didn't love was that Leland seemed unhappy, and he struggled to search for what he might have done to cause that. "Are you okay?"

"Let me walk you back," Leland said.

There were plenty of people to help finish whatever needed doing, so Jamie stuck close to Leland's side, trotting to keep up with his long legs. They went back around the cabins to the path in front of the dining hall, the evening air splotched light and dark beneath the shadows of the spreading pine trees.

Leland's hand brushed against Jamie's hand as they stopped on the edge of the glade of trees on the way to the staff quarters. With a slow grace, Leland seemed to be drawing Jamie deeper into those shadows, moving on the path away from the staff quarters, as if he meant to take Jamie to his own cabin. Then he stopped and, quite gently and slowly, clasped Jamie's face in his warm hands, and Jamie found himself curling his fingers around those strong wrists to keep Leland right where he was.

"I'm not quite sure what I'm doing," Leland said, his voice barely above a whisper.

Jamie could feel Leland's warm breath on his cheek. Feel the tremor in those fingers. See the sheen in those grey-blue eyes.

"Neither do I," said Jamie. "I mean, I don't know what I'm doing, either, not that I am not sure what you're doing." Because he was sure, quite sure, that Leland was about to kiss him. "Yes," he said, practically breathing the word, wanting Leland to know he could kiss him. Leland would be so careful with him because he was careful with everyone all the time. "You can—"

When Leland came closer, Jamie closed his eyes and absorbed that kiss like he had never done with anything else. Such a light kiss, not hesitant or shy, but careful and soft, Leland's lips like silk, his hands warm on Jamie's face. Jamie sighed, long and deep, as though he'd come to a place with fresh water after a long trek across a barren land.

When Leland pulled away, Jamie opened his eyes, looking for another kiss. Leland was smiling at him, though his eyes were troubled and dark.

"I'm your boss," Leland said, low, urgent. "I shouldn't be doing this."

"Yes, you should," Jamie said, holding on to his hands as hard as he could. "You can do anything you want. Anything."

"That's not how this works." Leland shook his head and drew away, his hands falling from Jamie's face.

Jamie felt cold, standing there in a circle of darkness as Leland moved out of the shadows and into a bit of light from the light from the porch of the staff quarters.

"I'm sorry," Leland said. "I enjoyed being with you so much, but this can't happen. It can't. I'm sorry."

As Leland strode resolutely off, it was all Jamie could do not to follow him, race after him. Beg him. Beg him like he'd never begged for anything before. But Leland seemed so unhappy about it, this thing growing between them, that Jamie stayed right where he was and watched him go, his long-legged stride taking him into the shadows.

Jamie's heart ached in ways that didn't make any sense. He'd come to Farthing because he'd been at the end of a very long, not very

175

sturdy rope, and had only hoped to find a way to make some cash so he could go back to school and start over.

He'd never expected to have feelings for a man, an older man—his boss—who, if they'd met on the street, never would have even said hello to him. And now, here he was, his lips still tingling from that gentle kiss, his skin shimmering in reaction, looking at a dark hollow where Leland had once stood.

22

LELAND

*A*ctivity on the ranch wound down on Saturdays, on account of guests were packing up, checking out, and finding their way from the ranch to the airport, or driving home. It was saved from being a mass exodus all at once because Maddy staggered the checkout times, which made everything smooth. That didn't mean Leland wasn't busy, because he was, maybe even more so as he took care of one issue after another, mostly tasks someone else could have handled, like helping guests carry suitcases from the cabins to the parking lot. And all because he didn't want to think or feel or anything.

It was his own foolishness that had gotten him to a state of distraction where he'd barely slept the night before, had raced through his shower, and forgone breakfast because he hadn't slept and then slept in late. It wasn't like him, not at all. Neither was the fact that when he'd walked Jamie to the staff quarters, he'd kissed him in the shadow of the trees, kissed him like he had a right to, when it wasn't appropriate in the least bit.

It was unexpected, though, the stamp Jamie's presence had put on his heart. A drifter, right? Someone who floated in on the wind, without direction. Not the sort Leland usually wanted to get to know.

But Jamie's story about his parents, his struggles, how he found himself without anywhere to tie up to in a storm of grief and loss that had overwhelmed him. He had such a watchful way as he studied people he talked to, studied Leland, as though, before the ranch, he'd never known what it was like to live the kind of life that came natural to Leland, natural as breathing.

Jamie had not been raised in a barn, but bad things had happened by the time he'd shown up at the gates to the ranch. His life had brought him down low and cut him adrift, and only now, in this place Leland loved so much, Jamie was starting to put down.

Impossible. It was impossible. All of it. After the season ended, Jamie would probably take his pay and make his way to the next stop in his life. But this was a lie Leland told himself, even as he signed forms, and answered questions, and met with Maddy at the ranch office to discuss the state of Cabin #4, which had been occupied by two older ladies who'd had quite the party the night before.

"Should we have alcohol on the ranch at all?" Leland asked her.

"Yes," she said, nodding. "Yes, we should, but we should monitor it so it doesn't get out of hand like that."

"I agree," Leland said, only able to half-concentrate on what he was saying. "I'll talk with Bill about it."

When she looked at him in that way she had, he amended the statement to, "The *three* of us should talk about it together, first opportunity we have."

These were such mundane details, regular end-of-the-week discussions and follow-up discussions as the guests left and staff started cleaning and setting up for the next round of guests, who would arrive on Sunday afternoon.

All of this kept him busy, but it would not help him repair the damage he'd done by kissing Jamie. Leland would need to find him, hopefully before guests arrived on Sunday afternoon, and apologize. And then explain how it could never happen again, which sounded too mean, even in his own head, as the kiss had been something *he'd* instigated.

Had he made up all these feelings? He felt dizzy with the idea of

Jamie, his heart soothed and made joyful all at the same time at the idea of not just working with him side by side, but *being* with him. Sharing the evenings together. Riding out along the ridge, checking out the tall prairie grasses growing on the low hills below Iron Mountain. Coming back to sit on the front porch of Leland's small cabin in those Adirondack chairs while the night grew dark and the stars came out.

He didn't often share his own romantic nature. Besides, his responsibilities on the ranch left little room for odd fancies and heartfelt dreams such as seemed to come at him now, left and right, hard as he tried to battle them off. First chance he got, he was going to tell Jamie how it had to be.

As the guests cleared out, one by one, leaving the ranch empty and still, at least for an hour or two, Leland indulged himself by going to the barn so he could go for an early ride. Most of the horses had been taken up to the fields for the evening, but one or two were in the stables, waiting for him to ride out. It wasn't quite evening, but he needed a good long ride, a distraction from everything in his head.

Clay was there, looking sweet and dusty, and ready for a cold beer at the Rusty Nail in Farthing. Leland knew he did some hookups, but Clay was always politely vague about what he got up to. If Leland had been drawn to anybody at the ranch, someone he cared enough about to break the rules for, it would have been Clay. Leland trusted him. Liked him. He had a square look about him, strong shouldered, stocky thighs. Dependable. Earnest. Cute. Anything a man could want. But he was not Jamie.

"Hey, Leland," he said as he saw Leland come into the barn. "Do you want me to saddle up Dusty or Mika?"

Mika was a cute orange roan, much loved by young ladies who came to the ranch for their Instagram followers. This didn't happen often, though it seemed the mare knew she was pretty and tended to prance about. Dusty, on the other hand, a dependable chestnut with a buzzed mane, was not lovely to look at, not compared to Mika, at any rate. But he was calm and strong and could go a long way at a steady pace, which was what Leland needed just then.

"Give me Dusty," he said to Clay. "And put on an old saddle; not one of the new ones."

Clay saddled Dusty up while Leland checked for messages in his office. Then he quickly called Maddy to make sure everything was running smoothly, and to inquire whether she needed his help with anything. She did not.

Tucking his cell phone in the top drawer of his desk, he went out to the main part of the barn where Clay was waiting with Dusty, all saddled up and ready to go. Just as he was mounting Dusty, the horse looked at Leland with his dark brown eyes as if to say thank you for choosing him over the flashy Mika.

"You bet, boy," Leland said, patting him on his sturdy brown neck. "We're going for a ride. Thank you, Clay."

"No problem, Leland," said Clay with a touch to his hat. "I'm about to head out to Farthing; if you wanted to go, we could wait for you, so you could join us."

"No, thank you," Leland said as he led Dusty out of the barn to stick his booted foot in the stirrup. "I'm good here, but you go on. Not too late, though, okay?"

"Sure thing, Leland," said Clay.

Leland rode away, walking Dusty carefully along the dirt road past the corral and up to the gate where the open fields were, and thought about the invitation that came from Clay on some Saturday nights. Maybe he was just being polite, inviting the boss. But maybe he meant it, and Leland had been blind all this time? Even if that were true, however easy on the eyes Clay was, Leland couldn't have done anything about it. Besides, it was only Jamie, his green-eyed drifter, who made him want to break all of his own rules, and all the ranch rules, as well.

Guiding Dusty up the bit of path that was steep as it led away from the ranch was a good distraction. As was the swath of land, golden in the afternoon sunlight, that spread out before them when they reached the top of the ridge. From that spot, Leland could have ridden for hours and not seen another human being, only members of the ranch's herd of horses, gathering at Horse Creek, or assembling around the blocks of salt he and Jamie had put out for them.

As Leland rode past the horses, most of the herd were in the tall grasses that twitched at their bellies as they ate with their heads down, tails flicking at flies, munching in a way that told Leland they somehow knew it was their night off. Except for Dusty, who willingly went where Leland directed him. Sometimes they cantered, and sometimes they trotted, and all the while, Leland's heart ached.

Eventually, as the shadows grew long, he realized he was out a long way. Nobody knew where he was, so, somewhat reluctant, he rode back to the main part of the ranch. Once there, with some care to attention, he took his usual turn around the ranch, checking out the creek that went up to the pond, looking at the fences and the state of the grass. Making sure the erosion along the river wasn't getting out of hand. Scanning the horizon for prairie fires, which weren't too common that time of year but which could happen. Everything was in order. Everything but him.

He rode all the way to the front gate, taking the last half mile along the dirt road at a fast gallop. Dusty obliged him, his legs thundering beneath Leland, his neck stretched out as though his rider had set him free after some long captivity and he was making the most of it.

Making a mental note that the gelding would be excellent for a strong, kind rider, Leland pulled Dusty up at the gate and wheeled him around. They trotted back through the trees along the main road as he let Dusty breathe it out, and together they enjoyed the patterns of shade and shadow, shade and light, as they made their way back to the parking lot.

And there, in front of the ranch store, holding a Carhartt jacket to his chest, was Jamie. Maddy was mounting the steps to her office, clipboard in hand, which left Jamie all on his own, with no one to see him there.

"Hey," Leland said as he trotted Dusty up to the steps of the office. "Do you need a lift?"

This was wrong, all wrong. He'd already had a talk with himself about this, already decided how it was to be, and there he was, leaning down to smile at Jamie, a smile which he could not stop as he looked at Jamie.

"You forgot your jacket," Jamie said, holding out the jacket. "It's a little wrinkled, 'cause I kind of fell asleep on it."

"It'll be fine, as Carhartt's are quite sturdy," Leland said, pleased, in spite of himself, that the jacket had been Jamie's pillow. But even as he echoed Jamie's smile, and ripples of pleasure wove through his heart, he knew he was making the same mistake. It was happening all over again, but he was unable to stop himself. "Here," he said, holding out his hand to Jamie as he removed his booted foot from the stirrup. "Give me the jacket and come on up, I'll save you a few steps."

Jamie obliged by flipping the jacket over the saddle horn before swinging up behind Leland. He held onto Leland's hand longer than strictly necessary, and Leland, in his own way, held on until Jamie was behind him on the saddle blanket.

A familiar weight settled against his back. When Jamie wrapped his arms around Leland's waist and tucked himself close, some part of Jamie snagged itself inside of him, inside his soul. Leland ducked his head and despaired of his own weakness.

Jamie was holding onto him like he'd rescued him from a drowning raft, damp and dripping and grateful. Leland didn't want Jamie to be grateful, he wanted him to feel—there were so many things he wanted from him and especially *for* him. He wanted Jamie's life to be good and full of purpose and joy, everything he deserved. Surely being with Leland would not take him in that direction. Would it?

Leland walked Dusty up the road to the barn, slowly to make the moment last as long as it could, them on horseback together. They passed the fire pit and went along the road to where they could look down the slope at the guest cabins and bunkhouses, where staff were just about finished prepping the cabins for a fresh wave of guests expected the next day.

Though Leland felt quite somber, he had to laugh when a few of the staff waved at them, and Jamie waved back, almost quivering with excitement, as though they were some kind of one-horse parade.

Leland might have told Jamie that his staff wasn't used to seeing him ride double like that, that they weren't used to seeing him ride with anyone at all. Not that it should be happening. It needed to stop, even this simple activity. He just needed to find the right way to make it stick.

They rode into the shade of the barn. There, he helped Jamie dismount, then got off Dusty and gave him some good hearty pets along his neck.

"This horse needs a strong rider, but a kind one," Leland said to Jamie. He wanted Jamie to linger while he figured out what he needed to say about how that kiss in the moonlight could never happen again. But what he said was, "Help me groom him?"

"Sure," said Jamie. He grabbed the jacket from the saddle horn and hung it in Leland's office as Leland tied Dusty up to a grooming post.

"Grab those brushes and that hoof pick while I undo his tack."

When Jamie came up, brushes and pick in hand, Leland patted Dusty's side. Good feelings washed over him, being with Jamie, working together like they were. But they crashed right into his sense of the forbidden, of the off-limits, of how what he was doing was wrong. The wrong of it was loud in his head, but the sweetness of it was equally loud until he felt just about deaf as he turned to Jamie.

"When I groom a horse, I can check him over, make sure he's sound," Leland said. "Which is one of the reasons I ride a different horse each day."

"I was wondering," said Jamie. He placed the tools on the thin wooden shelf along the pole where Dusty was tied. Then he watched Leland as he unsaddled Dusty and laid the saddle on the sawhorse to be wiped down before being put away.

"I could clean that," he said, eyeing the saddle.

"We'll get to that," Leland said. He picked up the brush and handed Jamie the chamois cloth. "Help me with this first."

It wasn't that Leland didn't think Jamie was responsible enough to clean a saddle on his own, because he was. His eagerness to do anything assigned to him showed he was smart, caught on quick. It was that he wanted Jamie with him, near him. Not just to have Jamie hone his grooming skills, but to have Jamie working at his side.

Together they wiped Dusty down and then brushed him all over, both of them going at it on either side of the horse, and laughed together when Dusty sighed as he sank into the grooming that he'd finally figured out was going to go on for a while. They combed his stubby mane and tail and oiled his hooves, and ran the chamois cloth over his coat one more time to add some shine. By the time they put him in the box stall with his nightly feed, there was a new expression in his eyes, and a look of contentment about him.

When Leland turned to take care of the saddle, Jamie turned at the same time, and he was inside of Leland's arms, which he tightened to make sure Jamie wouldn't fall. But then he didn't let go. And Jamie didn't move away.

They were so close, both smelling like horse hair, sweating a little, and when Jamie rose on his toes to kiss Leland, he let him. Kissed him back as feelings of sweetness raced through him, of wanting more, all while he held him close, and kissed that mouth and dreamed of how it might be.

Then someone was at the barn door, and Leland gently, oh, so gently, pushed Jamie away.

"I shouldn't have done that," he said to Jamie. "I don't know what's wrong with me. I'm sorry."

"I liked it," Jamie said, and his eyes were so wide and so green that Leland could have fallen into them. "I liked it."

"Go get some dinner," Leland said, a little more roughly than he wanted to. "I've got some work to finish in my office."

"Okay," he said, though Leland could tell he was confused again.

This was going so badly, and it was all his fault.

23

JAMIE

*J*amie went to dinner, but he didn't see Leland the whole time, and went to bed with dreams of Leland's touch swirling around in his head. Sunday was a struggle because Leland was busy taking care of paperwork and other tasks he had to do by himself. That was fine, Jamie could understand that, but when guests started arriving and Leland got even more busy, Jamie felt like he was on the outside looking in, kind of the way he did when he'd first come up to the ranch to ask for a job.

Sure, Clay and Brody asked for his help carrying luggage for guests, and sure, Stella sent him racing to get extra towels for Cabin #1. Everyone thanked him profusely afterwards, but there wasn't one nod or smile, let alone a glance, from Leland. Jamie told himself he wasn't hanging around the parking lot where Leland was sure to be, or shifting his place in line at the Sunday night buffet for a chance to stand near Leland, but that's what he did. All to no result. Leland stolidly maintained his distance.

Maybe Leland had meant it when he'd said what he'd said about them kissing and how it was wrong. Maybe it was. Leland was his boss, after all, and older. But if anyone could kiss Jamie like that and make him feel like that from one small kiss—

Jamie shivered all over at the thought of it.

Monday was more of the same. Jamie worked as hard as he could, both at chores Clay assigned him, and at trying to be where he thought Leland would be. Only either Leland wasn't ever there, or he was too busy to notice Jamie. Who knew he shouldn't be panting after Leland this way, like he was begging for crumbs at a banquet. But what did he know? He'd never dated anyone before, never experienced his heart pounding in his chest at the mere glimpse of the brim of Leland's hat as he marched into the barn.

Finally, on Tuesday, he was told he could join the guests in the corral for his first riding lesson. The afternoon turned out warm enough for him to roll up his shirtsleeves, and he strutted to the corral in the almost-new cowboy boots Clay had found for him in the lost-and-left-behind bin. Tipping his straw cowboy hat to the guests, he went over to the last unclaimed horse, which was, to his delight, Dusty.

Brody was in charge of the lesson and didn't seem to give Jamie any special notice, which was fine with him. He wanted to blend in while he learned about the parts of a horse, and the parts of a saddle, how to mount, how to dismount, how to guide the horse. All the basics.

"These lessons are just supposed to orient you to riding so you can enjoy your stay with us at Farthingdale Ranch," said Brody to the guests as he walked along the row of horses and guests, nodding as he examined the way each one was holding their horse's reins. "Now, mount up, like we learned yesterday, and we'll teach you more about how to trot and canter. Let's take a couple of turns around the ring."

Jamie pretended Leland was watching. He pretended Leland was standing outside the corral, leaning against the top fence rail, in that way he did, propped on his elbows, casual as anything, but really, quite focused on what he was looking at. Which, in this instance, would be Jamie as he made Dusty walk and then trot and then canter. The gelding's trot was bumpy, but the canter was smooth and the world spun past him in a breezy, almost uncontrolled way, like he was going to fly off the horse at any moment.

"Pull up a little bit, Jamie," said Brody. "And you, Dorothy, don't crowd the horse in front of you, okay? This isn't a race. Very good, everyone, very good."

They rode and walked and trotted, kicking up a bit of dust as they went. All the while, Brody talked about horses and horsemanship and how to be decent to the animals and to each other when they went out on trail rides.

Jamie didn't figure he'd be allowed to go with guests on something like that, as it would take him away from work for too long. But he listened just the same, wanting to absorb everything Brody knew so he could show what he'd learned to Leland later. So he'd be proud of him, and maybe they'd kiss. Maybe there'd be something more.

When the lesson ended, the guests dismounted and Brody told them to tie their horses up, and that someone would groom them— that is, unless folks wanted to learn how? Some of them did, and stayed behind, while others headed off in pursuit of other fun.

"Help me with this, Jamie," said Brody as he arranged the willing guests with their horses. "Go fetch the box of brushes and hoof picks. It's such a nice day, we can do this out here. Unless," he added, looking at Jamie carefully, "maybe you could ask Leland for the afternoon off, if you'd rather not work."

Not quite sure what he meant, Jamie shook his head.

"Oh no," he said. "I'm doing my job. Leland would want me to do my job and I want to do it."

The look he got as a response told him a lot, that Brody was pleased he didn't trade in on the fact that Leland and Jamie had been hanging out together. Jamie might have imagined it, but there was respect in Brody's eyes.

"I'll get those brushes and stuff," Jamie said, running off to fetch them.

They groomed horses in the corral, and then the guests had the pleasure of leading the horses up to the far field and letting them go for the afternoon. It was fun to watch the horses running across the field like four-legged kids let out to recess. Then Jamie had to go back to the corral and rake and shovel and haul manure, but that was fine.

187

He was getting used to the work and wanted to be at his best whenever Leland might walk past. Maybe he'd stop and say hello. Maybe Leland would stop and say something nice about the good job Jamie was doing. Maybe he'd look at Jamie with those beautiful grey-blue eyes, and Jamie'd see what he wanted to see. That Leland liked Jamie. Wanted to be with him. That those kisses they'd shared might lead to something else.

Jamie's legs, especially his inner thighs, ached all afternoon, but he kept moving so they wouldn't stiffen up. He knew he'd get used to riding, just like he'd got used to using all of his muscles.

All day, he missed Leland. At one point, in the long shadows of the afternoon, he saw Leland going away from the barn. But Leland never came close, never called Jamie to sit with him on the porch of the dining hall to take a break and have a cold, local-brewed root beer. And it looked like he would not offer Jamie another ride behind him when he went out in the evening to survey the ranch. It was as if Jamie had vanished from view.

What could Jamie do about it? He wanted to show Leland that he was a hard worker, wanted Leland's attention, but he didn't want to be one of those guys who went chasing after another guy, either. That wasn't him at all.

Maybe he could pretend he was indifferent and stop looking for Leland everywhere. Or he could try something new. Maybe he could get brave and tell Leland how he felt. Walk right up to him and tell him.

Maybe he was a little obsessed, but being with Leland had been like staring at a gate that had suddenly opened right in front of him, and through that gate was a whole different world. A world full of good people and hard work, a world full of guests having fun, clean sheets, and a room all to himself. And sweet kisses, while Leland held his face in his hands.

If Leland kissed like that, in a way that left traces of shivers across his mouth, what would it feel like when they were naked and in bed together? Would Jamie be able to linger and kiss those freckles on his shoulders? Would Leland let him kiss him everywhere? Anywhere?

He wanted to find out. He was going to do his best to find out. So that evening, when staff was setting up the lights for the dance after dinner, he rushed through the rest of his work and ate real fast, and went to his room for the longest, hottest shower, ever. He shaved carefully and brushed his teeth twice, just in case there was going to be more kissing.

In the damp fog of the bathroom, he did the best he could with his hair. When he swiped at the mirror so he could see, his hair was going everywhere like dark weeds around his face. Unless he took the scissors to it, but he didn't have scissors, so he would have to go to the dance looking like he was.

He put on his newest, darkest blue jeans, along with the gently used cowboy boots, which, with the stacked heel, made his legs look long and powerful. At least that's what he told himself as he looked down at his legs. As for the shirt, he pulled out the one he'd been saving, maybe even for this moment. It was a fancy dress shirt of some pale blue cloth and those pearl-snap buttons on shirts Leland always wore.

Piling all of this on, feeling a little bit foolish now wearing both a cowboy hat and cowboy boots *and* a shirt with pearl snap buttons, he made his way to the front of the dining hall. There, the twinkling lights were strung, and the band was warming up on the porch. Someone had pulled out benches from the dining hall and placed them around the dance area.

He was very tempted to go grab a bottle of root beer and plant himself on the edge of the porch again, or maybe on one of the benches, but he didn't. He was breathing too fast, too hard, all worked up, and wanted to be standing and ready for when Leland showed up.

If there was going to be line dances, he was going to dance next to Leland. If there was going to be a couples dance, he was going to ask Leland to pair with him. And never mind the reality of it, that he didn't know how to dance either dance.

But Leland would teach him. Leland would patiently show him. And then he would smile at Jamie and then they'd walk into the shadows, holding hands.

Blowing out a hard breath of jumbled feelings, Jamie grabbed a bottle of root beer anyway. Drinking it, he stood near the dance floor, watching the dancers line up as the band started playing, and waited, his heart pounding, for Leland to show up. And when he did, he was so handsome, Jamie's heart sang to look at him.

Leland was wearing his red shirt with the pearl-snap buttons, the one Jamie liked especially well. Leland had on new blue jeans, and, yes, they made his legs look long, especially because he was wearing those cowboy boots of his that made his butt curve out.

While Leland was standing talking to Brody at the edge of the porch, his took off his hat and ran his hands through his blond hair, making it stand up. Then he saw Jamie, and those grey-blue eyes of his locked on him like a battleship locking on a target.

Jamie was the target. *Him.* Which meant that Leland wasn't ignoring him any more.

His heart racing a million miles an hour, Jamie walked over to Leland, feeling like he was slicing through the air as he went. He had his intentions. He'd make his feelings known to Leland, who wouldn't turn him down for a dance in front of everyone, would he?

"Hey, Brody, hey, Leland," Jamie said as he went up to them. He took his cowboy hat off, too, and realized he was holding it the way Leland was, with one hand cupped around the crown, fingers holding the empty bottle of root beer. His other hand was tucked inside the crown of the hat, lifting it, twisting it, letting it fall, over and over.

"I see you've had some root beer," said Leland, and when he smiled at Jamie, it was as though he thought Jamie should have all the root beer he ever wanted and then some. He wanted good things for Jamie, always.

"Yeah, can I get you one?" Jamie asked, feeling a little foolish for offering, as though they were on a date. They weren't, but he wanted them to be.

"Let's get one together."

With a nod that felt more shaky than it probably was, Jamie led the way along the porch to the end of it where the barrel was, full of ice and cans of soda and bottles of root beer. Jamie pulled out two bottles, cold and dripping, and handed one to Leland. Silently, together, they screwed off the lids.

When Leland held his bottle out to him, Jamie was confused, but only for a second. They clinked bottles and drank down that good, local-made, slightly spicy root beer. As Jamie swallowed, he smiled at Leland, then wiped his mouth with the backs of his fingers.

"Would you dance with me?" Leland asked, dipping his chin down so only Jamie could hear the words.

He was so close Jamie could smell the dusky cologne on his neck, see the sparkle of beardgrowth where he'd missed a spot shaving. See the turn of muscle that went down below his open shirt collar. And all at once, Jamie experienced a sense of wanting, a rush so powerful, he felt willing to throw himself at Leland, then and there. But he'd asked him to dance and was waiting for an answer. And there was nothing Jamie wanted better than to dance with him.

"I was going to ask you," Jamie said, confessing this, the words tumbling out of him like escaped mice. "I was, only I don't know how."

"I'll teach you," Leland said, then took a long draw on his bottle of root beer.

Jamie felt as though he was falling forward, falling with a delicious, stomach-flipping motion. Leland's voice was full of promises, and his eyes, when he looked at Jamie, were full of affection and joy, like he liked Jamie just like he was.

They stood there, side by side, and finished their root beers, recycling the bottles before Leland reached out and laced his fingers with Jamie's and led him to the dance area. Nobody was looking at them with any particular notice, not like they disapproved or anything, but other dancers made way for Leland, on account of he was so tall, his presence so commanding that there wasn't anything else for them to do but get out of his way. And out of Jamie's way, since they were so close, and he felt pretty special as he took his place beside Leland. As they readied themselves, the lady who called the dances, all decked out in her cowgirl outfit, announced it was to be a line dance.

Though Jamie felt a sting of disappointment that he wouldn't be in

Leland's arms, maybe it was better to start off this way. Like a courtship, a sweet, fun dance, with him and Leland, side by side.

The music started, and the cowgirl called out the dance steps. Jamie fumbled and tripped his way through that dance, doing his very best not to run over anyone or step on Leland's booted toes. Leland laughed when Jamie would bump against him, and then he'd set Jamie to rights. He helped Jamie with the steps, always smiling as he gestured and demonstrated, his grey-blue eyes always looking Jamie's way, full of light and happiness and pleasure.

Jamie remembered Leland talking about how much he liked this part of his job, how he enjoyed taking part in the dances, both to show the guests a good time and to keep an eye on how it was going. And this time, he was spending that time with Jamie, and not anyone else. Jamie was so proud and pleased, his heart was about to bust out of his chest at every moment.

Just when he was getting the hang of it, the dance ended, and the cowgirl turned to the band to talk to them, holding her microphone to the side. Somebody gestured to Leland, and he tapped his fingers to his hat and nodded at Jamie and went up to take care of whatever it was.

Meanwhile, Jamie held his place on the dance floor as everyone dispersed for a moment. He felt a little foolish, but there was no way he was going to give up their spot. He wanted Leland to come back to him and he wanted to dance with Leland some more and he wanted to see where this might take them.

Never in his life had he been full of this kind of expectation, bubbling up inside of him like bubbles in a bottle of root beer, each bubble small, a little hesitant, but growing and pushing their way upwards until he could hardly stand to wait until the cowgirl stepped forward and put her microphone to her mouth.

"We're going to have a couples dance," she said as the band started up, a tune that rolled and moved through the air as though inviting everyone to get up and join in. "Grab a partner, now, don't be shy."

Jamie held his breath in fear that someone would ask him to dance because it was obvious, at that point, that he wasn't allowed to say no.

He worked for the ranch, so if a guest needed a partner, he was going to have to say yes.

He searched the crowd for Leland's tall form, and saw him, just at that minute, nodding to Brody, and handing him his hat. Then Leland hurried over to Jamie, and when he reached him, he took Jamie's hat off and placed it on a bench, and then, with a little bow, invited Jamie to dance with him.

There were no words, not in his mouth or in his head or anywhere, as he moved into Leland's arms and he held him like Jamie was the lady and Leland was the gent. But there wasn't anything to that. Someone had to lead, after all, and Leland was a much better dancer than Jamie was.

Maybe Leland would teach him how and he could lead some day. In the meantime, Jamie soaked in Leland's touch, soaked in the warmth of his skin as they held hands in the curve of his shoulder where Jamie's other hand rested. On the breadth and strength of his hand on Jamie's waist that guided him with little tugs and presses so he would know which way to go, so he would know how to follow him as the band warmed up, and the cowgirl sang the lyrics to something sweet and soft, the words going around and around with the music.

The small lights strung overhead twinkled as it got darker, and seemed to spread a kind of fairy tale of possibility, like they wanted Jamie to believe that it was possible, him and Leland. That there could be more of this, of dancing, and having root beer together, taking rides, and working side by side.

Life, his old life, had never been like this, nothing like it. Only here he was, dancing with a handsome man, their bodies in sync as Leland's grey-blue eyes smiled down, a gleam of sweat on his temple, pleasure radiating all the way through him and into Jamie. There had never been a night like this, where pleasure and joy mixed as they danced, around and around, their bodies close, hearts beating in time.

LELAND

*W*hen the ice maker went out, Leland sent two hands to the Rail Car restaurant in Farthing to get more. Then he turned back to the dance floor, where Jamie was waiting, all by himself. Standing there on the empty dance floor like he was guarding their spot, waiting to dance, and only with him.

His hair was sprawled over one eye and he had small sweat stains under each arm, but he was so adorable, so sweet and patient, waiting for Leland to do what his job required him to do. Leland wanted to gather Jamie in his arms, then and there, and kiss every spot of him he could reach. The guests would be scandalized, and his fellow employees would have fodder to fuel their gossip for weeks to come.

He was always so careful and reserved with his thoughts, his feelings, that he could hardly believe that his life had taken this direction. But it had, and he hurried over to Jamie as the dance floor filled, and took the liberty of removing Jamie's hat for him and placing it aside. Of bowing. Of asking him to dance, all without words.

Of course, Jamie stepped into his arms, head held high, green eyes sparkling, his whole being filled with life and light and joy. And he fit in Leland's arms as though he'd been designed for just this moment, his hand in Leland's hand, Leland's other hand in the small of his back, his skin alive and warm beneath the thin layer of blue cotton chambray that he wore.

Up close like that, Jamie smelled nice, the line of his cheek smooth and freshly shaved. He'd gone to some trouble for this dance, and Leland's heart banged at the thought of it, at how high Jamie's hopes were, and how Leland might be leading him on. But he wanted this dance with Jamie, and as the music started, and couples started moving, Leland guided him through the steps.

Jamie had no idea how to dance this dance; he was trusting Leland to guide him, trusting him to make sure of him in the moments, the swirl of couples all around them. Trusting Leland to make sure he didn't break his heart. He didn't want to break it; he wanted to take it and keep it close, and he wanted—

Sometimes, he just didn't know what he wanted. But at that moment, he wanted this closeness, Jamie and him, and he wanted to stay close, just like they were, almost hip to hip, Jamie in his arms, his gaze on Jamie, and only on him, as they danced and swirled and shared a secret conversation between them, known only to their hearts. A secret code Leland urgently wanted to untangle so he could find a way this might work, that what they shared would continue beyond the dance floor, into the night, and onto the next day. And the day after that. And all the days that followed.

Was it a dream? Was it just his foolishness? He wanted to find out. Wanted to know Jamie, to see him sprawled on clean white sheets, his pie-bald tan on display so Leland could kiss those ribs, kiss the bruises away, soothe the inside of his thighs, which must ache from his riding lesson. Wanted to curve his arms around Jamie and whisper sweet things to him as he gently pushed back that dark tumble of hair from Jamie's forehead. Leland wanted to cover Jamie's body with his own and make known the secrets of their bodies in passion and in sweetness.

Would Jamie want all those things, like he wanted them? And what would he want in return? Leland wanted to find out.

Levi gestured to Leland when the ice arrived, and for the first time in his life he wanted to snap out a command: *Just take care of it.* The last thing Leland wanted was to be pulled out of Jamie's arms. But this was the way they worked, as a team, so when the dance ended, Leland bowed to Jamie and went over to Levi to give the direction that yes, half the ice should be put in the cooler, half of it in the barrel, and that yes, someone should call the repairman in the morning, the earlier the better.

When he was finished with that, he went back to the dance area and looked for Jamie. He was waiting for him, on the edge of the dance area, this time, with his hands in his pockets, kicking at bits of gravel with the toes of his cowboy boots. Head down, concentrating on this, ignoring all that was around him, like he was making a wish with each and every kick, little bits of dust rising in the cool, night air.

"Jamie," Leland said, striding right up to him.

Jamie lifted his head, and Leland gave in to the impulse to push his dark hair back from his forehead. And gave in to another impulse, the one he never thought he would.

"Would you like to leave the dance, or stay?" he asked, his breath a little short and sharp in his throat.

"Leave?" Jamie asked, his green eyes reflecting the fairy lights strung around the dance area.

"And go back to my cabin—with me." Leland clarified that, just in case there was any question, though he felt a bit foolish, foolishly falling, his heart on fire for this young man who had jumped into his life with both feet.

Jamie's eyes went dark, then, a flare of something smoky and deep, as though Leland had stirred something inside of him with those words. He reached out his hand and gripped Leland's, tugging, holding on tight in a way that almost broke Leland's heart. It was as though he'd thrown Jamie a lifeline, and Jamie was grabbing on so hard, with so much wanting, so much openness—

"Yes," said Jamie, all affectation of casual indifference gone to be replaced by that open expression, eyes wide, his cheeks flushed.

"All right, then," Leland said. He slipped his hand from Jamie's and placed it on the small of his back, feeling the heat there, like he'd placed a brand on him, a mark of possession, even if only for one night.

What was he thinking, doing this? But his heart was racing, and he was hard in his jeans, his cock standing up against his belly like an iron bar. His heart ached with wanting Jamie, his soul singing as they walked away from the dance area and along the shadowed path that led to his cabin.

Jamie came willingly, trotting at his side to keep up, his breath coming in short bursts. Leland would treat him right, and he would honor what they were about to share, though some part of his mind was standing up, shouting, demanding he pay attention to it. But as they stepped onto the porch of his little cabin, and the porch light flicked on, he opened the door and ignored that voice. Ignored it completely as he drew Jamie into the half-darkness of the cabin.

He left the porch light on and turned on the light in the main room, pulling Jamie behind him as he led the way to the bedroom. Shadows and light played in through the doorway in long beams. There was a queen bed with a brass headboard and a colorful patched quilt, all supplied by the ranch, and as he pulled back the bedclothes to reveal the white sheets, Jamie made a little sound.

"What is it?" Leland asked, turning to him. He wanted to be sure of Jamie, to make sure he knew Leland would be gentle, that he wouldn't hurt him, but in the midst of his mind rabbiting on, Jamie smiled a sweet, small smile.

"I love your bed," he said.

This almost made Leland stop, that reaction from him. It was a bed, that's all it was, a bed. Yet Jamie was reacting as though Leland had pulled out a pile of gold and given it to him. What must his life have been like for him to appreciate something as simple as a bed? It wasn't even his. It was a borrowed bed. Borrowed bedclothes. Yet to Jamie—

Leland went to him and pulled him close and kissed him, like he'd been wanting to. His whole body sighed as he gave into the kiss, their mouths meeting, touching like silken rose petals coming together. His hand came to Leland's waist, almost hovering there, before he felt slender fingers digging into the cloth of his shirt.

When he opened his eyes, Jamie's eyes were closed, eyelashes long shadows on his cheeks. Leland cupped his face, and kissed his cheek, fighting against the howling inside of him that wanted him, wanted him so badly, it was like fighting wolves to make him go slowly.

"I've never been with anybody before," said Jamie, his voice low and sweet.

"Never?" Leland paused and watched as Jamie looked at him, his eyes green jewels in the semi-darkness.

"No," said Jamie. He swallowed. "But I want to be with you."

"Are you sure?" Leland asked, whispering into Jamie's ear like a promise of love. "I will be gentle with you, so, so gentle."

"I know you will," he said, whispering back, his breath like a ribbon across Leland's cheek. "I'm sure."

Leland was almost broken by those words, that trust. And realized there was no more need for words, if there'd ever been any, as he undid the pearl-snap buttons on Jamie's blue shirt, one by one, the popping sound like a shot in the quiet room. And Jamie, with a teasing smile, did the same to Leland. One by one, they undid each other's buttons, and Jamie was brave, so very brave, matching Leland motion for motion.

Leland undid the brass button on Jamie's dark, new blue jeans, and Jamie undid the buttons on Leland's. And when he undid Leland's last pearl-snap button, he pushed away Leland's shirt from his shoulders and stepped into Leland's arms and pressed his cheek against his naked chest, his arms wrapped around his waist. Trembling the whole while.

"What are you doing?" Leland asked, his voice low. He dipped his chin and kissed the top of Jamie's head.

"Listening to you," he said, kissing the center of Leland's chest. "Listening to your heartbeat."

Staggering, Leland hugged him tightly, then slipped his shirt from him, and kissed his neck, the curve of his shoulder, all the while tugging them both in the direction of the bed. Which lay open, the bedclothes pulled back, an invitation of white expanse and colorful quilt.

Jamie, so independent, stripped himself to the skin, and tugged at Leland's jeans. In that moment, they weren't foreman and drifter anymore. They were two men coming together because they both wanted this, them together, sex in the half-dark, yes, but with the light of both their hearts shining upon it.

With his hand on Jamie's hip, fingers tracing the demarcation between tanned and pale skin, Leland looked at him and sighed. He was even prettier naked, his cock standing up in a hard curve against his belly, dark hair between his legs, trailing down his upper thighs. A pattern Leland's eyes adored, a pattern of skin and hair and muscle that made up this young man who had stormed his way onto the property and made a place for himself inside of Leland's life.

"Your jeans, now," Jamie said, moving between Leland's legs, blocking any chance of Leland actually obeying him. "Take them off."

"Yes, sir," Leland said, a bit of laughter bubbling up inside of him. "Here."

Leland eased Jamie back and stood up and peeled off his boots and socks and jeans as fast as he could. And, expecting Jamie would be a bit shy, was surprised when he stepped up and cupped Leland's cock in the palm of his hand, his fingers between Leland's legs, curling and uncurling. Such a bold thing he was, though in his eyes, there was a touch of uncertainty, as though he was asking himself if he'd taken it too far, too fast.

Placing his hand over Jamie's, he made a low sound, and it felt as though Jamie had pushed through ribs and skin to stand inside of him. There was no more time to wait; his body was shouting at him that this was urgent. He sat on the bed and, pulling Jamie on top of him, tumbled to the pillows.

Sprawled between Leland's open thighs. Jamie smiled and began scooting down as though he meant to slither lower to take Leland in his mouth and pleasure him, when that's not how he wanted it at all.

"Here," Leland said, holding him tight about his waist, both arms wrapped around him. "You and me both, at the same time."

Jamie's eyes wide, he nodded, and together, in sync, like they'd been doing it that way forever, Leland reached between Jamie's legs and he reached between Leland's. Jamie's dark hair sprawled across his forehead as he looked down, as though seeing this, what they were doing, was half the fun for him. Leland kissed the side of his temple and let go of him long enough to push the hair from his forehead. Then took his cock in his hand and curled his fingers around it.

"There's lube in the nightstand," he said. "If you want it. If you need it."

"No," Jamie said with a shake of his head, sending his forelock into his eyes again. His eyes gleamed with pleasure as he looked up. "I think I'd like it lightly, lightly."

Leland knew what he meant, what he wanted. Going lightly was different than going at it hard, and it caused more shivers, more wanting, more desire, as if lighting a single candle rather than a whole bonfire. There was something delicious in that, so Leland nodded, licked his palm quickly, and stroked him, good and soft. Lightly, lightly, Jamie shivering in his arms as he did this. Returned the favor, his fingers warm and delightful, stroking Leland, causing his belly to quake with wanting as his thighs shivered, his hand between Jamie's legs.

They tumbled on that bed, rocking each other slowly, creating such light friction, that Leland came without warning, hard and sharp, his body loving it, his mind shocked into stillness just as all of him decided that lightly, lightly was his favorite new thing.

Jamie followed, coming in Leland's hand, hot, silky ribbons, just after, and he held Jamie and petted him and kissed him over and over, a delicious whirl surrounding them both as they breathed and sighed and held onto each other as the night, and the air around them, became still once more.

The light from the main room was on, but Leland dozed, then came awake with a start, his heart pounding as Jamie stirred in his arms.

"Can we do this again?" asked Jamie, his voice bright, his eyes shining like stars. "Every night?"

"Jamie—" Leland's breath caught in his throat, heartsore over the beauty of it and the mistake of it, all at the same time.

As though Leland had actually shaken his head and said no, Jamie sat up and slipped out from beneath the sheets to stand naked in the light from the half-open doorway.

"I should probably go to my own room," he said, and before Leland could protest or, even, really figure out what would be better for him, or what he wanted—did he really want to go or just think he had to?—he had dressed and, carrying his socks and boots, slipped out the door, into the main room, and out the front door, closing it almost silently behind him.

Leland rose to sit on the edge of the bed, his head in his hands. This was not how it should have gone. He would have wanted to take a shower with Jamie to clean up, then held him while they slept. And in the morning, they could have shared a cup of coffee while they stood on the flagstone patio and watched the sun come up over the low hills to the south.

That or it never should have happened at all, and then he wouldn't have all kinds of thoughts and regrets and hope, whirling inside of him like an unexpected spring storm.

He got up to straighten the bed and then turned on the shower. He would take that shower and in the morning, he would straighten everything out with Jamie. There he stood in his bedroom for a good long while as the water ran, berating himself. There was cum drying on his thigh, and stains on the white sheets, and he'd just taken crass advantage of a young man who'd made himself vulnerable. He should not have done it, never. What had he been thinking?

In his heart he knew that what he'd been thinking was to turn a different corner this time and welcome the connection that had sprung up between him and Jamie. Someone who wanted what he wanted, or so it seemed: a simple life with simple pleasures. Someone to share chores with. Someone who would look at a far blue and green horizon and turn to Leland with a smile in his eyes.

Instead, what he'd done was take advantage of a situation. Jamie responded to him because he was his boss. Surely that was why Jamie had been turning to him, time after time, a smile in his eyes. And surely Leland should have laid down firm lines, and reminded Jamie of his policy, over and over, until it stuck. But he hadn't. And now here he stood, having made the worst mistake he possibly could have with someone like Jamie. And he had no idea what to do about it.

LELAND

*I*n the morning, Leland staggered into the shower, half asleep, before the sun came up, and while he was under the stream of water, it hit him all over again. What had happened between him and Jamie could not happen again. Not because it was wrong in his heart because his feelings for Jamie weren't wrong.

The problem was—he'd taken advantage of who Jamie was and where he'd come from. Leland had led him on, his heart dancing ahead of his thoughts and concerns about Jamie, and it was up to Leland to make it right. Not that it would be easy, no. He was already breaking his own heart, and he didn't want to break Jamie's, but it would be better, smarter, kinder to do it now. While the connection between them was still young. Leland dreaded doing it, but it was his responsibility, and his alone, to do the right thing.

He showered and shaved, ate a hurried breakfast in the lively dining hall, and then headed out front to where Maddy was waiting. She'd already called the repairman on the ice maker, of course, because that's how efficient she was. She'd probably done it before she'd gone to bed the night before, knowing her. Which left Leland with nothing to do but go over the duty roster, and assign his people to various tasks, and if his voice sounded hollow in his own ears, it didn't seem to affect anyone else.

Except for Jamie, who stood in the back row, where he usually stood, his dark hair and green eyes drawing Leland's attention like a beacon. He could see the expression on Jamie's face, and though they'd not talked yet, it was easy to see Jamie was troubled.

What Leland wanted to do was call for volunteers for some special task, see Jamie's raised hand and pick him out of the crowd. Then the two of them could head on out to the far parts of the ranch to check fence lines, or look for wolf scat, or wander through green meadows holding hands. He wanted it, wanted it so badly he could taste it, but it was bitter now, when the night before had been sweet.

Jamie came over to Leland as the meeting ended, wending his way through ranch hands and wranglers to get to him. And when he arrived, Leland stood there, and let Jamie look at him as he searched for the words to say to end it between them, searched for the right words to get the job done properly this time.

"Jamie," he said.

"Is everything okay?" he asked, his concern all for Leland. "You look funny. You sound funny."

Leland pulled Jamie to one side until they stood in the shadow of the barn. Everyone else was starting on their morning tasks, and it was nothing to them if Leland was speaking to one of his employees. Except this was a conversation he never wanted to have. "Last night—"

"I had such a good time, Leland," he said, and there were stars in his eyes as he looked at Leland.

"We can't—" Leland stopped and swallowed hard. "What happened last night can't happen again. I'm your boss. I'm the responsible party here, this was my fault. All of it."

"But don't you—I thought you liked me." Now, where once there had been green stars were dark hollows, his mouth down-turned, as though Leland had just smacked him.

"I do like you," Leland said, and if his heart felt like he'd just torn it in two with his own bare hands, that was his burden to bear, not

Jamie's. "But I'm your boss and it's not right for me to sleep with staff—"

"But you didn't sleep with *staff*," Jamie said, almost spitting the word. "You slept with *me*."

"You are staff, Jamie," Leland said. He pressed his hat firmly on his head and wished there was a better way to do this, knowing all the while that if he'd done the right thing to begin with, he wouldn't have had to come up with a better way. "And I am staff. This is the way it has to be. I take full responsibility for it happening in the first place, and I'm sorry. I never meant to hurt you."

Jamie's hands became fists. In another life, another place, he might have lashed out at Leland, and Leland wouldn't have blamed him, nor would he have defended himself. He would have stood there and taken it. There was so much hurt vibrating through Jamie, but he didn't move, as though pinned to the spot by his sorrow, his anger.

But just as Leland opened his mouth to continue, to say something else that he hoped would make a difference, Quint came to the open barn door. His eyes cast over Leland as though his boss was a problem that needed solving, and he gestured to Jamie.

"Jamie, come here," he said. "I need you to help clear the pallets for the hay delivery tomorrow."

With a look at Leland, sharp with dark daggers, laced with broken dreams, Jamie walked off, half tripping, half racing, to get away from him.

Yes, he wanted him to get away and stay away. It would be up to Leland to make sure there were no more outings, no more special chores. No more welcoming him to ride double, clinging to Leland's waist, his arms around him familiar and new all at once.

Each time. Each time had been special, and he had treasured them as they were happening. He would treasure them now as he moved on and hoped the pain of them would keep him smart. Keep him from reaching out to Jamie ever again.

The day dragged. Usually Wednesdays were the best days, as guests settled into a routine of activity, relaxed and happy that they had selected a guest ranch as their vacation, enjoying the low-key lifestyle, the abundance of food, the fresh air, and the stillness in the evenings.

As he took care of tasks delegated to the foreman, he nodded and smiled, as he usually did. Stopped to answer questions and sign bills of lading. He met with Bill in his office, and while they talked over the ex-con program and joked about Jasper's reticence for the program, his heart was sore, and he felt sick to his stomach.

Usually he could make hard decisions with ease, but not this time. This time he was mired in his own confusion.

Of course he had done the right thing, but had he done it for the right reasons? Had he done it because it was better for Jamie? Or had he done it because he was afraid—of getting close, of staying close—in a relationship that would make his life complicated?

He liked things simple and straightforward, and yet, there he'd gone plowing through all the straight furrows of his life, the orderliness of them, to try something new, leaving himself scattered and confused. Worst of all, he'd hurt a young man in the process, who didn't deserve to be hurt.

He threw himself into his work. He went down to Jasper's cabin to help him set up his brand new yet old-fashioned looking leather bellows, sweating and swearing under his breath as they hooked it up to his exacting specifications. He ordered special canvas aprons for Levi and his assistants for the next trail ride that involved the chuck wagon, which, as it was next week, had to be put on special order and followed up by a phone call. He saddled up a horse and went on the lunchtime trail ride with Brody and a dozen guests.

Later he talked with Quint about his ideas for a more rugged trail ride for those more advanced riders. Quint wanted a ride that went into the hills, far enough so that you'd have to bring your own water, and make very small campfires. He was sure some guests would love it, but as Leland saw the ranch as a place to relax and not a high-adrenaline adventure sort of place, they agreed to disagree for now.

Then, in the evening, he rode again, saddling up Diablo, a tough horse with a mind of his own. Diablo was for advanced riders only, and Leland took him for a nice long spell, out to the far reaches of the ranch where the hills turned into rocks and the wind blew a bit sharp and cold.

He was gentle with the horse, coaxing him to be obedient, but he wasn't gentle with himself, riding until his thighs felt raw and his skin had been blasted by wind and sun. Self punishment wasn't his thing, and neither was avoidance, but he'd avoided Jamie that day, avoided thinking about him, just about as hard as he'd avoided having any feelings at all. It was easier that way. Just easier.

But naturally, as he rode Diablo down the main road to the barn, both of them sweating, his throat dry as a desert, there Jamie was by the corral, finishing up clearing the sand of manure and hay. He paused, both of his hands on the sturdy rake. In his eyes, the hurt Leland had caused blazed, turning him back into a drifter once more. His hair beneath his straw hat was messy, his t-shirt sweat stained. Arms sunburned.

Why hadn't Jamie worn one of his long-sleeved shirts to protect himself? Had he taken breaks? What was he doing out there, anyhow? It was halfway through the dinner hour. He needed to eat. To keep that good muscle now beginning to show on his bones. To take care of himself.

Why wasn't anyone looking out for him? Well, Leland knew the answer to that. It was because he was the person, self-appointed, who had started looking out for him. He needed to do that at least, so as he walked Diablo past the corral, he slowed the horse.

"Jamie, go clean up and get some dinner," he said. "You're done working for the day."

"I can look after my own self," Jamie said, looking at Leland as though he were encountering a stranger.

Which was no more than Leland deserved. He deserved worse, actually, so he took Diablo into the barn, groomed him, gave him some water and some feed, and then walked the horse gently to the fields, where he could run with his horse pals and graze as long as he wanted to.

Jamie was gone from the corral when Leland went past it, and he hoped Jamie was getting some dinner. He would make sure, of course, but he wouldn't be obvious about it.

Look where being obvious had gotten him. Look where that had gotten Jamie, hurt and confused, acting like a young man with nothing in the world worth caring about. That was what weighed on Leland's heart as he scooted into the back of the dining hall to grab whatever wasn't already being wrapped up for the night. There were sounds of staff in the back, washing up, and guests lingered by the front door, happy laughter dancing up to the ceiling beams. And there he was, with a day-old ham sandwich in one hand and a slightly warm root beer in the other.

When he finished, he threw away his trash, checked on the ice maker, chatted with Levi a bit, all the while pretending he was okay. Being the foreman of a ranch, he was in charge of everything, but it seemed he was standing behind a blind spot. For everyone else, he knew what they should be doing, where they should be going, what they were responsible for. But for himself? He had no idea.

"Coming to the dance, Leland?" asked Levi. He'd taken off his apron, a signal that meant he was done with this semi-official meeting and wanted to go have some fun.

"Sure," Leland said. "I'll be there in a minute."

But he would not go. If he did, he'd either see Jamie there or he wouldn't. If he saw him, he'd be tempted to take him in his arms again, to sweep him off his feet and into his bed. He'd already done that. Already messed up.

If he didn't see him, then he'd get worried and start looking for him. He might find him in the barn, in the shadowy dark, or in his room. Either way, it'd be too much for Leland. The best thing to do—the best thing for *Jamie*—was if Leland left him alone for a while and then took up treating him like he had before. Casual and profession. Yes, that's what he'd do.

In the meantime, he headed to his cabin and took a hot shower and lay on top of the covers as the evening grew dark. He had the windows open to catch the breeze as it came down the mountains. From not too far away, he could hear the music from the dining hall, and the low laughter of guests and ranch hands and anybody who was dancing.

Jamie was what mattered. Leland needed to make sure he was okay, and then he needed to take him to the bank, like he'd promised. Help him get his driver's license. Make sure he didn't work too hard. And resist his own impulses, *his*, which had messed things up between them so badly.

26

JAMIE

*A*fter eating a quick dinner, Jamie cleaned up for the dance and went to the dining hall, half hoping Leland would be there. Half certain he would not be. What would he say to Leland anyway, should they meet? It was bound to be more of the same, more *no, we can't* and *no, we shouldn't,* even if they already *had.*

Leland was most definitely not at the dance, even as Jamie stood by one of the wooden beams holding up the porch, standing half behind it as though it might make him invisible. Leland wasn't there, and as everyone danced and laughed beneath the sprinkling of fairy lights and the stronger beams from the wrought-iron lanterns, no one seemed to notice. Or if they did, it wasn't important to them, as they were having such a good time.

This made the ache in Jamie's heart worse, though he knew Leland would truly be missed, if he ever were to leave. Jamie was the one who wouldn't be missed, and perhaps it would be better for everyone, especially Leland, if he left.

The second he got back to his room, he drew his green duffle bag out of his closet, and dragged his clothes out of the dresser. With all the new clothes and gear Leland had bought for him, the duffle was quite full. By the time he zipped it shut, he certainly couldn't fit his Carhartt jacket in there, or his cowboy boots. He needed to leave those things behind anyway, as they reminded him, every second, of Leland and his kindness.

He finished packing and left the duffle by the door so he would see it first thing he woke up, so it could remind him what he decided to do. Then he laid the money Mr. Ayers had given him on top, so he would remember to take it with him.

It was quite late. He needed to sleep.

In the morning, he was going to march down that road and out that gate, head into town with his thousand dollars, and catch the first bus out of Farthing. He would kick the dust of the ranch from his heels because he didn't need anything from the ranch. Not the hard work, not the hard hours, and not Leland. And especially not Leland's attention, or his smiles, or his strong arms. He was going to head out to fresh places and new people, and never, ever again would he open up his heart.

He was an idiot. Why had he fallen for those grey-blue eyes, that hard jaw, and a mouth that spoke such sweet words? He should have known better than to fall in love with the boss. Or with a guy who said *yes*, and then *no, come here* and then *go away*.

What had he been thinking? He hadn't been thinking, that's what. He'd started believing in hope, started believing he could make a better life for himself at the ranch. Started believing that Leland cared about him. But whether he'd been telling himself lies or Leland had told them, it was all lies, and he had believed them.

Well, never again.

Sleep came hard, as though he'd thrown himself against stones in the night and just hung on till morning. By the time the sun began creeping over his windowsill, the soft breezes stirring the thin, white curtains, someone was banging on his door.

It was too much to hope it was Leland, but he hoped anyway. And opened the door with such force, it banged against the wall of his room.

There stood Clay, fully dressed, looking bright-eyed and ready for the day.

"Hey, they need you," he said, jerking his thumb over his shoulder. "I know it's early, but the driver delivering hay has somehow managed to dump all the bales as the truck came around the curve to the barn. Leland wants everyone out there to clean up before guests wake up."

"What time is it?" Jamie asked, though it really didn't matter. It was early, and he needed to get away, get away before he ever saw Leland's face again.

"Five thirty," Clay said, and he winced as though agreeing with Jamie's unspoken complaint as to how early it was. "Extra pay, Leland says. He doesn't want the guests to have to wade through bales of hay."

"Fine," Jamie said. He'd do it to keep the guests happy and for the money. But he wasn't going to talk to Leland, even if he was there, except to say *yes, sir,* and *no, sir,* and that was it.

"What's this?" asked Clay. He looked at the green duffle bag just inside the door, at the fifties and hundreds flapping in the light breeze.

"I'm leaving after I help out." Jamie held onto the doorjamb, digging his fingers in to keep himself from trembling. "I just need to find Maddy so she'll give me my pay."

"She'll just deposit it to your bank." Clay looked at him, brows furrowed.

"I don't have a bank account," said Jamie, for what seemed like the thousandth time.

"She could write you a paper check on Saturday." Clay looked troubled by this idea. "At least I think she can. Anyway, thanks for helping this morning."

Clay left, clomping in his work boots down the hall.

Jamie closed the door and got dressed, quick as he could, stopping to grab a mouthful of water from the faucet. Then he headed down the stairs to the barn, almost jogging. It was chilly, but it was going to warm up soon, so it didn't matter that he was only wearing his t-shirt.

A flatbed truck with a flatbed trailer sat jackknifed in front of the barn, and beside it stood a red-faced truck driver wiping his forehead with the back of his forearm as he talked to Maddy. All round the truck and the trailer were bales of hay, most of which had spilled out of their bindings, leaving a snowfall of hay and hay dust on the dirt road.

Jamie coughed as he walked into the low cloud of debris to join the group of employees who were using pitchforks and wheelbarrows to gather the hay and haul it away.

He wasn't sure what he should do, as all the tools were being used. Then Leland walked by, his arms bare as he hauled up a bale of hay with gloved hands and put it back on the trailer.

"Get those up there, Jamie," he said, as though nothing had happened between them. As though he barely knew Jamie.

"Yes, sir," Jamie said, shivering, shards of hurt ripping through his heart.

When he went to the first bale of hay he saw and lifted it, Leland came up behind him. He could feel Leland's presence, even before he turned around.

"No, not that way," Leland said. "Here, use these."

He peeled off his gloves and handed them to Jamie, then marched off, probably to get another pair. When Jamie slid his hands inside, the canvas gloves were still warm from Leland's skin. Jamie lifted his hands to his face and imagined that the gloves smelled like Leland, still outlined the shape of his hands. Then he jerked the gloves away from his face and started lifting hay bales from the ground and up onto the flatbed trailer.

Clay got up on the flatbed and started arranging the hay bales, and as he did this, Jamie had to throw the bales higher and higher each time, till he couldn't throw them any higher. His arms were quivering, his shoulders sore, and he was covered with hay scratches all over.

By the time they finished the cleanup, all the hay had been removed from the ground, and the driver had driven the truck around the barn to the supply barn, it was just seven o'clock. Time for breakfast. Time for guests to get up and start their day. Time for Jamie to leave.

Jamie dusted himself off, removing as much hay as he could. He took Leland's gloves back to the barn, where he laid them on the desk in Leland's office. Then he went to the dining hall and had the biggest breakfast he could shove inside of him.

As he ate, Brody shook his head as he went by with his empty tray, and Jamie looked down at himself. He was sweat-stained and grubby with flecks of hay in his hair. He was right back where he'd started the day he'd arrived at the ranch. Having people look at him a certain way, think about him a certain way. Well, that was fine and too bad. He was leaving anyway.

He bussed his tray and was about to go to his room and grab his duffle bag so he could head out, but just on the front porch of the dining hall, Brody came up to him.

"Got a favor," he said. "I'm just about to start the lesson, but Dorothy's afraid to get on her horse. Can you help me? Maybe walk Dorothy's horse on a lead?"

"Sure," said Jamie, short.

"Go clean up, put on a long-sleeved shirt, and get your hat, and meet me there."

No more lessons for him, it looked like. Instead, he was on the ground, in the dust. Well, fine, he'd earn an entire day's pay and walk away with more money. Maybe he'd work all the way till dinner, eat that, and then head out. When did the last bus leave out of Farthing anyhow?

He raced to his room to grab his hat and long-sleeved shirt, and headed back to the corral. Even while grumbling the whole while about not being able to leave, something inside him felt like it was stepping back from a very dangerous place, from unknown prospects, from shitty bus rides to nowhere. Farthingdale Ranch was a good place, and yes, the work was hard, but everything about it—

Jamie stopped in his tracks as he came up to the corral in the blazing sunshine. Leland and Brody were inside the corral with a group of guests, talking to them about the lesson. Jamie grew hot all over and then cold.

Brody had asked him for help, and he was going to do it, but his heart was racing and his throat was dry. It might be the bravest thing he'd ever done, but he did it. Slipped through the fence rails and walked right up to the two of them. He tipped his hat at Brody, but not to Leland.

Leland had the good grace to nod, but said nothing to Jamie, and quickly turned his attention to Brody.

"Where did the fear come from?" asked Leland.

It took Jamie a second to realize he wasn't talking to him, but to Brody, quietly, so the guests didn't hear.

"She just got spooked overnight, is all," said Brody. "And I mean the rider, not the horse. Maybe the sky was too big, I don't know."

"Dorothy," said Leland to one of the riders, the lady Jamie'd had his one lesson with. "Jamie is going to clip a lead to your horse's bridle during your lesson today. Okay? He'll make sure nothing happens."

Leland turned, grabbed a canvas lead, and handed it to Jamie.

"It's Travelle," he said, pointing to the bay horse with a black mane and tail.

Jamie nodded and walked across the dirt ring. Travelle was a sweet horse, and Jamie should know. He and Leland had ridden double on her. It was stupid to be scared of a horse like that. He didn't know anything about horses, and he wasn't scared.

But when he turned at the footfalls in the sand behind him, he saw a woman behind him. It was Dorothy with her sad dark eyes and pale, powdery skin over the bones of her face. Her hair was brown streaked with grey, and she looked like she could be anybody's aunt. There was such gratitude in her eyes that Jamie's heart broke for her.

"Thank you," she said, wringing her hands. "I feel foolish, but I was thinking how dangerous this all was. I'm trying to be brave, but my husband died only a little while ago—anyway, I'm trying something new. But it's hard."

"Hey," Jamie said, soft feelings whirling around inside of him. It was nice to be counted on. Nice to be needed. "Travelle is the sweetest horse. See her eyes? See those long eyelashes? She's just waiting for the lesson to begin, is all. She's not going to hurt you."

With Brody's help, Dorothy mounted up. Jamie stood at Travelle's shoulder, making a great display of holding the horse still when, actually, Travelle was standing still all by herself. He patted Travelle's neck, then got in the line of other horses waiting to go around the ring so their riders could practice their skills. When the lesson began, Leland left, probably to go work in his office.

What was required of Jamie, then, was nothing more complicated than pretending to lead Travelle around the corral, sometimes at a walk, sometimes at a trot, and once at a slow canter. All of this was hot and thirsty work and quite distracting from his own troubles.

When the lesson ended, Dorothy dismounted and, with a warm smile, gave Jamie a big hug and a kiss on his cheek. He felt so glad in his heart at having done her some good, he almost forgot that he'd planned to leave.

Brody came up to him as the guests led their horses out of the corral and into the barn. Even before Brody asked, Jamie knew he'd stay long enough to clean the corral.

"Sure," he said. "No problem."

"Yes, thank you," said Brody, ever polite as he stood there in his long-sleeved shirt, sleeves rolled down, as if the day wasn't heating up like an oven turned on high. "You did well there," he said.

Low waves of hurt came at him that Leland wasn't also standing there with that smile in his grey-blue eyes, giving Jamie that nod of approval, letting him know, all without words, that he was the kind of guy Leland wanted to be with.

"No, I mean it," said Brody. "I could use you this afternoon. We're having a short trail ride, and Dorothy's signed up. If you're there—"

"I only had the one lesson," he said, all tangled up inside. Sometimes Leland went on those rides, sometimes.

"You can ride, just fine." Brody nodded and looked at the corral. "Take care of this. Get some lunch, then clean up, wear a clean shirt, and come back to the barn around one thirty. You can help groom and saddle, and then we'll put you on Dusty. He seems to like you. Then you can ride next to Dorothy. The last thing I want is for a guest to walk away feeling terrified of horses."

"Sure," said Jamie.

219

"She's a widow." Brody moved his jaw as though something inside him ached at the thought of it. "And we're going to help her make it through this."

"I don't—" Jamie stopped, clamping his mouth shut. It sounded more complicated than he was capable of dealing with, right then, though he didn't want to tell Brody no, that he was leaving.

His plans were his own. His duffle bag was packed, but nobody knew that except him and Clay, and Clay probably wouldn't remember to say anything about it. The situation at Farthingdale Ranch had gotten to where all he wanted to do was run, to start somewhere else. Leaving would be easier than sticking around trying to navigate his way through both avoiding Leland *and* doing his job.

But it was a job that he could get anywhere, right? There were other ranches in Wyoming and Colorado and everywhere. He didn't have to stick around. Not at all. Not even to help Brody, or Dorothy— or anyone. He should also leave behind everything Leland had given him, the new boots, the coat, the clothes, and just get out of there. Just leave.

"I know it's hard to think about things like that, her husband dying and all," said Brody. He ducked his head and peered at Jamie from beneath the brim of his cowboy hat. "But it's a part of life. You'll get used to it."

Jamie frowned as Brody pushed feelings on him that weren't his. He wasn't bothered by Dorothy being a widow, and when she'd kissed him, he'd been glad he'd been there when she needed him.

"So," he said, looking at Jamie. "You going to help on that ride this afternoon or what?"

"Sure I will," Jamie said.

What did it matter? He'd have another day's pay owed to him, and could head out in the morning, just the same. He told himself he was saying yes to Brody because of the money and not because Leland might be on the ride that afternoon.

Farthingdale Ranch would see the last of him quite soon. And Leland would, too. Which might teach him to mess with people's feelings, that or he'd forget about Jamie as soon as he disappeared over the first bump in the horizon. Either way, soon Jamie wouldn't have to look at Leland ever again.

2 7

LELAND

*a*fter lunch clouds began to roll in over Iron Mountain. Leland met Brody on the porch of the dining hall and asked him about the trail ride.

"Might be too boisterous out there for some guests," Leland said, looking at the ridge of hills where the edges flowed into the moody clouds. That was his way of giving Brody advice without telling him what to do. Brody was a responsible wrangler, one of the best the ranch'd ever had. At the same time, the group that was scheduled to go out were all new riders, having their first trail ride in their lives.

"It might be," said Brody. "We'll tie on rain slickers to each saddle, and the guests will love it. They'll think they're going on a trek into the wilderness with certain danger on every side. It'll be good for 'em."

"What about Dorothy?" Leland asked. "She's a very timid rider."

"She's got the heart of a lion." Brody shook his head, as though this idea was mere foolishness. "Besides, I've got Jamie coming along. He'll ride at her side the whole time, keep her calm."

"He is?"

This stopped Leland and all the thoughts in his head, which were usually focused on everything he needed to get done. Everything, ever part of him, narrowed in on the idea of it. Of Jamie on horseback, riding along with that smile in his eyes, tentative, but bright. His first trail ride—Leland had wanted that ride to be with him, the two of them together. Only he'd foolishly squandered any possibility of that happening.

Any pain he felt was his own doing, and he deserved every bit of it.

"Sure," said Brody. Then, as casually as any comment Leland had ever heard from him, he added, "You could come along too. Help me out."

"You don't need my help," Leland said, wishing desperately that there was some way he could backpedal his way out of the conversation.

"Sure I do," Brody said. Then he grinned. "Besides, they'd love it if the foreman of the ranch came along. It'd make it feel more meaningful if you were there."

"Meaningful?" Leland had no idea what he was going on about.

"More official. Like, you're giving it your stamp of approval if you're along for the ride. Like the ride is worth your going on it."

"Ah."

All rides were worth his going on, but he didn't always go. This time he would, if just to help Brody, help guests manage the upcoming rough weather. Which was a lie, all of it. He was going because Jamie was going. If he couldn't ride with Jamie on his own—and he couldn't—then at least he could be with Jamie this way. Under the guise of helping Brody. Then he could watch and dream and dry his own tears later over what he had lost.

"Sure," he said, finally. "I'll be ready. I'll take any horse the guests don't want."

Guests wanted pretty horses, horses they could write home about and post on their social media, so he was always willing to take the horses that were less photogenic. And a time or two, he'd been able to show guests that all the ranch's horses were good ones and worth praising.

As he walked back to the barn and his office, he decided the trail ride would be his long ride for the day. It would probably rain by evening anyway, and while a ride in the rain might look romantic on a movie screen, it was a miserable experience.

He took care of some paperwork, then grabbed his Carhartt jacket, along with some leather gloves, and headed out to the corral. There, ten horses were lined up, and guests were helping ranch hands to groom and saddle, though mostly it was the ranch hands doing the work while the guests flitted around with excited smiles and voices filled with expectation.

"Better bring out those yellow slickers, Mr. Calhoun," Leland said extra loudly, drawing out the *o* sound. He pulled on his leather gloves and steadied his hat as though preparing for foul weather and maybe even the worst storm the ranch had ever seen. It was a bit of theatrics on his part for the benefit of the guests, and to his pleasure, and as he expected he would, Brody snapped to.

"Yes, sir, Mr. Tate," he said, then gestured to the ranch hands to dash off for those slickers.

All of them, except Jamie, went into the barn where the slickers had already been piled up. They came back, their arms full, and carefully handed out a slicker to each guest, and to Jamie and Brody and himself.

As Leland helped guests tie their slickers to the back of their saddles, demonstrating what the leather strings on their saddles were for, he watched Jamie out of the corner of his eyes. He couldn't help it, it was like he was drawn to Jamie like a sighthound, hopelessly drawn to him.

Jamie helped Dorothy tie down her slicker and then tied down his own, but it was easy to see that Leland's comments and theatrics had made her more nervous, which wasn't right. With quick strides, he went over to her and Jamie and patted Travelle.

"Ma'am," he said, touching his gloved hand to his hat. "Jamie," he said. Jamie looked at him like he'd just smacked him, which made Leland heartsore all over again. "You probably won't need to use that slicker," he said to Dorothy. "It's just a precaution."

"But will the trail get wet?" she asked, her eyebrows high in her forehead. "Will the horse slip?"

Leland couldn't imagine what grief she'd experienced having lost her husband, but he admired her for going back out into the world and trying something new and different. She might be nervous, but she'd not stepped out of the ring. It was Leland's job to reassure her that all would be well.

"You're smart to be thinking about these things, Dorothy," Leland said, focusing his attention on her. "It probably won't rain, but if it does, we've got the slickers. The trail we're riding along is mostly flat, except for a small rise that we go over to get into the valley bottom. Besides." He gestured with his gloved hand to Jamie, standing close by. "Jamie will ride with you, keep you company. Dusty, the horse he's riding, is the steadiest of all the horses being ridden today. And you already know Travelle is sweet as sugar, and will take you there and back again, quite safely. Now, can I give you a leg up?"

"Jamie," she said as she reached out and touched his arm. "He makes me feel safe."

The last thing Leland would have expected, upon first meeting Jamie, was that an older, widowed woman would turn to him for help. There was something he'd done or said to make this good connection with her, and it was something Leland heartily approved of. That was the behavior that made a new rider feel safe. Made a good ranch hand. Made a good man.

Leland watched as Jamie stepped close and helped Dorothy mount Travelle, then kept watching, like some kind of fool with nothing else to do. Jamie double checked that Dorothy's yellow slicker was securely tied on, then patted Travelle's neck, talking softly to Dorothy all the while.

Leland wanted to step close and hear his words, wanted to make a difference—*any* difference—where he wouldn't have to feel like a complete asshole in all of this. But that was his burden to bear.

Anything that had happened between them and the fallout from his backing away—all of that was his fault, and his fault alone. He deserved to feel lonely. Deserved to walk away and mount Marduke, a plain looking ginger horse with amazingly long legs.

Marduke's trot might be choppy, but his walk was smooth. He

could canter for miles and when he did, his ginger mane floated in the air like cotton candy. Except for that mane, though, he was not Instagram worthy. Leland's throat closed up as he mounted, his anger flaring at all the focus on what something looked like rather than what it felt like. But those were the changes the world was going through, and he either needed to understand those changes or throw in the towel.

The trail ride must go on, and so when Brody mounted and clicked his horse into action, taking the lead, Leland waited till all the other guests slowly guided their horses into line. The horses were experienced at this, knew the drill, and lined up without a fuss, each following the other as they left the corral and headed up the low slope to the path along the foothills.

Jamie got ahead of Dorothy and smiled back at her as he nudged Dusty into motion. Leland steered Marduke behind Dorothy, both to keep an eye on her and, also, yes, to watch Jamie as he rode.

Jamie's back was straight, and when he looked at Dorothy to check on her, he looked at Leland, too, and then flicked his eyes away. As though Leland was a stranger. As though Leland was the enemy, which he probably was. But that's the way it had to be. Leland was the boss and couldn't be panting after his employees. It wasn't right. Wasn't ethical. Put a strain on things, like it was doing right now. If he'd not come on to Jamie, then the two of them could be on this trail ride together, sharing a laugh, taking care of Dorothy between them. But no, he'd screwed up.

Despite Leland's dark thoughts, the trail ride was glorious. The clouds came and went, making dappled patterns across the landscape and seashell shapes along the horizon, shifting the shadows on the foothills from blue to pink and gold, then back to blue.

A brisk wind came down from Iron Mountain by the time they went over the rise. Bits of rain spattered in the sky, but it was mostly virga from the clouds, vanishing before hitting earth. Even so, when they rode into the bottom of the valley, Brody had the guests stop and dismount.

Everyone had a fine time helping each other untie their yellow slickers from behind their saddles, and everyone did their best to put their slickers on without flapping around too much. There was happy laughter and much circling of horses, and all the while, Jamie quietly helped Dorothy.

He wasn't an experienced rider and couldn't have done much, had there been a serious problem. Just by being there, though, he was helping Dorothy stay calm and giving her the experience she'd come out to the ranch to have: that of being on horseback in a clean, unspoiled world.

Leland's throat closed up at the thought of it. He'd thrown Jamie off the property, and had that decision followed through as he'd expected it, then Dorothy wouldn't have Jamie's shoulder to lean on, his patient presence standing by as she mounted up again, the tails of her yellow slicker flapping all around her.

"Mount up," Leland said, using the words to clear his tight throat.

"Mount up, everyone," said Brody, tapping his hat to Leland. "If it starts to rain hard, we'll head back. We'll be fine, don't worry. Rain won't melt us, as we're not made of sugar, and the horses are used to this kind of weather."

Everyone mounted up, and the horses walked for a good long way along a tributary of Horse Creek, where the rain was casting dimples on the smooth surface of the water and stirring the green grasses. The guests chattered amongst themselves while Leland kept an eye on the weather.

When Brody pointed, Leland looked and spotted lightning on the horizon. The flash of light was so thin and so small, they probably weren't in any danger. Still, lightning could arc across great distances, especially in open areas like the high plains, so it wasn't a good idea to be caught out in the middle of nowhere.

When another shard came, silver-white against the darkening sky, Brody and Leland looked at each other and nodded.

"Looks like we'll be turning back, folks," said Brody, his words coming out exactly the way they should, calm, steady, dependable. "We've got more weather coming in than we expected, so it's better safe than sorry. Take a quick drink from your canteens, then we'll turn 'em around and head back to the ranch. There, you'll have a nice hot supper, and if it's not raining, we'll have dancing in front of the dining hall."

Leland looked over at Dorothy. Her face was white, and she'd balled up her reins in her hands, gripping the saddle horn the whole while. In her face, he could see what she was afraid of, of being in the middle of nowhere while the elements swirled all around her, out of control. Even though he knew there was very little to fear, to her there was, and he needed to take care of it.

Just as he was about to go over and offer assistance and maybe some gentle reassurance, Jamie rode close to her side, reaching out to her. And he didn't just pat her hand, he made her drink from her canteen, and took a drink from his own to show her how it was done. Gave her something specific to do, to focus on.

Leland didn't know what Jamie said to her as they put their canteens back, but she looked at him and nodded, her eyes wide. Then she got right in line with the others, guiding her horse, and while her knuckles were still white, there was a firm set to her jaw, and she concentrated on Travelle, patting the mare, talking to her all the while.

Leland got brave himself and rode up on the other side of Jamie. Marduke's hooves were off the path, and they were now riding three abreast, which wasn't exactly safe. But he would only be there a moment, and reached out to touch Jamie's thigh.

Jamie's head snapped in Leland's direction, like he'd said something harsh. His green eyes glittered, and his mouth was a firm, thin line.

"What?" he asked.

"What did you say to her?"

Jamie took a long breath, checked to make sure of Dorothy, then shifted his body in the saddle and leaned toward Leland. "I told her Travelle needed her to guide her back to the barn. That it was up to her to make sure Travelle was safe."

"You flipped a switch," Leland said, and he'd never been so proud and amazed. By making Dorothy more aware of her horse's needs than her own, Jamie had done exactly the right thing. "Well done."

For a moment, long and sweet, there was a smile in those green eyes, a curve to Jamie's lovely mouth, but then he ducked his head and turned back to Dorothy. And there was nothing Leland could do but slip back into place at the end of the line, riding behind Jamie and Dorothy.

Everyone arrived back at the barn just as it started to rain, which wasn't odd up in the high country in June. The rain would be brief, and when they let the horses go for the night, they'd be just fine out in the fields. But in the meantime, guests needed to be kept dry and comfortable, and the saddles needed to be removed, the horses groomed.

With all of them in the barn, and ten horses in the open area in the middle, it got quite busy. Leland lost track of Jamie. Dorothy had finished up, and another ranch hand was helping her, but he couldn't find Jamie to tell him *well done* and *thank you* and *I'm sorry*. Though he shouldn't say *I'm sorry* again, that might open a wound, a wound that would heal if he just left it alone.

By the time Leland was done helping where he could, he marched out of the barn. There, amidst the dappling rain, he slipped off his gloves and tipped his hat back on his head to get a better view.

Through the trees, he could see the dining hall was gearing up for dinner. Guests were wandering back to their cabins or the bunkhouse, and some were already headed up the path to the dining hall. Where, no doubt, they would gather in the shelter of the porch and watch the rain fall, and consider themselves lucky to be experiencing the beauty of nature, all in the wild.

Then they would go into the dining hall and enjoy the civilizing effects of a hot meal and good company. That didn't mean nature wasn't all around them, only that they were sheltered from it, and could still see its beauty and, yes, its uncertainty. Which maybe was Leland's problem. Maybe he'd cut himself off from something he shouldn't have—

"Boss?"

Leland turned. It was Clay, huddled in his Carhartt jacket, dark spots spotting his felt cowboy hat. He was looking at Leland somewhat askance, his eyes a little more narrow than Leland was used to seeing, and Clay's lovable dimples were nowhere in evidence.

"Yes, Clay?" Leland asked. He took off his hat, scrubbed his hands in his hair, then put his hat back on again. Stepping off the path so folks could get by them, he asked, "What can I do for you?"

"What's going on with you and Jamie?" Clay asked, jerking his thumb over his shoulder as if to show which direction Jamie had gone. Leland's eyes traced an invisible path, and when he felt Clay looking at him extra hard, he squelched the desire to chase after Jamie.

"What do you mean, Clay?"

With anyone else, Leland might have told Clay it was none of his business, but they were friends, as far as a boss and employee could be friends. Clay treated Leland no differently than anyone else, and frankly, he treated Leland like his leads treated him, with casual respect. He was the boss, sure, but he was one of them as well. Leland liked Clay, liked his refreshing manner, his lack of interest in labels and suchlike. But he was uncomfortable with this sudden and different scrutiny.

"Days ago, he was as happy as a lark, a literal lark," said Clay. He ran his thumbs over the lapels of his jacket, his head ducked like he was searching for words there. "And today, he's all—wired tight, like he's ready to leave."

"Leave?" Leland asked, his heart speeding up. "How do you know this?"

The look Clay gave him was, frankly, as though he'd kicked him hard and then turned around looking for another victim.

"I know it, *boss*, because he said it," Clay said, slowing on the word. "This morning he said, *I'm leaving*. And just now, he's headed to his room to get his stuff, I guess, though how he's going to manage walking all the way to town in the rain is anyone's guess. Not only that, but the bus only runs every other day. He'll be standing at the Greyhound station across from the Rusty Nail. The

231

doors'll be locked, and he'll be out in weather like this. You want that?"

Leland's weight was on the balls of his feet, as though his entire body was prepared to run, and run fast, to stop Jamie from leaving. He didn't want him to go. Then again, Jamie was his own man, free to do as he saw fit. Which left Leland teetering, unbalanced, when Clay put his flat hand in the middle of his chest, and just pressed it there. He looked down and then up at Clay, and he'd never been more confused. It'd been years since anyone pushed him around, *years*.

"Everybody saw you leave the dance floor together the other night," said Clay, and his voice was quiet for all it was so firm. "Everybody knows he was with you. What?" His eyebrows rose as Leland took a step back, his mouth opening, breath gathering, to protest. "You think when someone like you does something like that, nobody's going to notice? Well, you're wrong—"

"It shouldn't have happened in the first place," Leland said, thrusting his words into Clay's stream of explanation. "So I broke it off. It's my fault, all of it."

"Which doesn't excuse you acting like an asshole." Clay thrust out his jaw at him and glared.

"It shouldn't have happened," Leland said. It was only with Clay that he could have this conversation. With anyone else, he'd be scrambling for distance, but with Clay, it was okay to admit he'd made a mistake. "I made a mistake. I should not have come on to him. I'm the boss and he's my employee. I've got standards to keep—there are policies—"

"You know, Leland," said Clay. He tipped his head back and propped his cowboy hat off his forehead with a finger. "If you were one of those jerk bosses who screwed every greenhorn that came through those gates and then tossed them away? Sure. I'd be a whole lot more worried. But I'm not 'cause you're not that guy."

"No, I'm not," Leland said, and even as his mouth opened to say more, to explain more, Clay put up his hand to stop him.

"No, you're not," said Clay. "Besides, you didn't see his face the morning after you two left the dance. He was glowing. He was *glowing*. You know what I mean?"

Nodding slowly, Leland ran his thumb across his lower lip, as though he could feel the ghost-traces of Jamie's kisses. He knew that glow, had seen it in Jamie's eyes, had seen his whole self be taken over by it, changing him from what he was into what he could be. Happy. When Leland saw Clay watching him, he snapped his hand away and tried to settle the confused thoughts whirling in his head.

"Have you talked to him about this?" Leland asked, feeling very much like a third grader who has given a cute kid a check-yes-or-no message and very much wants to know the results of that inquiry.

"Not in so many words, I just asked him *are you okay* and stuff like that." Clay shook his head and smiled at a pair of guests who walked by them. "And then he muttered something about his duffle bag. He's a good kid, Leland, and he thinks you hang the moon, though at this moment I don't rightly know why. Don't fuck him up like that. Don't be that guy. And most of all—"

Clay paused. Leland could see him gather himself like he was going to tell him the very worst, crappiest thing he could think of to say. He steeled himself in return, for he would deserve that and more.

"Take that stick out of your ass and quick," said Clay. "You were glowing too, you know? Like I've never seen you. Sure you're happy. You're in love with working on a ranch, same as me, same as a lot of us. But you could be happy—*happier*, if you'd let yourself unbend, just a little bit." Clay pinched two fingers to show him how short a distance it was between Leland's everyday life and some imaginary one filled with hearts and flowers and kisses.

"It wouldn't be right," Leland said, and his hands came up, like he was floundering helplessly in layers upon layers of deep water.

"Normally, I'd say yes," said Clay, with definitive authority. "If a guy is in a position of authority, sure. He shouldn't take advantage. But you? You follow the rules so hard—but he'd be good for you and you'd be good for him, good *to* him. And you would never take advantage like that. Find a way. Fix it so that you can't fire him or anything like that if it goes sour. But give yourself a damn chance, why don't you. Just one freaking chance."

"Why is this so important to you, Clay?" Leland asked, finally aware that Clay's passionate rant at him might have just as much to do with himself as it did with what had happened between Leland and Jamie. "I've never seen you act like this, never heard you—" He stopped. Clay was fully in his rights to say anything he wanted and behave anyway he wanted. He was a man, fully grown, and Leland respected him more than he thought he would have upon meeting him. "Tell me what's going on? How can I help?"

Clay's jaw was working, like he was gearing himself up for the worst thing of all, the thing he never wanted anyone to know.

"You hang the moon for me too, you know? For me and Brody both." Tears glinted in his eyes and he scrubbed at them hard with his fingers. "I keep thinking, I can do that, I can be like Leland. But then you went and—well, you messed up, Leland. Messed up bad. Jamie doesn't deserve it, and I—I know you're human. People make mistakes. But I'm following your lead here, and I don't want to cut out of line just because you're behaving like an asshat. People depend on you. I depend on you." Clay pointed at himself with a hard stab. "Don't fuck it up, Leland."

Then Clay marched off, going along the path and under the trees, dripping with rain. Leaving Leland in that spot, staring after him. His mouth was open, and he breathed the cool, rain-drenched air.

A thousand ideas whirled in the air around him, startling him with icy cold dots as they touched his face. But that was the rain. The hard rain that came in early summer, cool at first, then shockingly cold. He turned his face up into it and blinked his eyes closed. And imagined that somehow, he could be washed clean. That he could make all of this right.

28

JAMIE

*B*y the time Jamie made it to the dining hall, it was raining hard. Inside, the guests were talking in excited voices as they stood in the buffet line, going over the afternoon's trail ride, and the excitement about the weather, the slickers. The fact that the foreman had gone on the ride with them.

Jamie grabbed a tray and got at the back of the buffet line, and did not join in the general admiration of how good Mr. Tate looked on horseback. If he did, he would most certainly have to agree, and then he would start rethinking his decision to leave the ranch.

"Hey, Jamie."

Jamie looked up. Brody was already at one of the long tables, waving him over. Jamie got his food and went to sit across from Brody. He took a bite of his meatloaf and mashed potatoes, but they didn't seem to want to go down, so he gulped on his iced tea and tried not to let his looming departure wash over him.

"Great trail ride, yeah?" asked Brody, his mouth full as he shoveled it in. "Man, Leland was perfect, wasn't he? *Better bring out those yellow slickers, Mr. Calhooooooooooun.* Gah." Brody shook his head and scrubbed at his mouth with a paper napkin. "Nobody puts on a show better than he does."

235

"I guess not," said Jamie.

"Just the right amount of drama, you know? Just to make it perfect for the guests, gives them a story to take with them."

"Yeah," said Jamie, because that part was true. He had a story to take with him too, except that it had a sad ending, rather than a happy one. "Hey, do you know how late Greyhound stays open?"

"Greyhound?" asked Brody, blinking at Jamie as though Jamie had just woken him up from a very pleasant dream.

"Yeah, when does the bus leave?"

"Um." Brody looked at him for a minute, then shrugged, as if he'd decided not to ask why Jamie wanted to know. "The bus goes Monday, Wednesdays, and Fridays. Around three, I think."

"Oh."

Friday was the day before payday. He could take the bus then, sure. But if he waited till Saturday, he'd have more money in his pockets. If he could figure out a way to cash the check Maddy was going to give him, he'd be able to show ranch and Leland his heels. Be his own man.

"You thinking of leaving?" asked Brody, finally.

"Maybe not till next week," said Jamie. He scrubbed at the back of his neck and told himself he was not scanning the dining hall for signs of Leland. "Maybe not till Monday. Maybe."

After packing and unpacking his duffle bag at least twice, Jamie tossed on his single bed and watched the curtains drifting in the soft, damp breeze from the open window. In the morning, when he stepped out of the staff quarters, the rain had cleared and the skies overhead were blue.

The scent of pine followed him in the cool air as he scooted along the path to the dining hall. From the propped-open doors he could smell bacon frying and pancakes and coffee brewing and sugar melting in butter. All those things swirled around him in the crisp morning air, and his stomach grumbled for him to hurry up.

The dining hall was lively and full of people talking and walking around the tables with their trays. Tomorrow would be their last day before they went home, and they were talking and looking and smiling, as though trying to absorb every detail before their real lives made the ranch just a memory.

Tomorrow would be Jamie's last day, too. He didn't want to imagine what his life would be away from the ranch, when he didn't have a steady income and a roof over his head. When he'd have to resort to working in a meat packing plant in the middle of nowhere. He wanted to stay but didn't think he could. Didn't think he should.

The best thing for him to do was to eat as much as he could, work one last day, and pick up his pay in the morning. After that, his future stretched out like an empty hallway that went on forever.

As he ate his breakfast, a pile of pancakes and a pile of bacon, he looked for Leland, for his tall frame, listened for his steady walk. All the while, he told himself not to. It was stupid. It was hopeless.

Maybe being with him hadn't been good for Leland. Or maybe Leland was afraid Jamie might talk about it or brag that he was sleeping with the boss. He didn't know. What he did know was that inside of him was a huge gash, like Leland had taken a knife and slashed him open, rough, jiggling that knife around to do the most damage. He was stupid to have let Leland get that close in the first place, stupid.

Someone came up behind him and his whole body stiffened, but when he saw it was Clay, he let out a whoosh of air.

"Hey," Jamie said as Clay sat down opposite him with his tray of food.

"Hey," he said with that smile of his, all dimpled and sweet. "Jasper wants your help scything again. Said you did a good job last time."

"Did he?" Jamie asked, trying to be interested in maybe feeling a little bit good about himself because somebody he didn't really know very well liked his work. "Cause I was thinking about catching that Greyhound bus at three."

The pain of that idea kicked him as soon as the words were out of his mouth.

"When does Maddy hand out the checks tomorrow?" he asked, taking a large swallow of bitter coffee, like he was an important man and all in a rush to make things happen for himself.

"Usually around ten," said Clay. "Though most have direct deposit. You know."

He knew all about it. Knew how direct deposit worked. Knew that you had to have a bank account, and a routing number, and all of that. He didn't have that, so a paper check it would be. Then he'd go to the bank in town without a driver's license and beg them to cash it for him. Such a little thing, an expired license, to cause him so much trouble.

"Sure," he said, smoothing his features and nodding in agreement, like he'd be the happiest guy on the planet to work out in the hot sun, scything grass, getting heat stroke again.

This time, Leland wouldn't care enough to rescue him, so he'd have to look out for himself. Take those breaks. Drink the water. Wear his hat. The one Leland had given him and said looked good on him. Feeling gears shifting in his head, small bits of lightning jumping in his belly, Jamie sat up. "When?" he asked. "When does Jasper need me?"

"After breakfast," said Clay. "He'll really appreciate the help. But— are you okay?"

When he'd bumped into Clay the night before, he'd told Clay he was leaving. Now, though, he'd signed up for work that would keep him around.

"I'm fine," he said. "I'll work today, pick up my check tomorrow. It's all good."

With that, Jamie got up, bussed his tray, grabbed his straw hat from the peg along the wall, and headed down the road and along the path around a small hill to where Jasper's cabin was.

Jasper had a pretty good setup, though Jamie didn't really know why he was off by himself. Maybe because he was grumpy, which he sure was when Jamie knocked on his front door. Jasper came out of his workshop, a small building to the side of the cabin, wiping his hands on a cloth and frowning at Jamie like he'd interrupted him in some great and dangerous experiment.

"Here," he said, pointing to the scythe leaning up against the wall of the shed. "Need you to cut the grass along the creek."

Jasper went back into his shed, leaving Jamie blinking, standing there holding the scythe like some sort of newbie grim reaper who hasn't been handed his hooded black cloak yet. But he went to work, going down to the creek, eyeing the long rows of grasses, which had grown tall in such a short while, green-tinged from the recent rain.

It was a big job, and it occurred to Jamie to wonder why they didn't just get a weed whacker or something. But maybe that would be too noisy. What did it matter to him, anyway? He wasn't likely to be sticking around long enough to put his stupid suggestion in the suggestion box.

He scythed that grass for a good hour before Jasper came out with water and wordlessly handed it to Jamie. Jamie tipped his hat back, and took large swallows of the water, breathing in the fresh, newly cut grass smells rising in the warm air all around him.

He'd never smelled a place as nice as this. Never felt this way, his shoulders sore from the work, knowing he'd had another hour or so of work and then he could have lunch in a nice, clean dining room. Maybe he was the lowest guy on the totem pole, but he wouldn't be forever if he stuck around.

But that would mean having to deal with Leland and all those feelings that were swirling around inside of him, making him want to crumple in a small ball, hiding in the grass like a newborn faun. Which he was not, and nobody was coming to save him.

He put the empty bottle on a rock so he could recycle it later, and started swinging at the grass, all the while ignoring the ache in his heart. Swing, scythe, lift, step up.

Over and over, he did this, focusing on the way his arms hurt, and not on how much he longed to go back to that moment, the two of them riding double up the main road of the ranch. The two of them working together, painting that shed. The two of them in Leland's bed, their skins warm, Jamie's heart racing when Leland kissed him.

The ranch had given him such a sense of belonging, of purpose. Something he'd not felt since he'd been at community college. But even then, he had never imagined his life might look like this, that cutting long grasses with a completely outdated and heavy farm tool would give him such a sense of satisfaction as he stepped back, his arm on the rake, and looked at his progress.

"You might be a chain maker," said a voice from behind him.

Leland.

Jamie turned around, holding the scythe in front of him like a barrier, a weapon of very small destruction.

Leland was so strong and so tall, he could have taken the scythe away from Jamie in a heartbeat. But he didn't. He didn't come any closer, just stood amidst freshly cut grass, sprinkles of grass blades on his dark blue jeans.

He held his hat in his hands and let the sunshine beat down on him. He was such a stickler for avoiding sunburn that Jamie was worried about him getting one, and yeah, his cheeks were pink. Jamie had no idea what he was doing there, so he leaned harder on the rake and just looked at him.

"A chain maker," Leland said in that quiet, patient tone Jamie had grown so fond of, on account of Leland was so handsome when he was like this, plus Jamie knew he was on the edge of learning something new. "Is someone who likes to work and to see the results of that work spreading out like a long chain behind them."

"Like painting a building," Jamie said before he could stop himself. He visualized it quite hard, just then, him and Leland over at the rebuild of John Henton's cabin, stepping back and measuring their progress with their eyes. And then, in tandem, looking at each other and smiling. "I guess you're one, too," he said, again almost without any free will at all.

"That I am," Leland said.

Leland looked down at his hat, where he swirled it around and around, one fist inside the crown, his strong fingers along the brim. Then he looked at Jamie, his grey-blue eyes perfectly serious, kind of like the first time Jamie'd seen him, when he'd been appraising Jamie up and down and finding nothing he saw he could approve of.

But it was different this time. He didn't look away, didn't frown and wave Jamie away. No, he took a step closer, his boots crunching in the grass, and then he stopped.

"I'd like to ask if you'd want to take care of that driver's license and bank account today."

"Today?" Jamie asked, feeling stupid. But there Leland was, plain as day, with answers to two things Jamie needed to take care of. "Why would you do that?"

"Because I said I would," said Leland, quite steadily. "And because you can't get a bank account without some form of ID, and you can't get that ID without some form of proof of residence. I'm here to help you with both. Thought we'd drive into Chugwater today."

Chugwater was thirty miles away. It was almost lunchtime.

"I need to eat first," Jamie said, lifting his chin in a way that he hoped showed that none of this was affecting him. He lifted his chin so far that the sun was in his eyes, and he had to squint to see.

"Thought we'd get lunch," Leland said in his quiet way.

He put his hat on, and Jamie noticed he was wearing a blue plaid shirt that made his eyes even more grey. And new blue jeans, so new, the color snapped in the sunlight. He was so handsome, standing there, so broad-shouldered. Why not go with him and let him help? Then later Jamie would have the memory of their last day together to take away with him.

"Okay," he said.

His mind raced ahead, refusing to land on any one thought, any one image. All of them were of Leland, the two of them in Leland's shiny F150 Ford, barreling down a country highway with the windows down, the sun glinting off Leland's smile. Which was stupid, way stupid, but Jamie couldn't seem to stop himself.

"Maybe change," Leland said, quite carefully, as though he was avoiding stepping on Jamie's toes somehow. "Get cleaned up for the ID photo."

"Okay," Jamie said again, and then, like he was somebody he wanted Leland to respect, pointed his thumb at the last uncut swath of grass. "But I've got to finish this."

"I'll finish," Leland said, reaching out to take the scythe from Jamie. "You get cleaned up and I'll meet you by the supply barn in twenty minutes."

They were so close. Leland put his hat on, took the scythe from Jamie, and they were so close, he could see the tension in Leland's jaw, see the pulse beneath the muscle in his neck. Smell the soap from his shower, the scent of his hair. The warmth of him was all around, and Jamie wanted to bawl like a kid for not having any of that anymore. For losing him with no hope of ever getting him back.

"I'm on it," Jamie said, trying to make sure Leland didn't know what he was feeling.

But Leland knew. Jamie saw it in his eyes as his fingers curled around the thickest part of the handle of the scythe. And just before Jamie let go, their fingers brushed.

Jamie jerked back like Leland'd just asked him to hold hands, but really, his hand felt alive, like a million volts of lightning had gone into his body and jerked him awake from being dead.

This man had made such a difference in his life. It was going to kill Jamie to walk away from him, but he would. Leland didn't want Jamie around, that much was plain to see. If he was keeping his promise to Jamie to help him with the paperwork, then that's just the kind of man he was, and no indication that he wanted Jamie to stick around.

Besides, Leland was helping him get his driver's license so he could leave. Right? That's what he was doing, Jamie was sure of it.

Leland had the scythe. Jamie turned on his heel and waded through cut grass, and marched across the dirt road to the staff quarters. He would shower and shave, the fastest he'd ever done it, and be there at the supply barn before Leland. And in no way was he sprucing himself up for Leland, no way.

It was all about the license, and that was it. The license was his freedom from the ranch. His ticket out. And Leland was going to help him get it, even if Jamie wasn't sure he wanted what it represented anymore.

29

LELAND

The drive to Chugwater usually took about half an hour, if Leland went fast, which he usually did. With Jamie in the truck, he drove a little slower, enjoying Jamie being there sharing the drive, enjoying how he sat with his elbow in the open window, leaning slightly towards the open sky, smiling in the sun.

Leland guided the truck along the two-lane paved road, slowing down along the stretch where it was all gravel and scrub, and then sped up along the small paved rise to Chugwater. Everything was beautiful in the sunshine, the grasses damp-green from the rain shifting in the low breeze, rising the grass-scent in the air, the blue sky overhead. It was a gift, all of it.

None of this he deserved to be enjoying, but he was enjoying it all just the same, along with the memories of moments that felt like he'd stolen them from their rightful owner. As though what he and Jamie had shared between them had been borrowed, and he'd casually returned everything, every word, every glance, every touch, every caress, every kiss—only to feel the ache of loss churning into a downward spin of regret. By the time he pulled into the parking lot of the DMV in Chugwater and got out of the truck, he was sweating along the back of his neck, fretting like he had no more sense than a newly haltered colt.

Jamie followed Leland into the small, air-conditioned office, cautious, sticking behind Leland, as though he imagined they would throw him out, first chance they got. They walked up to the counter together, the only people in the small, linoleum-floored lobby.

"Pull out your license, Jamie," Leland said, just to get the process started.

Jamie showed the clerk his old license. She tipped down her head and looked at him over the rims of her stern black eyeglasses and glared at him.

"This is expired, young man," she said, her tone derisive.

"He works for me, at Farthingdale Ranch," said Leland, as calmly as he could. It was easy to see she would have turned Jamie away, for sure, had Leland not been there. "He needs a new driver's license. Please make it happen."

The clerk must have known Leland would not stand for any nonsense or delay, for she processed Jamie's paperwork right away. Jamie looked handsome in his blue chambray shirt, and a little pleased, a smile playing around his eyes when she took his picture.

Leland wanted to ask her for a copy of the picture that he could keep for himself and moon over in his own time, long after Jamie was gone. Helping Jamie with this, and with the bank account, was going to make it easier for Jamie to leave, but it was important he be able to do what he wanted, important that he not feel beholden to the ranch or that he was stuck there with no way out.

Jamie tucked his crisp new driver's license in his beat-up canvas wallet, and even though Leland wanted to take him shopping to get a new leather one, he resisted the impulse. It was one thing supplying Jamie with boots and gear, courtesy of the ranch, but there was no way Leland wanted Jamie to feel beholden to *him*.

After that was done, Leland drove them both to the small local bank. Standing nearby, he watched as Jamie filled out the paperwork and handed over a fistful of money that he pulled from his pocket and laid on the counter. As the bank teller counted out the bills, it didn't look like Jamie had spent any of it.

"You can access that money from anywhere, now," Leland said, pleased as Jamie flashed him his new debit card before stuffing that in his old wallet, as well.

"Yes, thank you," said Jamie. It looked like he wanted to say something after that, but he only shook his head, and together they got into the truck in the nearly empty parking lot.

For a moment, they sat there, even as Leland started the truck and let it idle. The windows were open, and a pleasant breeze was coming through the truck cab, stirring Jamie's hair, the warm air bringing a flush to his cheeks.

"Should we get some lunch?" Leland asked, keeping his hands on his own thighs rather than reaching out for Jamie.

"Shouldn't we get back?" Jamie asked. "Won't they miss us?"

"They know where we've gone," Leland said. And then waited as they both sat there, doing his best to figure out what to say to make this right. To ask without asking if Jamie would stay, rather than leave. Or maybe he should ask, say it right out loud.

In the silence that fell between them, Jamie took a breath, long and slow, like he was gearing himself up for something big.

"I wouldn't have told anyone," Jamie said, almost whispering. "About us. Not a word."

"I never made you promise that," Leland said as softly as he could, heartbroken that Jamie would think that was the problem. "Besides, they all know anyhow, as I wasn't very discrete. I should have taken more care. With you, I mean."

"But you took care, *good* care, of me." Jamie turned to look at Leland, his green eyes big and shining, his dark curly hair tumbling around his head in the soft breeze that came through the open truck windows. "You taught me so many things. I never felt more cared for than when I was with you."

"You gave me—" Leland had to stop, his heart aching at the thought that he'd hurt Jamie, that Jamie felt this way and still thought good things about Leland, even though Leland had treated him badly.

"You gave me everything. Showed me a way to look at the ranch, at my life, with new eyes." Leland's eyes grew hot, and he curled and uncurled his fingers against his bejeaned thighs just to keep himself from reaching out for Jamie.

"Then why did you want me to go?" asked Jamie, his chin up like he expected Leland would deliver the very worst news in the world. "It's like you didn't want me anymore after you had what you wanted."

Jamie's words stung all the more because they weren't true. He hadn't planned what had happened, but he'd hurt Jamie, and it was his fault, all of this. He deserved to know that the pain in Jamie's eyes, the tears that were about to fall, were his fault. His and his alone.

Clay had said to pull that stick out of his ass and, upon occasion, definitely more than once, Bill had said the same thing. Leland wanted to do that, very much so. His thoughts, tender and gentle, about taking Jamie to get his driver's license so he could get a bank account so he could access his money from wherever he went, had led them to this moment. Where they were sitting inside the hot cab of a shiny truck, the sun glinting off the chrome fittings, each looking at the other, neither of saying what was in their hearts.

There were things he wanted to say, needed to say. And, by the look of him, Jamie did, too. One of them had to go first. It had to be Leland.

"I shouldn't have come on to you like I did," Leland said, leaning forward, his arms on the steering wheel, fingers laced together like he was about to confess to a priest. "But you drew me—"

"You drew *me*," said Jamie, the words hard for all he looked so vulnerable, hair tumbling around his temples. "But you're making it sound like it was my fault, when you're the one who kept coming by. You're the one who asked me to go deliver salt blocks with you, and you're the one who asked me to paint John Henton's cabin with you. You're the one who asked me to *dance*. Why would you do that if you didn't like me?"

Leland could hear the bitter sorrow in those questions, see the tender quiver of Jamie's lower lip.

"You asked me to your cabin," said Jamie, almost whispering, as though it was a secret between them. "And you—and *we*—" He stopped to take a breath. "I've never been in love with anybody before, but I guess even I would know better than to lead someone on like that."

"I didn't lead you on." Leland's chest caved in at the sound of those words, at what Jamie felt. That Jamie *loved* him. He leaned back and, glancing over at Jamie, drew his thumb along his mouth, remembering the feel of his mouth, the sweetness between them. "I would never do that, but I didn't want you on the ranch, to start with."

"No, you sure didn't." Jamie's eyes snapped dark green as he pushed the tumble of hair away from his face.

"But once you were there, it was as though—" Leland paused. He was saying everything wrong when he needed to make everything right. He took a deep breath, summoning up his courage as he kept in the very forefront of his mind how it felt to be with Jamie. "I always have looked at the ranch as being a special place. You looked around you like you were seeing it the same way I did. Then you started fitting into all those empty places I hadn't known were empty. That's why I asked you to run errands with me. That's why I asked you to dance."

"You can't just do what you want, even if you are the boss," Jamie said, his face flushed.

"That was exactly the problem," Leland said quickly. "Or at least as I saw it. Only it isn't a problem. Not if I—not if *we* don't want it to be."

Jamie's expression when he looked at Leland was one of confusion, even though the last thing he wanted to do was confuse Jamie or unsettle him. Yet, that's exactly what he'd done in his clumsy way. His heart was just not used to asking for what it wanted this way.

"My problem is that, as a boss, I have a rule about fraternizing with employees. It means—"

"I know what it means," Jamie said, sounding like he was tearing at the words with his teeth. Then he shook his head and scraped his hair out of his eyes. "It's a rule. You have a lot of rules, you know."

"Yes, it's a rule, and yes, I know," Leland said. He took his hat off and laid it on his knee and looked out the window and blew out a long breath, trying to ease the tension in his chest. "It has been pointed out by a friend of mine that this rule might be getting in the way of something sweet, something *good*—"

Again Leland stopped, feeling his breath stutter in his throat, the words about to bounce off his tongue in uncontrollable leaps. When he looked at Jamie once more, he thought of all the dreams, liquid in moonlight, of cowboy poetry and long sunset rides, which his heart had always told him was too much to say aloud in the bright light of day. But they needed to be said. He needed to say them. So he would say them. Out loud. Right then and there.

"You brought feelings into my life that I didn't know I wanted or needed," Leland said, as simply as he could. "And maybe you need that, too. Maybe you need the same things. Only I don't know because we never really talked about it. And we should, only I'm so damn bad at it." Leland scraped his hand through his hair, frustration at his own inadequacies rising up inside of him.

"I can quit the ranch, then we can be together," said Jamie, as if it were just that simple. "Fire me. You won't be my boss then, so we can be together, if that's how the rule works."

"Jamie." Leland's heart banged in his chest, and suddenly it was too hot in the truck's cab, too confined.

"Just let me be with you and I can get a different job." Rising up, Jamie was closer now, close enough that Leland could see the reflection in Jamie's eyes of the sunlight bouncing off the chrome fittings of the truck. See the hard flush to Jamie's cheeks. Sense his breath beating so rapidly in his chest. Sense the hope. "I can work at the Rusty Nail. Anywhere. I don't care. I just want to be with you."

What Jamie deserved was the best Leland could give him. What he did not deserve was to be jerked around based on Leland's pole-up-his-ass notions of how things should work.

What Leland needed to do was step up and handle how he felt without relying on the idea that they could only be together if his job and Jamie's job weren't connected. They *were* connected. Every task that everyone on the ranch did was connected, from Bill, the owner, right on down to Jamie, the new guy, scything in the fields and picking up the odd end jobs that nobody else had time for.

Jamie stepped onto the ranch and into Leland's life, making changes he didn't know he was making. But maybe they needed to be made. Maybe Leland needed to let them be made, or rather, maybe *he* needed to make them. He sure as hell didn't want to let go of the way Jamie had made him feel, like he used to before Laurie Quinn had gone missing and nearly ruined the ranch, like he could look up from the work from time to time and enjoy the world around him.

He wanted to look into Jamie's eyes and see happiness blazing from him, from every pore, every minute of every day. That's what he wanted.

"I'm not going to fire you," Leland said, plopping his hat on his head a little harder than necessary. "I don't need to fire you for us to be together. What I need to do is fix it in my head—"

Leland stopped, almost bruised by his own hesitation. He turned to look at Jamie, really look at him, at the patient way he was waiting for Leland to fumble through his own self, his own doubts. Like he was waiting for Leland to get to where he had gotten to long ago. Where what they had between them was easy and natural and right. The drifter was teaching him, the foreman, this time.

"You can go if you want, you know," Leland said, because it needed to be said. Or did it? "You have a bank account now—"

"With a thousand dollars in it," Jamie said, a wry smile flickering in his eyes. "Plus my pay on Saturday."

"A thousand can turn into more, after a season on the ranch," Leland said. Then he shook his head. He was a practical man, but in this moment, he needed to push that part of him away and say what was in his heart. Say the exact thing that would get Jamie to stay. Which was, "I'd like you to stay. I *want* you to stay. Stay on the ranch and find what suits you, work wise. As for you and me, I'd like to—I'd like to court you, do it slow. Do it properly, this time."

"Court me?" Jamie asked with a sweet, small laugh under his breath. "You're an old-fashioned cowboy, that's what you are."

"Yes, I am," he said, feeling a smile on his face. He wasn't ashamed of it, but had never really admitted it to himself before. "I've got an old-fashioned heart, and it wants to court you. Will you stay on the ranch and let me?"

"You know," said Jamie. There was a small pause as he looked down and picked cottonseed fluff from the knee of his jeans. Then he looked up at Leland, and his eyes were so very green, as green as a moss-covered rock in a cool summer pond. His smile was shy. "I kept looking for you, hoping you'd ask me like you did. Kept going to the barn to see if you were there. Kept an eye out for you in the dining hall. Walked slow in case you were nearby. I was always looking. Hoping you'd find me."

"I did find you," said Leland, chuffing out a hard-fought breath. "I'm glad I found you, despite my own foolishness."

"Me too."

Slowly, slowly, so Jamie wouldn't get spooked, Leland leaned close. And then, even more slowly, doing his best to be gentle, he reached and cupped the back of Jamie's neck, pulling him near. Twining his fingers in Jamie's wild hair. Jamie leaned forward in response, willingly, closing his eyes as Leland kissed him.

Their lips met like soft, silken promises, and Leland sighed into the kiss, feeling regret at the time he'd wasted, feeling joy bubbling up in his chest at the promise in that kiss that they gave to each other.

When he felt Jamie smile, he pulled back, brushing his thumb along Jamie's cheek.

"Is that all right?" he asked, and though he was unsure why he asked it, he knew when Jamie nodded that he asked because he needed to know for sure that Jamie was okay. That the two of them were going to be okay. That the two of them were going to be together.

"You're a good kisser," said Jamie, completely without guile.

"Yeah?" asked Leland, pleasure flooding through him.

"Probably the best ever, though I've not kissed a lot of guys, you know—"

Now adorably shy, Jamie tangled his hands in his hair, so Leland pulled him close and kissed his neck and inhaled the scent of him, and sighed. Jamie, in return, tried to climb into Leland's lap, which was fine with Leland, except that the bank teller was walking across the parking lot, looking through the open window of the truck like she'd stumbled on a peep show.

"She's going to tell us to get a room soon," said Leland, half under his breath as he smiled into Jamie's hair.

"Maybe we should," said Jamie, sitting back in his seat with a laugh as though Leland had suggested something quite daring.

"What we should do is get some lunch." Warmed through with feelings of happiness that had been missing for too long, Leland started the truck and drove out of the bank's parking lot.

On instinct, on autopilot, he drove past the Stampede Saloon and Eatery, where he'd been planning to take Jamie, and instead drove down Lone Tree Road to the edge of town to the farm where his mom lived.

It wasn't much of a farm anymore, really, not since the dry years, but it had a nice two-story brick farmhouse on the edge of ten acres of land that abutted Chugwater Creek. Most times the fields went green with wild alfalfa, and some years, Mom planted clover and turnips for local cattle feed. This year Leland didn't know what she'd planted, only that she was out in the front yard waving her apron at him like she knew they'd been on their way.

"Who's that?" asked Jamie as he half-leaned out the window.

"My mom," Leland said, pulling into the circular driveway. Along with all the other happiness he found, it did his heart good to see her smiling face, the same thick silver braid over her shoulder, flour stains on her apron.

"Your *mom?*" The question came out a squeak, and Leland could see the worry in Jamie's eyes. Would she like him? Would he measure up? Why had he brought him here?

"The truck kind of knows the way," Leland said as he put the truck in park and turned off the engine, pleased that this was how the day was turning out when it had started out so sorrowfully, with the idea that Jamie would soon be leaving the ranch. "Besides, if I'm going to court you, then you two need to meet."

Mom came up to the driver's side and held Leland's face and kissed him, like she'd not seen him in ages instead of just a week.

"You've got such good timing," she said. "C'mon in, I'll make you some lunch. Who's this? Bring your friend. I've got a fresh strawberry-rhubarb cooling in the pie window."

"We don't want to bother you," said Leland, mostly for form's sake, though he put his hat on the seat next to him, which meant that they were staying. "We could easily go to the Stampede and have lunch there."

"Nonsense," said Mom. "Their food is for tourists, and I've got plenty."

The two of them, walking not-quite hand in hand but almost, followed his mom into the cool shade of the front porch and through the old wooden screen door. The house smelled like sugar and honey and strawberries, and a breeze came through the back screen door. He followed his nose to the kitchen, and looked back to make sure of Jamie, who was practically tiptoeing behind him.

"It's okay," Leland said, slowing so Jamie could catch up with him and they could enter the kitchen together. "I think you'll like my mom."

"But will she like me?" asked Jamie, his eyes full of questions as he peered through the open doorway to the kitchen where Mom was already busy pulling items out of the fridge.

"Yes," Leland said, feeling shy, though he knew this was the right next step. "I'm sure of it."

30

JAMIE

*L*eland's mom, Mrs. Tate, had grey-blue eyes like he did, was tall like he was. She had wrinkles around her smiling eyes, but she carried herself like Leland did, all straight and strong, and her arms and face were tanned, like she worked outside a lot. Looking at her was a little like looking at Leland, only with curves and a soft bosom and ample hips.

"Hey, Mom," said Leland, kissing her on the cheek as they came into the kitchen. "This is Jamie. He's our newest ranch hand, so I thought I'd bring him over so you could meet him."

"How do, Jamie," said Mrs. Tate. She wiped her hands on her apron, and though she looked him up and down, her eyes were kind. "It's nice to meet you."

"It's nice to meet you, Mrs. Tate," said Jamie.

"It's Ginny," she said. "No need to stand on formality in my kitchen. Now, you boys wash up and sit down."

It was easy for Jamie to do as he was told. Easy to sit at the big farmhouse table in the middle of that large, airy kitchen with the sun shining through the windows while Ginny was busy at the stove, cooking bacon. Easy to look at Leland, who sat across the table from him.

"Here you boys go," said Ginny as she slid a BLT sandwich in front of each of them. "Those tomatoes are from the store, rather than my garden, but they're still pretty good."

"Thanks, Mom," said Leland, chewing with his mouth full.

"Thank you, Mrs—I mean, thank you, Ginny." Jamie drank a huge gulp from the glass of milk she set in front of him, and nodded at Leland to show him how good the sandwich was. "This is fantastic."

"Don't tell Levi," said Leland. He smiled as he took another bite of his sandwich. By the relaxed way he sat in his chair, it was easy to see how much at home he was.

"I won't tell him," said Ginny. "But I will tell you this. I've had that lasagna of his and it could use more garlic, for sure."

"He can't cook that spicy on account of all the different guests, Mom," said Leland. "He's cooking for almost fifty people each week."

"He used to cook for a hundred people before that dang fool of a guest up and disappeared." Ginny wiped her hands on a towel and leaned back against the farm sink, her arms across her chest. "And the police still don't have a clue."

"It's a cold case now, Mom," said Leland. He took a drink from his iced tea. "Besides, I'm sure Quinn didn't do it on purpose."

"That's not what you said at the end of last season," said Ginny. "You had quite the string of words to describe him then."

"C'mon, Mom," said Leland. He gestured to Jamie as Ginny brought out several slices of strawberry-rhubarb pie and sat down next to Jamie to join them. "You're going to give Jamie the wrong idea about me."

"I'm sure he's got the exact right idea." Ginny smiled as she ate a forkful of pie. "You fellows look any harder at each other, well. You might as well be holding hands across the table." She laughed at their reactions and patted Jamie on the arm. "Don't mind me, Jamie. But what you don't know is that Leland has never brought anyone home before. So you'll have to excuse my assumptions."

A small silence fell in the bright kitchen as Jamie and Leland looked at each other.

Jamie's mom and dad, with icy hearts, had turned their back on him when he admitted to them he liked boys, and he had no real experience being that honest with anyone else. That is, until he met Leland, who, when Jamie had admitted he was gay, had turned around and been honest right back. And now, in Ginny's kitchen, it seemed the same was happening all over again, except Jamie had no idea what to say.

"We're still new, Mom," said Leland, looking at Jamie with affection blazing in his grey-blue eyes, a smile curving his mouth. "So be gentle with us, would you?"

"Of course I will," she said to him, reaching out across the table to touch his hand with hers. Then she looked at Jamie, her eyes full of stars. "I just like to see a young man with a healthy appetite."

Jamie looked up, his mouth full of pie. He felt flushed, uncertain what Leland would make of his mom paying him so much attention, but both of them laughed like it was an old joke between them.

"I cook for one these days, Jamie," she told him as she got up and gathered their empty plates. "So it does me good to cook for more."

"Jamie and I will come every week, Mom," Leland said. "I just don't like putting you to any trouble."

"It's no trouble," she said. Her back was turned to them as she rinsed off plates and cutlery in the sink and set them to one side. "I like the company, is all."

"Mom."

Leland got up and went to her, wrapping his arms around her, giving her a hug and a kiss on the cheek. Her hand came up to press his face to hers, and though Jamie was seeing this all without seeing their expressions, his throat grew tight. That was how a mom acted who loved her son, who loved and accepted him for who he was.

"C'mon now, son, let me finish this up."

Leland stepped away, and Ginny turned around, patting the corners of her eyes. When she saw Jamie sitting there, she smiled.

"You've got such wide green eyes, Jamie," said Ginny, the fondness in her voice folding around Jamie like a warm blanket. "And I know many a girl who would die for that hair."

"I might cut it," said Jamie, shifting under this glow of attention.

"No," said Leland, then he stopped himself with the force of a Mack truck slamming on the brakes. "I mean, if you want to cut it, of course it's your hair. But I kind of like it—dang." With a rough hand he rubbed the back of his neck, as though worried about Jamie's reaction to this information.

"Then I'll keep it, if you like it." Feeling warm all over at having an audience, even a nice one, for such a declaration to Leland, Jamie shifted in his seat.

"All that hair barely fits under his hat," said Leland, smiling to lessen the tease. "A hat which he forgot today."

"I wouldn't talk," said Ginny, teasing Leland in her turn. "You're the one who always leaves his shirt off when working outdoors, and now you have permanent freckles on those shoulders."

Again they laughed, bringing up in Jamie small bubbles of joy, of happiness. When Leland looked at him, his mouth open as he laughed, his face was bright and his grey-blue eyes were full of light. As the laughter turned to warm smiles, Jamie remembered those freckles from when they'd painted John Henton's cabin, and how he'd wanted to kiss them. Now, he would get that chance.

Leland winked at him, as though he knew what Jamie was thinking, and Ginny smiled, though she couldn't possibly know. But what if she could guess? Horrified that his wayward thoughts might be plainly seen, Jamie scrubbed his face and got up, pushing his chair in.

"We should get back, Mom," said Leland, giving Ginny another hug and a kiss. "I'll mention the amount of garlic to Levi."

"He'll know I'm right," said Ginny. "Now, you boys want some pie to take with you?"

"Yes, please," said Jamie.

She wrapped a whole pie in plastic wrap and then in aluminum foil before handing it to Jamie.

"Thank you, ma'am," he said, then when she arched her eyebrow at him, he amended this to, "Thank you, Ginny."

"Leland, you store that in your fridge, but make sure to share with Jamie."

"Yes, ma'am," said Leland, tapping his forehead in a mock salute.

"You boys get along, now," she said. "I'll have chicken pot pie for next week; you just let me know when works best."

"Mom, you don't have to—just tell us what day works for *you*." Leland kissed her and gestured to Jamie that they needed to get going.

"Friday afternoons, just like this," said Ginny. "Now scoot."

"I'll call you in a few days, Mom," Leland said. "And if the roof leaks, call the neighbor boy, don't go up there yourself. You hear?"

"Sure, sure," she said, laughing, waving at them to go as they walked back through the house and through the screen door to the porch.

Even with the windows open, the interior of the truck had gotten hot while the truck had sat in the sun, so Leland started the truck while Jamie tucked the pie carefully on the floor.

Leland blasted the AC while they waited a bit, cool air pushing the hot air out the open windows. He picked up his hat and turned it in his hands, a gesture that said he was thinking.

Jamie stayed patient and waited, knowing Leland'd have something to say that, at this point, might be something he wanted to hear. Then he realized Leland had been sitting there without putting the truck into drive for a good long time. That hat just kept spinning around and around, and his head was bowed.

Leland was such a proud man. Jamie liked it when his head was up, shoulders back, ready to face the world, and so searched his mind to find a way to soothe Leland, to distract him, at least.

"Leland?" he asked. "Is everything okay? I think your mom liked me. Do you think she did?"

"I did everything backwards," Leland said, with a hard sigh.

"Backwards?"

"You know." He shook his head and very carefully put his hat on the dash as though he wanted to stare it into submission. "I took you to my bed. Then I introduced you to my mom. And now I want to court you. And I will, once I untangle this mess in my head. I did everything all backwards. Should have done it frontwards, like everybody else."

"Well, let it be backwards. You're not everybody else," Jamie said. "And I wouldn't want you to be."

Leland was obviously still beating himself up about the way it had gone between them. Which wasn't right. Maybe Jamie was too stunned by how quickly his plan to leave had turned into meeting Leland's mom. And maybe he was still a little heartsore and hand-shy, but he needed to be clear to Leland how he felt. To make certain Leland knew he wanted to be with Leland, not just at the ranch, and while they worked, but in bed, too. And he needed to do that right now.

"Leland," Jamie said.

"Yes?" he asked, looking at Jamie as though he might have the answers to all the questions in his head. Well, Jamie didn't and Leland probably didn't either. But he could make certain Leland knew how he felt.

Scooting to the edge of his seat, he slid off, and bent his knees so he could slip in front of the large, black steering wheel and straddle Leland's lap, like he'd wanted to do in the bank's parking lot.

Leland made a gasping sound, and even though Jamie landed as lightly as he could, Leland's thighs quivered beneath him.

It felt all kinds of wonderful to slide into that spot where his thighs could grip Leland's hips like he was riding a horse. To slip his arms around Leland's neck and bury his face in the warm curve of Leland's shoulder. Smell his salt-sweat, kiss the thrumming of his heartbeat just below his skin. To tuck their groins together. To hug Leland with his whole body.

Jamie sighed as Leland's arms came around his waist, holding him tight, firm, strong, and still. Just like Jamie liked it, like Leland was trying to absorb Jamie into his skin, into the center of him.

Leland's sigh echoed Jamie's, long and low and sweet. Then he kissed the side of Jamie's head and cupped his bottom in the palm of his broad hand. He was all around Jamie now, his breath, his warmth, the solid feel of him. Everywhere, everywhere.

"So is that a yes?" Leland asked, whispering in Jamie's hair.

"That's a yes, you can court me," Jamie said, whispering back, not hiding his smile. "I don't care for flowers, but I like chocolate. No coconut. And let me go riding with you sometimes, okay? That's what I'd call a courtship." Not that he had any true idea of how a courtship worked, but all of this sounded pretty good to him. "And for you?" Jamie asked Leland softly, kissing his ear. "What do you want?"

"For you to be with me," Leland said, simply. "For us to work side by side. For us to take that horse ride, and then after, we can sit on my porch and share a root beer in the moonlight."

"Moonlight?" Jamie asked, sitting back, looking Leland up and down. His hands curled on Leland's shoulders and then ran down his muscular arms. "There's poetry beneath those grey-blue eyes of yours, Leland."

"Cowboy poetry," Leland said with a firm nod, though Jamie could see it scared him a little to admit this. While Jamie had no idea what cowboy poetry even was, if Leland wanted to recite it to him, he was going to let him. "And I'll do my best not to get too bossy."

"Don't worry, I won't let you," Jamie said, though it was a sure bet he'd do anything Leland ever asked him to do, any time he asked.

"We can't drive like this," Leland said, kissing Jamie on the mouth, his hands on Jamie's hips.

"No?" Jamie asked, teasing.

"It's dangerous," Leland said, firm. "I might get distracted. You need to buckle up."

Jamie smiled at the idea of how dangerously distracted Leland might become with Jamie on his lap in a truck going sixty miles an hour, but he obediently slithered off Leland's lap. Buckling himself in his own seat, he lifted the well-wrapped strawberry-rhubarb pie to his lap, his arms carefully around it.

Leland drove them back to the ranch at a fast clip, kicking up dust and cruising those back roads like someone who'd done it all of his life. He had one eye on the road and one eye on Jamie, appraising him in that way he had, but now what Jamie saw reflected in those eyes was a glow of acceptance.

They were going to try, the two of them. As to where it might lead,

Jamie had no idea. Only that, in that moment, he felt about as good as he ever had. Safe. Wanted.

At the ranch, three people came up to Leland the moment he parked the truck and got out, dragging his attention away from Jamie and onto his job. Which left Jamie with the responsibility of what to do with the pie.

Getting out of the truck, he took the pie to his room and put it on top of the dresser. Then he changed into a grubby shirt and went back out to see where he could help out.

At the back of the dining hall, Levi needed him to help carry in some bags of ice from the delivery truck, as the ice machine was still broken. Then Brody needed him to help groom half a dozen horses in the barn, as the guests that had just ridden had no desire to get dirty, but hurried off to clean up for dinner and the dancing later.

Jamie was busy right until the dinner bell and barely had time to get cleaned up before the guests rushed in. The dining hall was lively and bustling with activity as he got his tray and sat at a table with some ranch hands. And of course he scanned the dining hall for Leland again, but this time it felt comfortable and right. He didn't need to hide what he was doing anymore.

Leland was at a table with some guests, saw Jamie, and waved. Jamie waved back and smiled, feeling like a kid in high school who has just made friends with the most popular kid for miles, even if he couldn't always sit with him.

"You two make up?" asked Clay, nudging Jamie with his elbow as he sat down with his tray next to Jamie.

"What?" Jamie asked, putting off answering by taking a very large swallow of his iced tea.

"Yeah, you know what I'm talking about," said Clay, nodding, those dimples firmly in place as he chewed and smiled at the same time. "Who made the first move, him or you?"

"He did," Jamie said, not hiding this, though he had to struggle not to squirm in his seat. It all felt still so new between him and Leland. "Though I don't think I should talk about it at all."

"Actually, you can and you should," Clay said, nodding. "There's no need to hide what you and Leland have. We're all on this ranch together for months at a time. And maybe nobody knows what Jasper gets up to in that cabin off all by itself, but as for everybody else? Yeah, you catch a cold and everybody knows. You forget to tie a shoelace, and we all laugh, but then we help you tie it before you trip. Get it?"

"I guess so," Jamie said as he looked over to the table toward the front where Leland was talking and laughing with guests.

He'd never been courted before, but he needed to learn to share Leland with others. Leland had a big job, running the ranch, and lots of obligations on his time. It had been that way before Jamie had shown up and it would be that way after—except the *after* might include him, now. He shivered, doubts clamoring for attention inside of him. It was almost as scary to be wanted as it was to be on his own.

"If he hurts you, I'll kick his ass," said Clay, conversationally as if they were talking about something else altogether.

"Nobody kicks him," Jamie said, though he knew what Clay was trying to get at. He and Leland were in the courtship phase, and he knew, just knew, that Leland would turn himself inside out to avoid hurting Jamie.

Jamie had a sudden vision of Leland standing below his window, throwing light pebbles at it to get him to open the window and sneak out, like one of those old black and white movies they used to make.

Only he wouldn't have to sneak. Leland would let Jamie know when and where, and Jamie would come down those stairs, two at a time. Or maybe Leland would knock at his door and he would come out. All kinds of dreamy scenes whirled around in his head as he ate his dinner.

If he kept smiling like he was, then it wouldn't only be Clay making observations and sharing his opinion, it would be everybody else who worked on the ranch. Could Jamie handle it, being part of such a big family? He had no idea, but he guessed he was going to find out.

31

LELAND

On Friday night after dinner was through, Leland sought Jamie out near the dining hall, looking at every face beneath the twinkling fairy lights for the one he wanted. Jamie. He wanted Jamie.

Guests were chatting and laughing as they danced and swirled and stomped in enthusiastic lines, excited about it being their last night, drawing out the moment, as if they longed to rearrange their entire lives and stay on the ranch forever.

Leland found Jamie up near the porch where the band was playing. Jamie was helping Levi with the ice, pouring it from plastic bags bought at the grocery store into the barrel. Leland cursed under his breath. He needed to follow up on the issues the ice maker was having, and he had some harsh words to share with that repairman. The last thing he wanted was extra and unnecessary work for his staff.

When Jamie saw Leland coming up, he stopped dumping the ice and smiled.

Jamie was sweating beneath his arms from the work on this warm night, and damp curls of hair were sticking to his temples. He never looked so sweet, and never so much did Leland want to carry him off.

But they'd made promises to each other about courtship, and Leland wanted to take it slow.

"Working hard, I see," Leland said, taking his hat off.

"Yeah," Jamie said, taking a piece of ice and putting it between his teeth to crunch loudly.

"Would you care to dance with me?" Leland asked, ducking his head. He had meant to say the words so that only Jamie could hear him, but Levi was smirking when he walked off with the empty ice bags. "In the next couple's dance?"

This stopped Jamie, and Leland drank in the surprise and pleasure sweep that swept over him, but maybe he saw a little worry, as well, on that sweet face.

Leland's heart jumped in a painful way to think back on how he'd hurt Jamie. He didn't want Jamie to doubt him, and if he did, even just a little, Leland was going to double down on making sure Jamie knew just how much Leland cared about him.

All of this swept over him. He took a step forward. Then Jamie took a step forward. And it was as if the guests faded away, leaving only the two of them on the edge of that dance floor with jaunty music in the background as Leland reached out and Jamie took his hand.

"The very next couple's dance," Jamie said. "But remember, I don't know how."

"You're a fine dancer," Leland said. "I'll do my best to lead, and maybe next winter, we could take lessons."

"In Chugwater?" Jamie asked, his eyebrows going up. "With your mom?"

"Yes," Leland said with no hesitation whatsoever. "It's fun. It's a good winter activity, when—" Leland stopped and looked down and realized that he was turning his hat like he was nervous and didn't know what to say. And while both were true, he was a man, fully grown and needed to stem those nerves. Needed to say what was in his heart. "I would love to dance with you this winter," he said.

Jamie's smile streamed from his eyes, and Leland didn't let go of his hand. Jamie didn't let go of Leland's hand either, and when the dance leader came out and announced it was a couple's dance, Leland led Jamie onto the dance floor.

Jamie's body fit into Leland's arms as though he'd been designed for them, as though they, in their separate lives, had been waiting for just this moment, for when the music started and the band began to play. They swirled and circled on that dance floor, in step and sometimes in misstep, when Leland would step on Jamie's toe by accident, or Jamie would bump into another dancer.

Leland gathered Jamie close after each mishap, and reset their hands, and they would begin again, over and over, as many times as it took. And all the while the music swept around them like a bright and jaunty cape, seeming to separate them from the other dancers within a bubble all their own.

And all the while, Leland held Jamie's hand and circled Jaimie's waist, and looked into those bright green eyes, and though he felt he was falling, he was perfectly safe. He could see into Jamie's soul, and Jamie could see into his soul. It was as though this moment had been destined to be, forever and forever.

Leland kissed Jamie then, right then, as they stood on the dance floor. Paused a brief moment to stop their motion and kiss *his* Jamie, his eyes closing while he savored Jamie's nearness.

Jamie tipped up on his toes, his hands going around Leland's neck, and whispered in his ear. "This is so nice, so nice."

Such a simple thing to hear at a dance on a ranch, the dance floor only dust, the band rushing the notes from time to time. But it was perfect to Leland, and he loved the feel of Jamie against him, so brave and bold, and didn't care who was watching.

That's who Jamie was, a brave soul, the bravest. To have come all this way without knowing what was at the end of his journey. Well, the end of that journey was them, Leland and Jamie, together.

And as Leland swirled them back into the dance, pleasure and delight seemed to stream from his fingertips and his skin and everywhere. And in return, Jamie's eyes were like green jewels in a beautiful wine-dark sea. It made Leland's heart explode in his chest and he tipped his head back and sighed and laughed, up to the sky, now filled with stars abounding beyond the twinkling fairy lights around the dance floor.

When the dance ended, the guests lingered or left, chatting and hugging as the staff cleaned up and the band packed up. The dance announcer wished everyone goodnight as the fairy lights turned off one by one.

"Thought I might walk you back and pick up that pie to put it in the fridge," said Leland.

As they walked off the dance floor together, him and Jamie, Leland nodded at the staff and guests, at everyone in general, so they would understand that he saw them, but that he was going to spend some time with Jamie now. Except when Levi came up with a broken gear in his hands, Leland paused to respond with a quick suggestion, and when Brody came up with a question about when bags of feed grain were set to arrive, he had to pause again and check the calendar in his head. After that, he determined that everyone would have to manage on their own, or get someone else to help them.

"Let's go, Jamie," he said.

"Okay." Jamie wiped his damp hands on his jeans, and Leland's eyes were drawn to those slender hips, and the dust on his shirt, and everything about him.

They walked back, side by side, not quite holding hands, but close enough so their shoulders brushed. It wasn't too far to the staff quarters, and he followed as Jamie led the way up the steps to his room. There, Jamie paused, looking up at Leland like he expected something from him. And while Leland had soft and honeyed words just waiting in the wings, he was too breathless, his heart was beating too fast, to say any of them out loud.

"Let me just kiss you good night," Leland said. "I'll take the pie and go."

"Is this the courtship part?" Jamie asked, his eyes bright.

"Yes," Leland said.

"It's mighty slow."

"It needs to be."

Then Jamie did what he did best. He slid right past Leland's

266

defenses and into his arms, pressing against him with his whole body, his arms around Leland's neck, drawing him down for a kiss.

Someone came up the stairs, but Leland didn't care, didn't care. He wrapped his arms around Jamie, a sound coming from his throat as he held Jamie close, kissed his neck. Pushed back his hair and kissed his forehead, and finally, Jamie, impatient, kissed Leland on the mouth, letting them both savor it, the anticipation and the sweet taste of each other.

This was how it should have started, but if Leland drew back and said anything about it, Jamie would tell him they might have gone backwards, the two of them, and so what? They were starting at the beginning, two new lovers, kissing in the hallway of the staff quarters as though they could never bear to be parted from one another.

"There," Jamie said when he finished kissing Leland. He pulled back a little bit and with Leland's arms still around him, touched his mouth with the backs of his fingers. "Now that's what I call courtship."

Jamie filled Leland with everything as they stood there, with light and energy and love. Leland's cock was hard against his belly, and he could feel that Jamie was worked up as they stood there hip to hip. But the anticipation would make it all the sweeter.

Leland wanted to know Jamie more, find out who he was, find out what he wanted, what he needed, and then give it to him with his whole heart. The sudden tumble into Leland's bed hadn't been right, not for either of them, but he was grateful Jamie was going to give him a second chance.

"I'll take that pie now," Leland said, letting Jamie go at long last.

"Come and get it," Jamie said with a laugh as he opened the door. "See what I said there? Come and get it?"

Smiling, Leland grabbed the pie from Jamie's dresser, kissed him on the mouth, and paused to push the hair back from Jamie's forehead.

"See you tomorrow," Leland said, tenderness rising all the way through him.

"Tomorrow," said Jamie. As he stood in his open doorway, Leland kissed him again, then hurried away as fast as he could, before his instincts, now screaming at him, made him cave in and roll with Jamie on his bed right that minute.

Outside, the night was dark and breezy, and Leland went through the shadowy trees along the path to his cabin, feeling chipper and relaxed and happy all the way through. He put the pie in the fridge, took a quick shower, then sat on the front porch in one of the Adirondack chairs and looked at the other one, which was empty. It might have seemed innocent to anyone else that his greatest joy would be to see Jamie sitting in that chair while the two of them watched the sun go down together. But it was true, and he wouldn't be ashamed to admit it to anyone who asked.

In the morning, Leland barely had enough time to eat before things got hopping, but then Saturdays were always busy, with guests packing up to leave, hugging new friends goodbye. Staff did their best to help guests get on the road, and Maddy kept the exodus running smoothly, clipboard in hand.

Leland had a list of things that needed fixing and tending to, starting with the ice machine, so he didn't have a chance to be with Jamie all day. Feeling like a thwarted teenager, he threw himself into what needed doing, including the ice machine and the call to the repairman who seemed reluctant to come all the way from Chugwater on a Saturday.

"You didn't fix it right the last time, so you owe me a visit, I'd say," said Leland, his voice firm as he held the cellphone to his ear and thrummed his fingers on his desk.

"But it's Saturday," said the repairman like a petulant child.

"That's just too bad," Leland said, looking at the barn through the open door to his office. "I've got ranch hands and wranglers and all kinds of staff who like ice in their drinks. I've had guests who've had to ration their ice while they've been here, and that just won't fly, you understand? I've got a new set of guests arriving starting tomorrow noon, and if that ice maker isn't fixed, I will find another repairman. Pronto."

Threats weren't normally his style, but the ice machine, all things considered, was pretty important. All the different parts of the ranch were important, truth be told, each a part of a larger weaving. But that was one thing taken care of, so he put the phone in his back pocket, and threw himself into helping guests get on their way.

He carried luggage and hugged everyone goodbye who wanted a hug, and told them all they were welcome back, any time. When it was Dorothy's turn, she stood in the parking lot while a van stood nearby, its engine idling, waiting for her to slide into one of the seats.

"It was a pleasure having you with us," said Leland. He held her hand in his, and looked at her to make sure she knew he meant it. "I hope you enjoyed Travelle, too. Hope you had a good time, I truly do."

"I did," she said, and her smile was warm as she smiled at him. Her eyes were bright, and her skin not so pale with sorrow. "I wanted to thank Jamie in particular, but I don't see him."

"He's—" Leland stopped. Normally he didn't call particular ranch hands off the job to say goodbye to a guest, but this was different. He pulled out his phone. "Hang on," he told her. "Can the van wait?" he asked her. He looked up at the van's driver. "Can you wait?"

The van driver nodded, and Leland swooped through his contacts to call Clay who, luckily, answered on the first ring.

"Hey, it's Leland," he said.

"What's up, boss?" asked Clay. "Is it about the bags of grain? Cause they haven't arrived yet."

"No, it's about Jamie," Leland said. "I need him to come say goodbye to Dorothy. She's waiting. Can someone scoot him down here?"

"Sure, boss."

Clay clicked off before Leland could thank him, and he turned to Dorothy.

"He'll be here in a minute," he told her.

"That's good because—" her voice broke off and she blinked fast, and seemed to be focusing on the ripples of bright water on Horse Creek in order not to let her emotions get the best of her. "Jamie helped me so much."

"I'm glad to hear it," said Leland. "Here he comes."

In a cloud of dust, Clay drove the F150 into the parking lot, swirling to a stop, applying more than enough brake to make a grand entrance. Jamie hopped out, his hair in its usual disarray beneath his straw hat, his shirtsleeves rolled up, grime spattering the front of his t-shirt.

Clearly he'd been hard at work, and even more clear than that was the fact he'd responded to Leland's request as if it was of the utmost urgency. Which it was. For some reason, Dorothy's plight had affected Leland in ways he couldn't rightly explain. And as for Jamie, Dorothy had turned to him in her hour of need. And now here Jamie was, a smile on his face, eyes bright.

"Hey, Dorothy," Jamie said, coming right up to her. "That your van? Are you heading out?"

"Yes, I am," she said. "And I wanted to thank you for everything you did for me. I don't know how I could have managed as well this week without you."

"You did good," Jamie said. "And you were very brave."

"I didn't feel brave," she said, a worried expression curving her mouth down. "Especially on that trail ride—"

"You *were* brave," said Jamie. "And you handled Travelle just right. I could tell she felt confident you were her rider."

"Really?" asked Dorothy. Her dark eyes looked sad again, and Leland imagined he knew she was thinking about her husband.

"Sure," said Jamie. "First time I got on a horse, I nearly fell off the other side. You were much better than me when I first started."

"You think so?" she asked. Now her smile came back, and her cheeks were pink with pleasure.

"I know so."

Jamie's confidence in her perked her up as much as praise from Leland might have done. Somehow, coming from Jamie, the words meant more to her, had the power to convince her she'd done well.

"Here," she said, digging in her purse, which was slung over her shoulder. Pulling her hand from her purse, she held out three twenty-dollar bills. "I want you to have this."

"Oh." Jamie paused, flicked a look at Leland, then shook his head.

"We're not supposed to take tips," he said. "And anyway, I'd be handing this over to Maddy, and it'd go in the kitty for the end-of-the-year party we have for staff. I wouldn't be keeping it."

"Well, in that case." Dorothy reached into her purse and pulled out more twenty-dollar bills and placed all the money in Jamie's palm, using a gentle hand to curl his fingers around the bills. "Please take it," she said. "I want you all to have a wonderful party."

Jamie was looking at Leland, so he nodded, and Jamie took the money and handed it to Leland. Then, all on his own, he reached to hug Dorothy, and she hugged him right back, and for a minute they were still, hugging each other, and Leland realized, with some worry, that Dorothy was crying.

"Don't be sad, Dorothy," said Jamie, almost whispering. "You can come back next year and ride Travelle again. She'll be waiting for you."

"We'll all be waiting for you," said Leland. The van driver was looking impatient, and it was time for Dorothy to head out or she'd miss her flight. Moments like this, where guests and staff connected so hard, were some of the best parts of his job, but also the hardest. Emotions ran high when it was time for goodbye, but seeing this now, between Jamie and Dorothy, was a kind of gift.

"Thank you again, Jamie," said Dorothy, pulling back. Taking a tissue from her purse, she scrubbed at her eyes with it and did her best to smile. "This was the best vacation I've ever had, and I owe it to you and Mr. Tate here."

"Leland, ma'am," he said. "Please call me Leland."

"Thank you, Leland," she said, and with that, she boarded the van, the van driver slid the door shut, got in, and drove away in a small cloud of dust.

"Is it always that sad, saying goodbye?" Jamie looked up at him, his eyes bright.

"Sometimes," said Leland. "But even if it's sad, it's good. You know?"

"Yeah." Jamie sighed and looked at Clay, who was waiting in the truck, doors open. "Well, I better get back at it. See you later?"

"Yes, later," said Leland. He bumped his shoulder against Jamie's and watched him get in the truck, watched Clay drive off in an even bigger cloud of dust than the one he'd arrived in, and sighed.

When the last guest had departed, he went to the back of the dining hall and poured a bucket of cold water over his head and went outside to bid the repairman hello when he arrived. The ice machine was fixed and churning out ice in under an hour.

He headed up to the barn where he and Bill and Maddy had a quick meeting about other repairs that needed doing. Levi joined them to discuss the wholesale ordering of potatoes from a fellow up in Idaho, rather than going through the local supermarket chain, and everyone approved. It was the way Leland liked to do things, letting people come up with ideas so everybody had a shared responsibility in the running of the ranch.

Out of the corner of his eye, as Leland stood on the front porch of the office building, he saw Jamie trundling past with a wheelbarrow loaded with hay. Though his shirtsleeves were rolled up, his hat was properly on, hands gloved, and he looked adorably efficient as Leland's eyes tracked him as Jamie went up the hill to the supply barn, where the compost bins were. Maybe the hay came from a horse trailer, or maybe something else, he didn't know. What he knew was that Jamie was working hard and not taking advantage of the fact that the two of them were an item.

"Huh," said Bill. When Leland looked at him, Bill gave him a gentle slap on the shoulder, which Leland took as approval about the relationship between him and Jamie, which was nice to get.

A full hour before dinner, when all the staff would gather in the dining hall for a well-earned break of eating on their own without having to worry about guests and their needs, Leland stopped and went back to his little cabin.

There, he took a shower and shaved slowly and carefully, shaved again, then smacked his cheeks with cologne, and called himself all kinds of a fool as he looked at himself in the steam-fogged mirror. And maybe he was a fool, a fool of a foreman who had fallen for a drifter. And there wasn't anything he wanted to change about that.

When he arrived at the dining hall, neatly dressed, clean and spruce, everything had a relaxed air, with no guests to wait on or impress. Staff and leads mingled at tables and chatted, trays in hand, while all around the good smells of chili and cornbread floated in the air.

Leland got himself a tray and heaped on food on his plate, thinking only too late about chili stains and such, and went over to where Clay and Brody and Quint were already sitting, elbows out as they plowed into their food.

"Look at you," said Clay with a grin. "All dressed up, even though there's no dance tonight."

"No dance tonight," said Brody, shaking his head with a sorrowful air.

Quint just grunted and kept on eating.

"Never you mind," Leland said, not minding the teasing about him being gussied up like a lovesick fool.

He put his tray on the table and looked around the dining hall, and when his eyes focused on Jamie, and Jamie saw him, he waved Jamie over. Yes, he'd just invited Jamie to sit with him and his leads. Jamie belonged at Leland's side.

If Jamie wanted to sit with the other ranch hands, or wherever he wanted to be, that was fine, too. But Leland was pleased, just the same, when Jamie's smile brightened and he hurried over to the table. When Jamie got close, his eyes widened as he took in Leland's appearance.

"You look nice," Jamie said. "Should I have cleaned up?"

"You're fine," Leland said. "You're fine just the way you are."

They sat side-by-side, their elbows touching, and as they ate, the conversation resumed around them. Leland shared the details about the ice maker fiasco, and Levi talked more about the quality of potatoes he was expecting to get from their new supplier. Quint brought up adventure riding yet again, and while Leland didn't shoot him down, he cautioned Quint as to the reputation of the ranch, should someone get hurt.

"What's adventure riding again?" asked Jamie, leaning close, keeping his voice low.

273

"Where you ride to more rugged places, and do a bit of survival type camping overnight," Leland said, leaning close right back.

"Would someone like Dorothy like something like that?" Jamie shook his head even as he was asking this.

"No, she wouldn't, and I don't think most guests would," Leland said. "But people have ideas, good ones, and everybody deserves to be heard."

They ate their dinners, and Leland loved every minute having Jamie right there, and considered himself the luckiest man on Earth.

JAMIE

$\mathcal{I}$t only took Jamie a minute of eating his dinner while sitting next to Leland before the feeling of being at the cool kids' table, and maybe doing something he shouldn't, wore off. He had worked with both Brody and Clay before, of course, and besides they seemed so casual about him being there, very casual about the fact that he'd been invited by Leland himself. Jamie had sat with Leland before, but that time he'd invited himself. This time, it was different.

The conversation moved around him, paused, and then started up again. He was just happy to be there, at Leland's side, their shoulders brushing, the heat of Leland's body soaking into his.

Leland smelled nice, and when he spoke, his voice rumbled from his chest. When he leaned, it was toward Jamie, to catch Jamie's eye, to check on him, to make sure he was okay—all of this Jamie read in those grey-blue eyes, the curve of Leland's smile.

"Looks like you got a bit of a sunburn," Jamie said, seeing the pink in Leland's freshly shaved cheeks.

"Dunked my head in water, didn't put my hat back on." Leland shook his head at his own foolishness. "But I was distracted at the thought of something—of someone—else."

When Leland looked at him, Jamie became the focus of his attention, all of it. Jamie put his hand on Leland's thigh, bold as anything, and petted it, long and slow. In that moment, it felt like they were alone together, like it had felt at the dance. This was all new to him, all bright and sweet and good, and he wanted to roll in it, over and over, with Leland in his arms, with him in Leland's arms, until they became dizzy with it.

"You fellows ought to get a room," said Quint from where he was concentrating on his chili.

"You can mind your own business," said Leland, the words tart.

Brody and Clay chuckled and poked at each other with their elbows. Leland was blushing, hot under his collar, and Jamie could tell he was uncomfortable.

"You leave him alone," Jamie said, tart in his own way.

Leland didn't deserve to be teased, but when he looked at Jamie and smiled, Jamie could tell he didn't really mind, it was all part of the gentle play between him and the people he worked with. And all at once Jamie wanted to take Leland in his arms and kiss him everywhere he could, just because he could.

"We can move the courtship along, now," Jamie said, low, ducking his head to look up at Leland. Who was so tall, just so tall. Jamie loved the warmth that moved through him at the thought of being in bed with Leland and not having to hide or hurry off afterwards. He imagined their legs tangled beneath the sheets, the silky feel of Leland's skin beneath his palms. Leland's breath stirring his hair.

Leland paused, his fork in front of his mouth, and Jamie knew, right then and there, that Leland was holding himself back for Jamie's benefit. And while Jamie was new to this old-fashioned courtship, new to being with another man, he was not such a tender butterfly as all that. He wanted to be with Leland. Right now. His head was dizzy with wanting Leland, and he had to adjust himself in his jeans as he waited to lower his fork and respond.

"Sure," Leland said, a blush creeping along his neck like a sweet pink scarf. "You finished?"

"Yes," Jamie said. He stood up and pushed back his chair so loudly that all eyes were upon him. Yes, everyone in the dining hall was looking at him, and looking at Leland as he stood up, too. But rather than anything else, the only expressions he saw were smiles, hundreds of them, it felt like, as though, any minute, everybody was going to burst out with applause. "Let's go."

Leland nodded and Jamie followed him up to the bussing area. After, Leland wrapped his arm around Jamie's waist and scooted them both out of the dining hall, as though he'd been holding himself back all this while. It was nice to be wanted. Nice to be treated with such care. Jamie wasn't used to it, but he liked it.

By some unspoken agreement, perhaps as they kissed beneath the sweet-scented pine trees, still warm as the evening grew cool, they came to Leland's little foreman cottage. Inside the front door, with all the lights off, the only light came through the windows from the front porch, Jamie started unbuttoning the pearl-snap buttons on Leland's shirt, shadows and light, his fingers quick, insistent. As Leland undid Jamie's regular buttons, he seemed fumble-fingered, and maybe nervous, so Jamie put his hands on Leland's, and held Leland's hands pressed to his chest.

"It's fine," Jamie said. "Whatever it is, it's fine. I'm okay. I want to be here with you."

Leland kissed him then, long and slow, his mouth on Jamie's feeling like devotion and want, all rolled up together. And yes, a little like he was holding himself back still. So Jamie undid the rest of Leland's buttons and spread his shirt wide and bent close to suck on the curve of Leland's chest and run his hands across his naked ribs and bring Leland into the light of joy that he'd brought to Jamie, simply by coming on horseback to get him and taking him back to the ranch.

It was the job, but it was more than that. It was Leland's acceptance and his strength in everything he did. Drove Jamie wild, somehow, and he undid the button on Leland's jeans and unbuckled his belt, and pushed back the cloth so he could cup Leland's hips where they poked above the waistline of his jeans.

Leland made a sound, a low grunt of surprise, like Jamie had just given him everything he wanted, only he'd never known how to ask for it. It did something to Jamie's heart to think of him like that, wanting and never asking.

Jamie wanted to give everything to Leland, whatever he wanted, and while it might take some time to find out what all that was, Jamie knew something he liked, something he could do right then. He climbed up Leland's body and hooked his legs around Leland's waist and buried his head in the curve of Leland's neck and held on. Like Leland was the only thing worth holding onto, the thing Jamie loved best.

Leland's skin was warm beneath Jamie's cheek, and when Leland's arms enfolded him, Jamie was flooded with the feeling of being safe, of being held as Leland carried him into the bedroom. There, Leland placed him on the bed as though Jamie were made of bone china, and loomed in the darkness as he took off the rest of his clothes. Jamie stripped off the rest of his clothes and dragged Leland down to him so they could lie together, skin to skin, their hearts beating hard, Leland's breath on Jamie's cheek.

"I like the way you court," Jamie said, so there would be no doubt in Leland's mind that Jamie wanted this, wanted what they were doing. "We're both naked now. You gonna kiss me, or what?"

"I'll do my damnedest," Leland said, his voice breathy and low, rumbling up from his chest like a growl, like he'd just let loose the wild wolf inside of him.

He rolled to Jamie, and took Jamie in his arms, half covering him with his body as he kissed and then kissed Jamie again, leaving him breathless. Leland's thighs were dense upon Jamie's thighs, the bulk of Leland's body pressing him into the mattress, his knee sliding up to press Jamie's thighs apart. Silky warm in the half-darkness, skin on skin, Leland's breath came in shudders as he kissed Jamie, on the mouth, on his cheek, sweet kisses on his neck.

Leland never asked what Jamie liked, not out loud, but with his fingers, the palms of his hands, he learned. It was as though he was reading Jamie in the half-dark, sighing with Jamie's sighs, kissing him there behind his ear, again and then again.

When Leland's hand curled around the base of Jamie's cock, whisper-light at first, then tight and firm, Leland's breath stuttered against his chest as though he was staggering with want. Then he kissed Jamie's belly and kissed lower down, teasing his fingers through the wiry hair between his legs, and finally, with a gasp, took Jamie's cock in his mouth so lovingly and slowly that his hips jerked to get it in that mouth, that round, warm sucking space.

While Leland sucked and teased, his mouth warm, he pressed his palm between Jamie's legs, snugging his balls upward so he could stop to lick them, and suck and pull a little bit, all with a constant rhythm, a determined rhythm.

Small sounds echoed that rhythm in the half-dark, and Jamie knew those sounds were coming out of his mouth and he couldn't seem to stop them. It wasn't long before his belly sank to his spine, and his hips rolled as he clasped Leland's shoulders, half lifting off the bed as he came in Leland's mouth. Feeling as though Leland had released all his inner demons, taking them in, banishing them.

As Jamie fell back on the bed, Leland moved up, covering him with his whole body, elbows on either side of his head, a protective cave where he left small, warm kisses on Jamie's closed eyes. He sweetly kissed Jamie's mouth, and sighed, really, really deeply, like he'd come to some treasured, secret place after having searched for it so long. Jamie blinked and opened his eyes and clasped Leland's face.

"I'm here," he said, whispering, tender. "I'm here, Leland."

With a shudder, Leland buried his face in Jamie's neck, and rolled off, and pulled Jamie to him.

As they settled in the curve of each other's bodies, their breathing slowed, always in sync, and the warm night drifted around them. From an open window came cool breezes from Iron Mountain, and the faraway, lonely, high-pitched howl of coyotes. Jamie had never really heard coyotes before coming to the ranch, but he knew that's what they must be.

"Coyotes?" Jamie asked.

"Yes," Leland said, his fingers trailing through Jamie's hair, tangling in it. "They're crying for the moon."

Jamie's throat ached at the thought of it, of wild things crying for something they could never have. And how rough Leland's voice had been when he'd said that, as if he, too, had been crying for something he could never have. Did he have it now? Could Jamie give it to him? What did he want?

All these things and more, Jamie wanted to know so he could carve a place for Leland in his heart, hold Leland in his arms, and make him feel safe, the way he had held Jamie and made him feel safe.

With a low sound in his throat, Jamie sat up and shifted, swinging his leg over Leland's hips like he was riding him, loving the idea of it, Leland the horse, Jamie the rider. Jamie with Leland's reins in his hands, guiding him.

Jamie could see the surprise in Leland's face, and the delight in his eyes, in that half-light where the front porch light made long shadows inside the cabin. He clasped Jamie's hips and settled him upon him, and Jamie scooted down his thighs and took Leland's cock in his hands, delighting in the heft of him, the heat of his shaft, even as the long hairs on Leland's thighs tickled against his balls.

It was a wonderful, sliding feeling as he rocked back and forth, finding his place on Leland, curling and uncurling his fingers around Leland's cock. Leland lifted his chin as though he was concentrating on all the feelings, Jamie's movements, his hands, eyes half-closing to absorb the motion of Jamie rocking his hips and urging him on as he stroked Leland's cock, slowly, slowly, lightly, lightly.

Jamie loved Leland's shudders and his sighs, loved the way he licked his lower lip as though his mouth was dry from panting. He could see the gleam of sweat along Leland's neck, tendons tightening, and he slithered down and took Leland in his mouth, the tender, round tip of him, licking his long shaft, leaving a silver of moisture behind as he did this over and over, absorbed in him, his scent, the heat of passion building within him.

He loved the trembles in Leland's belly and the soft cries he made, and never in his life had he been so connected like this, with every move, every sound, all the heat and the salt. He was so focused he almost missed it when Leland came between his fingers, almost invisible white spurts on his belly that Jamie licked and licked like a cat until Leland weakly protested, and hooked his hands under Jamie's arms and pulled him up, all the way up, on top of him, and kissed him firmly on the mouth.

"Will you be my blanket?" Leland asked.

"Yes," Jamie said.

Jamie pulled the sheet up to cover them both, never letting go of Leland. He stayed curled on top of Leland like a young thing who has found a safe hollow in the snow in a bad storm. He was warm all the way through, and content and sleepy, and loved the weight of Leland's arm across his waist.

Then he slid into the curve of Leland's waist, one leg over Leland's legs, possessing him in the dark. He belonged to Jamie, now, and Jamie to him. Each to the other.

Jamie's breath slowed, and Leland's breath slowed, and Jamie trailed his fingers in Leland's hair, that short, duck-edged fair hair of his, and smiled to himself.

"Busy day tomorrow," said Leland, the sleep plain in his voice. Jamie knew that meant Leland thought they should fall asleep so they could be rested and ready for Sunday, when guests started arriving.

"Don't you ever get a day off?" Jamie asked, sleepy and low.

"You're my day off," Leland said in response, turning to kiss him, wherever that kiss might land.

"I want to be your every day," Jamie said, hearing the demand in his own voice.

"You are my every day," Leland said, the words rumbling from his chest. "You are my always."

Jamie curled his arm around Leland's neck, but gently, and tucked his head down, brushing his forehead against Leland's shoulder. And finally fell asleep, as though he'd been waiting for that moment all of his life.

33

JAMIE

*J*n the morning, Leland was up with the sun, but of course he was. He reached for his phone the second it started buzzing, and was sitting on the edge of the bed, the sheet wrapped around his hips before Jamie was fully awake. He curled around Leland's back and kissed the curve of his bottom, and sighed, still sleepy, blinking at the sunshine that came through the parting in the curtains.

"I'm on it, Bill," said Leland. Then he listened for another long moment and nodded as though Bill could see him. "No, I agree, we shouldn't leave it there, though they could have called yesterday, when I was in Chugwater."

Leland clicked off the phone and slid his hand along Jamie's legs, petting him. Making sure of him.

"I've got a quick errand to run, and, of course, guests will start arriving at noon," Leland said. "The post office delivered the official paperwork for our ex-con program to the Dairy Queen in Chugwater, if you can imagine that."

Pulling himself around Leland, Jamie kissed his hip loudly, and laughed when Leland looked down, eyebrows raised, as though shocked to find Jamie there.

"Will you move in with me, do you think?" Leland asked, trailing his fingers along Jamie's shoulder, tracing the line on Jamie's skin of lace-like patterns of light and shadow as they came through the curtains.

"This is all so sudden, Leland," Jamie said, pulling the sheet close, like he was a shocked, sweet thing. Which he was, in a way.

The sound of Leland laughing as he tossed his head back filled Jamie's heart, and when Leland gently cupped the back of Jamie's head and leaned sideways to kiss him soundly, he smiled against Leland's mouth, almost purring.

"I've got to shower and go so I can be in place before the guests arrive," Leland said.

When he stood up, Jamie stood up, too, and wondered if he'd be shy about showering together. Standing next to Leland, he was a full head shorter and skinny. Leland had so many muscles, all long and wonderful, and Jamie felt puny.

When Leland looked at him, he must have understood his scowl for what it was because he picked Jamie up and bodily carried him into the bathroom, put him down, and then turned on the shower. The shower stall was a regular sized one, not luxurious, but there was room for both of them, if they got cozy, and plenty of hot water and soap. Together, they showered, and then shared the small mirror and shaved, playful and laughing.

It was only when Leland had gotten dressed and left, the keys to his truck jangling in his hand, that Jamie realized he'd been left in the little cabin all alone. This would not have happened only a short while ago, so Jamie dressed quickly and carefully shut the front door, and strutted to the dining hall, whistling under his breath.

The morning air was cool and still, as though the day was full of its own expectations, just as Jamie was, because he'd never had this happen to him. Where a strong man, a good man, swept him off his feet and offered to share himself. Feeling very much the cock-of-the-walk as he entered the quiet dining hall, at the same time, he didn't want to make an announcement of it to anyone. Though, as they looked at him, and Clay waved him over, it was easy to see that every-body already knew.

"Wow," said Clay as Jamie put his tray down next to Clay's and sat down. "That was fast."

"I lured him," Jamie said jauntily, though that wasn't true either. He hadn't drawn Leland or lured him and still, just the same, they'd spent the night together. Showered together. None of this was anything he wanted to share with Clay or anyone just then, as it was still new, sifting through his brain like a gentle snowfall, melting where it touched, being absorbed, bit by bit.

"Sure you did," said Clay, as though he could read Jamie's mind. Jamie smiled when Clay smiled at him, enjoying his dimples and casual, confident air.

"What all needs doing today?" Jamie asked as he dug into his eggs and bacon, feeling very much the responsible man.

"Meeting at the dining hall at eight," he said. "And probably checking the cabins are ready, carrying luggage, that kind of stuff."

Jamie nodded and finished his breakfast, enjoying being part of the weekly rhythm of the ranch more than he had words to express. After he bussed his tray, he went out into the bright, sunshiny morning, and stood in front of the dining hall porch, wishing he'd stopped off to get his straw hat so he didn't have to squint as he listened to Maddy and Quint as they went over the assignments for the day. And felt a bit smug because when Quint asked where Leland was, Jamie was the one who knew.

"He had to run to Chugwater for some paperwork," Jamie said, and though his voice sounded to him like he was uncertain, everybody nodded.

"Thanks, Jamie," Quint said. He consulted his clipboard and Maddy's clipboard, and then announced the end of the meeting, then released them all to their work.

Jamie helped wherever he could. He ran to fetch missing trash liners for the trash cans, did a last-minute sweep of the dining hall porch, did a walk-around looking for trash. And then, finally, he waved at Leland from across the parking lot as he pulled up in front of the ranch office in a cloud of dust. Jamie watched Leland march inside with an envelope in his hand, and then come out, not smiling, shaking his head as if in dismay at the lack of communication from the Chugwater Dairy Queen.

Then the cars and buses started arriving in the gravel parking lot, and Jamie got caught up in helping guests carry their luggage, answering their questions as best he could, and though he felt like he could do more for them, the guests seemed happy to be there. Jamie watched them relax as they opened the doors to their cabins and took deep lungfuls of fresh mountain air, and considered himself lucky to have taken that bus to the middle of nowhere.

It got busy and Jamie ran errands and carried messages, helping in the corral as guests excitedly met the horses, then fetched a bandage for a little girl who had hurt her finger, and all kinds of things. He threw himself into the day, sweating under his arms, and was just about worn out by the time dinner came.

He hardly saw Leland, and missed him more than he thought he would. But they had to figure out a way between the two of them to make this work and do their jobs. The job was the thing, and Jamie felt puffed up with pride that he was a working man as he ate his dinner with Clay and the others, and was a part of that. Part of the team. Part of the ranch family.

It was during a small lull in the general conversation between the ranch hands at the table that Clay leaned over to Jamie.

"Leland wants you to meet him by the barn after dinner," he said.

"By the barn?" Jamie asked, trying to think of what else might need doing.

"Don't forget your hat," said Clay. "And your cowboy boots."

"Okay," Jamie said, somewhat mystified.

Jamie went back to his room to get his hat, then changed into a clean shirt, his fingers brushing against the black leather jacket hanging in the closet. He'd last worn it what felt like a lifetime ago. It didn't suit him now, too snake-like, and he made a note to get rid of it or donate it.

He looked at himself in the mirror, at the reflection of himself in his hat and snap-button shirt. This was who he was now, this was who he wanted to be.

Leland had never had Jamie meet him anywhere, so as he slid on his cowboy boots, the ones with the stacked heel and pointed toes, he tried to figure it out. It was his body that finally told him as he pulled his jean cuffs over the boots and straightened up. They were going on a ride together. Leland was going to share his private time with Jamie.

Whether they would ride double, or each on their own horse, it didn't matter, not one bit. They were going to ride together while the sun set, and share the glory of it, and add to the pile of good memories that were now so many they all blended together inside of Jamie in one big happy cloud of joy.

Briskly, he made his way down the steps of the staff quarters, and along the dirt path to the barn. There, in the glow of early evening, Leland, standing tall, waited for him. And he stopped, his whole body absorbing what he saw before him.

Leland's head was tipped forward, his expression hidden by his hat. He had two horses saddled, a tall, bright red horse, and Dusty. Dusty was for Jamie, as he'd already ridden him, and the long legged red horse was for Leland.

As Jamie came up to Leland, he lifted his head and smiled at him, his grey-blue eyes bright beneath the brim of his hat. He'd changed his shirt to the blue one Jamie loved, and he smiled when he saw Jamie'd changed his shirt, too. It was as though they'd both gotten gussied up for a date, just like two lovebirds newly met.

These poetical thoughts whirled in Jamie's head. Leland had given him so much, and now he'd given him poetry as well. Just by wanting to be near him, Leland had shown him his heart, and for joy it was all Jamie could do not to shout with joy. Jamie rushed up to Leland and hugged him tight and pressed his cheek against Leland's heart.

"Thank you for asking me," Jamie said into the folds of Leland's shirt. "Thank you."

"Nobody else, Jamie," Leland said. He ducked down and took off Jamie's hat and kissed the top of his head, then replaced the hat as though to seal the kiss in. "Some days, I'll still like to go by my lonesome, so I hope that's okay. But sometimes, it'll be you and me."

"Of *course* it's okay," Jamie said stoutly, digging his chin into Leland's chest as he looked up at him. "Wouldn't want to be attached at the hip like that anyhow."

Truth was, Jamie had never wanted to be attached to anyone as much as he wanted to be attached to Leland, but this was who he was. Leland was a guy who liked to go riding by himself and have his thoughts, and Jamie needed to let him.

Leland slid his hand to Jamie's hip, and ducked low to kiss him on the mouth, and it staggered Jamie to be loved so much that he had to hook his hands in Leland's belt and just hang on as they kissed. Then Leland patted Jamie's bottom, quite gently, and helped him mount Dusty, and then mounted the red horse, whirling to pull the reins as the horse's hooves danced in the dust.

"This is Big Red," Leland said. "Big Red likes to run, and on account of that, he's only good for experienced riders. He needs to learn to slow down some, but we'll let him stretch his legs today. What do you say? Dusty can keep up, I think."

"Sure," Jamie said. His one lesson had been in the ring, but he'd gone on that trail ride, too. Dusty was gentle enough, and he trusted Leland to know whether he could handle the ride.

They clucked their horses into going and headed up the long dirt road that led to the gate, where beyond stretched wild grasses and the horses, grazing freely. Leland had Jamie practice opening the gate from horseback, but he was hopeless at it and climbed down to open it and let them through. Then he closed the gate behind him, mounted Dusty, and pulled him up gently and beamed with pride. Maybe to another ranch hand it wouldn't be much, what he'd just done, but it was a big deal to him.

Leland smiled, and then they rode, two abreast along the dirt path that led up to the edge of the valley. There they paused, the wind ruffling the horses' mane and tails, and Jamie took a deep breath, all of a sudden, like his body wanted to absorb the sweeping view before him.

The sun was going down behind Iron Mountain to the west, and the silver shards of dark mixed with the bright yellow sun streaming through the ridge. Below them, the green grasses swirled around and around in the breeze as though stirred by an unseen hand. Cool air mixed with warm and Jamie looked at Leland.

"We'll walk 'em down this slope," Leland said, pointing. "This is how we do it when we take guests out on the trail. We teach them to walk a horse downhill always, unless there's an emergency. Be gentle with them going uphill, as well. Across the flats, yes, let them run."

Leland clicked to Big Red, and led the way down the slope. Jamie held Dusty's reins loosely and balanced himself with a hand on the saddle horn, feeling like he was a real ranch hand now that he got to go riding with Leland.

At the bottom of the slope, Leland looked at Jamie and nodded, and Jamie nodded back. Then Leland clicked to Big Red again, pressed the horse's side with his heels, and off Big Red went like a shot.

Dusty followed at what felt like a full gallop, but he was slower than Big Red and couldn't keep up. So Jamie let him go at his own pace, and laughed as he saw Big Red sweep up a hillside, his long legs eating up the distance from where he'd been to the top of the next hill, like he was conquering it. And Leland let him, his hands easy on the reins, leaning forward so Big Red could run as fast as he pleased.

Jamie cantered slowly, and let Dusty take the up-slope as he wanted to, which was at a brisk walk. He found himself at the top of that hill all alone until finally a red blur caught his eye. He saw Leland, miles away, it seemed, pull up and circle the horse, a brilliant curved streak of scarlet against the tall green grasses, like a circle of fire as Leland came back around.

Jamie eased Dusty into a canter, the wind fast against his face as they went, only to pull up, and really, Dusty pulled himself up, when they met up with Leland and Big Red in the curve of a lonely hillside.

"This horse needs to be ridden more often," said Leland by way of greeting. He patted Big Red's neck while Big Red chuffed and snorted, his ears pricked forward, eager and alert. "Our guests are mostly beginners, and he's just too much horse for the majority of them. I'll make a note in his chart and talk with Brody, see what he can arrange."

If Jamie'd not already been in love with Leland, he would have fallen in love with him then and there. His concern was not just that the horse might be too much for the guests, but that Big Red loved to run, and so should be allowed to run.

He was all about taking care of the horses, of the guests. Of Jamie. On this, their first ride together, he'd put Jamie on a horse he already knew so he would feel comfortable. And now, as he looked up, still patting Big Red's neck, he smiled at Jamie.

"Sorry I left you like that," Leland said. "But Big Red was pulling so much, and he really needed a good run."

Jamie shook his head, smiling. It was hard to put it into words, the feeling of watching Leland turn that horse, that horse that so loved to run and who would have run to the horizon's edge if Leland had let him—Leland had turned that horse in Jamie's direction. And all so they could sit on horseback, side by side, and stay that way for a good long while as the sky grew dark, and the smoky colors of sunset grew bolder, settling down over the landscape.

"We should head back," he said. "While it's romantic as all get out to ride beneath the stars, it's not always safe. We can take the truck out sometime, though, if you'd like. Some evening after it gets dark."

"I'd like that," Jamie said, because of course he would like it. His mind started coming up with all kinds of images, like dreams taking shape. Leland and Jamie, kissing under the stars while a slender, quarter moon slid into the blue-tinged blackness above the mountains.

They were silent as they rode along the glow of the path to the road that led through the gate. Leland unlocked the gate from Big Red's back and closed it behind them. And then, together, side by side, they rode back to the barn.

There, in the quiet coolness of the barn, they groomed the horses, and wiped down the tack. Gave the horses hay and water, and started back beneath the trees. As they arrived at the bottom step of the porch of Leland's cabin, he hugged Jamie close.

"I want to take you to bed," Leland said. "And then, after, I'd like to sit out here and watch it grow really dark. Maybe have a root beer or two, or maybe share some of Mom's strawberry-rhubarb pie, what do you say?"

"Sure," Jamie said, because yes, all of him wanted that, all of that.

A part of Jamie heard the unspoken message as it wove its way between Leland's quiet words. There was something to his invitation about sitting on the porch together and having a cold root beer. It was as though there was a picture in Leland's mind about it, and Jamie understood those kinds of dreams, sure enough. So he stood up on tiptoe and kissed him lightly.

"Those chairs look mighty empty," Jamie said. "And I'd be proud and pleased to sit out here with you."

"But later," he said, with a small smile. "After. After."

"After," Jamie agreed, and clung to Leland as he half carried him inside the cool darkness of the cabin.

EPILOGUE

*L*eland had to wrangle his temper like it was an ornery calf as he stared at Brody, his hands on his hips.

"What do you mean, they came back without saddles?" he asked, keeping his voice even. This wasn't Brody's fault, though it sounded like the teenagers on that afternoon's trail ride *had* gotten the best of him.

"I was focused on those two ladies from New York," Brody said calmly because he knew, and Leland knew, both of them, after several years of working together, that Leland was going to hear him out, come what may. "And that's when the three of them rode off together. By the time I could round them all up and start heading back, that's when I realized they were bareback."

"All three of them." It was not a question. The three teenage girls had probably thought it was a lark, a spree, but it was strictly against ranch policy. Only a fool would gallop across the prairie like that without a saddle on a horse they hardly knew. Leland was worried, too, about the horses. Sure, they could adapt to being ridden bareback, but the whole thing sounded like an accident waiting to happen. "And the saddles are still out there."

"I'm sorry," said Brody. "We were halfway back by the time—

Anyway, I figure the saddles are along the trail somewhere. I'll send someone to pick them up before it rains."

"I'll go," Leland said. "You can join Quint in giving those girls and their folks a lecture on horse safety and ranch rules, okay?"

"Thanks, boss," Brody said, tapping his finger to his hat. "I'll take care of it."

Leland knew he would. He knew that under his care, and Quint's care, the horses would be taken care of and settled after their wild ride. He also knew that once Bill found out about it, he'd have a thing or two to say, and would deliver one of his stern lectures, though he probably wouldn't kick the guests off the ranch, mid-week.

It was left to Leland to grab the truck and head on out, quick as he could. There were storm clouds brewing over the mountains, and the saddles were at risk. Sure, with the insurance, they could always buy new saddles, but these ones were already nicely broken in, giving them the air of *real* saddles, which he knew ranch guests appreciated. It would take an entire season to break in new saddles properly.

Leland grabbed some plastic tarps from the supply shed, got the keys from the hook, and thought about how he would get a message to Jamie that he'd probably miss dinner, and could Jamie grab him a sandwich or two.

He thought about calling Jamie on his cell phone, but though Jamie finally had a phone of his own, he tended to leave it in the cabin, like he didn't remember he was now connected, part of the ranch, part of the ranch family. Part of Leland's life.

And he was. All of Jamie's things fit in half of Leland's dresser, and Jamie easily determined which side of the bed was his, which half of the towel racks were his. Which coffee mug of Leland's he loved best to use. Where his boots went when he stored them, side by side in the closet with Leland's. What color woolen throw he wanted when Leland offered to buy him one for the Adirondack chair he'd claimed as his, as a kind of housewarming present.

Jamie blustered he didn't need one, but Leland had seen the shine in his eyes. Jamie had a thing about blankets and sheets that Leland was only slowly coming to understand. They represented hearth and home to Jamie, the one thing he'd been lacking since his parents had turned their back on him, and Leland intended to make it up to him every way that he could. Now, if only he could get Jamie to carry that cell phone around with him.

Walking back to the barn, Leland needed to tell Clay, or someone, that he was headed out on an unexpected jaunt into the expanse of acres that was the wild prairie section of the ranch. And, really, to follow his own rules, he needed to get someone to go with him. The area wasn't the most dangerous place on the planet, of course, but they had standards to keep and safety policies for a reason.

Leland stepped into the shadow of the barn, jingling the truck keys as he settled his hat on his head. A small wind scurried around his boots and he knew he needed to head out quick or lose those saddles to the weather.

Cursing under his breath, he strode out of the barn, intending to grab the first person he saw to ride shotgun, when he heard a shout. He looked, and there, running towards him, up the slope from the row of cabins, was Jamie.

He was grubby from work and his hair flew around his head as he came to a quick halt in front of Leland. Giving a quick look around, Jamie grabbed Leland around the waist and held on tight, practically taking the air from him.

"Heard you had an errand," Jamie said, almost breathless himself, looking up at Leland, digging his chin into the middle of his chest, looking so cute Leland had to sigh. "Clay told me. You can't go out alone. It's a rule."

"That it is," Leland said, cupping the back of Jamie's head, twining his fingers through that dark hair. "Next time, carry your phone with you. Then it won't even be a question."

Jamie rolled his eyes, like Leland was the thousandth person that day who'd reminded him of that. Leland bent and kissed Jamie, not caring who could see, though he did make it quick.

"C'mon then, if you're coming," Leland said, as if it was a question that he'd even want anybody else with him.

Leland strode to the silver truck, Jamie at his side, and they piled in and headed up the slope toward the gate and the trail beyond. Jamie obliged Leland by taking care of the gate, and together they bumped along the rough road in contented silence while Jamie hung out the window, almost to his waist, and kept his eye out for those saddles.

The wind was brisk so Jamie had to keep a hand on his hat, and Leland had impulse upon impulse to shout at him to get back inside, but he didn't. Jamie had grabbed hold of the side mirror and was as safe as he could be, though Leland's hand twitched on his thigh as he drove, in case he had to snag hold of the waist of Jamie's jeans.

They drove for a good mile or more, both of them keeping a lookout, and just when the clouds began lowering over the edge of the mountains, Jamie pointed. Seeing the flash of color, stripes of blue and white of the saddle blankets, Leland sped that truck up as fast as he could. Jamie leaped out before Leland fully stopped, and they were able to get those saddles, and the saddle blankets, in the back of the truck and under the plastic tarp just as it began to rain.

Leland was soaked to the skin inside of a minute as he tightened the tarp over the saddles, and Jamie was as well. But he just laughed and tilted his head back and stuck his tongue out to taste the rain. And then Leland bent close, took his hat off, curled his arm around Jamie's waist, and tasted that same rain, moist and sweet, on his tongue.

Dripping and laughing at their success, they drove back to the ranch, hauled the saddles into the barn, still covered by the plastic tarp, and wiped the tack down.

"Time for that root beer," Leland said. It was the middle of the week, and guests were still all around them, but he wanted to take the time to slow down, to share time with Jamie. "We can fetch some dinner later. What do you reckon?"

"Sure," Jamie said, his eyebrows going up. "Just you an' me, huh?"

That was how Jamie liked it, how Leland liked it. Side by side they walked through the rain-dappled shadows, smelling of pine and damp earth, until they reached the cabin. Inside, they stripped to their skins and rubbed each other down with clean towels.

Leland could have tumbled Jamie on the bed and driven him to the edge with kisses and touches, but he wanted this now. Them in their t-shirts and sweatpants, carrying bottles of local-made root beer out to the front porch where the Adirondack chairs always patiently waited.

After courting Jamie for nearly a month, Leland found that he just wanted to keep on courting him. And Jamie, in return, courted Leland, finding ways to show up at his side when he needed a sounding board or someone to run a quick errand for him, the way Clay used to do.

Jamie was always available for any job, no matter how rough. All he wanted in return, it seemed, was a nod indicating he'd done well. So Leland gave him those nods, and touched his shoulder, and singled him out—and all the while Jamie grew straighter each day, his shoulders filling out, his gaze more confident. And Leland loved him more each day, especially in the quiet of the evening like this as they padded barefoot to the front porch.

After Leland opened the bottles of root beer and put them on the arms of the chairs, Jamie reached inside and turned off the porch light. With a snap, it became much darker, the wind stirring the branches of the pine trees overhead, the stars coming out to wink through the gaps in the clouds. They watched as a soft rain came down, bringing with it the velvet scent of damp pine.

Leland sat with a sigh and took a long swig of root beer, wondering why he'd taken so long to make this particular dream come true. They'd been so busy with Jamie moving in, each of them adjusting to the other, week after week, finding their shared rhythm, slowly, slowly, lightly, lightly.

Leland slept better with Jamie in his arms, and that was just the truth. And every day, Jamie glowed, stars in his eyes, sunlight in his smile. He was not a drifter any more. He was putting down roots. The two of them were putting down roots that tangled together, deep underground, beneath their feet. All the way down to the center of the Earth.

Tipping his head back, taking a swallow of root beer, Leland half-laughed to himself.

"What?" asked Jamie, his voice low so as not to disturb the distant sound of coyotes crying for the moon.

"Well," Leland said, feeling serious in his joy, just then. "I'm so glad you bought that bus ticket to anywhere. So glad you got off in Farthing."

"I am too," Jamie said, quite simply.

Leland turned his head to look at Jamie. He was leaning on his elbow, a shadow of an outline, his eyes glinting in the starlight and rainlight. He was sitting the way he did when they went anywhere in the truck, up on one knee, scanning the horizon, happy to be in motion, or to be still, each day a new adventure. Leland might not have deserved Jamie when he met him, but he damn well wanted to make sure he deserved him now.

"You've changed my life, and that's all there is to it." Leland took a hard swig of root beer, maybe too hard, still not used to the powerful feelings that would swarm up inside him.

"And you mine," Jamie said, whispering.

Jamie got up then, putting his bottle of root beer on the porch, and Leland's, too, and straddled Leland's hips, his arms going between Leland's back and the back of the chair. It was his favorite position. It was Leland's, as well.

Leland wrapped his arms around Jamie and held him close, kissing the top of his head. That was his brand on him, the only mark he would ever make, the only way he would keep him tied to his side with an invisible kiss.

When Jamie felt the gesture, he pressed closer, as though he meant to push his way beneath Leland's skin, into his body. That was his brand on Leland, and though it too was invisible, it would hold him stronger than any rope, and he was happy to let it.

Want to read more about the sweet romance between Leland and Jamie? Click here. (https://readerlinks.com/l/1725141)

Want to read about the time Jasper fell in love? *The Blacksmith and the Ex-Con* is the second book in the Farthingdale Ranch series. Click here. (https://readerlinks.com/l/1775200)

Want to read about Brody, the ranch's wrangler, and how he fell in love? The Wrangler and the Orphan is available for preorder! (https://readerlinks.com/l/1890263)

Want to read about how Laurie Quinn got lost and how John Henton found him? Click here. (https://readerlinks.com/l/1568445)

You can stay up to date on upcoming releases and sales by joining my newsletter or my reader's group.

Newsletter: https://readerlinks.com/l/1775220
Reader Group: https://readerlinks.com/l/1776076

If you enjoyed *The Foreman and the Drifter*, I would love it if you could let your friends know so they can experience the romance between Leland and Jamie. Currently the book is available on Amazon, and is also listed on Goodreads.

JACKIE'S NEWSLETTER

Would you like to sign up for my newsletter?

Subscribers are alway the first to hear about my new books. You'll get behind the scenes information, sales and cover reveal updates, and giveaways.

As my gift for signing up, you will receive two short stories, one sweet, and one steamy!

It's completely free to sign up and you will never be spammed by me; you can opt out easily at any time.

To sign up, visit the following URL:

https://www.subscribepage.com/JackieNorthNewsletter

facebook.com/jackienorthMM
twitter.com/JackieNorthMM
pinterest.com/jackienorthauthor
bookbub.com/profile/jackie-north
amazon.com/author/jackienorth
goodreads.com/Jackie_North
instagram.com/jackienorth_author

AUTHOR'S NOTES ABOUT THE STORY

The Farthingdale Ranch series, and this first story, came from a thought-provoking question put to me by Randall J, one of my readers. After finishing *Honey From the Lion*, Randall asked:

"What happens to the ranch if there's no story of Old Joe?"

Honey From the Lion is one of the books in my gay m/m time travel romance series. In it Laurie Quinn is swept to the year 1891, where he changes the events of the past. Naturally, if you mess with the past, or the future, the entire timeline will be changed.

I hadn't thought of time paradoxes or anything when I wrote Honey, but after Randall asked me that question, I thought long and hard about it.

I thought about the guest ranch Laurie had visited, and I thought about the characters I'd introduced in Honey (namely Bill and Maddy, and other nameless ranch hands that now had my attention), and I thought about their lives on the ranch.

What were their concerns? What were their hopes? And, most importantly, was anybody going to fall in love?

The answer to Randall's question (and my own) is the story you just read. I hope to write more stories in the Farthingdale Ranch series, and hope you will enjoy the results.

A LETTER FROM JACKIE

Hello, Reader!

Thank you for reading *The Foreman and the Drifter,* the first book in my Farthingdale Ranch series.

If you enjoyed the book, I would love it if you would let your friends know so they can experience the romance between Leland and Jamie.

If you leave a review, I'd love to read it! You can send the URL to: Jackienorthauthor@gmail.com

Jackie

facebook.com/jackienorthMM
twitter.com/JackieNorthMM
instagram.com/jackienorth_author
pinterest.com/jackienorthauthor
bookbub.com/profile/jackie-north
amazon.com/author/jackienorth
goodreads.com/Jackie_North

ABOUT THE AUTHOR

Jackie North has written since grade school and spent years absorbing mainstream romances. Her dream was to write full time and put her English degree to good use.

As fate would have it, she discovered m/m romance and decided that men falling in love with other men was exactly what she wanted to write about.

Her characters are a bit flawed and broken. Some find themselves on the edge of society, and others are lost. All of them deserve a happily ever after, and she makes sure they get it!

She likes long walks on the beach, the smell of lavender and rainstorms, and enjoys sleeping in on snowy mornings.

In her heart, there is peace to be found everywhere, but since in the real world this isn't always true, Jackie writes for love.

Connect with Jackie:

https://www.jackienorth.com/
jackie@jackienorth.com

facebook.com/jackienorthMM
twitter.com/JackieNorthMM
pinterest.com/jackienorthauthor
bookbub.com/profile/jackie-north
amazon.com/author/jackienorth
goodreads.com/Jackie_North
instagram.com/jackienorth_author

Printed in Poland
by Amazon Fulfillment
Poland Sp. z o.o., Wrocław